LEGENDS OF ANDOLIN

LEGENDS OF ANDOLIN

A. M. PORTMAN

CETUS

Contents

Copyright © 2025 by A. M. Portman
Cetus Publishing
All rights reserved. No part of this book may be reproduced in any manner
whatsoever without written permission except in the case of brief quotations
embodied in critical articles and reviews.
First Printing, 2025

To Alyssa,

Happy Birthday.

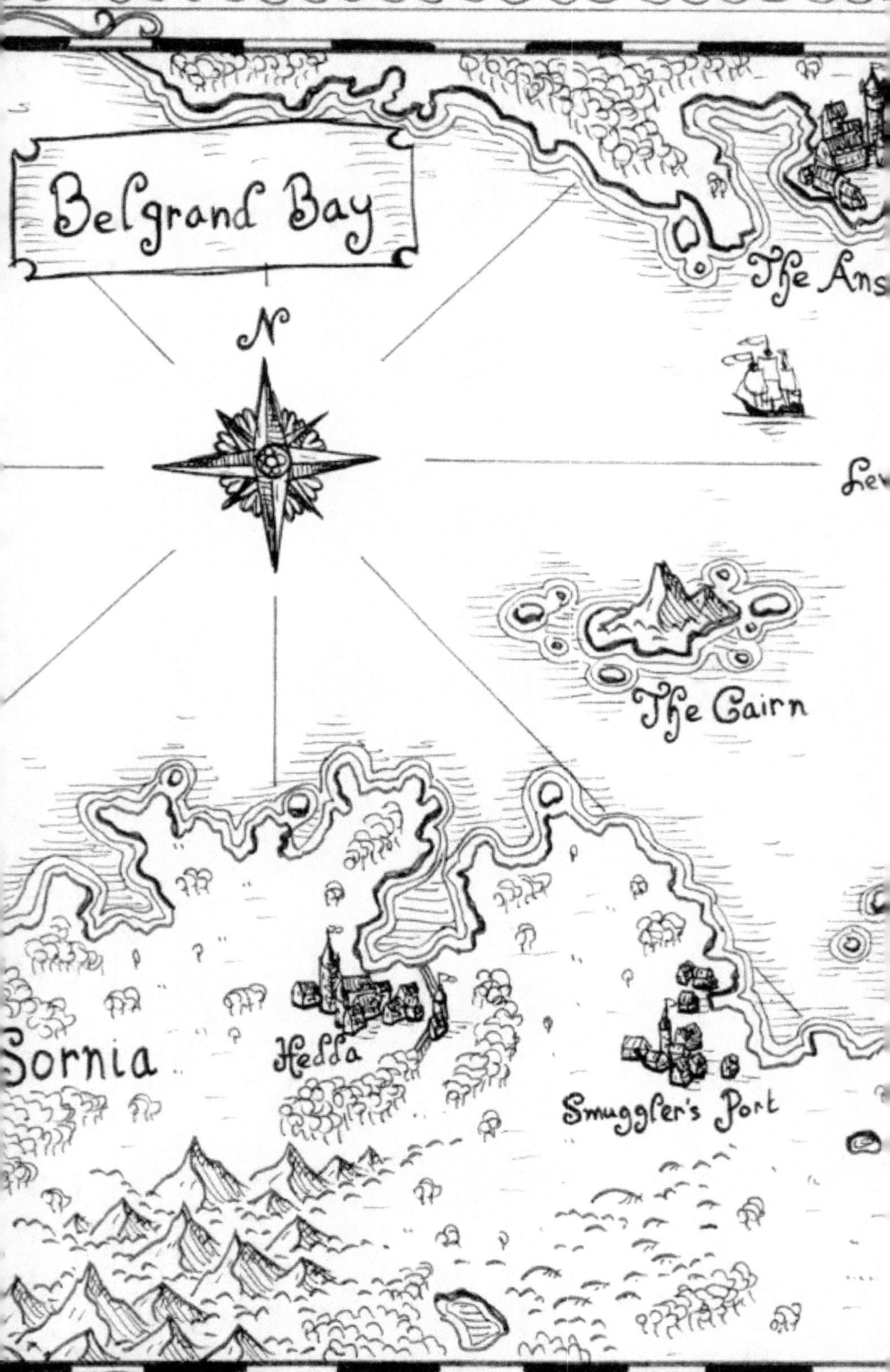

Belgrand Bay
N
The Ans
Lev
The Cairn
Sornia
Hedda
Smuggler's Port

Pentz
Fly
The Isles
The Teeth
Valenna
Raymouth
head
Elldon
s Point
Campos

Eyes in the Grass

Crouching behind a thicket of spring brambles, he moved his hand to the hilt of the sword at his side. Dark clouds were blowing in from the west, with raindrops already pattering on his heavy oilskin cloak. The tangled shrubs he hid behind lay in the center of a large swath of grassland, spreading out vast and yellow-green in every direction. He watched as the young woman in the field before him dismounted, tossing the reins forward over the head of her small bay. The horse itself wasn't much to look at. *But the woman,* he considered, *she'd be worth the trouble.* He squinted against the distance, but she looked young, and pretty. As she bent down to run her hands along the grazing horse's mane, he eyed her slim figure. Her brown hair hung loose down her back, and the sheen of her garments showed them to be silk. She was clearly highborn, passing her evening carelessly riding around in fine clothes rather than scrubbing pots somewhere. For a moment, he wondered what such a life would be like.

Thunder rumbled behind him and the woman straightened and looked around. From the cover of the thicket, the man held his breath as she turned her head in his direction. *Not now,* he pleaded silently. If she saw him now, he would have to kill her to keep her from raising the alarm. He didn't want to do that; he'd much rather take her to the auction block in Hedda and make a small fortune. His stomach had felt like an empty pit for the last week, and he couldn't resist thinking about how well he could eat with all that gold. *No more fighting over scraps,* he thought, *at least for a little while.* Letting his breath out once more, he watched as she led her horse onward, lifting her petticoats in one hand while walking leisurely along in the tall grass.

As his gaze drifted into the background, it came to rest on the large manor house sitting on the crest of the hill beyond, overshadowed by tall trees. Today, he was only scouting; tomorrow will be the real test. He had never been entrusted with any kind of command before. If he could follow through on his orders without any problems, things might go better for him from now on. He smirked to himself. *They couldn't get any worse, anyway.*

1

Lavender Tea

Adella reined her little gelding to a trot as she approached the front of Greywood Manor. Beside the steps leading up to the imposing double doors of the entrance, Teressa, the estate's housekeeper, clipped a bouquet of lilac blooms from the hedge and shook last night's rain from their petals. The sun shone in a blue sky, and the early morning air was just beginning to warm. Adella drew her horse to a halt and looked around, drawing a deep breath. In the distance, horses grazed in the rolling green pastures around the estate as birdsong issued from the tall elm trees. It felt good to be back home. She hopped down from the saddle and tied her horse to a hitching ring.

"Good morning, Miss Adella," Teressa turned to greet her, piling the lilacs into her outstretched apron. "You're back early. How was your trip?"

"Just fine, thanks," Adella replied, pulling leather riding gloves off her fingers. "The weather was a little rough, but Mother and Father's ship left port on schedule." Adella picked up a small sprig, adorned with pale purple blossoms, and inhaled their sweet fragrance. After moving here from the Capital seven years ago, her mother had planted them, homesick for the royal gardens they used to frequent as a family. Even now, the scent took Adella back to her days in the palace, spent wandering the halls with her older sister, Margavita, while her parents attended the Council of Lords. "Any letters from Margo?"

"No," Teressa replied gently. "I'm sorry. I know you miss her."

Adella followed Teressa up the steps of the fieldstone manor, peering past the open doors into the foyer for the sight of her father's butler. "Where's Armand?"

"He was ill yesterday; he must be home resting," Teressa replied. She arranged the bouquet in a blue and white porcelain vase that stood on a pedestal table inside the doorway. "I can take Shy to the stable for you," she offered, nodding toward the courtyard, where Adella's horse stood patiently.

"That isn't necessary, thank you. Oh, Armand is never ill." Adella frowned, wringing her gloves absent-mindedly. "I hope it isn't serious."

"I'm sure he'll be fine." Teressa looked expectantly through the open doorway. "Didn't your brother return with you?"

"He'll be along shortly," Adella assured her. "He stopped in town for some reason or other. You know Lucas, he's always been hard to keep track of." She shrugged, and Teressa smiled in agreement. Unlike Adella, Lucas had taken to their new life with alacrity, already embracing the freedoms that came with being the next Lord Grimless. While the inheritance could lawfully fall to her, tradition still dictated it pass to the son—an assumption Adella was relieved to encourage, as it spared her a responsibility she never wanted.

After leaving their old life behind when the king sent the Grimless family to oversee the new town of Elldon, whatever loneliness she felt had only deepened lately; Lucas had been disappearing to the port city of Raymouth more frequently, leaving her to ride the fields alone. Still, she had learned to manage. Lord Grimless, a former cavalry officer, had demanded self-sufficiency from his children, raising Adella to be ready for service to the Crown at a moment's notice. With her dear horse, Shy, to keep her company, she had long ago resigned herself to the quiet wilds of the frontier, even if her heart remained elsewhere.

Even so, she was grateful for this little town on the edge of the map, and the people whose lives were now intertwined with her own.

It was late afternoon when the courtyard outside of Greywood Manor again filled with the sound of hooves. As Adella sipped tea in the dining room, she caught sight of Lucas as he passed by the window on his bold red-and-white mare, foam falling from her lips. It wasn't long before he flung open the door and sat down at the opposite end of the long table, putting his stocking feet up in front of him.

Teressa came over and set a cup and saucer before him. "Good afternoon," she greeted him.

"You stayed a while in town," Adella noted. She paused to sip the fragrant lavender tea. "Where did you go?"

"There is a new shop in the merchant's square," Lucas said finally. "I bought a spyglass there." He pulled the heavy instrument from his bag and set it down with a thud that made the porcelain rattle. "And I got you a new pen knife."

He fished a small object from his pocket and tossed it across the long table. Adella tried to catch it one-handed but missed, and it skidded over the polished wood, clinking against her saucer. She picked up the knife gingerly, running her thumb over the mother-of-pearl inlay on the handle.

"Oh, I almost forgot," Lucas continued. "I bumped into Captain Declan at the docks. He asked me to give this to you." He pulled a small parcel wrapped in brown paper from his bag and slid it toward her.

"Thanks." Adella turned it over carefully in her hands. "It's probably another seashell; the captain likes to collect them. He always sends me the strangest kinds." She stuffed the little package, unopened, into her large pocket through the side of her petticoat. While she hadn't seen Rogero Declan in years, they continued to correspond regularly after the Grimless family moved to Elldon. They had been close friends in childhood, and Adella had fond memories of their time spent together in the gardens of the Capital.

That evening, as the sun sank peacefully into the horizon, Adella sat down at the little vanity in her bedchamber. She removed her gold and pearl earrings, then carefully pulled out the metal pins that had been keeping her hair up on top of her head all day, running her fingers through the long, auburn tresses as they fell around her shoulders. Looking absent-mindedly at the sky in the bay window, reflected in the mirror in front of her, she watched the clouds turn golden, orange, then pink as night approached. Then, a dark grey cloud gathered just outside her window, streaming upward, carried on the wind.

Her brow furrowed as she stared into the mirror, puzzled at what she saw. "What in the world..." Adella muttered to herself as she ran toward the window. Looking out, a blazing light hit her eyes from below. Gasping, she watched as the stables behind Greywood Manor were engulfed in flames. Her heart pounded in her ears as she was overcome with the urge to run to the horses and fling open their stall doors to let them loose. She sprinted down the hall; a commotion came from downstairs, with loud voices and heavy banging from the foyer.

Halfway down the flight of stairs that overlooked the entryway, Adella froze, still clutching her skirts in her sweaty palms. Below, the barred doors splintered at the lock with each blow, then flung open violently. Her heart leapt into her throat as men with blades and torches rushed in, jostling the table in the foyer as they went. The blue and white vase toppled over with the sharp crash of shattering porcelain, scattering lilac blossoms and broken shards across the floor. In the dark, they hadn't seen her on the flight of stairs above them, and Adella hurried down the steps with the intention of running to Armand's house for help, putting aside thoughts of the horses now that her household was under attack. She froze when a shrill scream rang out behind her. A feeling of cold dread flooded from her gut. *Teressa!*

Turning on her heel, Adella ran down the main hall, her reflection only a fleeting shadow in the glass of the gilded mirrors that lined the walls. She halted abruptly when she noticed the doors to the dining room to her right were ajar. As quietly as she could, Adella pushed open the door. In the flickering firelight within, a man grabbed Teressa's arm with one hand, holding a torch with the other. Teressa, who was smaller even than Adella, seemed nothing more than a ragdoll in his grip. Without a thought, Adella charged at him with all her weight, burying her shoulder into his side. Though the man was huge, the blow caught him by surprise and he fell hard onto the stone floor. The torch rolled loose from his hand toward the wall.

"Run!" Adella yelled to Teressa, moving quickly to put her arm around the man's neck. Instinctively, she squeezed as hard as she could to try to choke him. It was all she could think to do, and she hoped it would at least buy Teressa some time. Teressa scrambled to her feet but hesitated, looking wide-eyed back at Adella. "Tess, *run!*" she yelled again, and Teressa obeyed.

The man rose, Adella's arm still clinging around his neck. As her feet were lifted far from the floor, she realized just how large he was, and her mouth went dry with panic. Grabbing her by the elbow, his fingers dug into her arm and he flung her around, slamming her backward into the wall. Pain seared through the back of her head as she fell to the floor. Dazed and wincing, her vision blurred as she watched his silhouette lower, crouching down toward her. Adella gasped and, scrambling backward to get away, pressed herself against the wall. Squeezing her eyes shut, she turned away, expecting pain at any moment. When it didn't come, she forced herself to look. Though she could barely see his expression in the dim firelight, as the hulking man looked at her, the lines of his face changed, and his scowl faded away, his eyebrows drawing upward. He grabbed the torch and stood up. Heart hammering against her ribs, Adella made ready to kick him, but the man simply turned to leave, closing the doors behind him.

"That's everyone," a deep voice called to the other men who, judging by the sounds of the footsteps, had just gathered outside of the dining room. "Let's go!" The heavy pounding of feet grew more distant as they hurried down the hall, then out the door.

Adella lay there a moment and let out a long breath, putting her hands to her stomach to calm a growing queasiness. Hopefully, Lucas was still safe in his bedchamber upstairs. *And if not?* The thought struck her like a blow to the gut. *What if he came down, like I did? He might be hurt, or worse.* She had to find him.

She jumped up, pausing for her head to stop spinning before running upstairs to check his room, calling his name. Lucas was not there. Frantically, she searched every room, every wardrobe, under the beds, and even in the pantry; he was nowhere to be found. Adella slumped down on a chair to think and remembered the man who grabbed Teressa's arm. He hadn't tried to hurt her, he had simply tried to catch her. *Perhaps they were looking to take people captive... Did they take Lucas? And what about Tess?* Adella wondered, hoping her attempts to buy Tess some time had allowed her, at least, to get away. *Maybe Lucas ran for help? But... If that was the case, surely he would've returned by now...* Her heart sank into her stomach. *I wish Father were here...* He wouldn't have wavered; he'd have been tacked up and on their trail, galloping boldly after them already by now. *But... Why couldn't I?* He had taught her all he knew about tracking, and she was deeply familiar with the area. With her parents gone and Armand ill, there was no one else. If there was any chance her brother had been taken, she knew she needed to leave now. Lucas could be in real danger; there was no time to think it through. *As the nearest town was over an hour's ride away, they must've come in on horseback. The tracks, sounds and signs of a large group of horses will surely make them easy to follow.*

Adella jumped up and ran to the foyer. Lucas's travel bag had been left in its usual place on the coat rack. She grabbed it along with her grey oilskin cloak and sprinted out the back of the manor, trampling through the fragrant herbs in the kitchen garden with the cloying smell of smoke thick in the air around her. Behind Greywood, the stables still burned and had begun to collapse. The gates to the horse paddocks were all open, and only one horse could still be seen remaining in the moonlit pen. It was Lucas's skewbald, Ember. Adella breathed a sigh of relief; though Ember could be capricious, with a propensity for bucking, she was the fastest horse in all of Elldon. It would certainly be worth the risk.

As she ran back through the rear entrance that opened up into the mud room, Adella grabbed the leather bridle that hung on a peg on the wall inside. She always kept her own saddle and bridle indoors to keep it from molding and was glad of that fact now that the rest of the tack was burning in the stable.

Though Ember needed the usual coaxing to catch, Adella got her tacked up quickly and they were off at a trot. Soon her eyes adjusted to the moonlight, revealing a path where many horses had trampled the grass. It went straight as far as she could see, toward the Campos. *How unusual,* she noted. The Campos were uninhabited. Adella gently squeezed the mare's sides with her heels to ask for a canter, but instead got a small buck and a hard gallop.

Adella rode across the open fields for what felt like hours, slowing now and then as the terrain required, passing only clumps of trees that had grown up around a small pond or a trickling stream now and then. When the clouds began to gather in the night sky, blotting out the moon, she lost sight of the trail in the darkness. Adella cursed herself for wasting so much time searching the Manor. All she could do was continue onward, straight ahead, and hope.

Eventually, she came to the top of a wide hill, with the glow of a campfire burning in the distance. The wind kicked up and she drew her rain cloak tighter around her shoulders to keep out the cold night air. Searching over the landscape, she noticed a thick stand of trees just north of the fire, the pattern of the branches barely visible in the faint moonlight that made it through the clouds. Adella guided the horse north, keeping the trees as a sight barrier between herself and whomever the fire belonged to.

As she approached the trees, Adella dismounted. The dark tangle of branches loomed above her. She fished around in Lucas's bag until she found a bit of rope and tied it in a figure-eight around Ember's forelimbs, then left the mare to graze. Gathering up her skirts, she walked into the little wooded area, cringing with each branch that snapped beneath her leather boots. Emerging on the other side, she was only a short distance from where the fire was.

What sort of people would attack Elldon, on the edge of the Campos, Adella could not guess. *Raiders of some sort?* she wondered. *But who? Who could possibly be out here, so far from civilization? Where could they have come from?* She crouched down on the ground and took out Lucas's brass spyglass he'd shown her earlier. As the moon broke through the clouds, she held it up to her eye and, peering through it, saw the silhouettes of men in the glow of the fire, which was in the center of a circle of tents. Nearer to her was a make-shift horse pen with at least twenty horses. She could barely make out the form of a large pole that had been erected in the ground by the pen, with the silhouette of a man seated at the bottom of it. *Could that be Lucas?* Adella wondered. He was too far from the light of the fire; she couldn't tell from this distance. She would have to get closer.

Adella dropped to her belly. The cold dampness of the soil soaked through the front of her dress as she dragged herself forward on her elbows, the coarse blades of grass scratching at her wrists. The moon once again hid itself behind a thick blanket of clouds. The wind rustled the grass, muffling her movements. Then, it shifted, carrying a heavy, pungent wave of woodsmoke and the musk of unwashed men that stung her nose, buffeting her senses after the clean night air of the open plains. Not even the horses noticed her approaching as she went wide around to keep the pen between herself and the campfire. As she came up near the man at the pole, Adella still could not make out his face or any details that would let her know if this was her brother or not. He seemed to be tied with his hands around the pole behind him, judging by the way he slumped against it. As she inched closer, however, she saw that he was much too large to be her brother; his shoulders were too broad and, even with him hunched over, he was too tall. Her heart dropped into her stomach.

Just then, a horse nickered softly. Adella knew that gentle sound anywhere; it was her gelding, Shy. The horse had finally noticed her presence and came over to the fence near her. She had to let him out. Adella began to crawl away.

"Wait," a rough voice whispered. "Untie me."

Adella froze when she heard the strange accent. He was clearly not a captive from Elldon. *Should I free him?* He could be dangerous, or she could get caught trying. Or, if she ignored him, he could shout and raise the alarm. Mostly, though, she remembered the relief she felt hours before when the stranger had, for whatever reason, left her in peace in her dining room. *Was it out of compassion?* Somehow, she felt she owed this man the same.

"Please," he hissed. "They're going to kill me."

"I'm looking for my brother," she replied under her breath, still wary.

"Not here," he said quietly. "They went west. Hurry, we can sneak away before they notice."

That was all the urging she needed to make her choice. *He knows where Lucas is!* Adella crept closer, her pulse thundering in her ears. With trembling hands, she brought the blade to the ropes, sawing frantically at the thick fibers. As she worked the blade back and forth on the cord binding his wrists, it began to rain, the cold drops hitting her face and hands. Thunder rumbled in the distance as the ties finally broke away.

"The horses," Adella leaned in to whisper. "We have to let them loose."

He let out a loud breath, then turned and crawled along the fence line. She followed him through the damp grass over to the gate, which was mercifully only a few paces away. Adella couldn't see it clearly, but he seemed to know exactly where it was. Fumbling around in the dark, they removed the ropes that held the wooden gate shut.

A flash of lightning lit up the sky, spooking some of the horses as the sound of frantic hoofbeats pounded within the pen. The man swung the gate wide open and the animals bolted out. Adella knew her own horses would find their way home.

"We need to get to those trees over there," Adella whispered. Loud voices erupted from the direction of the tents, making her heart hammer.

The man grabbed her upper arm and pulled her to her feet. "Run," he ordered, and Adella tried to keep up as they took off toward the stand of trees. Lightning flashed around them, cracking loudly above their heads as it seemed to rip the sky in two.

They'd nearly reached the cover of trees when Adella realized they were being pursued. Between the rumblings of the thunder, quickening footsteps followed. Soon, they were overtaken as the pursuer charged toward them, tackling the man she had freed. The two crashed sideways into Adella, and she hit the ground hard. The men struggled in the wet grass beside her, wrestling until one of them cried out in pain. Only one stood up again, and as lightning lit up the sky, she saw the glint of metal in his hand. Which man it was, she didn't know. He came at her quickly.

He grabbed her arm and pulled her to her feet again. "Let's go!" he urged. As they ran, her companion was having trouble keeping up. He was stumbling and his breathing sounded ragged.

They made it to the trees, and scrambled their way through the cold, damp underbrush to the other side. Even in the dark of night, Adella could see Ember's white markings not far ahead. As they hurried onward, the man fell and needed help to rise again.

"Come on," she goaded, pulling him up by the arm. "Just a little farther." When they finally reached the horse, Adella removed the hobble and, lowering the stirrup, they mounted up with some difficulty. With the man taking the reins as she climbed behind him, the two rain-soaked riders rode onward.

The rain had stopped and the stars began to peek through gaps in the clouds when the man began to slip to the side. Adella clutched onto his shirt to try to hold him in place but it was no use; he slid out of the saddle, dragging her down with him. She fell into the wet grass, landing hard on her hip as the horse bolted straight for home, leaving them stranded in the field. Adella crawled over to where the man had fallen, and, seeing the dark lump lying in the moonlight, turned him over in the grass.

"Are you all right?" she asked, patting his shoulders, then his face to try to get a response. He grabbed her hand and placed it on his ribcage. His shirt was soaked through, warm and sticky. *He's bleeding!*

Moving quickly, she ripped a piece of cloth from one of her petticoats, wadded it up, and pressed it firmly into the wound beneath his shirt, the way her mother had done when her father stumbled home from the skirmish at Enth with a saber slash across his gut. Adella had been very little then, but she remembered it vividly.

She flinched as the man groaned sharply through his teeth at the pressure. Though she had no idea how deep or serious the cut might be, she knew she needed to staunch the blood. She pressed the rag there for what felt like ages, putting her weight into it. When she felt the blood seeping through the cloth, she tore another and tried again, placing it on top of the other one.

Eventually, the blood stopped soaking through the fabric. Adella couldn't guess what time of night it was, but she was exhausted. The man had either passed out or fallen asleep already, so they would have to stay where they were. She shivered in the cold night air, travel-sore and soaked with rain. Adella pulled her cloak tightly around herself, set her haversack under her head, and lay down to rest, though the knot in her stomach kept her from sleeping deeply, falling instead into fitful dreams.

2

Further Afield

Adella awoke, damp and sore, to a clear dawn spreading its golden light over the dewy grass. She got up and looked around; there was a wide clump of trees not far off to the east. To the northwest, a long ridge of rock jutted out of the landscape, but she could not guess how many leagues away it was or how large. To the south, the land swelled upward, limiting the view. All else was relatively flat grassland. In the distance, a horse whinnied, the sound echoing over the rolling landscape.

The wide vantage and the thought of being pursued made her uneasy. For now, she thought it best to relocate to the trees for cover and went over to where she left the man. He was still lying motionless in the grass. He had seemed to know where they were headed, but he'd be no good to her dead.

"Don't be dead," she muttered anxiously to herself, "I need you..." Pressing her fingers into the side of his throat, she checked for a heartbeat.

"I'm not dead," he mumbled.

She let out a breath in relief. "Can you move? It's not safe out in the open." He nodded, and she helped him up. Stumbling and muttering curses, he limped beside her to the cover of the trees, and they ducked under the skirt of a large pine.

They had only just settled under the fragrant, resinous boughs when two men on horses came riding into view from the south and stopped right at the spot where Adella had slept that night. The riders looked around for a moment, then turned to face the grove of trees where they were now hiding.

Adella held her breath as they headed in her direction. She looked at the man beside her, widening her eyes at him meaningfully. Nodding his understanding, he motioned for her to move under another tree a few paces away. She scurried over and crawled under the branches. Glancing through the pine needles, she watched him pull a large knife from inside his boot.

The two men dismounted, approaching the trees further south, leaving their horses to graze. "Kol," one of the men called loudly. "We know you're hiding here. We saw you killed Roen, that was harsh. Come out and bring us the Valennian, and maybe we'll forgive you." The two men drew out swords and split up, hacking at vegetation here and there.

"That's right," said the other, looking around as he walked. "Just give up the foreigner and we'll act like we never saw you. I swear it." As he slashed at the bracken, he slowly made his way toward the two trees where they were hiding.

Adella looked over at the man they called Kol to see if he would answer them. His dark eyes met hers from between the branches and he put a finger to his lips. The second man continued closer, moving into the space between their two trees until finally, he turned to face Kol's hiding spot.

A flurry of movement from the other tree caught Adella's eye, accompanied by a sickening thud. The man fell backward onto the ground with Kol's knife lodged in his throat; he had thrown it and was now unarmed. Hesitating for only a moment, Adella ran out from under the pine and pulled the sword from the dead man's hand.

She heard a shout and, brandishing the blade, turned to see the second man coming up behind her, his sword gleaming in the air. She tried to steel herself as he ran at her, red-faced and grimacing, teeth bared, but she had no idea how to swordfight. Adella's heart dropped into her stomach, pulse hammering, arms growing weak. Her courage drained away as he drew nearer until, finally, she turned and ran, hoping instead to draw her pursuer away from her injured companion.

The dull thud of a body hitting the ground stopped her in her tracks. She looked back to see Kol grappling with her pursuer in the dirt. As they tussled, the man reached out for his dropped sword. Adella rushed over and kicked it away from his outstretched hand.

Kol caught the blade by the hilt and stuck it in the man's chest. When there was sure to be no more movement from him, Kol let out a breath in relief, then clutched at his side.

"You shouldn't have done that," she chided. "You'll make the wound worse." When he didn't reply, only took a ragged breath and closed his eyes, Adella realized she'd have to take a look at his injury. She would need supplies for that. Looking around, she spied the riders' horses grazing just by the edge of the trees. She retrieved the saddle bags from the horses, then rejoined him by the pine.

In the first bag, she found a canteen of water, some biscuits wrapped in a scrap of waxed cloth, and a tin flask. Adella pulled the cork from the mouth of the flask and took a sip. The liquid burned her throat. "Do you mind if I take a look?" she asked, gesturing toward his side. Taking a deep breath, he covered his face with one hand and nodded. Carefully, she pulled the blood-soaked linen from his side as he winced beneath his palm. A deep slash ran over the bottom of the rib cage and into the abdominal muscles. It didn't pierce through the ribs, but bone peeked through the flesh in one spot.

She pressed her fingertips into the skin to get a better look, and Kol groaned through clenched teeth. The muscle on the side of the belly had been cut into, but the blade hadn't pierced any organs, as far as she could tell. Though she had often helped her mother tend to the various injuries that occurred at Greywood Manor over the years, she'd never had to do it on her own before now. Adella wasn't fully confident, but she had to try, or he wouldn't make it. She used his knife to cut more strips of cloth from her petticoats to make bindings. As she poured some of the contents of the flask over the wound, she flinched at his pained reaction. The sharp, metallic tang of fresh blood wafted between them, making her lightheaded in the thin morning air. Under her fingers, the heat radiating from his inflamed skin felt dangerously feverish, and she had to steady her nerves to keep from pulling away.

"It sounded like they called you Coal?" she asked, helping him sit up. "Is that your name?"

"Yes," he answered, wincing at the motion. "Kol," he repeated, emphasizing his own accent.

"Well, Mister Kol, I'm Adella Grimless." She tucked the end of one strip beneath another and wound it around his ribcage. "You said you know where my brother is? He is nineteen, blond hair."

"I saw him," he replied. "They were heading for the base camp in the West Campos, but from there they will take him to the auctioneer in Hedda."

"The *what*?" Adella looked at him, aghast, unable to believe what she was hearing. Her stomach clenched and she suddenly grew light-headed. "Did you say auctioneer?" Kol didn't meet her eyes, which was answer enough. She had to find Lucas before then. "Hedda? Is that in Sornia?" Adella pressed her lips together. "Are you Sornian?"

"I am—I was," he corrected himself, "a soldier. Now I'm a traitor; I can never go back."

She secured the end of the bandage and stood up, wiping her hands on her skirt. "Are you *all* Sornian soldiers? Were you one of the raiders?" He looked up at her and nodded. Adella let out a loud breath as she walked away, crossing to the southern edge of the trees to be alone with her thoughts. Nearby, the dead men's horses grazed under the clear blue sky. *Why would the Sornian king allow his soldiers to pillage in Valenna?* she wondered. *It would be an act of war.* If what Kol said was true, then she needed to get this news to her father, who would be arriving at the Capital on Belgrand Bay in the next few days. The sea cut deep into Valenna from the west; there was no quicker way than by ship. The southern rim of the Bay was probably only a day's ride north, she figured. However, the shoreline in that area was mostly cliff, and the sea was turbulent; she had seen it herself on several hunting excursions with her father and Lucas. Large teeth of rock jutted out from the water; no ships could approach the coast there. The closest port was in Raymouth just north of Elldon, where her parents had departed from. If she went back to Elldon now, she could send a letter. *But then, what about Lucas?* The Sornian borders had been closed for over a hundred years. *If Lucas is taken across the border, there may be no rescue at all. Even King Harrian himself couldn't save him then, short of open war.* The best chance would be to catch up with them in the Campos. She realized, though, that she didn't know where in the Campos she might find him, or what she would have to face when she did. As much as she knew she couldn't trust a Sornian, it seemed Kol was her only hope for finding her brother; the idea of doing it on her own was beginning to look impossible.

As she watched the horses grazing, her eyes shifted focus onto something peeking out from a rolled-up blanket behind one of the saddles. Adella walked closer to get a better look. It seemed to be some kind of small bow. She untied the blanket from the metal rings on the saddle and freed the weapon, turning it over in her hands. It was a small crossbow with wooden lathes. Its string was broken, but otherwise, it looked to be in good condition. A handful of wooden bolts with iron tips had been wrapped with it. She gathered them up, leaving the blanket lying across the saddle, and wandered back toward Kol, who was leaning on one arm, drinking from the flask.

"Look what I found," she said. "It needs a new string."

He glanced from the crossbow up to her face, looking at her pensively before replying. "Toss that bag over," he said finally, pointing to one of the saddle bags by her feet. She gave it over, and he rifled through it until he brought out a ball of linen cord. "Here," he said, holding it out to her. "Make a new one."

"Uh—" Adella raised her brows, taking the cord.

"You don't know how?" he asked.

"Well, no," she admitted. "Do you?"

"Yes, but you're going to do it yourself." He talked her through the steps, first instructing her to wind the cord until it was thick enough to fit nicely in the nock of the bolts, coming up just short of the length of the bow. Then, she made two smaller loops for the ends and wrapped the whole thing with another length of cord. Finally, she had it just right and fit the string onto the nocks of the bow.

Adella walked off to try out the weapon. Though she'd never used a crossbow herself, it looked simple enough. Placing her foot into the metal stirrup on its front, she slid a bolt into place and pulled the string backward until it locked, then lifted it and took aim. Lining up the length of the weapon's stock with her target, she flinched the first time she squeezed the iron lever, not fully trusting the string she had made. When she opened her eyes, however, she realized she had hit the tree she aimed at. After a few more practice tries, Adella noted how the bolt dropped downward over a longer distance. The crossbow wasn't very strong, but it was fairly accurate at a shorter range. Satisfied with her progress, she collected the bolts. "Thanks for your help," she said as she sat down. They shared what water was left in one of the canteens. "Can you ride? We probably shouldn't stay here much longer."

"I don't know," he said, putting a hand on his wound. "Where will you go?"

"I'm going to find my brother," she answered.

He raised an eyebrow. "How do you plan on doing that?"

She sighed, her shoulders drooping. "I don't know," she admitted. "But I can't just go back home without trying."

"I wouldn't advise going home at all right now," he replied. "The raids will continue until your whole town is burnt to the ground."

"What?" she asked breathlessly. "*Why?*"

He shrugged. "King Berento has decided he wants the Campos for Sornia."

Adella stared into the distance, deep in thought. She had come to love Greywood Manor, and Elldon. As Lord Grimless' daughter, she had a personal responsibility for the people there. She wondered if she should go back and warn them. *No,* she thought, *surely Tess or Armand will have handled things, and sent word to the Capital by now. King Harrian will send troops to defend the town.* Adella's heart sank as she realized Teressa would likely think she had been captured along with Lucas. *Oh well,* she consoled herself, frowning at the thought. *Nothing can be done about that now.* Her thoughts returned to the problem at hand, finding Lucas. It was rather lucky for her, she realized, that she came across this man who might be able to help. *But would he?*

She chewed her lip for a moment. "So, if you were one of them, what happened? Why aren't you now?"

"We had a disagreement," he said flatly, though there was an edge in his voice. Folding his arms, he turned away, ending the conversation.

Adella thought better of pressing the issue but continued to watch him, studying his features. His eyes were such a dark brown, they looked black. His hair was also black, and fell in dirty waves nearly to the shoulders. He was tall and lean, almost gaunt. *The Sornians apparently don't feed their soldiers well,* she thought, though there was a knotted look to his muscles that suggested he was much stronger than he seemed at the moment. If he weren't so gravely injured, she wouldn't feel safe at all to be near him. "What about you?" she asked. "Where will you go?"

He shook his head and looked down. "Nowhere to go."

"Could you—" she hesitated. "Would you be able to help me bring my brother home? I can pay you. Any amount. Gold, land. Name your price."

He thought for a moment, then nodded. They both fell silent again.

Though Kol was reluctant to move, Adella had decided it'd be best to continue onward. She put his arm around her shoulder, supporting as much of his great weight as she could bear, and took each step slowly until they reached the horses. She lowered the stirrup iron as far down as it would go, and Kol was able to mount up carefully. He couldn't ride any faster than a walk, though, and Adella went along on foot beside him, leading his horse in-hand. The other horse, she ponied to his with some rope. Without any better idea of where to go, Adella headed toward the large rock formation to the northwest. She wanted to view the land from higher up in the hopes of spotting a water source. Their last canteen was nearly empty.

The sun was at noon and the day was getting warm. Adella's clothes were still damp from the rain the night before and were beginning to chafe. She was not used to sleeping with her stays on under her clothes, and a sharp pain began to grow on her left side. Her ribs strained against the thick fabric with each breath. As she walked, she tried to take her mind off of it. Adella looked up at the sky dotted with little white clouds. She listened as the birds chirped their pretty songs, and noticed how the grasses had taken on the lively bright green of spring. Flowers of every color dotted the fields here and there. She could see the blues of grape hyacinth and bluebell, the whites of anemone and everlasting, along with many flowers she had no names for. The little weathered trees that dotted the land were pink with buds.

She looked at Kol to see how he was faring. One hand had a tight grip on the horse's mane, while his other was clamped over the wound on his side. His face was a grimace but he didn't make a sound.

"Do you need a rest, Mister Kol?" she asked. He shook his head.

They came to the rock outcropping, which formed a cliff on its north side, but sloped gently upward from the ground on its southern end. The horses were able to walk up the incline without losing their footing. At the summit, Kol dismounted carefully with one hand pressing into Adella's shoulder. He was very heavy and she thought she might buckle under his weight. It was at that moment she felt a sharp pain beside her sternum, as her ribcage pressed against her stays. As soon as Kol was settled, she turned away and hastily untied her jacket bodice, then her stays, pulling the string through the holes until she was free. Swearing under her breath, she threw the damp garment angrily on the ground and quickly put her bodice back on over her shift, lacing it tightly before turning around again.

Kol raised his eyebrows, but turned to rummage around in the saddle bags. There was one biscuit left, hardly enough for a meal for the both of them. He was about to break it in half when Adella stopped him.

"I don't want it." Adella hoped he couldn't hear her stomach growl as she spoke. "I'm not hungry." She had never been really, truly hungry in her life, but this man looked like he knew the feeling well. She wondered how he could be so lean and still so heavy.

Adella walked around the edge of the cliff, studying the lie of the land. She spotted a large pool of water not far off in the distance to the northwest, surrounded by small trees and shrubs. *Good,* she thought, *we'll head there next.* Kol stood by the horses, drinking from the canteen as she returned up the slope of the rock formation.

"There's water that way," she gestured. "But after that, you'll have to lead us on. I've never been this far west before."

He nodded. "I know this place. They call it Compass Point, as it points straight north. If we keep heading west, we'll come to a trail. We'll take it up to the sea, and follow the coast toward Hedda. They keep a camp just outside the border there." He gently lowered himself to sit on a large rock, wincing.

Adella eyed him curiously for a moment. "So, what happened between you and them? Why were you tied up?"

He exhaled slowly before answering. "Our orders were to terrorize the town until you were all dead or gone," he admitted. "We've always been told terrible stories about you Valennians. I had no reason not to believe it." He shrugged, casting his eyes downward. "Things are very bad in Sornia. Why would it be any different anywhere else?" He brought out the flask that had been tucked into the waist of his dirty doeskin breeches.

"Go on," she prodded.

"It was my first assignment as a squadron chief. Valennian women sell for fifty gold pieces in Hedda." He turned the flask over in his hands. "I tried to catch that maid of yours and make some money. Then you blindsided me. When I saw who it was—" he pressed his lips together. "Well, I wasn't expecting it to be you," he said, one corner of his mouth pulling into a smile.

"What difference did that make?" she asked, leaning in on her elbows.

"I'd been scouting the area for some time before. I had seen you around, and I—" Kol stopped himself and looked away, but his face reddened. "I don't know," he said quickly. "Maybe because no one in Sornia would ever take a risk like that for a servant. Where I'm from, they are beaten regularly. I thought maybe things in Valenna weren't as we've been told."

"So you defected?" Adella asked.

"Something like that." He paused to take a drink, wiping his mouth on the back of his hand. "Anyway, outside, the men wanted to set fire to the house as well, with you in it. We fought it out, but when we returned to camp I was a traitor and that was that. They were going to execute me in the morning." He watched her face, waiting for a response.

Adella narrowed her eyes. "So that was you?" she asked, repulsion twisting her features. "I still have a headache from that." She frowned, rubbing the back of her head where it hit the wall the night before. There was a bump.

Given what this man had said, the kingdom of Sornia was much worse than she could ever have imagined. *Absolutely barbaric,* she thought. *Him, and all of Sornia. How could Valenna and Sornia have been colonies from the same empire, and yet be so different?*

"Come," he said. "I want to show you something."

Adella hesitated, not sure she wanted to know what it was, but she could find no malice in his expression. Besides, with his injury, he could barely walk. He was no real threat to her. Curiosity won out, and she followed as he walked slowly up to the highest point of the rock. Sweeping his foot to clear the brush away, he revealed part of a carved stone. It was broken off a few feet above the ground, but it had an ornate base and fluting carved into the sides.

"A column?" She bent down to touch the stone. The harsh weathering on the surface hinted at its age. "Did your people make this?"

"No, it's not Sornian," he answered. "But there are more scattered around the area."

"In Valenna, we've always been told the Campos had never been inhabited," she mused, brushing the dust from her hands as she stood.

He nodded. "It's the same in Sornia."

From the corner of her eye, she caught his gaze lingering on her face. "It couldn't be Andolinian, could it?" she asked. As she glanced up at him, Kol turned away quickly. *What's he staring at?* Adella wondered. He turned to walk again, and she wiped her face to clear away any dirt that might be on it.

Kol stopped suddenly, bringing his hand to his side. *He's in a lot of pain,* she realized. Adella knew he needed to rest, even if that meant going without water for a while longer. "I think we've gone far enough today," she said, trying to sound indifferent as she grabbed his arm and wrapped it around her shoulders to support his injured side. "If we camp under the northern outcropping, we could chance a fire." Though she was eager to continue on to find her brother, she didn't want to make the mistake of sacrificing one life while trying to save another. *He may not survive his injury even as it is,* she reminded herself, *let alone if I push him too far.* Without Kol's help, in any case, she'd have little hope of rescuing Lucas.

They made camp for the night and, as Adella walked back in the dark after relieving herself much further away than necessary, something caught her eye by the campfire. As she drew closer, she saw a silhouette approaching their camp, outlined against the firelight. The figure held a bow as it snuck up behind Kol, who sat unaware, staring absently into the flames. *Sornians!* The springy green grass muffled Adella's steps as she crept up behind the hooded form. Deftly, she loaded a bolt into her crossbow, which she had thankfully brought with her for safety. Raising the weapon, she aimed it at the figure.

"Drop it," she warned. The stranger relaxed the bowstring and turned, revealing a stout old face with grizzled sideburns.

"Miss Adella?" he asked in disbelief.

"Armand!" She lowered her weapon. "What in the world are you doing here? Oh, am I glad to see you!" she gushed. "Lucas has been taken."

"We thought you were, too," Armand said, putting the arrow back into his quiver.

"No." Adella shook her head. "We've come to look for him."

"You and who?" Armand asked.

"Me," came Kol's voice nearby. Neither she nor Armand had noticed him appear beside them in the dark. "Who are you, and who is that?" he asked, nodding toward another person approaching the firelight with a large horse in hand.

"Miss Adella!" Teressa exclaimed as she joined them. "I'm so glad you're safe! When I realized you and Lucas were missing, I went to Armand's for help, and we tracked you this far—we were so worried!"

"I'm sorry for that," Adella replied, "but I'm so glad you managed to escape!"

"What is going on?" Kol interrupted gruffly.

"Mister Kol," Adella explained, "this is my father's butler, Benramil Armand. And our housekeeper, Teressa Kith."

"And he is?" prompted Armand.

"This is Mister Kol—" Adella stopped, realizing she didn't know his full name. "Is that your family name or your first name?"

"I don't have a family name. I never had a family," Kol said flatly, eyes lowering.

They cast uneasy glances at each other but had no response. Finally, Teressa spoke. "Let's go sit by the fire. Armand is not well."

The night turned cold as the four of them warmed themselves by the campfire. Armand began to shiver, and they wrapped him in saddle blankets.

"Just to be clear," Kol began, "you came out here, just the two of you? You did not bring any more people, or send a message before heading out?"

Teressa and Armand both nodded.

"Adella," Kol began, turning toward her as Armand and Teressa winced at his use of her first name, "when I realized you had come after your brother alone, I thought it was out of panic. But now, I see these two are just as reckless. Do all Valennians run headfirst into trouble?" he asked incredulously. The three of them looked briefly at each other, then back at him and nodded or shrugged.

"Armand isn't merely our butler," Adella insisted. "He is part of the family. Armand was my father's valet when my father was a cavalry officer during the Northern Hostilities. From what I've heard, they took turns saving each other's lives during the battle of Enth."

"I haven't heard that story," Teressa said.

Armand's weathered face brightened at the opportunity. "Well, it all started when Lord Grimless' horse was killed and fell upon him, pinning his leg to the ground." He grinned as he warmed up to telling the tale. "We were beset by mounted archers, and as I struggled to pull the beast off, I was struck by arrows. First in my buttocks, then in my shoulder. And again in the ankle! I managed to get Grimless free but was myself incapacitated. Then, he hoisted me up on his shoulders like a lamb and tried to make for cover. As we finally got clear of the archers, out popped three on foot from the bushes, waving a cutlass each. Grimless and I drew swords likewise, and as he spun this way and that, we cut them down though I be on his shoulders still."

Adella smiled. "Such a ridiculous story."

"But true nonetheless," Armand said, scratching his grey sideburns thoughtfully. "And that's not even half of it."

"I don't believe it," Kol replied. "At least, Sornian officers don't think twice about leaving a man behind. During the border skirmishes, I was left for dead at least three times. Once with nothing more than a sprained ankle."

"Why would they do that?" Armand asked sharply.

Kol pulled out his flask again. "We were in the middle of a festering bog, being attacked with little darts. We couldn't see the enemy anywhere. Perhaps they were hiding in the water. The men started to fall one by one. That's when we realized the darts were poisoned..."

He was still telling the tale while Adella leaned in toward Teressa. "Great, now they're both making up stories," she whispered. She almost laughed, but suddenly felt a catch in her throat as she thought of her brother. *No time for laughter and stories,* she scolded herself. *Poor Lucas! Who knows if he's all right? Or even still alive.* She shuddered at the thought, and, curling up in her cloak, retired for the night with a knot of anxiety in her gut.

3

The Pool

Adella awoke beneath the towering, dark mass of Compass Point as the sun climbed behind a ceiling of grey clouds. Though their campfire had died in the night and the air held the damp chill of dew, Armand remained soundly asleep. Kol was awake but still lying down, pressing a hand to his side. Not far off, the horses were drinking from, and rolling in, a large rain puddle. A voice called her name. Adella turned; Teressa appeared from behind the bluffs to her right.

"Miss Adella," Teressa called out again. "Come here!"

"What is it?" Adella asked as she joined her, then followed her through the tall grass around the stone outcropping.

"There." Teressa pointed down to the ground, where a large paw print had been left behind in a patch of bare soil. The print showed four large toes and a wide footpad, with claw marks clearly visible by each toe.

"It's a wolf print," Adella said, recognizing the shape from her many sightings of them while riding afield. "I hear them howling sometimes even from Greywood."

The two returned to find Armand and Kol in conversation, but they stopped when the two women approached.

"What?" Kol asked.

"Wolf prints, not far off," Adella answered. "It looked like just one, but we should keep watch at night from now on." She turned to Armand. "Did you two bring water?"

"One skin full," he answered. "But that won't last long."

Kol rolled onto his side and slowly tried to stand, then froze with a grimace.

"What's wrong with him?" Armand asked, nodding toward Kol.

"He's injured," Adella said, frowning.

"Let's see it," Armand ordered, and knelt beside him. Adella helped to unwrap the wound, and Armand inspected it, gently pressing here and there along the edges of the inflamed skin. "As long as you take it easy and keep it clean, you should heal up all right," he assured him.

Noticing the cloth was damp where fluid had seeped from the cut, Adella set about changing the dressings as best she could, though she had little to work with. She stuffed the soiled rags into a saddle bag with the hope of being able to wash them later. As she buckled the flap of the bag, she paused, thinking for a moment of her mother. *I'm doing what I can, but I don't know—* she thought to herself. *If only Mother were here...* Any time her father would cut himself with a knife, or Armand with the handsaw, Adella would be there to watch her mother clean and bandage the wounds. For years, there had been no surgeon in Elldon; everyone had to make-do tending to illness or injury amongst themselves, or ride to Raymouth for care. Adella wished she had paid better attention. "What about you, Armand?" she asked. "Are you feeling any better?"

"I wake up with aches still," he replied. "Especially my head. But the fever only comes on at night, and with it the shaking."

"What could it be?" Teressa wondered, but no one had an answer.

"I don't know about you three," Armand said at last, "but I'm starving."

"We ran out of food yesterday," Adella admitted sadly. "Try to get the fire going. Lucas keeps an iron striker and flint in his bag." She pointed to the travel bag she had left on the ground. "I'll go see what I can find."

"I'll come with you," Teressa offered, while Adella unrolled the crossbow and bolts from the blanket she had wrapped them in the night before. Teressa grabbed Armand's axe and followed her out into the fields.

They did not stray very far from Compass Point. Adella walked slowly, looking this way and that at the ground around her. Here and there, she would bend down to inspect something in the dirt, or break off a piece of a plant and smell it. Finally, she called Teressa over.

"Here," Adella said, pointing to a large patch of low-growing plants with wide, rough leaves. "Young burdock. We can cook the tubers," she explained. It was something she'd learned from her father, who had spent many years in the field on campaign in the cavalry when he was younger. After they had moved to Elldon, she had helped prepare many foraged meals under his guidance and knew the plants well enough, though she'd never had a knack for cooking. "Would you mind digging them up?"

Teressa nodded. "I can do that."

Adella left her to it, continuing to look along the ground for something she recognized as a food source. The plants in the Campos were a mixture of familiar and strange. Many were similar to popular Valennian garden herbs. There were varieties of lavender, comfrey, feverfew, chamomile and many others scattered across the plains. Other plants she came across were foreign to her. Some seemed very strange indeed, as though they belonged in other climes and had traveled here from distant shores.

A flash of movement caught her attention and, turning to look, she saw a little flurry of grey fur. She followed the motion with her eye, and loaded her crossbow. Slowly, she aimed for a patch of grey she could barely make out in the green ahead. She pulled the trigger, and the bolt flew straight, but the animal was already gone. She searched the spot but could find no sign of the rabbit, or her bolt. It was lost in the grass.

By now, Teressa had dug up a good amount of tubers and set them on her apron, which she had taken off and laid out in the grass. "I wanted to talk to you about something," Teressa said, continuing to dig with the axe as Adella approached.

"What is it?" Adella asked.

"That man," Teressa began sharply. "He's the one who attacked us, at Greywood. Don't you remember?"

Adella pressed her lips together. "I'm aware."

"Then why is he coming with us?" Teressa threw the axe down onto the ground, furrowing her brow. Curls of ginger hair fell loose over her freckled face. "He's one of *them*; he can't be trusted. He'll use us until he recovers, then kill us. Or take us like they did Lucas. If you ask me," she continued, growing more spirited, "I say, let's leave him here and go on just the three of us. Leave him out here to rot." She stood and gathered up her apron full of roots.

"I don't trust him," Adella admitted. "But if he wanted to kill me he would have done it by now. And he didn't want to go back to Sornia until I offered him a lot of money. But, I figured—" She hesitated, looking away. "Even if I were to be captured too, I'd be that much closer to finding Lucas." She bit her lip, hoping she sounded more confident than she felt. "That was the risk I chose, come what may."

As they walked back to camp, they surprised a large snake warming itself in the grass. Adella slowly lowered the butt of her empty crossbow just above its neck, then shoved it downward. The creature was caught beneath, twisting and turning in anguish. "Tess," Adella said quietly. "The axe, please."

* * *

Kol rummaged around in Lucas's bag, looking for the fire-making tools. Even after handing them to Armand, he continued to pull items out to inspect them. Armand was too busy trying to get a spark to light in the little pile he made of dry grass to pay him any notice. Kol took out the spyglass from the bag and looked around at nothing in particular. Then he found a small package tied up in brown paper. It didn't make much of a sound when he shook it, so he set it down. He moved on to the inside pocket next. He pulled out a small book bound in faded red cloth and turned it over in his hands. The cover had no title, only a floral pattern embossed in gold. "This would make good kindling," Kol offered.

"Don't you dare," Armand replied, shooting him a disapproving look. "That's an antique. Was her grandfather's." Finally, a little flame sprouted up in front of him, and he blew on it gently.

Kol opened the book. Inside were four names, each written in a different hand: R. S. Grimless, Alfrin R. Grimless, Adella Grimless, Lucas Grimless. He ran his fingers slowly over the handwriting and wondered what Adella's life was like, what it might feel like to be a part of a family. It was something he'd always longed to know. Growing up in the orphanage in the middle of the bustling port city of Hedda, he'd always wondered who his real parents were. Like every other child there, he dreamed he might secretly be the son of some noble, hoping to be whisked away from the dreariness, the dirty chores, and the pallet on the hard stone floor to a life of luxury in the countryside. Of course, those silly thoughts had fallen away completely as he grew older and joined the military. Even so, her life seemed so different from his own that he felt drawn to her. He wanted to know more about her.

"You can borrow it if you like," came Adella's voice from behind them, as she and Teressa walked toward the campfire. Embarrassment heated his face as Kol shut the book quickly and stuffed it back in the bag, along with all the other items he had taken out.

They roasted and ate the snake meat and tubers, storing some away for later. Soon, they were packed up and headed to the pool in the northeast. Armand rode Patches, his own large, steady draft that followed along behind the others with little guidance necessary from his rider. Kol sat on one of the smaller horses as Adella led it in hand, with the second one ponied to his. Teressa mostly walked along next to Adella; she was not used to riding and was nervous around horses. They traveled like this most of the day, until they came to the water that had been visible from the peak of Compass Point. The pool was large, almost a lake, and was surrounded by little windswept trees and blooming, fragrant shrubs. The water was shallow and clear; there was no sign of algae, or weeds, or even fish. The bottom was all pebbles and rock.

They refilled their water containers at the edge of the pool, then washed their faces and hands in it. Then they settled in for the evening, making a little campsite a short distance from the north end of the pool. Adella unlaced her riding boots and pulled them and her stockings off her aching feet. Blisters had formed on her heels and toes, she had a stitch in her side nearly the entire day, and her skin felt dry and tight from too much wind and sun, but all of that was nothing compared with the turmoil the recent events had left within her. Adella's stomach churned as her mind kept envisioning the worst: Lucas lying dead in a field, Elldon burning, her parents returning home to find it all in desolate ruin, only to be captured themselves. She tried to push the thoughts away, but they kept returning.

The others were sitting in front of a small fire, trying to decide who got first watch. Finally, Kol volunteered but Adella wasn't paying attention; trying to keep her mind on lighter things, she was thinking about the cool, clean water of the pool. Perhaps a refreshing dip would rally her spirits. The shadows of the trees around them were getting long, and the sunlight had turned golden. There was still plenty of time before dark to go for a quick swim, she figured. It seemed safe enough, and her aching muscles could certainly use it.

Adella grabbed one of the swords that she had gotten from the dead soldiers two days before, just in case, and went back to the pool. She set it by the water's edge and removed her outer garments, leaving on her thin shift of undyed linen and her under-breeches that ended in lace above her knees. Stepping in, she walked carefully over the slick stones beneath the water. It was brisk, but refreshing. Sleeping on the ground at night and traveling all day had left her sore and blistered, but the aches seemed to wash away as she walked deeper in. As she waded to the deepest part at the center of the pool, which only came up to her chest, Adella felt an odd sensation under her feet, as though the ground started to crawl. The small pebbles she stood on shifted sideways, and then rolled away completely. A strange rumbling emanated from below as the bare rock beneath her gave way, disappearing below her feet. Cold water rushed over her head and into her eyes and ears as she plunged downward. Flinging out her arms, she tried desperately to grasp onto anything at all. For one dark moment, she thought she would be completely lost, until finally, her hand caught hold of a sharp rock ledge.

Holding her breath tightly, Adella fought the urge to gasp. Looking down through the murk around her, all she could see was inky blackness. The water was now much colder, and, oddly, she tasted the tang of saltwater in her mouth. She looked up again toward her hand, still gripping the edge of stone. The hole above her head that she had slipped through shone golden with sunlight compared to the dark abyss below. Adella kicked her feet as hard as she could to propel herself upward through the opening. The fabric of her shift twisted and tangled around her legs, but finally she was able to pull herself through, back into the pool above. Still holding her breath, she pulled herself through the lip of the hole and, as her head broke through the surface, gasped for air. Pushing her hair back from her face, she waded toward the shore, and was almost there when she heard a splashing behind her.

Adella glanced back, and her heart dropped down into her stomach. A large, serpentine shape came up out of the hole in the bottom of the pool that she had fallen through, darting this way and that, back and forth through the water and right toward her. She scrambled toward land as fast as she could and threw herself upon the dry ground. Glancing back toward the water, a cold panic flooded through her as she realized the creature was still coming toward her fast. She grabbed the sword beside her that she had left in the dirt. Just as it breached the surface at her feet, Adella thrust the blade downward, skewering through the creature's skull with the sickening crack of bone.

Gripping the handle of the sword, Adella dragged the heavy thing out of the water and into the grass. It flopped and curled for a while, then finally lay still. The strange, fish-like animal was longer than she was tall, and as wide as her waist. It had a long, toothy snout and a fin on the end of its tail that flared out like a paddle. Little flippers hung where limbs would've been, and she was struck by the strangeness of it. Never had she seen anything like it before. Adella walked a few paces away to safety and slumped down onto the ground to catch her breath. Her limbs felt weak, her fingers trembled. She laid back into the soft grass and closed her eyes, letting the golden evening sun warm her chilled skin.

A shadow moved over her face, blocking out the sunlight. "Are you all right? I heard splashing." Squinting one eye open, she saw Kol standing over her, pressing a hand to his side. He looked over at the dead creature with a sword through its head. "You didn't say you were going fishing," he added. Adella couldn't help but let out a weak laugh.

Armand and Teressa came up behind him. Teressa, eyes widened and speechless, looked at the animal with a mixture of disgust and horror.

"Good heavens, girl!" Armand exclaimed, suspiciously eyeing the creature, then Adella. "What happened?"

"I was wading," Adella began, sitting up and brushing her wet hair from her face. "The bottom gave way, and I fell into water below. It was frigid brine underneath, like I had fallen right into the sea."

"Are you saying you broke the pool?" Teressa asked dubiously. "What is it, anyway? An eel?" she guessed, but Adella could only shrug.

Armand clapped his hands together, eyes gleaming with enthusiasm. "Let's eat it!"

They all helped cut the meat from the creature and cook it in the campfire, finishing just as the light disappeared in the west. After eating, the four of them rested for a while, gazing quietly into the flames. Adella sat contemplating what she had experienced in the pool. *The change in the water, the sudden appearance of the... the eel...* she wondered, not fully believing that was what it was. *What does it all mean?*

Armand broke the silence as he turned to Kol. "What did you mean, you never had a family?"

Kol glanced at him, then away again, a pained look flashing across his face. Adella thought for a moment he wouldn't answer. Finally, he spoke. "I was found on the street when I was very small," he began quietly. "I don't remember anything before then." Gingerly, he laid back in the grass, putting one hand behind his head. "I was brought to the orphanage in Hedda. As soon as I was old enough, I went straight into the military. Since then, I've lived either in the barracks, or in a tent in the field. Never had a home."

"That sounds lonely," Teressa said. "Do you not have anyone at all? Not even—" She stopped abruptly and Kol looked at her, raising a brow in confusion.

"She means to ask if you have any lady friends," Armand said to him. Kol only frowned at the two of them.

"Not everyone likes to talk about personal matters," Adella said quietly as she caught his expression, trying to put an end to the subject.

"I couldn't imagine," Armand replied. "That's probably my favorite thing to discuss."

Adella smiled. "I'm well aware."

"How is *Misses* Asher, anyway?" Teressa interjected, a look of mischief in her eyes.

"No, you're mistaken," Armand said. "I haven't seen her in two weeks. I met this beautiful woman when I was in Raymouth last. Her cheeks were pink as roses."

"Which cheeks—" Kol began. Adella shook her head and waved her hands at him, but it was too late; Armand took the prompt, and began to describe the woman in exaggerated detail. By the time he had finished, the other three knew what the old woman looked like naked. Adella groaned, hiding her face behind her hands.

"What about you, girl?" Armand asked Teressa. "Are you asking him for any particular reason?"

Teressa shook her head quickly. "Oh, no. I have someone already." She looked down at her hands, a smile spreading across her face. "Only last week, he told me he loved me. Under the apple tree," she added wistfully, "as the petals were falling."

"That sounds lovely," Adella said. "Is it someone from Elldon?"

Teressa nodded but quickly changed the subject. "And you, Miss Adella? What about that captain of yours?"

"No," she said softly, looking away. "He's just a friend."

"Does he know that?" Armand asked. Adella bit her lip but didn't respond.

Armand, who had been sitting wrapped in a blanket, began to shiver. The other three looked on nervously, helpless as they watched the tremors progressively worsen. Suddenly, he fell backward, shaking violently as his limbs flailed against the ground.

They rushed over to his side. "What's happening?" Adella asked, her voice strained.

"He's having spasms," Kol replied. "Does he do this often?"

"Only since he fell ill," Teressa replied. "It happened before, as we were traveling here. What can we do?" she pleaded. "Should we try to hold him down?"

"No." Kol turned Armand onto his side. "Stay clear of him, there's nothing we can do right now."

A grey morning came, overcast with clouds. After preparing for travel, they gathered at the edge of the pool to replenish their water supplies. Armand bent down to the water, cupping his hands in it and rubbing it into his face. Bringing more up, he drank from his hands, but spat it back out. "It's brackish," he said in disappointment.

"That doesn't make sense," Teressa replied. "It was freshwater yesterday." She drank the water in the canteen she had collected the day before to be sure. "See, this is fresh still." She reached down to stick her hand in the water again and shrieked, surprised by a burst of movement as a tentacled creature darted away from her hand. "What could've happened?"

"There could've been a salt pocket in the ground," Kol reasoned. "There are salt mines not far to the southwest."

"But what of the eel?" Adella asked.

He shrugged. "You seem pretty good at finding trouble. Let's get away before more come." The others agreed but Adella wasn't convinced. *There's something strange about this land.* She was quiet that morning as they packed away their things and headed west again.

Half the day had passed when Adella looked over at Armand riding on his horse and was surprised to see his face and neck covered in red splotches, her eyes widening at the sight. Kol, whose horse Adella was again leading, caught her reaction.

"Did you see his face?" he asked, leaning in close to speak quietly, and she nodded. "I've seen something like that before," he continued. "Along with the spasms, it's very similar to the red ague."

"What is that?" she asked.

"A plague that spread through Sornia ten years ago," he replied. "I was fifteen when I had it. It only gets worse."

She furrowed her brow. "What can be done? Is there any way to treat it?"

"The physic for it is still sold in the markets in Hedda. But it's expensive, and we're days from there." He straightened up in the saddle again, putting a hand to his side. "There is another kind of treatment, though."

"What is it?" she asked, bringing the horse to a halt to look up at him.

"A decoction of wild herbs," he replied. "Those of us who couldn't afford the physic had to make our own remedies. It wasn't as effective, but it helped."

"Which herbs?" she asked eagerly. "Can we recreate it?"

"Two herbs were used to make it," Kol replied. "One was eternity root, the other a tree flower. I don't remember the name of it, but I would recognize it if I saw it."

"I've never heard of eternity root," she said. "What does it look like?"

"It's a common Sornian garden flower, but I've seen them in the Campos," he explained. "It's a small shrub with large, dark leaves and red flowers. The blooms look like roses, but much larger."

She nodded thoughtfully, noting the description. "And the other herb?"

"It grows in the wild," Kol replied. "Usually by water. A small tree, with clusters of little white flowers."

"And you're certain you can recognize them now?" she prodded.

He nodded. "Yes."

"Good," she replied. "Keep an eye out for them."

The day wore on with no sign of the needed plants. Though the daylight was not yet spent, they decided to stop for the evening when they came to a shallow creek. They unpacked their things and refilled their waterskins at the stream's edge. Armand had been worse that day, and so Adella decided to look for the materials for the physic while the others rested. Leaving Teressa to look after Armand, Adella set out on foot with Kol alongside on horseback to find the plants in the wild. They followed the stream northward, searching along the banks for the first herb.

As the sun lowered, Adella stopped walking for a moment. Her legs ached in ways she never felt before, the skin on her heels worn raw. She leaned with one arm against the horse and rubbed her foot with her hand, sighing with dismay, she looked at the vast plains spread out before them.

"Up," Kol said, offering a hand.

"What?" she asked, blinking up at him.

Kol moved back to make room on the horse. "Take a rest."

"Oh..." Though they had ridden double out of necessity on their first night in the Campos, now that she was beginning to know him a little better, the thought of once again being pressed so close to him brought warmth to her face. "Well, I—"

"Come on," he urged and, taking his foot from the stirrup, took her hand.

Adella gave in and stepped into the stirrup, with Kol helping her up as best he could. She settled in front of him and, taking up the reins, tried not to lean against him as they continued on toward a clump of trees by the riverside in the distance. One tree ahead looked promising, with patches of white on its branches. As the horse walked onward, the air turned cool and the wind stirred, pulling at their clothes. Adella felt a hand running across her shoulders behind her neck and froze, holding her breath, until she realized Kol was merely pushing away her hair that had been blowing in his face.

They approached a tree with white blossoms, and Adella dismounted to get a closer look. "Is this it?" Adella asked, handing a clump of flowers up to him.

Kol crushed the petals between his fingers and inhaled. "Yes. Gather as many as you can."

Adella set to harvesting clusters of the little blossoms from the branches. "This is an elder tree," she mentioned casually, remembering he didn't know the name of it.

"Elder..." he trailed off. "Ah, that's right. In Sornia, it is called the eldritch tree, but I can never remember that word."

"No wonder," she replied with a smirk. "That's an absurd name for such a common plant. Might as well forget it again, and remember the correct name." She paused as something caught her eye in the distance. "Didn't you say the other herb was red? Look there, on the crest of that hill." She pointed to a rise westward where flecks of crimson could just be seen among the endless green, with the lowering sun above. She smiled at the thought of their task being done.

"Yes, I see it now," he said, squinting against the light. "But we need to be careful, we are nearing the western trail. We might not be alone out here."

Adella packed the blossoms into the saddle bag and they headed west.

They approached the hill under a pink and orange sky, the clouds edged with gold. Adella stopped the horse, and after helping Kol down, they trudged up the rise. A vast expanse of land spread out before them in a wide valley, with a long ridge of bluish hills beyond. Coming to the patch of red, Adella knelt in the grass to inspect the plants. Large, ruffled blossoms nodded in the wind on feeble stems. As she bent down to smell one of the flowers, burying half her face in it, a familiar scent greeted her.

"It's only a peony," she said sadly. "I didn't know they could be red. We'll have to keep looking."

"What do you mean?" Kol replied. "This is eternity root. This is what we need."

She furrowed her brow. "Do the Sornians name all plants so extravagantly? What do you call that one?" she asked, pointing to the grass at their feet.

"That's grass," Kol said flatly. "We don't have time for games, it's getting dark. Let's dig this up and go." He drew out one of the swords taken off the dead soldier that he had lately been wearing on his belt. Bracing his side with one hand, he knelt carefully and pried the blade into the soil around the plant.

As he loosened each large root, Adella lifted them, shook away the dirt, and packed them away. She paused for a moment, watching as he worked. Dark hair hung loose in his face, obscuring his sharp features. The black stubble on his jaw was beginning to thicken into a beard. Though he looked rough, she thought that, altogether, he wasn't bad looking. *Maybe even handsome...* She was grateful that he'd offered to help find the herbs and, though Adella reminded herself he only agreed to come with her after she'd offered to pay him, she was glad he had agreed to help find Lucas. *He might not be the friendliest fellow, but I suppose he's been rather helpful.* She was surprised at the thought, considering how they'd met. Kol looked up and, as his dark eyes met hers, pulling her back to the present, Adella realized with some embarrassment that she'd been staring. He opened his mouth to speak, but then his gaze shifted to something in the distance behind her.

Kol grabbed her wrist. "Get down!" he whispered, pulling her to the ground. He winced and grabbed his side.

"What is it?" she asked under her breath, her heart pounding with alarm.

"There are riders in the valley; I don't know if they saw us," he explained, creeping backward in the grass. "We've gathered enough, let's get going."

4

The Chase

By the time Adella and Kol arrived back at camp, Armand was asleep already. Teressa sat by him with anxious tears in her eyes. Kol set to making a fire and instructed Adella in chopping the roots. Placing a tin cup full of water on a stone in the firepit, he added the chopped herb. It simmered until the liquid became a dark golden brown, then Kol added the elder blossoms and left them to blanch. Finally, the physic was finished and, when it had cooled, they woke Armand and gave him a draught of the medicine. The remainder was poured into Kol's empty flask.

It was Adella's turn to keep watch for the first half of the night. She spent most of the time walking the perimeter of their camp to try to take her mind off things, though it didn't seem to be working. Anxiety knotted in her gut as she turned the same worries over and over again in her mind; Lucas's fate, Armand's health, even Kol's injury, and the safety of her neighbors at Elldon all weighed heavily on her. Traveling during the day, it was easy for Adella to keep her mind on her surroundings and the tasks at hand, but the night offered no such respite.

When her aching legs couldn't stand the pacing any longer, she returned to the campfire and was surprised to see Kol sitting up, look-

46

ing at the stars. "Is everything all right?" she asked. "Why aren't you asleep?"

"Everything's fine." He rubbed his face. "I have trouble sleeping sometimes. Nightmares."

Adella sat beside him. "You can't sleep, and I can't stay awake." She thought for a moment, remembering how eagerly he had shared military tales with Armand. "Do you know any good stories? I still have a while yet before I can wake Tess."

"I don't know any," he answered flatly. "None you would enjoy, anyway."

"Oh," she muttered, folding her arms on her knees.

He let out a breath. "Well, there is one I heard in the orphanage when I was young. An Old Andolinian tale, but every Sornian knows it."

"Andolinian?" she asked in surprise, but caught herself. "Oh, right. It's strange to think Sornia was a part of Andolin once too, like Valenna." She stretched out in the grass, crossing her arms under her head. "Go on."

"The story takes place long ago," Kol began, his features illuminated softly in the moonlight. "Before the war that divided the Andolin Empire. There was a young man by the name of Leveret, who lived in a small village in the countryside. He set out to become a hero to win the heart of a beautiful woman from his village, whom he loved. Her name was..." He scrunched his face up in thought. "Paloma, I think. Anyway, he went adventuring and slayed a great beast. In its den, he found an exceptional treasure called the Heart of the World. This jewel could bestow unnatural abilities on whoever possessed it. Great strength, the power to fly, or to breathe water, even to take the shape of animals or call up storms." He paused.

"I'm listening," Adella said quietly.

"After finding this treasure," he continued, "strange things began to happen. Horrible creatures came out of every corner of the world, terrorizing the people. The seas became turbulent, and violent storms ruined villages. He realized he couldn't be everywhere at once to stop them." He paused again.

"Mmhm," she murmured.

"Leveret returned home one day to find his homeland destroyed and Paloma dead. He blamed himself, and in his grief he decided to be rid of the Heart of the World forever. He used his abilities one last time to fashion an unbreakable box from meteor iron, and locked the Heartstone inside. He hid it where no one could ever find it. The key he kept on his person for the rest of his life. When he grew old, he climbed to the top of the tallest mountain to die, taking the key with him." Kol was silent for a moment, looking up at the starry sky. "Every boy in the orphanage, myself included, dreamt of finding that treasure someday."

"Hm." Adella closed her eyes.

* * *

"Adella," Kol whispered in her ear. "Wake up, it's morning. And my arm is numb."

Adella opened her eyes to a dark blue sky with a soft yellow light tinting the east. Her neck felt as though she had slept on a rock all night. "Your arm?" she asked in confusion, sitting up. "Oh, I'm sorry…" Heat rose in her face as she realized the rock she had slept on was his elbow. She hadn't meant to sleep, but she had been too exhausted to fight it. *Ugh, how embarrassing!* She cringed, hiding her face behind her hands. *And his arm! I'll never be able to look him in the eye after this.* Then, another thought hit her. "Oh no, I forgot to wake Tess!" she muttered.

"I did before I went to sleep," he replied. "You slept so soundly, I thought you must've needed it."

At that moment, Teressa hurried toward them. "Wake up! All of you!" she scolded in a hushed voice. "Riders are approaching."

Adella jumped to her feet and went over to where Armand still slept. "Armand!" She poked his shoulder. "How do you feel? You must wake up."

He sat up and rubbed his eyes. "I feel hungover. That stuff you gave me was awful."

"Well, you look better," Adella replied, noticing the red spots on his face had faded. "But we have to clean up the camp and hide." She helped him up, and together they all packed away their things, buried the ashes of the campfire, and led the horses into a tall thicket.

They hid in the foliage, with all three horses tacked up at the ready. The sun had fully risen and as they peeked through the branches, they could just make out five riders to the northwest, heading in their direction.

"The bushes are blocking their view of our camp, and the fire is out," Teressa said. "Perhaps they didn't see us, and will pass by?"

"They're following our trail from last night," Adella replied. "They'll be upon us soon."

"What can we do?" Teressa asked.

"We'll just have to wait," Armand replied, "and hope to catch them by surprise."

"That won't go well," Kol said, peering through the branches at the riders in the distance. "They're soldiers fresh from Sornia. Well armed, well rested."

"They're not wearing uniforms though," Teressa countered.

"They don't wear uniforms in the Campos," Kol replied. "Those were our orders."

Adella considered their options. With Armand ill, Kol injured, and Teressa unskilled at riding, there was only one thing left to do. "Suppose one of us were to ride out and draw them off?"

"You mean yourself?" Kol asked sharply, turning to look Adella in the eye, and the concern on his face caught her off guard. "No, your little crossbow is no match for their hunting bows."

"Then I'll stay out of range," she replied with a shrug. "No sense in arguing about it, I'm going."

Kol let out a long breath. "If you can't lose them, return here immediately. We'll be ready."

Adella grabbed her crossbow, stuffed the bolts into the waistband of her skirt, and hopped up into the saddle of one of the Sornian horses. Leaving the cover from the east bank of the stream at a working canter, she headed north. When she came into the view of the oncoming riders, several of them drew out bows as they picked up the pace. Clicking her tongue, she bumped the horse with her heels and the horse obeyed the cue, lengthening out into a gallop. She pushed her hands forward along his soft black mane to give him room to stretch his neck.

The stream lay between her and the five riders still; it wasn't wide, but the riverbed was deep and rocky. As the riders approached the water, they slowed. The first rider, on a big black horse, jumped from the bank to the other side; the second horse dumped its rider in the water and bolted. The remaining three riders walked their horses through the stream, climbing down and up the steep sides, and continued after her.

"That's one down," Adella said to herself, brow lowering in determination. "Four left." Their trouble crossing the stream had given her a long lead in front. She looked around the landscape for any interesting features. Not far to the northeast, she could see a large patch of woods. Urging her horse faster, she veered right.

As she came up to the edge of the trees, Adella glanced over her shoulder. The riders behind her spread out in a long string, with some advancing faster than others. The man on the large black horse was coming up quickly behind her. Ahead, she saw something in front of her that made her heart flutter with panic. The trunk of a large fallen tree stretched across a gap in the woods; it looked to be about as high as her own horse's chest. Steeling herself, she leaned forward in the saddle and galloped straight toward the fallen tree. Adella had jumped her own horse Shy over obstacles many times, but she knew him well and could guess his every move. This horse, she hardly knew, but he seemed sporting enough. As they neared the tree, the little gelding jerked up his head and showed the whites of his eyes. Glancing quickly back again, her heart dropped to see the rider on the black horse almost overtaking her, his brandished sword gleaming in the sunlight.

She kept contact on each rein to guide the horse directly toward the tree, squeezing her heels into his side to encourage him forward. When she was one stride away from the log, Adella moved her hands up along the mane to give the horse his head. However, instead of up and over, she felt herself suddenly jerk to the left as he bolted sideways, and Adella found herself momentarily hanging in the air beside the saddle. She pulled herself back into it with the reins and stirrup.

"Damn!" she muttered, her heart racing. She looked behind her just in time to see the large black horse clear the jump beautifully. They had been close behind and didn't have time to change course when she did. Adella briefly admired the skill of the black horse and its rider as they sailed clear over the log. Directly behind him, the second rider tried to turn quickly, but his horse slid in the grass and ran right into the trunk of the fallen tree. The rider was thrown over it, and it looked as though he landed badly, legs askew in the air.

Her horse gave a low, rattling snort. "It's all right, good fellow," she said, patting its neck to calm him. Behind her, the two other riders made the turn and were coming up quickly. One was a good distance behind, but the other was gaining on her.

"I want her dead!" a voice shouted.

As he closed in on her, the first rider came within range of his bow, and loosed an arrow at her. It whizzed just past Adella's ear; her horse tossed his head in protest. *Shit!* Adella gasped. *That was too close!*

As the man fumbled to reach another arrow in the quiver on his back, Adella swung her horse around in a sudden, tight turn and galloped toward him. Hoofbeats pounding in her ears, she dropped the reins and raised her crossbow. At that same moment, he drew back another arrow. Adella drew a deep, steadying breath and squeezed the lever.

Her bolt hit him in his left side, sinking deep between the ribs as the man's arrow grazed across the side of Adella's neck, biting through the skin with a sharp sting. He dropped to the ground, and his horse trotted away in confusion.

Adella now found herself galloping toward the second rider. She was still trying to think of something clever to do when she was thrown forward as her horse tripped and fell out from under her. She tumbled through the air and landed hard on her back, knocking the breath from her lungs. Through her blurred vision, she was vaguely aware that the second rider had dismounted, the beats of his hooves slowing to a stop, and was now approaching her on foot as she struggled to regain her breath. Finally, just as she gasped a mouthful of air, a hand clamped down around her throat, cutting off her breath once more.

"Well, aren't you a pretty thing," she heard a rough voice say in her ear. "It would be a shame to kill you so soon." The grip around her neck tightened, and her vision blackened around the edges.

Adella felt frantically around at her waistband, her trembling fingers searching until she found what she was looking for. Pleading silently for her hand to steady for even a moment, she pulled out a bolt and jammed it upward into the man's gut with as much force as she could muster. Warm blood spilled out over her hand, then a massive weight came down on her as he collapsed and went limp.

She pushed the dead man away, and got up as fast as she could. A wave of dizziness came over her, but she pressed on toward the horse he had been riding. Her own gelding was nowhere to be seen. By her count, there was still one more rider left, the man on the black horse. She mounted up and, looking around, spotted him in the distance. He had circled around the north end of the woods, and was heading her way.

Adella's hands shook as she took the reins. Urging the horse up to gallop, she turned back in the direction of the campsite. Behind, the black horse gradually closed the gap between them over the long distance as her horse began to tire. Finally, she drew up alongside the bushes where she knew her friends were hiding just as the rider on the black horse raised his sword. From the corner of her eye, metal flashed in the sun and the man was knocked out of his saddle. Behind her, hoofbeats slowed as the black horse continued on without its rider; his body lay on the ground, with the handle of an axe protruding from his chest.

Adella swung her horse around and trotted up as Kol emerged from the bushes, watching as he strode over to the soldier on the ground and stuck his sword in him. Adella dismounted and, bringing the reins over the horse's head, joined him. Her hands and the front of her dress were red with blood, and a trickle ran down her neck from where the arrow grazed her, tickling her skin.

"Are you injured?!" Kol said, turning toward her, fear in his eyes as he took in her appearance. She couldn't yet summon her voice; she only shook her head.

Adella rested her hands on her knees for a moment, taking a deep breath to calm her nerves as Armand and Teressa came toward them. Finally, Adella tried to speak. "Good work with the axe, thanks," she said breathlessly to Kol, then turned toward Teressa. "Can you try to catch that horse?" she asked, pointing to where the black horse had stopped to graze. She took another deep breath. "Please," she added. Teressa looked at her dubiously for a moment, then went to collect the animal.

Adella looked the creature over. It was a mare, well muscled and tall, with a thick mane and tail. She stroked the animal's neck, moreso to calm her own nerves than the mare's, while Kol rummaged around in the large cantle bag tied behind the saddle.

Teressa wandered toward the dead man in the grass. "Oh, Miss Adella," she said sadly. "Look at his face; he was so handsome."

As Adella approached, she could see that he was young, with smooth skin and dark, close-cropped hair. "Yes," Adella replied. "He was an excellent rider as well. Such a shame." Beside her, Armand placed his old rain hat over his heart, as though the girls were giving a eulogy.

Gold glinted in the man's palm, and Teressa turned over his hand to reveal a wedding band. She stood again, tears filling her eyes. Adella put her arm around her and patted her shoulder. Though she was shaken as well, she tried to put her nerves aside and put on a brave face, if only to provide some encouragement for her friend. Yet, when Adella closed her eyes, the face of the man she'd stabbed—the first life she'd ever taken—remained etched in her mind. She willed the image away.

"Not to interrupt," Kol began, "but he did try to kill you, five against one. Also, there's food here. Cheese..." He uncorked a leather bottle and sniffed. "Wine." Then, he brought out a jar and opened it. "And honey!" he added in excitement. He stuck a finger into the half-empty jar and licked it.

"Mister Kol," Adella called over to him. "Don't eat that."

"Why?" he asked, frowning as he walked over.

"It has better uses." She took the jar and closed it.

They left the riverside quickly and traveled north the rest of that day, not daring to approach the western trail used by the Sornian soldiers. Adella had a vague understanding that they were drawing near to the southern coast of Belgrand Bay. The farther north they went, the more nervous she became, which was partly due to her excitement at finally reaching the sea. The excitement, however, was mixed with the much stronger apprehension of drawing closer to Sornia, and the uncertainty of what would happen when they arrived. *My poor brother,* she thought. *I wonder what he's going through right now.* She tried to remind herself that, if he was to be sold at auction like Kol had suggested, they wouldn't want to hurt him. *He should still be alive and well... Shouldn't he?* Her stomach tied itself in knots. *Oh, Lucas,* she pleaded silently, *don't make any trouble. Please, don't give them reason to hurt you.*

In the early evening, they had to make camp out in the open. Now that they were in higher plains, there was no tree cover anywhere to be seen. Thick dark clouds blanketed the sky. As they dismounted and untacked their horses, Adella noticed Kol was again holding his side with his hand. They sat in the grass to rest, sharing what little food they had while they watered the horses at a brook. Though she would've loved to keep the beautiful animal for herself, Adella had given the black horse to Kol to ride, since its size and good training suited his height and condition. She couldn't help but notice the kindness with which Kol treated the animal, watching as he patted the mare's graceful, arched neck and lifted her long, elegant legs to check her hooves for stones. Adella looked back at her own little bay, which she had caught again after the chase. Eyeing its short legs and round belly, with hardly a forelock to hang down above his bulging eyes, she sighed in resignation.

Adella walked over to where Kol stood with the black mare. "You should name your horse," she said, petting the animal's soft muzzle.

"How about..." He thought for a moment. "Madigan?"

Adella nodded, and ran her fingers through the mare's soft coat. Madigan stretched her neck, sticking her lip in the air, and Adella laughed at the reaction. Kol sat in the grass, watching her with a wry smile.

"I should change the dressing on your wound today," Adella commented.

"You forgot yesterday," he replied, pulling the wineskin from his bag.

Adella frowned when she realized he was right. "You should've mentioned it. How's it feeling?" she asked, kneeling beside him. Shrugging, he took a drink, then handed her the wine. Adella took a swig, but then corked it and set it beside her in the grass. "Do you mind?" she asked, motioning toward the wound on his side. Adella watched the knotted muscles over his ribs flex as he pulled off his shirt, then tried to put it out of mind as she gently removed the dressing. Kol winced and looked away. Underneath, a small patch of skin shone swollen and red. Some of the drainage was white rather than clear.

"Oh, no," she muttered.

He reached across for the wine skin. "What?"

"Infection has started," she replied. "Do you still have that flask of spirits?"

"Gone," he admitted with a shrug.

Digging through her things, Adella pulled out more dressings that she had previously washed in the pool before it had turned to brine. As she did, the little package that Lucas had given her back at Greywood fell out of the bag.

Kol picked up the parcel, turning it over. It wasn't very large, but had been wrapped and tied carefully. "What's in this?" he asked.

"Probably nothing important," Adella guessed as she pulled out the jar of honey from her bag along with a clean rag. She opened it up and dipped the rag into the jar, then applied the honey to the wound on his side.

"Oh, that's what you meant about the honey..." he trailed off.

"It's good for healing wounds." She brought out another scrap of cloth and continued to plaster the cut with the honey, then covered it with clean dressings like she had seen her mother do when Lucas had a skin infection last year.

"Can I open this?" he asked, already pulling at the string from the package.

"If you hold still," Adella huffed, struggling to wrap the bandages around his torso. His skin was slick with sweat, making it difficult. Not only that, but leaning in so close that she could smell the wine on his breath was making her pulse quicken; she hoped he wouldn't notice her unsteady hands.

Kol opened the brown packaging paper, and inside was a folded letter on white parchment, sealed with wax. He broke the seal. Inside, there were only a couple of lines written in a hasty hand, with an ample amount of space between each line. "Someone must waste a lot of paper," he commented, then proceeded to read the note aloud. "'Dearest Adella, I hope this letter finds you well. Please accept this small token of friendship, enclosed herein. Forever yours, Rogero Declan.'" Kol wrinkled his nose. "'Friendship?' What a dull man."

"Would you stop moving?" Adella scolded, trying to secure the end of the bandage. After she finished, she took the lacquered wooden box from him just as he was opening it. Inside was a dainty gold ring; the band had a delicate scrollwork design around a little coral jewel. She tried it on and smiled. "Oh, that's pretty!"

"Is that from the captain?" Teressa asked as she came over, apparently listening to their conversation. "Let me see—" Teressa said, taking Adella's hand. "Oh, it's lovely!"

Kol looked back down at the letter. Scrawled in the upper right-hand corner was a little symbol resembling the sun. "What's that mean?" he asked, pointing to the image.

"Nothing," Adella said quickly. She took the letter from him and folded it back up, tucking it in her bag along with the empty box. In truth, she recognized the symbol as one that Rogero had made up when they were younger, when they would amuse each other by writing secret messages in invisible ink made from the juice of lemons. The sun symbol was their way of indicating to each other that the paper should be held to heat. The two of them hadn't used it in years, however, and she was quite perplexed why he would now. Their previous secret notes had always been childish nonsense or silly jokes; she couldn't imagine what it could be now.

"Is it an engagement ring, Miss Adella?" Teressa asked excitedly. "You've got it on the wrong hand."

"It certainly isn't," Adella replied firmly. Without having read the secret message, though, she wasn't really sure.

"The letter didn't say it *wasn't* an engagement ring," Teressa noted.

"What's that, Miss Adella? You're getting married?" Armand asked loudly from where he sat, wrapped in a blanket once more. He took a mouthful of the physic from its flask and pulled an ugly face. Though he was shivering again, it wasn't as bad as it had been. "To whom? Not Mister Kol you mean?"

Kol choked on the wine, coughing.

"No, Armand, don't be ridiculous," Adella said.

"Tell us about him," Teressa urged. "What's the captain like?"

"I haven't seen him in years," Adella admitted with a shrug, "but..." A smile pulled at the corners of her mouth as she remembered. "He was shy, and sweet. What he lacked in appearance, he made up for with his gentle disposition. We were inseparable—" She stopped abruptly as she recalled the last time she'd seen Rogero, her smile fading away with the pain the memory brought back. She stood and walked off under the pretense of packing away her supplies.

Adella just wanted to step away for a moment, not wanting them to read the emotions on her face. After what happened between her and Rogero years ago, she didn't want to spare him another thought. It hurt too much, and so she pushed the memories away.

Thinking about the present wasn't much better, though. An uneasiness gnawed in her stomach. She had been so concerned with Armand and his illness that she had neglected to tend to Kol's injury, and now it festered. If she was being honest with herself, she wasn't sure he'd survive. She had, whether intentionally or not, favored one over the other, even after Kol found the herbs and made the medicine to help Armand. *But is that all?* she wondered. *Am I not putting Lucas's life above theirs, even now? Am I putting one life above three?*

She looked out over the plains as the sun began to set, letting her mind course through her worries like an unbridled horse. Eventually, she returned to the group, wanting to say something but unsure how. She spun the little gold ring on her finger while she thought.

"I've been thinking..." Adella began hesitantly. "I don't think you three should come with me. To Sornia, I mean." Kol looked up at her intently, waiting for her to go on. "I've got you all into enough trouble," Adella continued. "If something were to happen to any of you now..." She bit her lip. "Well, it would be my fault, and I couldn't live with that."

Armand and Teressa, who had been working to get a fire going with little materials, looked at each other for a moment, then back up at her. "Miss Adella," Armand began, "Pardon me for saying so, but even if you were safe at home, me and Tess would still be here, on our way to find your brother. You're lucky I let you come along," he added with a laugh.

"We are all here because we love Lucas," Teressa said. "We're not going home without him."

"Uh," Kol interrupted. "I'm not here because I love Lucas. But I am used to risking my life for money, and in far worse company than this."

"You two surprise me," Adella said to Armand and Teressa, smiling at them. "Not you, Mister Kol," she added with a smirk. "I thought you might say something like that." Even so, she was relieved to hear his answer.

The night slowly turned chilly and damp with the threat of rain. When it was her turn to keep watch, Adella poked at the sticks in the campfire, waiting to be sure everyone was fully asleep. Armand was snoring loudly; Teressa's mouth was open, drooling onto the saddle pad that served as a pillow. Adella waved her hand over Kol's face as he lay wrapped in a horse blanket to be sure he was actually sleeping. There was no reaction, so she dug through her bag again and pulled out Captain Declan's letter. *I had better do this quickly before it rains and the fire goes out,* she told herself. Kneeling down, she held the paper over the glowing coals.

Brown printed letters began to appear in the spaces between the lines of black script. She accidentally scorched the paper here and there, but eventually, she revealed the hidden writing between the lines:

Forgive my haste, you are the only one I can trust. You'll find an artifact within this box, under false bottom. Sornia wants this very badly, keep it safe, show no one. Spies in Raymouth!

Though she thought the letter sounded ominous, Adella was surprised to feel a bit relieved there was no mention of marriage. *The ring must've been merely a diversion in case the package was intercepted,* she realized. With her pen-knife, she pried out the velveted bottom panel inside the box, revealing underneath a golden disc the size of her palm. Turning it over, she noticed one side of the item was covered with an embossed honeycomb pattern, and the other side had curved markings etched into it, resembling the lines of a map. The disc had notches in strange shapes cut into the outer edge, and a star-shaped hole in the center. Digging out some spare cord from her bag, Adella threaded it through the disc and hung it from her neck, then stuffed the golden object down the front of her bodice. The wooden box and the letter she set into the fire and watched them burn away into ash.

As she sat watching the flames dance, Adella's attention shifted to a sound coming from behind her. It was the sound of harsh, labored breathing and, looking around, she realized it was coming from Kol. She knelt beside him in the firelight, and could see he was still asleep. Then, the sound suddenly stopped altogether, as he seemed to be holding his breath. She waited for one long, uncomfortable moment before shaking him by the shoulder.

"Mister Kol!" she whispered. "Wake up, you're not breathing." Startled, he woke with a gasp and sat upright, looking at her in confusion. Then, pulling the blanket back over his head, he turned away to lie on his other side, and Adella wondered if she had made a mistake waking him.

The wind rose, rustling the trees and bringing the smell of rain. In the distance, lightning flashed, followed by a low rumble. Kol sat up again, pulling the blanket off his head, leaving his hair hanging wildly in his face. "Is that thunder?"

"A storm is rolling in," she replied, "but we've nowhere to go." The high plains they now camped on contained no trees or rock formations to shelter under, only small shrubs and endless grass. Adella frowned at the thought of traveling in damp clothes again. She went over to wake Teressa and Armand.

They huddled together, each wrapped in a blanket or rain cloak, hoping the storm would pass quickly. Lightning cracked and lit up the sky around them. Adella sighed; she used to be fond of storms, when she could watch them pass from the comfort of her chamber window. Greywood felt so far away from her now.

They spent a miserable night waiting for the pouring rain to end. Armand had somehow drifted off again under his cloak while Teressa leaned against Adella, dozing but unable to fully sleep. Kol sat on her other side, with the blanket over his head like a hood.

As the rain slowed to a drizzle, Adella shivered under her oilskin cloak. She looked over at Kol, who was staring off into the dark. "Were you having a nightmare when I woke you?" she asked, and he nodded. "What's it like?" she wondered. "What do you dream of?"

"I've never spoken of them to anyone before," he said, then was silent for a while. Adella figured that was his way of saying he didn't intend to discuss it now, so she just sat watching the lightning. "It's different every time," he continued quietly, "but some things are the same. It's always dark. And I'm on a ship in a storm. Sometimes, I fall in and the waves crash over my head," he said, waving a hand in the air above him, "or terrifying shapes circle me in the water. Other times, I only look on helplessly while someone is washed over the rail into the darkness. Someone I love, though I know not who." He paused for a moment. "I've always wondered if that's how I lost my family. If they were lost at sea."

5

The Coast

Dawn rose, cold and dim, as the travelers made ready to leave. They had just started to saddle the horses when Adella noticed hers was lame, favoring the back left leg. Looking over his hooves and running her hands along his legs, she found a tendon that was warm and swollen. She called Armand over to take a look, as he'd been her mentor in horsemanship her whole life and she trusted his advice.

"It isn't too bad right now, but if we continue to use him, it will worsen," Armand told her, setting the hoof back down. "You have to leave him behind. That would be his best chance." Adella removed the bridle and turned the horse away, continuing on foot with the others riding. They had only gone a little ways when she felt a warm breath on her arm. The little bay nickered gently, hobbling along beside her. Her heart was touched, and she wrapped her arms around his neck, burying her face in his mane.

Armand came over on Patches. "If he wants to follow, let him," he instructed. "That's his choice."

The little bay walked behind them the entire way, struggling admirably to keep up. Adella walked along at his neck, with her hand sometimes on his withers or petting his mane.

As the day wore on, they began to hear the call of gulls. The terrain gradually rose higher, until they found themselves on rocky bluffs overlooking the sea. Spread out far below them, the inky waters of Belgrand Bay churned and heaved, the white of sunlight and seafoam glinting on indigo waves. A strong and constant wind blew at them from the Bay, pulling at their hair and clothes, bringing the smell of saltwater. While they followed the cliffs heading west, Adella couldn't help but watch the sea, feeling compelled to look for a way down the bluffs. She was reminded of the many times she had traveled with her family to the port town of Raymouth, and had spent countless hours playing on the beach with Lucas and Margavita. The memory of happier days sent a pang through her heart as she wondered if she'd ever see her brother again.

Adella looked down and caught a glimpse of her own hands. Her fingernails were lined with black, caked with grime underneath. Dried blood still stained her neck, a thick layer of greasy dirt from handling the horses covered her palms, and, as she put her arms back down, she caught a whiff of body odor. *Ugh*, she thought in disgust, *is that me I smell?* She was no stranger to getting her hands dirty; however, she always cleaned up quickly after she was done. To linger around in filth was a new and uncomfortable feeling for her since leaving Elldon. The thought of swimming in the sea grew all the more tempting, and she knew they could all use a rest.

As they went along the coastline, Adella thought she glimpsed the shape of a ship far off toward the horizon but soon lost sight of it. There were many large and jagged rocks jutting out of the waves along the coast, she figured that must have been what she really saw. The southern rim of the Bay was known for its menacing rock formations, known as the Teeth. So many Valennian ships have been lost to the Teeth over the years that now few dared to sail the southern coast.

As the sky had cleared and the sun now shone hotly on them, they decided to stop for a rest just as Adella spied a way down the rocky slope. The cliff face had collapsed in one spot, allowing her to climb carefully down to the sandy beach. Working her way slowly over the boulders, the others followed, leaving the horses hobbled to graze above. Kol went last, sighing and muttering to himself as he climbed delicately down the slope.

"I've never seen the Bay so calm," Adella commented as they all caught up with her, trudging across the damp sand.

"It's low tide," Kol replied. "Otherwise, there wouldn't be a beach here at all."

Adella sat down to untie her boots. "Tess, come swimming with me," she pleaded. The fresh sea air felt invigorating after so much travel.

"We could all probably use a swim," Armand said, pulling off his boots. "Wash the filth off us."

"Not Mister Kol," Adella replied. "You shouldn't swim with that wound." The thought of saltwater stinging such an injury made her cringe.

"You quit ordering that boy around," Armand chided her. "The seawater might do him some good. We all stink like pigs."

As the others headed toward the water's edge, Adella stripped down to her pale linen shift and under-breeches, and looked wistfully at the large bloodstain on the front of what used to be her favorite bodice. *There's no saving it*, she thought with a sigh. The matching petticoat was likewise ruined with grime and horsehair. Dropping them in the sand, she made her way toward the sea.

Kol had removed his riding boots and stockings and rolled up the knees of his breeches to wade in the water a bit, rinsing his hands. Then, he sat in the sand and watched the others. He didn't like the sea; anything could be hiding under the dark surface, unseen until it was too late. He shuddered at the thought.

As he watched the girls splash in the waves for a moment, rinsing their hair, his gaze drifted to the horizon. Soon, the tide would turn and the beach he sat on now would be submerged again. In the distance, the grey shapes of porpoises darted in and out of the waves. Then, a dark silhouette against the sparkling blue water caught his eye. It looked to be a ship, gliding between the jagged islands. He watched it pass warily while the others returned to the beach. Dripping wet, they gathered up their belongings as he pointed it out to them.

"Is that a Valennian ship?" Adella asked, squinting at the silhouette. "What are they doing out here?" With one hand shielding her eyes from the sun, she watched the ship intently.

"Only smugglers and reavers sail this way," Kol replied. "They use the sea caves all along the southern coast to hide their cargo." As he pulled on his boots, he stopped to look up at her. The sea-soaked fabric clung to her skin, revealing the soft curves of her figure. After traveling with her over the last few days, he'd realized she wasn't how he had expected her to be. A pretty girl like her, and a rich one at that, he would've imagined to be fairly useless at best, and a burden at worst. *Of course, I probably feel that way because I've never really known any.* Having grown up in the King's Home for Boys, then going immediately into the military while still so young, he'd never had the chance to get to know many women. *Only in passing,* he thought bitterly, *in the dicing-houses...* He'd never had much say over the path of his own life.

Perhaps that was why he found Adella so intriguing. Being from the lowest social class in Sornia, Kol rarely met with anyone willing to freely associate with him, especially anyone of a higher rank than himself. Yet this highborn Valennian girl saved his life, cleaned his wounds, sat with him and listened to his stories. *Fell asleep beside me.* The memory brought warmth to his wind-cooled skin. He hadn't had the heart to wake her that night to move his arm. *Valennians are turning out to be much different than I was expecting.* Lost in his thoughts, he had been watching her all the while until, finally, she turned and caught his gaze. Embarrassed, he looked away quickly.

The tide had turned and was beginning to wash over the beach, erasing their footprints as they crossed the sand toward the rocks they had climbed down. Kol went first, as the others dressed quickly.

When he came to the top, he was surprised to see a figure only a few paces away as a man walked toward Kol with sword drawn.

"Hobbs," Kol said loudly, hoping the others who were still climbing below could hear him. "What are you doing here? Did you get lost?" he scoffed.

"Do you have any idea how much trouble I've had tracking you this far?" Hobbs asked, coming at him with sword leveled. "You're a slippery fellow."

"You don't say," Kol replied casually. "Where are your men?"

"They're coming," Hobbs answered. "You've got quite a bounty on you. The general wants you dead, along with that woman you've been traveling with."

"He never did like me." Kol bent down to secure a button at the knee of his breeches. "But there's no woman. I'm traveling alone."

"Don't play that game, she got me thrown off my horse," Hobbs growled. "Nearly broke my neck."

"Oh, her?" Kol replied nonchalantly, adjusting his boot. "I haven't seen her since. I thought she went south."

"Not a lot of women out here," Hobbs replied, looking around. "Where could she be hiding?" He stepped closer, peering over the edge of the bluffs.

"Couldn't say," Kol replied, reaching into his boot. "You know me, always the loner." They both froze, looking each other dead in the eyes. Then, in a flash, Kol pulled the knife from his boot top and rushed at Hobbs just as the sword swung down over him.

Kol blocked the sword edge above his head with the flat of his knife, pressing a hand into the other side for support. A trickle of blood ran down his arm as the tip of the blade dug into his palm. Finally, the sword slid down across the knife as he pushed it away, barely missing his right hand. Finding his opponent momentarily open, Kol shoved his elbow hard into the man's nose, then thrust the knife upward, sinking it deep beneath the soldier's ribs. Hobbs gasped and clutched at his wound, doubled over in the grass.

In the distance, coming up over a rise in the land, Kol spotted a group of seven riders heading toward him. As he scrambled back down the tumbled boulders, the others, who waited midway down the slope, looked at him questioningly.

"Go down!" he ordered. "Soldiers are coming." He led them westward along the shore, now covered with seawater, as the cold waves lapped and tugged at their ankles. They had to run their hands along the slimy rock for support to keep from being pulled out into the sea.

Adella walked behind the others, following Kol along the bluffs. The waves now crashed at her knees, and the sand below her feet gave way each time the water receded. She had no idea where they were going, or if it would have been better to stand their ground and fight. Behind her, she could see dark shapes moving quickly as the string of soldiers made their way down the fallen boulders and along the shoreline.

A fierce wave crashed into her, pummeling her hip into the jagged rock. The sand below her feet gave way, and Adella fell below the surface. Cold, dark water rushed over her head, flooding into her eyes and ears. As she scrambled to regain her footing, another wave came, shoving her into the jagged cliffside. Frantically, she reached out around her to try to grasp anything, her fingers scraping blindly at the slimy rocks. Finally, there was a break in the waves as she grabbed onto a small ledge and pulled herself to her feet. She wiped the water from her eyes just in time to see her three companions disappear behind the rock in front of her.

As Adella came to the place where she last saw her friends, a hole opened up in the rock beside her. The others were standing just inside the mouth of a sea cave, with the water lapping at their knees. Adella marveled; all around them, carved into the stone, were pictographs of strange aquatic beasts, and ancient writing. Even in the dim light inside the cave, the deep etchings could be clearly seen overhead and all about them, creating an otherworldly atmosphere. Some of the depicted animals had long necks and flippers, others had large, toothy snouts like a crocodile, with tails that ended in flukes that reminded her of the creature she had killed from the pool. Armand had stopped to inspect some writing that had been carved in a strange script, just beneath one of the ferocious figures.

"What is this place?" Adella asked, gaping around.

"Smuggler's cave," Kol replied flatly.

"The soldiers are coming," she warned as she waded toward him. "They're right behind us."

"Good," he replied with a smirk. "We'll lose them in here." Then, he headed toward the darkness, with Teressa and Armand following closely.

Adella stopped. The mouth of the cave seemed to close in around her. For a moment, she imagined what it would be like to be caught deep inside with the tide pouring in, pinned between the sea and the stone. Her breathing quickened, and she grew lightheaded. Her thoughts turned back to the panic she felt when she had fallen through the hole in the pool and believed she would drown. Then, unbidden, came the memory of the soldier with his hand around her neck, along with the terror of being unable to breathe. A sudden tightness clutched at her chest and, putting her hands to her throat, she gasped for air.

Kol sloshed through seawater back toward her. "We have to hurry, or we won't make it."

"I can't," she said. She willed her feet to move, but they would not.

"I've been here before, I know this place. You have to trust me," he pleaded, his eyes focused intently on hers. "We need to go right now." He held out his hand.

She hesitated, fighting the rising panic that held her in place. Finally, Adella took a deep, steadying breath and took his hand. He led her quickly along, half helping, half pulling her through the dark, along twists and turns far beneath the rock as voices echoed behind them.

The water was rising fast. Already, it was at her chest, even as the cave roof sloped down just above her head. Kol had to duck along beside her, running one hand along the rock above. Armand and Teressa had fallen back just behind them. The space seemed to close in around them, and Adella's breathing quickened again. Her chest continued to tighten until she panted for air, her senses blurring as her legs started to give way. She was dimly aware that she was being pulled along by the waist when she noticed the tunnel ahead glowing with a faint light. The water continued to rise up to her chin as they hurried along.

The cave brightened and they came to an opening, filled with light, just ahead. "Go!" Kol shouted as a sudden surge filled the entire cave with water. Adella took one last gulp of air as the seawater poured in, filling the area entirely up to the roof. Swimming forward, she struggled to make her way through the cave mouth, with the rock scraping over her head. Her lungs burned as she kicked her way upward toward the light, until she finally surfaced and took a full gulp of breath. She was relieved to see the others bobbing in the waves around her. The mouth of the cave they had exited from was hidden completely under water.

Coughing and sputtering, they clung to the rocky cliff face. "Up this way," Kol said, and began climbing up the stone. Cracks and small outcroppings dotted the bluffs here and there, and they were able to work their way carefully to the top. Teressa was the last one to the summit, her foot slipping just as the others grabbed her arms. They pulled her onto the ground and helped her to her feet.

They lingered on the bluffs to look out for any signs of the soldiers. Adella sat on the edge of the rock high above the sea to catch her breath. With her legs dangling over the side, she looked down at the dark waves capped with white foam. There was no sign of the soldiers, and she shuddered as she imagined their fate.

They found their horses grazing not far from where they were left; the horses of the soldiers were nowhere in sight, and the tracks suggested they fled south. The four travelers continued westward along the shore. Adella's horse was still too lame to be ridden, so she took turns switching places or riding double with the others when she needed a rest. Even Teressa had given in to weariness, and rode at times.

Evening approached, and the travelers stopped to make camp as best they could. They had traveled in damp clothes the whole day and, though the sun had by now dried them for the most part, a chill had settled deep into Adella's flesh. There was little to be found for making a fire, aside from grass or an occasional shrub. Teressa set about collecting whatever dried materials she could find while Adella decided to change the dressing on Kol's wound.

Adella pulled the supplies from her bag and walked over to Kol, who was already pulling his shirt off to inspect his wound. She sat down beside him; the slice over his ribs had formed one long black scab. Though the bottom edge was still quite inflamed, it looked better than it had the day before.

"I think you'll live, after all," she said, opening the jar. "You won't have to wear the dressings much longer. Suppose you could change them yourself now?" She plastered the wound with clean cloth.

"I'd rather not," he replied, with one corner of his mouth turned up into a half-smile.

As his dark eyes lingered on hers, Adella wondered what he meant. *And why is he smiling like that? Is he enjoying this?* She shook her head to clear the thought away. *He couldn't possibly. He's just being lazy.* Sighing in disappointment, she wrapped the cloth around his ribs. As she leaned over to tuck in the loose end of the bandage, her hair fell to the side, revealing the cord hanging around her neck.

Kol ran his finger along the string, following it over her collarbone and down her skin. "What's this?" he asked.

Adella got up. Putting a hand to the artifact at her chest, she was relieved to find it still hidden under her clothes. Her fingers trembled slightly, but she wasn't sure if it was out of fear of the object being discovered, or the touch of his warm hand on her skin. "Nothing," she blurted out as she gathered up her things, then walked away.

Kol watched her until she was out of earshot, then rubbed his face with his hands. "Uff," he moaned into his palms.

"You all right?" Armand asked from where he sat nearby, honing the edge of his axe on a whetstone. He ran his thumb along the blade to inspect his work. "Is that girl annoying you?"

Kol let his shoulders fall. "I think I frightened her."

Armand laughed. "That'll teach her."

Kol blinked at him, unamused.

"Oh," Armand said, seeing the look on his face. "You like her, is that your problem?"

"How sad for you!" Teressa interrupted, as she walked by with an apron filled with dried grass. "Miss Adella is taken, so look somewhere else." Kneeling down, she piled the grass on the ground in front of them. Kol pretended not to hear her.

"No, she is not," Armand insisted.

"Is so," Teressa countered, turning to face him. "She writes to that ship captain."

Armand waved it off, whetstone in hand. "That don't mean any-thing."

"What do you know?" Teressa replied. "You're not a woman."

"That's right, so you won't catch me gossiping," Armand answered.

"And yet, here you are," Teressa countered with a shrug.

Adella crossed to where the horses were grazing, with the saddles sitting on the ground nearby. She knelt and packed the rags away into Madigan's cantle bag to wash later. Her mind was still on the object hanging heavily around her neck. Captain Declan had written of it with such urgency. *Show no one*, she remembered the letter had read. *If this object was so important that all of Sornia was looking for it*, she asked herself, *would Kol recognize it? He is one of them, after all. Would he try to take it?* she wondered, buckling the flap of the saddle bag. *Would he hurt me to get it?* Adella wasn't sure why, but she felt the urge to tell him, to trust him with this matter. *What are you thinking?* she scolded herself. *He's Sornian; of course he can't be trusted. Surely I could trust Tess and Ar-*

mand though? Adella sighed. She did not like being secretive. *But,* she reasoned, *as Rogero is the only one who knows what's going on, I should do as he instructed and show no one.* Not knowing anything about the situation, she'd better just do as he said. *It's just some silly object, anyway. How important could it be?*

She returned to where the others sat, apparently interrupting a tense conversation between Armand and Teressa, since they stopped abruptly as she approached. "Are you two bickering?" she asked, but they only looked at her, mouths tightly shut. Adella decided to try a different topic. "Did you notice the pictures in the cave?"

"They were horrible, weren't they?" Teressa replied, wrinkling her upturned nose. She had been striking the iron and flint above the pile of grass with no luck.

Kol pulled his shirt back on over his head. "There was strange writing also."

"Aye, that was Old Andolinian," Armand informed him.

"What did it say?" Kol asked, leaning forward.

"I may be old," Armand replied, "But I ain't that old. That dialect hasn't been spoken for nearly a thousand years."

6

Sornia

Morning came, and the weary travelers continued along the shore westward. Soon, they would be approaching the Sornian border, and though they wore brave faces, none could predict what would happen when they arrived.

Adella had to take a rest from walking and rode double in front of Kol. She found herself pinned between his arms since he wished to hold the reins himself. Again, she tried not to think too much about it.

"We will reach the border encampment before evening," he began over her shoulder. "Your brother may be there still, or he may have been taken onward to Hedda." She nodded in acknowledgment. "But I want you to prepare yourself," he warned, his voice lowering to nearly a whisper, "for the worst. If he made any trouble, we could be too late."

"I understand," she said quietly, though his words made her stomach turn.

Armand, who had been riding next to them, suddenly turned Patches aside. As he guided his horse to the edge of the bluffs, the others followed curiously. In the distance, weaving between islands of jagged rock jutting out from the waves, was a Valennian three-masted ship. Its sails were striped vertically, red and black, and a string of colorful pennants ran along from masthead to prow. Adella fished the spyglass from her shoulder bag to get a better look.

"I know that ship," Armand said, squinting.

"As do I," replied Kol, who was pressed so closely at Adella's back that his deep voice reverberated through her chest. "They are reavers. Let's hope we never see it any closer."

"Reavers?" Adella asked, peering through the spyglass. "Are you certain?" She could barely discern the forms of the sailors moving on the upper deck.

"The colors are unmistakable," Kol replied. "I've seen this one stalking Sornian waters, preying on merchant vessels."

"That there is *The Tigress*," Armand said. Kol looked at him blankly.

"Captain Declan's ship," Adella said under her breath, an icy chill raising goosebumps on her skin. The others were all quiet for a moment, glancing sideways at her. Adella sighed, collapsing the spyglass with her palm. "No matter. Whatever the captain does is, thankfully, none of my concern." Though she tried to outwardly shrug it off, it stung to find out how little she really knew Rogero now. Her thoughts turned toward the heavy disc tucked beneath her clothes. *Is that how he got this object? And why did he send it to me?*

They turned to continue onward. As Kol passed the reins from one hand to the other, his arms momentarily squeezed around her waist. His free hand pressed lightly on her side as the horse stumbled over some rough terrain. She tried to find something else to think about other than the man pressed so closely against her, but failed.

"Did you know?" Kol asked at length.

"Hm?" Adella said, trying to remember what they last spoke of. "Oh, about the captain? No, I was under the impression he transported tea." Kol laughed at that, and although she did not previously find the situation amusing in the least, Adella found herself laughing along with him.

As they traveled, the landscape shifted from open plains to scrubland, which then led into patches of trees. Rain puddles became marshes and streams as the elevation lowered. They lost sight of the coastline where it curved northward while they continued on toward the west.

By the late afternoon, they could see a haze of smoke in the distance as they approached the Sornian encampment. The ground swelled gently upward before them, obstructing the view beyond. They headed toward a thick stand of trees at the base of the incline, where they untacked the horses out of sight of any that might be traveling by. Sitting down on the ground in the thick leaf litter, they removed their weapons and bags, and passed around what was left of the water reserves. The air was cool in the dappled shade of the trees, and a gentle wind rustled the branches. During the moments when the wind was still, however, they could barely hear the far off din of harsh voices and metal clashing.

Adella's stomach was all in knots. The other three were taking a rest, with boots off to air out their blisters as they flopped backward into the leaves in exhaustion. Adella, weary and sore though she was, couldn't bring herself to do likewise. She watched them for a moment, chewing her lip. Then, making up her mind, she pulled the spyglass from her travel bag. "I'm going to take a closer look," she said, leaving the bag on the ground. "You three stay here, I'll be right back." With that, she walked off.

Kol opened his mouth to protest as she disappeared through the trees. Beside him, Teressa groaned, and Armand swore under his breath. The three of them looked around at each other blankly; both Armand and Teressa had removed their footwear and stockings already. Sighing loudly, Kol resigned himself to the task and hurried after Adella. There was no way he was going to let her go on alone; it wasn't safe. He was still alive because of her, and he wasn't going to let her get into trouble if he could help it.

The landscape was filled with shrubs and small trees, which would provide ample cover if they crouched down low. He caught up with her halfway up the slope, and grabbed her wrist to stop her. "What are you doing? Get down," he whispered, lowering to the ground.

She did likewise. "I told you, I'm just looking. I'll be careful."

He shifted to one knee and pulled the knife in its sheath from the top of his boot. "Here, take this," he said, handing it to her. "Just in case." She pulled up her skirts and tucked the knife into her own boot. "I'll want that back, though," he added, pointing a finger at her. "It's my oldest possession. Don't lose it."

She pulled the ring Declan had given her off her finger and handed it to him. "Take this as insurance, and we'll trade back later." He nodded and pocketed it, but couldn't help wondering exactly what it meant to her.

Adella crawled behind Kol through the bushes on their elbows to the summit and, laying shoulder-to-shoulder, they looked over the ridge. Sprawled out below, they could see the military encampment, its cook-fires raising smoke over the valley. Plain canvas tents formed two rows on each side of the encampment, with two larger striped pavilions on either end. Wagons and horses dotted the landscape haphazardly, and they could even make out clotheslines filled with laundry on the far side. Men were walking the camp here and there, while some could be seen practicing archery and swordplay on the northern slope.

"How many soldiers per tent?" Adella whispered to Kol, closing one eye to peer through the spyglass.

"Two, usually. One for officers," he replied.

"So how many men in total, then?" she asked.

He thought for a moment. "Sixty-five at most."

"Where do they keep their captives?" She swept the view over the camp, searching for a sign of Lucas.

"The striped tent, on the north end," he said, pointing. "Beyond the rise to the west lies the wall surrounding the Sornian border."

"And to the north?"

"The sea," he replied. "And the Smuggler's Port, just outside the border."

Adella lowered the glass and paused. She took the scene in one last time to commit it to memory before backing down the slope.

They crawled halfway down before rising back onto their feet. As Adella stood up, the artifact around her neck fell out from the front of her bodice. It dangled from her neck, glinting in the sunlight before she clamped her hand down over it. It was too late; Kol had seen it. He grabbed her hand and turned it over, revealing the golden disc in her palm. His brow furrowed as he looked at it, then at her.

"Where did you get this?" He took it in his hand, turning it over to inspect it. "Do you have any idea what this is?"

Adella didn't respond, only looked downward, pressing her lips together.

"All of Sornia is looking for this," Kol went on sharply, "and you bring it back here? Of all places!" He spoke through his teeth, anger rising in his voice.

Without a word, Adella snatched it back from his hand and tucked it into the front of her bodice.

"We have to go," Kol said, putting his hands on her shoulders as he looked her in the eyes. "Right now. Sornia can't get this, do you understand? Forget your brother, we must go back to Valenna. Immediately."

"No." She took a step back, shrugging free of his grip. "I'm not leaving without my brother."

"Don't be stupid!" He rubbed his face with his hand in frustration. "Why didn't you tell me you had Leveret's Key?"

"Leveret..." she whispered to herself, trying to remember the story he told her days ago. "You mean you believe that silly fable? You're the one being stupid," she snapped. "I'm not turning back now."

"You're arrogant and reckless." He narrowed his eyes at her. "Some things are more important than one person."

"If you think that," she replied coolly, "then clearly you've never cared about anyone but yourself." He stepped closer and Adella braced herself, not quite sure if he would try to hurt her. Keenly aware of how much taller and broader he was compared to her, she knew how easy it would be for him to simply take the disc. He looked her hard in the eyes, and she resisted the urge to back away.

"Fine," he relented at last, stepping to the side. "Do what you want, but I won't help you." He walked away, heading back toward the trees.

"Fine," Adella replied. She stayed behind, still fuming. "Better arrogant than stupid," she muttered to herself. Kol was out of sight when she decided she had better get moving. Adella had only gone a few steps, however, when something rustled behind her. Before she could turn to look, a hand clamped down over her mouth. Another grabbed her arm and twisted it up against her back, pain shooting through her shoulder as the spyglass fell to the ground.

Adella's wrists were tied tightly behind her, her hands tingling from lack of blood flow as she was forced along by two swords poking into her sides. The soldiers at her back stopped her in front of a very large man in a garish cockaded hat.

"What's this?" the man asked in a deep, coarse voice.

"We found her spying from the ridge, General," one of the soldiers replied.

The general looked her up and down, and Adella shifted uncomfortably under his scrutiny. Though she looked completely disheveled and travel-worn, she wore expensive clothes over an elegant figure, betraying her life of leisure. "You have one chance to explain yourself," he said finally.

She took a deep breath to steady her nerves. "I am Adella Grimless, daughter of Lord Governor Grimless of Elldon, representative of His Majesty King Harrian of Valenna. I have come here in peace to negotiate for the life of my brother, who has been taken captive by your men—"

"Stop," the general interrupted. "I've heard enough." He turned to address the man at her right. "Good work, Lieutenant Rett. This is that Valennian vixen we've been hunting in the Campos."

"Shall we execute her, sir?" the lieutenant asked.

"No, I've changed my mind," the general replied. "She looks to be worth a bit of gold. The convoy leaves in two hours; you both will take her to the traders. Use the money to buy some decent horses." The two soldiers nodded, and grabbed her by the elbows.

"This is an act of war," Adella said sharply. The general backhanded her across the mouth, knocking her teeth together. Blood trickled down her split lip.

"We are already at war," he scoffed, then walked away. The two soldiers escorted her into the pavilion, pushing the heavy flaps aside and shoving her down onto the bare dirt floor. Without her arms to catch herself, she fell hard on her side. They untied her wrists, only to wrap them around the center pole and tie them again even tighter. Then, they got up and stood sentry on either side of the entrance.

Adella looked around. It took a moment for her eyes to adjust from the bright sunlight outside to the dim interior. She had hoped to see other captives within, but aside from her two guards, she was alone. Lucas wasn't there. *Damn!* She cursed herself for her carelessness. *What was I thinking? I've got to get out of here.*

She sat in silence for some time, the sting of her lip increasing as it began to swell. She lost the feeling in her thumbs from the tight bonds. Though she pulled and twisted at the rope, it wouldn't give at all. Adella remembered Kol's knife in her boot and considered trying to reach it to cut the ties. *But then what?* she asked herself. *I'm completely surrounded.* Even if she did escape the tent, she wouldn't get very far, and the attempt could get her killed. If she was going to get out of the trouble she was in now, she figured, it wasn't going to happen there.

Adella looked up at her guards. One looked rather rough and hard-eyed, but the other was obviously quite young, perhaps around her own age. She decided that if she could elicit any sort of sympathy from him, her escape attempt later might be easier.

He glanced over at her, and Adella took the opportunity to engage him in conversation. "What's your name?"

"Ignore her," the older man warned his companion.

The younger soldier hesitated. "Lieutenant Jais Rett," he finally answered.

"Shut up!" the older man scolded in a harsh whisper.

"You shut up, Garen," Jais said to him. "I outrank you, remember?"

"Only since yesterday," the other man mumbled, temporarily chastened.

Adella searched for something she could talk to him about. "A lieutenant at your age?" she asked. "That's impressive."

He brightened, clearly enjoying the flattery. "And I only enlisted a year ago."

"It's because your family is rich," Garen interjected, and Jais threw him a dirty look.

The younger man seemed eager to talk, so Adella decided to probe him for common ground. However, she hardly knew anything at all about Sornia. She was going to have to grasp at straws. "Did you know a soldier named Kol?" she ventured. *Perhaps if they're allies*, she thought, *he'll help me.*

"Which Kol?" Jais asked, brow wrinkling with confusion. "That's a common name here; you'll have to be more specific."

"She means that man wanted for treason, you idiot," Garen cut in.

"That nameless wastrel?" Jais asked her. "Of course I knew him." He frowned. "He broke my nose."

"So you probably weren't friends, then," she guessed with disappointment.

"Hardly!" Jais replied. "Kol has no friends. He is of the lowest social class, along with the slaves and bastards. It would be beneath me to associate with someone like him."

I see why he broke your nose, she thought. Adella wondered if, because of her own social standing, she came across as arrogant as this man.

"Where is he now?" Jais asked eagerly. "If you cooperate with us, things might go more smoothly for you."

"I'll tell you, but you might not like it." She frowned. "He succumbed to his wounds. He's dead." If they believed her lie and stopped looking for Kol, perhaps her friends would be a little safer out in the wilderness.

"Oh," Jais said. "The general will be disappointed to hear that. Though I can't say anyone else will be."

"Don't let your prejudice cloud your memory," Garen reprimanded Jais. "He might not have been a friendly fellow, but he was highly skilled, and a damn good soldier."

"Even so," Jais replied, "no one will mourn him."

Voices grew louder outside the pavilion, putting a stop to the conversation. Adella spent the remainder of the time in silence, trying not to fall into a helpless despair, until her guards dragged her by the arms to an uncovered wagon hitched to a couple of draft horses. They pushed her up the ramp and, once again, shoved her forward; this time she was prepared for it and only stumbled to her knees. *These Sornians are all savages*, she thought bitterly. The two soldiers lifted the ramp and latched it, then climbed in behind her. The wagon was filled with various wooden crates and trunks upon which they took their seats.

The driver at the front clicked his tongue, and the wagon began to roll forward as the horses walked on. Looking around, Adella noticed it was one of several in the convoy, and near the back of the line. There was only one other cart coming along behind them, but it was filled with armed soldiers. She looked up toward the ridge where she had spied from, searching for a sign of her three companions. *Of course*, she reminded herself, *it's only two now that Kol said he wouldn't help me anymore. I'm sure I'll never see him again after this*. She was surprised to feel a pang of sadness at the thought, but pushed it away, turning her mind to Teressa and Armand instead. *They don't stand a chance, just the two of them.* For an instant, she thought she saw a little glare of light far off on the ridge, but then it was gone.

By the time Kol reached the trees where the others waited, his anger had subsided, and he regretted his harsh words. After all, he couldn't blame Adella for wanting to rescue someone she cared about; he was beginning to understand the feeling himself. *I can't fault her for not trusting me, either, after the things I've done...*

Somewhere behind him, a twig snapped. "Adella, I'm sorry," he began, turning toward the sound. "I—" He stopped short as a man leveled a blade at him. "You're not Adella," Kol remarked, hoping to buy some time while he figured out what to do. In his haste, he had left his sword on the ground with the others, then had given Adella his knife, leaving him unarmed. *Stupid!* he scolded himself. He should've known better than to leave the sword behind.

"Did you lose someone?" the soldier mocked him. He slashed his blade forward, but hit only air as Kol sidestepped it. Dropping to the ground, he swept the man's legs out from under him.

"Where is she?" Kol asked, stepping on the man's hand that gripped the weapon. The fingers crushed against the handle as he pressed his weight into it, and the soldier groaned in pain. Kol then took the weapon easily from the bruised fingers, pointing it at the man's chest.

"Having tea with the general," the man replied with a sneer. Kol buried the sword in the man's gut and walked away. Ducking back into the trees, he bumped into Armand and Teressa.

"What happened?" Armand asked, looking past Kol at the dead man on the ground.

"They have Adella," Kol replied curtly. "I don't know what happened, she was right behind me. When I turned, she was gone, with a soldier in her place."

"You lost her?" Teressa asked in disbelief. "Good work."

"You know how that girl can be," Armand reminded her. "Found a sea serpent in the middle of a prairie, remember?"

"Enough talk, we have to find her," Kol snapped and headed back toward the ridge, leading the way through the brush. Something shiny caught his eye in the grass and, as he stopped to pick it up, his heart dropped. It was Adella's brass spyglass.

Crawling back up the slope, Kol stopped at the top and held the spyglass to his eye. Searching over the encampment below, he spotted a familiar figure in a long skirt. By the way she moved, she seemed to have her arms tied behind her, and two soldiers walked along at her back with swords drawn. He watched as they walked her to the north pavilion and halted her before a man standing by the entrance. It was difficult to make out details at this distance, but the man's conspicuously large cocked hat gave him away.

"General Blackburn," Kol muttered with disdain. He handed the spyglass to Armand as he crawled up beside him.

"The fellow with the hat?" Armand guessed, looking through the glass as Teressa crept up on the other side of Armand.

"I've never hated anyone more," Kol replied. "Had me caned on my very first day, I couldn't sit for a week. I hope she has enough sense not to cause any trouble."

The convoy rolled on, first heading north, then curving northwest, following a well-worn dirt road through the wilderness. As they continued, the sea came into view ahead of them. The waves were cresting high and foamy, and the water looked nearly black as the sun lowered into a bed of dark clouds on the horizon. Adella tried to tally up the number of days it had been since she left Greywood Manor, but each day seemed to blur together in her memory.

"What day of the week is it?" she whispered to the soldiers next to her.

"Shh!" Garen hissed, whacking her on the shins with his sword scabbard.

"Monday," Jais replied quietly, eyes fixed on the horizon. The last wagon was not far behind them, and she understood that neither soldier wanted to be seen speaking to her.

Adella tried to think back to the night Elldon was attacked. *The day my parents left for the Capital, that was a Tuesday,* she remembered with surprise. *It's been almost a week.* She thought back on all that had happened over the last several days. It felt like so much longer. Her parents should be sailing back to Raymouth on *The Cormorant* by now, she figured. *That's a three-day journey.* Adella imagined her parents coming home to an empty house in disarray, and her heart ached for them.

As the convoy rolled onward, they passed along the sea to the north. The coastline looked more forgiving than before, as it sloped gently down to the water rather than ending in steep cliffs. The road that they followed forked off and, in the distance, Adella could see a small town built around a harbor, with several wooden docks jutting out into the sea. Ships of all kinds were coming and going from every direction. She marveled to see old Sornian caravels pass in the same waters as modern Valennian brigantines. Then, she noticed one particular vessel with red and black striped sails, already moored at one of the docks.

They continued westward, the land becoming more lush and verdant as they traveled. Ahead, a massive stone wall slowly appeared through the trees. As they drew nearer, soldiers in green and white coats could be seen walking along the parapet. The convoy finally stopped before the massive iron portcullis, and they were held up there for over half an hour while soldiers in uniform inspected each wagon. Lieutenant Rett left the wagon to speak with them, leaving her with only one guard for a while. While Garen watched the others work, Adella twisted and pulled at her arms behind her back. Her fingers tingled and the coils of rope dug into her skin, but the knot held. She brought her hands to one side, then the other to see how far she could reach, stretching toward the knife in the top of her boot. It seemed an impossible task, and she pulled a muscle in her leg trying.

"Quit," Garen said, whacking her in the shoulder with the scabbard. Lieutenant Rett returned, and the convoy rolled through the gates, into the city of Hedda.

The first thing she noticed about the city was its beauty. Though the architecture was simple, the gardens were plentiful. Topiaried hedges filled with sweet-smelling flowers lined each roadway, perfuming the air, and trees grew freely all around, shading the houses and blanketing the ground with fragrant petals.

They came to a bustling marketplace, and the wagon stopped abruptly. Jais and Garen offloaded her carelessly over the side, then marched her through the crowds with a firm grip on each arm. Adella observed the people as they went; she noticed the men of Sornia kept their hair cropped much shorter than those in Valenna, who commonly wore theirs tied back in a long queue. The clothes here also looked more extravagant, with brighter colors and mixed patterns. The women wore their hair high up in bouffants adorned with flowers and feathers, and tied short, colorful capes around their shoulders.

As Adella was shoved along the cobblestone roads of Hedda, her foot came down on a dislodged stone, rolling her ankle. With a cry of pain, she stumbled forward into the crowd, slipping out of Garen's hold. As Jais caught her by the arm and pulled her up, Adella tried to speak to him again.

"Please," she whispered, "you don't have to do this."

Jais hesitated a moment, then his expression hardened. "Yes, I do." Adella took the opportunity to shove her shoulder into his jaw. She put the full force of her body behind it, knocking him backward onto the ground. Scrambling on the cobblestones, she ran off into the crowd of people.

It was no good; Adella didn't get far before Garen grabbed her by the arm again, and dealt a blow to her diaphragm. She doubled over, breathless, as they continued to drag her through the crowd. Exhausted and in pain, she gave in, no longer resisting their direction.

The sky had darkened with heavy clouds when the soldiers halted her in front of a large wooden platform. Affixed to the side were iron rings, where a few other dirty and bedraggled people were tied by ropes. They shoved her against the wall, and tied her wrists tightly to one of the rings. Leaving Garen to stand guard, Jais walked up the wooden steps to the top of the platform. Adella looked around at the other captives, each as travel-worn and battered as she was. Only one woman appeared to be Valennian like her, judging by the style of her dress. She was an older woman wearing a fitted jacket-style bodice like Adella's, with sleeves ending in ruffles at the elbows and peplums flaring out from a tightly-laced waist. The woman looked over at her, furrowing her brow in sympathy. Adella thought she had seen her face before, but couldn't place it. *I wonder if she's from Elldon,* she thought. *Perhaps Lucas is here somewhere...* A raindrop rolled down her cheek as it began to rain.

One by one, the other captives were untied and walked up the steps of the platform. The rain was coming down hard when Garen finally untied Adella from the ring and walked her up. Her stomach turned as he led her forcefully along, and she thought she would be sick. A fat man in a wide-brimmed hat stood at a podium in the center. The crowd that had gathered on the other side of the platform was dispersing, pulling the hoods of their capes up over their heads as Garen swore under his breath.

"Bad timing," Jais said to him with a look of concern. "I don't want to think what Blackburn will do to us if we don't get a good price. Should we wait til morning?"

"No," Garen replied. "Let's be done with it. We can always steal the horses."

The auctioneer began calling out numbers, and here and there a hand would pop up among the people who remained. He got to forty-five when lightning began to flash, after which only a few people lingered. Adella thought she would be sold to the elderly lady standing close by, with strings of pearls draped down her front. Two servants stood at her sides, their arms full of parcels. The auctioneer called out once more, twice more, and was just about to hit the gavel when two men in hooded cloaks came forward. The shorter one put his arm up, then turned to whisper to his companion, pointing at Adella. The old woman put her hand up again in response, and the two bidders went back and forth in competition. The price reached sixty-four, and the hooded men argued between themselves in hushed tones.

"Seventy," the cloaked man said. The auctioneer gave his last call, but the old woman didn't raise her hand; it was over.

The two men paid and came to collect her, walking her down the steps. A heavy hopelessness settled over her like a cloak as she wondered if this was the end of her journey. Adella followed along in a daze; her feet and hands felt as numb as her mind. Not only had she failed to find Lucas, but she had doomed herself to captivity as well. *If the Sornians are capable of this*, she reasoned, *then they are capable of anything. This place is worse than I could ever have imagined.* Her breathing quickened as she wondered what her future might be like.

They ushered her through the streets, which were now dark and soaked with rain. Splashing through deep puddles, they made their way around formal gardens littered with the debris of windblown flowers. She was hurried past a wide staircase leading up to a huge palace adorned with ornate columns, gabled windows and numerous mismatched turrets. To Adella's surprise, they marched her across the vast front lawn of the palace, through arbors and past topiaries in perfectly symmetrical gardens, and around to an inconspicuous side entrance hidden between two cedar trees.

The taller of the two men pulled a large key out from under his cloak and unlocked the iron door. As they entered, the heavy door scraped to a close behind them, then the two strange figures guided Adella down a long corridor, with only the dim evening light filtering in from the high arched windows to see by.

Finally, Adella was ushered in through a narrow door on their right. Inside, a fireplace cast a warm glow around the room, and her heart sank even further when she saw it was a small bedchamber. She didn't know what it meant, but it couldn't be good, and without windows, there was no means of escape. As soon as they had latched the door behind them, one of the men worked quickly to untie her arms. "Adella!" a familiar voice admonished as the two men pulled back their hoods. "What in the *world* are you doing here in Sornia?"

Adella was speechless. She could hardly believe what she was seeing, but there was no mistaking that voice. "Lucas!" she exclaimed, nearly breathless with astonishment as she realized one of the men who brought her there was her own brother. "Oh, thank goodness," she said with a sigh as a flood of relief washed over her. Adella ran over to put her arms around him, holding tightly to her brother that she had been afraid she'd never see again. Memories of their younger days flooded her mind, all the scraped knees and bruises gently tended to, all the laughter and heartaches that came with growing up side by side. Though her eyes filled with tears, Adella couldn't help but laugh for joy as she let go to inspect him. "I came to find you, obviously. Are you all right? Did they hurt you?" She cast a sideways glance at the other man. He was taller and older than Lucas, and his ash-brown hair had been cropped close to the scalp in the Sornian style. He shifted his dark grey eyes from Lucas to Adella and turned to go, shutting the door and leaving Adella alone with her brother.

"Right..." Lucas began, glancing from her to the door. "I'm fine. Listen, you shouldn't be here. It's dangerous." He lowered his voice, "They don't treat women very well here."

"So I've noticed," Adella remarked. "Well, now that I've found you, let's get out of here," she urged. "Let's go back home." A smile spread across her face at the thought of returning to Greywood Manor, her quest complete.

"Absolutely," Lucas replied. "When the time is right, of course." He furrowed his brow. "The problem is, I don't have any money on me. I managed to convince Matei out there," he explained, pointing with his thumb toward the door, "to pay your auction, and he won't be very happy with the idea of us leaving so soon."

"We'll sneak out then," Adella replied. "But we can't stay here." She paused, considering her next words. *What's the matter with me?* she chided herself. *He's my brother, of course I can trust him.* "I've got something on me," she whispered. "Something I don't want them to find."

Lucas's eyes widened. "What do you have?"

"I'm not sure exactly." Adella pulled on the string that hung around her neck, lifting the golden disc from her bodice. It glimmered as it dangled in the firelight.

Lucas was silent, mouth gaping in awe. He reached out to grasp it and look it over. "Where did you get this?" he demanded suddenly.

"Captain Declan," Adella replied. "He asked me to keep it safe." She took it from his hand to tuck it back into the front of her clothes, but he grabbed her wrist to stop her.

"Let me have it," he said sternly.

"No." She wrenched her arm free, taken aback at the sudden turn in his voice. "Declan entrusted it to me."

"That was a mistake," he retorted. He took the disc and yanked on it; the string cut into the skin of her neck before it broke. Lucas pocketed the object and walked out of the room, shutting the door behind him. Adella heard a key turn in the lock, but she tried to open it anyway. She pushed and pulled on the handle, to no avail.

"You bastard!" she screamed, pounding on the door so hard that bruises bloomed on her fists. She tried to break down the door with her hip, then her shoulder, but that didn't work either. Looking frantically around the room, she could find no means of escape, not even a chimney, and the walls were made of stone. Adella plopped down on the bed and buried her face in her hands. *I only have myself to blame,* she thought bitterly, letting the tears she had held back before flow freely now. *I should've listened to Kol.* Now she was trapped, a helpless captive, betrayed by the very person she'd risked her life to save. She had no idea what was going on or why Lucas would treat her this way, but the sting of his actions cut deep into her heart.

7

The Key

Kol watched through the spyglass as the convoy rolled off into the distance. He crawled to his feet and ran through the brush down the sloping ground, back to where Armand and Teressa were busy tacking up the horses. As Kol approached, he could hear them arguing. He ducked behind a tree to listen, peering through the leaves.

"I don't care what you think," Armand said to Teressa. "I'm your elder, and it's my decision."

"He's dangerous and you know it," she countered. "He's a *Sornian*. He can't be trusted. Do you really believe he was telling the truth about how Adella got captured?" Distracted, she yanked on her horse's girth as she tightened it. The gelding snaked his head around, flattening his ears and snapping his teeth at her.

"The fact of the matter is," Armand began, turning to point a finger at her, "we can't get into Sornia without him. So keep your feelings to yourself." She opened her mouth to respond. "This is the end of the conversation," Armand warned her, cutting off her reply.

Kol waited until things quieted before joining the others, pretending he hadn't overheard. He wasn't here for their sake, and they all had bigger problems to deal with now. They mounted up and headed north, following along after the convoy while keeping well out of sight. As they passed the fork in the road, Kol glanced over at the harbor town to the northeast. He brought out the spyglass to take a look; among the various ships moored at the docks, he noticed one with red and black sails.

Finally, they drew closer to the gates of Hedda. Thick patches of forest closed in around them, their leaves still the bright yellow-green of springtime. Flowers of every color and shape trembled in the increasing winds. They led their horses to a little group of trees for cover until dark, not wanting to be seen by the soldiers patrolling the parapet atop the wall. Kol took out the spyglass again, and watched through the foliage as the convoy passed through the gates. He brought the glass down and looked toward the horizon, where black clouds loomed over the city. Kol buckled the sword around his waist. "Looks like rain," he said to Armand, who was untacking his horse beside him. "Where did Adella put her cloak?" Armand shrugged, so Kol rifled through the saddlebags. He silently mourned the loss of his personal possessions, left behind forever at the Sornian encampment in the Campos, surely already divided up amongst the other soldiers. *Not that I had much anyway,* he lamented. *But a jacket would've been useful.* He finally found her oilskin cloak under a wool blanket and drew it around his shoulders in anticipation of the oncoming storm as the wind whipped the branches around them. Kol then threw Adella's haversack over one shoulder and went about stuffing items in it that he thought might prove useful. He found the pearl-handled pen knife and, as he put it in his pocket, his fingers brushed against the little gold and coral ring. He had completely forgotten about it. Kol pulled it out to look at it, running his thumb over the dainty scrollwork. *I'd better not lose this, or I won't get my knife back.* He strung it on a piece of spare cording and hung it around his neck. He then untacked Madigan, and hobbled the mare's forelimbs as it began to rain.

Kol turned toward the others. "After nightfall, we're going to go south, wide around the gate," he instructed. "Just follow behind me, and don't make a sound when we approach the wall. Not even a whisper."

Armand and Teressa nodded. It was then that Kol saw Teressa was shivering as she held a blanket tight around her. He looked to see if Armand also noticed, but he didn't seem to be paying attention, so Kol didn't mention it. *Maybe it's the weather... Or perhaps she caught the ague?* He remembered overhearing her harsh words about him earlier. *Even if that's the case, it's not my problem.* He pulled the hood up over his head and shrugged the thought off.

Kol turned away to watch the grey evening light fade out of the sky, and the memory of another stormy night came into mind. *It was only days ago, but it feels like a lifetime.* He remembered the hopelessness he had felt, alone in the storm with his wrists bound around the pole, waiting for sunrise and death. He had given up, realizing he had been on the wrong side all his life. *She only found me there by accident,* he reminded himself. *But I'll be damned if I won't return the favor.* He stood there in silence, watching the gathering storm.

They waited until the dead of night to set out. The sky was pitch black, though lightning flashed now and then, illuminating the landscape. Leaving the horses behind, they set off across the open in the pelting rain, passing carefully over the dirt road the convoy had traveled along. Veering west, they approached the wall under the cover of trees, walking along as silently as they could. Soldiers still patrolled the parapet even in the storm, and their voices could occasionally be heard coming from above. Kol ran his hand along the stones as he led the others over and around shrubs that grew next to the wall, feeling for one stone that stuck out more than the rest.

Finally, he found what he was looking for. Carefully pushing aside the branches of a yew tree, he pried at the edges of the stone with his fingers to dislodge it. It was not the full size of the others; rather, it had been chiseled down to nothing more than a veneer to hide the entrance. This hidden door was commonly known among the lower ranking soldiers, who used it to get into and out of trouble. He sent Armand and Teressa through first, then pulled the cover back into place behind him. Kol crept through the short tunnel under the wall, holding his sword scabbard to keep it from scraping against the rock. They emerged from the other side through thick vines into a formal garden. Lightning flashed, revealing hedges trimmed into the shapes of animals.

The three of them continued silently along the wall, the sound of their footsteps completely lost in the heavy rain. Then they crossed the sprawling lawn, scurrying from hedge to hedge to stop and listen for anyone approaching. As they gathered under a very large boxwood that was trimmed into the shape of a horse and carriage, Teressa began to shake violently, her teeth chattering loudly.

Armand swore under his breath. "She's got what I had," he whispered. "What do we do?"

"We could leave her here," Kol suggested.

"We can't do that," Armand said flatly.

"Then we'll split up, and you can take her with you." Kol thought for a moment. "Do you have any coin on you?"

Armand checked in his bag. "Some."

"Go to the apothecary, down by the docks," Kol said, pointing north. "Bright blue door, sign shaped like a shield. Tell them she has the red ague, they'll know what to do. I'll meet you there before sunrise."

Armand agreed, throwing Teressa's arm over his shoulder and pulling her gently to her feet. The two disappeared into the darkness, and Kol headed northeast to find the marketplace.

The rain had slowed to a drizzle by the time Kol found the auction block. The streets were empty, but harsh laughter and voices could be heard coming from the various buildings surrounding the market square. The warm light from many windows provided a little illumination. Nearby, a sign hung over a door, painted with the words *Jodiah's Tavern*. Kol peeked in the window. Sure enough, there sat the fat auctioneer, downing a beer in a booth by himself. Kol had brought captives to auction a few times over the years and recognized the man immediately. Next to the auctioneer, however, was a table full of soldiers in their emerald uniforms, swords at their hips. *I'll have to wait for him to come out,* Kol thought.

He stood by the entrance for what felt like hours before the man stumbled out the door, putting his hat on askew as he headed down a side street. Kol quietly followed after him.

"Excuse me," Kol said as he caught up to the man, hoping to sound nonchalant. "I'm looking for someone, and I think you can help me."

"I certainly can't," the auctioneer replied, protectively gathering up the heavy bag that hung from his shoulder. "This information is private."

Kol tried to smile sympathetically. "I'm not asking," he said, reaching for the hilt of his sword.

The man threw the bag at Kol and ran away. *Well, that was too easy,* Kol thought, catching the bundle against his chest. He took a large leather-bound book from the bag, and flipped through it in the light of a nearby window. Getting to the last written page, he found the date. Beneath it was a list of the people who had passed through auction that day with a brief description, followed by the signature of their buyer:

May 21
Madorran man: Murderer
Mid-age, bald, limp- 35g- Tor Halfast
Sornian man: Thief
Youth, shorn, malnourished- 20g, 5s- Ketta Lomini
Valennian woman: Prisoner of War
Old, stocky, blonde- 40g- Ketta Lomini
Valennian woman: Prisoner of War
Young, brunette, highborn- 70g- Matei Azbarian

He ran his finger along the last line. *That must be Adella,* he figured. *Azbarian,* Kol thought. *That's the last name of the Royal Family,* he recalled. *That means they're likely at the Palace.*

"There he is!" a voice shouted behind him. He looked to see the auctioneer had returned, and was pointing him out to a group of soldiers. Kol dropped the book and ran in the other direction. The last thing he wanted was for one of them to recognize him.

Kol ran down a dark alley and ducked into a gap between two buildings. Pulse pounding in his ears, he counted the soldiers as they ran by, *One, two, three, four...* He drew his sword. As the fifth soldier appeared, Kol lunged forward, skewering the man in the side. He then ran off again, back the way he had come. It didn't take long for the other men to figure out what happened, and they chased after him again, their footsteps echoing behind him in the damp, empty streets.

He rounded a corner and stopped suddenly, pressing himself against the wall. When the leading soldier appeared, Kol swung his sword at the man's midriff. The soldier parried, pressing the blades together. Kol supported the blunt back of his sword with his left hand, and shoved the man forward. The soldier was caught off guard, and Kol took the opportunity to punch him in the face with the hilt. Then he slashed across the torso, and the man doubled over in pain. As the other three soldiers caught up, Kol again turned to run.

He continued on in the dark, heedless of the direction, looking for anything that he could use to his advantage. Despite his recent injury, he was the faster runner, and gained a little distance. Kol turned down a narrow alleyway, with the pounding of the soldiers' boots not far behind. Then, he heard the clopping of hooves on cobblestone. Just ahead, the alley opened up onto a main street, and a team of draft horses came into view. Kol had just enough time to run through the opening in front of the horses. As he ducked beneath their heads, they shied and reared at the surprise, blocking the alley with a large cargo wagon. Climbing up the back, Kol pulled himself onto the roof of the wagon and then, flattening himself, peered over the edge just as the horses continued onward. Behind the wagon, the soldiers rushed out into the street, looked around in confusion, then split up, with one turning left and two heading right, following after the wagon.

Gripping his sword hilt tightly, Kol crouched on the roof and readied himself. Below, the two soldiers splashed through rain puddles as they caught up. Kol leapt from the wagon, crashing down on one soldier, and they hit the ground, Kol landing hard on his shoulder as they grappled on the wet stone. As he pressed his blade closer to the soldier's throat, movement flashed above his head. Kol grabbed the shirt of the man he was grappling with, and rolled to the side just as a blade whistled through the air, slashing down on the soldier's back. The man he'd used as a shield screamed; Kol pushed him away as the other man spun his sword around in the air to bring it down once more. Kol parried just in time, the metal clashing loudly right before his face. The soldier braced his sword in his hands, pushing his full weight down into it. The point of the blade inched slowly downward, until it pressed into Kol's shoulder. The edge bit into his flesh, and Kol could feel the warmth of blood spreading down along his back. With a shout, he jabbed his knee sharply upward into the man's groin. The soldier fell sideways, and Kol stuck his sword in the man's side.

Kol scurried to his feet, pressing his hand to his shoulder. Sticky blood oozed through his fingers. He wasn't sure where in the city he was now, but he kept moving forward in case the last soldier had doubled back.

He stumbled through the maze-like streets. Kol realized in dismay he was far from the Palace and was beginning to feel lightheaded. Looking around, he noticed faint light growing in the eastern sky. *Sunrise already? I'm supposed to meet them by the apothecary,* he remembered. Blood dripped onto the cobblestones as he continued on deliriously. When he couldn't go any further, he collapsed in exhaustion beneath a tree.

Adella awoke from a deep sleep to a dark room. It took her a moment to remember where she was and all that had happened. Her heart sank when she remembered her brother's betrayal, the pain of the heartbreak so sharp that it felt more like the stab of a knife. She hadn't intended to fall asleep, but after spending so many nights on the cold, damp ground, a soft bed had been too much to resist. She rolled over, flopping onto her other side, when her arm hit something.

"Ow," said a strange voice, and she realized it was a man.

Adella screamed and hit him again.

"What are you yelling about?" he said angrily as a hand grabbed her arm. "This is *my* bed, you stupid girl. Sleep on the floor."

She twisted her arm free and ran in the dark to where she remembered the door had been. She shook and twisted the handle, but it wouldn't budge. She felt around, but her hands couldn't find a latch. Drawing Kol's knife from her boot, she returned to the stranger.

"Unlock the door," she ordered, digging the tip of the knife into his chest.

"Is that really any way to treat your rescuer?" he asked. He took the knife from her and shoved it under his pillow.

"Fine," she said. "Go back to sleep, then." Adella went over to the wall and slumped down on the floor, then sat in the dark and waited.

When the man began to snore gently, Adella tip-toed across the room. She felt around the little side table, opening the drawer and patting around inside, but found nothing but paper and quills. Reaching across the mattress, she delicately searched for the key to the chamber door on his person. She thought perhaps it was tied at his neck, and felt around there, but there was nothing. Suddenly, an arm wrapped around her waist as the stranger pulled her closer, and she felt his hot breath on her neck.

"Stop!" she yelled, and hit him again.

"What is your problem?" he asked, letting go. "It was your idea."

She scrambled backward off the bed. "I was looking for the damned key, you idiot!"

"Sure you were." He pulled the blankets and rolled onto his other side. "Wake me again, and I'll make sure you find what you're looking for," he warned.

Adella sat back down against the wall. "I hate this place," she muttered.

Soon, a light grew under the crack of the door. *It must be morning,* she realized. Adella snuck over to the bed again and slipped her hand carefully under the pillow, feeling around for the knife this time. She was relieved when she found it. As she fumbled in the dark to stick the knife back into her boot beneath her long skirts, she lost her balance, bumping the edge of the mattress with her hip.

Adella froze, listening for signs of movement, unsure whether she had woken him. No sound came from the bed, so she relaxed. Then, there was a sharp knock at the door.

"Your Highness," a voice called out from the corridor. Adella heard a metallic click and the door opened, flooding the room with light.

Matei sat up. "What is it?" he mumbled.

An older man came in carrying a chamberstick, which he set on the table by the bedside. He held a brass key in his other hand. "You're wanted in the councilroom," the man said. "I'll return in ten minutes." He then left the chamber, locking the door behind him.

Matei looked over at Adella, standing close by the bed, and she put her hands up to explain. "I swear I wasn't—"

"You know damn well by now I don't have the key to the door," he said angrily. "So pester me *one more time,* and I'll think it's something else you want." She sat back down against the wall, and he glared at her mistrustfully as he pulled on his boots.

The older man returned as Matei finished buttoning up his waistcoat. "It is time, Your Highness," he said, glancing sideways at Adella. "What shall be done with the girl?"

"Put her to work with the others, until I send for her," Matei answered, tying his cravat. "And tell them to keep a close watch on her, she's troublesome." The older man took her by the elbow and escorted them both down the corridor.

Kol awoke to something sharp jabbing into his side. He opened his eyes to see a group of small children looking down at him, poking his ribs with a stick. As he sat up, snatching the stick from them, the children all screamed and ran off down the street. Judging by the shadows on the ground, it was around midday. Glancing around, he realized he was in a little garden by the docks. The wharf and the deep blue water of the bay lay behind him, and the shield-shaped sign of the apothecary shop just down the road. Amid the constant chatter of the people coming and going around him, he suddenly heard a familiar voice.

"Get your hands off me," a woman ordered in a prim Valennian accent. "I can walk just fine on my own." Kol scanned his surroundings, thinking he had only imagined it. Then, through the crowd, he saw Adella being dragged by Sornian soldiers along the wharf.

Kol jumped to his feet; a wave of heavy dizziness overcame him, making his ears ring. Everything turned black and he swayed forward, catching himself against the tree. He rubbed his eyes. Eventually, his vision cleared just in time to watch them walk up the gang-board and onto a Sornian ship flying green and orange flags. *The colors of the Royal Family,* he noted. The sails were unfurled, and sailors in emerald jackets with white lapels and cuffs were coiling the mooring lines.

Though his head was still spinning, Kol wove his way through the crowded wharf, with careless people knocking into him now and then. Blood once again seeped down his sleeve, pattering red droplets on the ground. He finally crossed the length of the dock only to see the ship had sailed and was out of reach; he didn't see Adella among the green-clad sailors working on the weather decks as the small caravel turned seaward, leaving Hedda behind.

He stared out over the water blankly for a moment, at a loss for ideas. Looking around at the other ships in the harbor, he noticed by their flags that each one belonged to the Royal Sornian Navy, and so would be of no help to him. He walked toward the apothecary, thinking all the while. As he opened the door, he was surprised when he bumped into Armand and Teressa, who hurried toward him.

"Well?" Armand asked impatiently. "Any sign of her?"

"Yes," Kol muttered, lost in thought. Then, an idea struck him. It was a long shot, but it was all he had. "We have to go," he urged. "Right now."

They hurried back through the city, Kol leading the way haphazardly across gardens and through alleys. He brought them back through the hole in the wall, this time with little consideration for hiding in the broad daylight. Then, they scrambled across the dirt road and back to the patch of forest where they left their horses.

Kol's black mare wasn't far from where she'd been left, grazing contentedly in the shade. Adella and Teressa's horses were wandering amongst the trees. Patches was a pretty far walk off in the distance, rolling in a puddle.

"I don't have time to wait," Kol told them, tacking his horse up quickly. "You two will have to catch up. Meet me at the Smuggler's Port, northeast at the crossroads."

"What's going on?" Armand asked.

Kol turned to look at him meaningfully. "I have an idea," he replied, eyes wide with excitement. "Probably a really bad idea," he added, hoisting himself up into the saddle. Then he galloped off, clenching his jaw against the pain in his shoulder and clutching the reins hard to stay upright.

8

Setting Sail

Adella had spent the morning bruising her knees on the marble floor of a large ballroom as she scrubbed it clean alongside several other young women. She had considered trying to make an escape, but the doors were guarded by armed soldiers. When dinner time came and the other servants dispersed, the older man from that morning came and led her away.

He brought her back to the small chamber she had passed the night in. Entering, she found Matei standing in front of the open wardrobe, hurriedly stuffing some of his belongings into a small trunk. The older man closed and locked the door as he left.

"Where is Lucas?" Adella asked, looking around the room. She had hoped that her brother would come to his senses and find her so they could leave together. His betrayal over the Key certainly stung, but the thought of leaving him behind after all she had been through still seemed worse. If given the chance to speak to him, perhaps she could bring him around.

"You'll see him again soon enough," Matei replied. Turning, he threw something at her, the soft fabric hitting her face as she caught it. "Put that on," he ordered. "We'll be traveling soon."

"Why?" she asked. "What do you want with me?" He didn't reply, but kept his back toward her as he packed his things. "Where are we going?" she demanded, her tone indignant as she stomped toward him. He shot her a dark glare over his shoulder, anger flashing in his eyes. Surprised, she stepped back while he continued to rummage through the wardrobe.

Swallowing hard, Adella decided not to press the issue. Holding out the cloth, she saw that it was a short, hooded cape of grey velvet. She pulled it around her shoulders and tied the ribbon closure; it hung to her waist, partially hiding the bloodstain on the front of her bodice. "I heard that man call you Your Highness," she commented, keeping her words light as she tried a different topic. "If you're royalty, why do you get locked in at night?"

"The First Royal Consort doesn't trust me very much," he replied, not bothering to turn around. "If anything happened to her oldest son, I would be the next in line for the throne. So she has me under guard while I'm at the palace."

"'Royal Consort?'" Adella asked, brow furrowing. "Don't you mean 'Queen'?"

"Sornia has no queens." He threw a pair of buckled shoes into the trunk. "I'm only telling you all this because I'm friends with your brother. Please, try to hide your ignorance from the rest of the population. It reflects badly on me, now that you're my property."

"Your what?!" Adella's mind turned to the knife in her boot. *I've seen enough of Sornia*, she thought, but it was too late; the door unlocked and three soldiers in emerald coats entered the chamber.

As they were escorted down the corridor, Adella found herself carrying the handle on one side of the trunk behind Matei; one soldier carried the other side, and the other two walked behind them. They continued along, turning this way and that through elegant hallways lined with gilt moldings and crystal chandeliers until her hand ached with the weight of the trunk and the handle dug into her fingers. Eventually, they came to an opening in the architecture where the ceiling soared up over a grand foyer filled with ornately carved pillars. They stopped in the center of the space, and Adella and the soldier set down the trunk on the black and white marble floor. Sitting to rest on top of the trunk, she looked around, gaping at the massive tapestries woven with the images of various plants and beasts that covered the walls. One in particular caught her eye, which featured the figures of a brown hare and a pale grey dove. Between the two animals was the image of a crystal or gemstone. Golden beams of light surrounded it, shining like the sun.

Matei glanced over at Adella as she studied the tapestry. "Leveret," he said, pointing. "The hare. And Paloma, the dove. Lucas said you don't know that story in Valenna."

She shook her head. "I only heard it recently." *Well, most of it anyway*, she corrected herself. Her face warmed as the memory of waking up on Kol's arm surfaced suddenly, but she took a deep breath and tried to put it out of mind. "Why are they shown as animals, in the tapestry?" she asked.

Matei shrugged. "I don't know, it's Andolinian. Symbolism, I guess."

The sound of footsteps echoed down the corridor behind them. Turning a corner, Lucas came into view, accompanied by several well-dressed Sornian men and women along with their servantry. Adella and the soldier lifted Matei's trunk once more as the two groups merged and headed out the palace doors. They crossed through the formal front gardens, the warm air thick with the perfume of flowers. Adella glanced sideways at Lucas walking beside her. "What's going on?" she asked in a whisper. "Why is it you can walk about freely here, while I'm forced into servitude?"

"A little manual labor won't hurt you," he scoffed. "I am a citizen of Sornia now. I earned my position here; can you say the same in Valenna?"

"What did you do?" she demanded, no longer trying to be discreet. Lucas quickened his pace, leaving her behind without so much as a glance backward.

"Mind your place," the soldier beside her warned.

The group made its way through the cobblestone streets and into the busier areas surrounding the market square. Crowds pressed into them from all sides, crossing rudely between them now and then. The metal trunk handle bit into her skin, which was now red and raw.

"Stop," she said quietly to the guard beside her. "I need to switch hands." He huffed and rolled his eyes, but set the trunk down and walked around it. As he lifted the other side, however, Adella ran off into the crowd.

"After her!" Matei yelled, and the footsteps of the guards pounded behind her.

Adella wove side to side through the colorfully dressed crowds that gathered around the market stalls, pushing and shoving to make her way down a side street. The same crowd that impeded her pursuers slowed her own movement as well. She accidentally bumped into a woman carrying a large basket, its contents spilling all over the street as dried walnuts rolled under foot. Glancing back, she saw the first two guards fall over each other, cursing.

As Adella ran onward, she became aware that the people she passed by pointed out her direction to the soldiers that followed. She wove her way left and right through a crossroads, then finally ducked behind an unmanned merchant table in hopes that they would pass her by.

Peeking out, she saw one soldier, then another, run by and disappear into the crowd. She waited to see if any more would come, looking every direction around the table. When there didn't seem to be any more soldiers following after her, she got up and bolted back in the other direction. As she turned the first corner, Adella slammed right into a green wool jacket.

"Got you, you little mink," the soldier growled, grabbing her upper arms. He turned her forcefully around, twisting her hand up behind her back, and marched her forward.

They rejoined the group, who were waiting impatiently in the marketplace. Matei glowered at her. "You really are a lot of trouble," he remarked. Then, he turned to the soldier at her back. "When we get to *The Accord*, have her disciplined." He paused to think. "Ten strokes of the cane should do it."

As the soldier nodded, Adella's stomach dropped. *Oh, that's not good.* One of the servant girls in their group looked at her sadly.

After the two other soldiers rejoined them, the group continued onward through the city. Adella was dragged along, with both arms held behind her by two soldiers. That left Matei to help carry the trunk, which he didn't seem pleased about.

They approached the docks, where the fresh sea breeze blew in from the Bay. Marching across the wharf, they turned right and continued along one of the docks. Flocks of gulls called over a calm sea, and the fishy smell of seaweed and brine thickened the cool morning air. Peering over the ledge as she passed, Adella looked down into the water where the waves rippled gently, reflecting dappled light onto the sandy bed below the surface. As they crossed the rickety planks of the gang-board, she stopped, pushing back against the firm hands that held her. The blue-green water beneath them shimmered, cool and inviting, and she considered throwing herself over into the sea to try her luck, soldiers or no. However, she was awaiting a punishment already and decided not to add to it. They shoved her onto *The Accord*.

After boarding, the group headed below deck to a private cabin filled with hammocks and some spare furnishings. The other servants set to putting away the luggage while the Sornian nobility relaxed, sitting at the table or resting in the hammocks. The soldiers at Adella's back did not let go of her arms all the while, waiting on a word from Matei.

"Go on," he said to them, waving them away. "Take her to the caner already."

"Oh, let's all watch," a woman said cruelly, and Adella shot her a hard look. She appeared to be middle-aged and an aristocrat of some sort, judging by the opulence of her clothing. Her hair, the same dark ash brown as Matei's, was piled high up on her head in a thickly powdered bouffant. "Serves her right for keeping us waiting," the woman added.

They dragged Adella above deck by the wrists and held her down, forcibly bending her over a trestle table. The soldiers threw her skirts up over her shoulders, exposing her long under-breeches. Her face burned with embarrassment.

"Count one," she heard a man shout, and braced herself. There was a loud crack as pain seared through her upper thighs and coursed through her body. As she screamed through clenched teeth, muffled laughter came from behind her.

"Count two," she heard. The anticipation of the second strike was far worse than the first had been, and tears welled up in her eyes. The second blow hit far too close to the first, but she was able to stifle her voice this time. The third hit just above her knees, and stung worse than the first two, making her gasp. She clenched her fists, fingernails digging into her palms.

After the fourth blow, there was a commotion around her as someone rushed forward from the group.

"Stop," she heard a woman's voice plead. "I will take the remainder of her punishment." Adella turned her head to see a servant woman come forward, the same one who looked at her sympathetically in the market. It was hard to guess her age; her face bore the lines of a hard life, but her black hair had no grey.

"I'll allow it," Matei responded.

"No!" Adella yelled, but the soldiers shoved her aside; her legs gave out beneath her and she fell to the deck, pain surging through her flesh at the impact. They placed the woman over the table instead and the caner resumed his duty.

Matei reached out to help Adella up, but she swatted away his hand. "You are all savages," she spat, clambering to her feet on her own. Her whole body ached.

"This is how things are done in Sornia," he said calmly. "It isn't personal. The sooner you learn, the better."

After the caner had finished his last strike and the woman was released, Adella came over to help her, taking her arm to steady her. "Why did you do that?" Adella asked. The others that had been gathered around them all left to return to the cabin, but the soldiers stayed behind to keep an eye on the two women.

"I can see you're new here," the woman explained, her voice shaking. "Ten strokes was far too many for you." She winced as she took a step. "I couldn't stand to watch them break your spirit, like they did mine. Besides," she added, smiling feebly, "I hardly feel it anymore."

"You are exceptionally brave, Miss—?" Adella began.

"Oh no, not Miss. I've never been called Miss," she replied as they walked gingerly back to the cabin. "It's just Maribel."

"My name is Adella. I don't mean to seem ungrateful, but never do that again."

Adella was up before dawn with the rest of the servants, washing traveling clothes and scrubbing the remains of last night's supper from the table. After Lucas and the Sornian nobility awoke and dressed, they left the cabin to tour the ship, leaving the servantry to complete their tasks under the supervision of a couple of guards. Adella kept botching whatever task she put her hand to, and Maribel took it upon herself to follow behind and correct her work.

"So..." Maribel began hesitantly. "I heard you are a prisoner of war. You were not a servant in your homeland, I'm assuming?"

"No," Adella replied, shaking her head in frustration. "I don't know how to do any of this, and I hate it."

"You'll learn," Maribel encouraged her. "It's not so bad, really. Much the same work we'd be doing if we were married, and managing our own households."

Adella frowned at the thought and scrubbed the table harder.

"You're lucky it was Prince Matei who saved you," Maribel went on, undaunted by Adella's silence. "He can be harsh when provoked, but otherwise fair. And he's so handsome, too."

"I think he's horrible," Adella replied. "Only in Sornia would anyone confuse *this* with rescue."

"I would trade with you in a heartbeat," Maribel offered. "I work for Princess Dagny. That's the Prince's half-sister," she explained. "She is..." She glanced around the room before whispering, "a real shrew."

"I'm sure." Adella sloshed her cleaning rag back into the wash bucket, weary of small talk. "Do you have any idea where we're headed?"

"No," Maribel admitted, pushing her long braid back over her shoulder. "I only know it's some secret expedition for the war against Valenna. We're on our way to acquire some sort of..." Her brow furrowed in thought. "Weapon, I guess."

Adella, who had been drying her hands on her skirts, stopped suddenly. She had figured Lucas would pass the Key on to the Sornians, but she didn't expect it to amount to anything. *Apparently, I was wrong,* she thought as her gut sank with foreboding. *This is exactly what Rogero was trying to prevent by sending the key to me. Ugh!* She turned away, hiding her face in her hands. *Kol tried to warn me, and I wouldn't listen to him either. How could I be so arrogant?*

"Shh," Maribel said, putting her arm around Adella's shoulders. "It'll be all right. You're with us now, you'll be safe."

At midday, Adella had been ordered by one of the older servants to empty the chamber pot. She noticed that, as she carried it up the steps, the soldiers who guarded the cabin let her go by unaccompanied without any trouble. Walking to the rail, she closed her eyes briefly to enjoy the fresh sea breeze while trying not to think about the contents of the large stoneware pot in her hands. Holding her breath, she looked away as she tipped it out into the shimmering waves below. Her grip on the handle slipped and the pot nearly fell into the sea, but she caught it by the rim. Her stomach heaved as the warm pungent stench wafted up toward her.

Adella set the stinking thing down onto the deck for a moment, wiping her hands on her skirt as she looked out to sea. She inhaled the cool, salty air that brushed her skin, whipping through her hair. As she had spent the journey until now below decks, the sight of the open water stretching widely before her sent a thrill through her heart. The whole world seemed to lay before her, blue and endless. Though she had no idea toward what land they were sailing, part of her was eager to find out what lay ahead. *After all,* she told herself, *the Heartstone Kol told me about is just a legend.* Then she remembered Kol's distress, written plainly on his face when they had argued over the Key. The thought gave her pause. *Isn't it?*

Scanning the horizon, she turned aft to look westward, and was surprised to see the dark form of a ship in the distance. *Are we being followed?* she wondered. It was too far to discern any detail. Adella shrugged off the thought and wandered around the ship, enjoying the momentary freedom; the crew seemed to ignore her presence as they went about their business, giving her the chance to look around. A small boat, suspended from a pair of davits on the quarter deck, caught her eye. There wasn't much else to look at on the small caravel, so she retrieved the chamber pot and returned to the cabin. After shoving the empty pot back into its closet, she continued washing the linens with newfound gratitude for the bucket of soapy water.

By late afternoon, the gentry had returned from dinner on the mess deck, and the servants were dismissed to make a meal of whatever was left. Adella was not allowed to go with them, but Matei brought her a plate of bread and whitefish. When she tried to take a seat at the table affixed in the center of the cabin, she sprang up again as pain flared through the back of her legs. She tried again, this time perching delicately on the edge of the seat to avoid angering her wounds. As she tore at the bread crust, she was surprised when Matei took a seat beside her.

"I have been talking with your brother," he began matter-of-factly. "I have come to realize that perhaps this isn't your calling in life." Adella shot him a glare, though he didn't seem to notice. "But I have paid too much for you—I am not the Crown Prince, you know. I'm not made of gold," he digressed bitterly. "Anyway, I have come up with an idea." He paused, apparently awaiting a response, but she only took a bite of bread. Undeterred, he continued, "I can't just let you go free. But, if we were to marry, you could have a more comfortable life."

Adella's mouth was too full of food to tell him that she would much rather throw herself in the sea. *The sea!* she thought, suddenly remembering the boat on the quarter deck, and the ease with which she approached it while emptying the chamber pot. *That's exactly what I'll do. If I don't draw anymore attention to myself,* she figured, *I could find a way to escape and row to shore.*

"I see you are considering it," he said. "You needn't answer now. I have to say I'm surprised, I thought you'd still be angry."

Adella resisted the urge to pull a face at him while she swallowed the bread. *What an idiot,* she thought. "Tell me—" she began, changing the subject. "How did you meet my brother?"

"Ah," Matei replied. "As I'm sure you've realized, though I may be the king's son, I am completely expendable. I was given the task of overseeing a network of spies in Valenna. Mostly to keep me out of courtly drama." As she picked at the food, he took her silence as a cue to continue. "One night, as I was sent on a particularly important mission, I and a few others ended up in a tavern in Raymouth. We had a bit too much ale and were talking far too loudly. Your brother overheard us, gathered that we were Sornians looking to cause trouble in Valenna, and wanted in on it."

Her eyes widened. "But why? Why would he?"

"Because," Lucas said, striding across the cabin from the companionway, "our family has supported each King and Queen of Valenna for hundreds of years, going all the way back to Sir Adelo Grimless, under First King Valen of the Haspen Dynasty. And how did they repay us?" He slammed his fist onto the table. "Ostracizing us from court! Banished to the frontier to be forgotten."

"That's not what happened," Adella protested as hot anger surged through her, burning her face.

"It is," Lucas replied. "Regardless, Valenna is in decline. It has forgotten its own history, turned its back on its heritage." He leaned in with his palms on the table. "It's only a matter of time before it collapses. Only Sornia can save it from oblivion, by restoring the Colonies to the glory of the Andolin Empire."

Adella blinked at him, then a sudden, sickening realization struck her. "So, you were not captured during the attack on Elldon?"

"No," Lucas replied smugly. "I wasn't there when it happened, I left earlier. I was at the soldiers' camp in the Campos at that time. I am the one who told them when Elldon would be without its Governor."

Adella felt her blood run cold. She covered her mouth and tried to swallow the overwhelming flood of emotions. Finally, with a steadying breath, she composed herself. "You were the one behind the attack on Greywood?" she managed to utter.

Lucas threw a dark glance at Matei. "The deal was they'd leave Greywood untouched," he said through his teeth.

"Don't look at me," Matei replied with a shrug. "I wasn't involved. Talk to Blackburn."

"Did you know the man who led the attack?" Adella demanded, wondering if Kol had known about her brother's treason all along.

Lucas shook his head. "I don't know who it was," he replied. "Nobody important."

She turned to Matei, her brow so tightly furrowed that it ached. "And what was the important mission you said you were on, when you met in Raymouth?"

"My father, *King Berento*," Matei said with a grimace, "had tasked me with spreading disease in Valenna. The red ague, to be specific," he explained. "We've had it in Sornia for years, we know how to treat it now."

Adella turned to Lucas, mouth agape. "You're involved in spreading the red ague in Raymouth?" she asked in disbelief, her voice hardly a whisper. .

"Right," Lucas answered. "It can be spread through the water supply, or by drinking after someone who's ill. All we had to do was throw a sick pig into the River Ray..." He trailed off, laughing.

"I'd expect something so horrendous from a Sornian," she said, glancing darkly at Matei, "but how could you do that to your own people?" Her voice rose, no longer able to hide her outrage. *Poor Armand! He goes to Raymouth often; he must've caught it there.* Lucas had always been his favorite of the Grimless children. *If he knew that Lucas was behind his illness, he would be devastated.* Her heart ached for him and all the people suffering in Raymouth because of her brother.

"They're not my people," Lucas retorted. "Not anymore. Besides, there are always casualties in war." He shrugged. "It's unavoidable."

"You're nothing but a traitor!" she shouted, knocking her chair back forcefully as she got up from the table. "You are *not* my brother; never speak to me again." Adella strode over to the companionway, and stopped as the soldiers by the entrance crossed their swords in front of her. In her distress, she had forgotten about the guards.

"Do you *mind*?" she growled, jaw clenched as she tried to push her way through. The soldiers looked over at Matei for direction. He nodded, and they let her pass.

Adella crossed the main deck, nearly tripping on a pile of netting, and headed aft, stomping up the steps of the sterncastle, weaving around the crewmen in their green jackets. The wind from that height blew her hair and skirts wildly around her. She approached the taffrail high above the sea. Leaning over, she looked down into the water and wondered how long she would survive if she were to jump right in.

"We are being followed," Matei said, walking up behind her. "I noticed it earlier." Adella looked toward the horizon and saw the mysterious ship had moved in closer.

"Followed by whom?" she asked, her curiosity at the situation surfacing over her anger. "Valennians?" For a brief moment, she entertained the hope of rescue.

"I doubt it, coming from the west." He crossed his arms. "Probably reavers," Matei guessed. "They've been a real problem lately." He squinted at the ship. "It looks like they're gaining on us. Don't worry, we will lose them in the shoals."

Reavers, she thought. *Wonderful. Things couldn't possibly get any worse.* If she could get the ship's boat in the water, perhaps she could make it to shore. She'd rather take her chances with the sharks and storms that Belgrand Bay was known for than stay another moment on the ship. *But reavers?* she wondered. *Would I stand a chance then?* She imagined escaping from one ship full of cruel, violent people only to be taken up by another.

"How old are you?" Adella asked, remembering their conversation earlier. "Thirty?"

"Thirty-two," he replied.

"That's rather old to still be unmarried." She narrowed her eyes at him. "Did no one else want the job?"

"Ah," he said, sounding hurt. "I was married once. My wife died when the plague came to Hedda ten years ago." He gazed wistfully at the sea. "I still miss her terribly. You do remind me of her, a little. And perhaps that's why I offered—that, and the fact that I will need to marry a Valennian noblewoman in order to fulfill my plan..." He rambled on, still staring out to sea. Realizing he was no longer paying attention to her, Adella quietly snuck away.

She found Maribel on the mess deck below, eating smoked whitefish at a long table with the other servants. When she saw that Maribel was kneeling at the table, rather than sitting on the bench, she knew it was due to the wounds left by the cane. Adella crouched next to her. "I don't have a lot of time to talk," she whispered, "But I plan to get off this ship as soon as I am able. Hopefully after nightfall."

"You're daft," Maribel replied, shaking her head. "Where will you go? You'll be eaten by sharks."

"I can't stay here," Adella countered. "You've been kind to me. I wanted to give you the choice, if you'd like to take your chances and come along. You can't really wish to remain here, can you?"

"It's not so bad," Maribel said with a shrug. "It must seem worse from your perspective, coming from a life of leisure. But it's all I've known." She looked up at Adella sadly. "Would you really rather die than stay with us?"

"If it comes to that," Adella replied. She couldn't bear to be on the same ship as Lucas after what she had heard. She needed to return to Elldon, and to her parents. She had to let them know what happened.

"There you are," Matei said as he came down the steps. "You are a sneaky one." He took her by the wrist and dragged her away.

Matei led Adella across the main deck and toward the bow of the ship. He stood there a moment, still with a firm grip on her arm, and watched as dense fog rolled across the Bay before them. "We'll be there by tomorrow evening," he said quietly. "Then we will have the Heart of the World."

"Everyone seems to believe that story," Adella muttered. She tried to pull her wrist free from his hand, but he held fast.

"Have you ever been to Andolin?" he asked, looking her in the eye. "Have you seen the ruins there?" His face was grave and drawn; she shook her head. "If you had," he said, releasing her wrist, "you would believe it, too."

"So you'll find the thing." She shrugged. "Then what?"

"Then, the war will begin in earnest." They stood in silence for a while, watching the sea. "Please understand," he began at length. "It's not that I enjoy being cruel—" He turned to face her. "In Valenna, how are criminals dealt with?"

"They pay a fine," she replied. "Or, if their crimes are severe, may be executed or imprisoned."

"And," he asked, "what is the penalty for escape?"

"They might be whipped," she replied. "Or executed."

"So," he said with satisfaction, "in Valenna, corporal punishment is sometimes used?"

"For criminals," she admitted.

"Indeed." He put his finger to his lips while he thought. "I was informed you were originally meant to be executed, but were sold instead. They said you caused a lot of trouble in the Campos?"

"Your soldiers attacked my home," Adella replied.

"The Valennians started this war when they invaded neutral territory," he countered. "Are you aware Elldon is located outside the border of Valenna?"

She nodded. "Yes."

"We ignored that for years," Matei continued. "Then, your ships began attacking our navy. We still didn't retaliate until your people stole a very important artifact. The same one that you had on your person." He leaned against the rail. "Stealing from the king, that is a very serious crime. If we were to treat you the way Valennians treat their criminals, you'd have been executed several times over." She opened her mouth to protest. "Luckily for you," he went on before she could speak, "things are different in Sornia. I bought your punishment, which means I'd be held responsible if you were to escape. I'm trying to find a way for you to repay your debt to me, like a civilized person, but you are making it difficult. So, I have to ask you to make a choice. Would you prefer to do things the Sornian way, or the Valennian way?"

"I get your point," Adella replied.

"Good," he said, looking pleased. "I'm glad we've come to an understanding."

Adella spent the rest of the day attending to various chores along with the other servants. Maribel stopped what she was doing several times to correct Adella's work and give her proper instruction, and, under her guidance, Adella was able to do a passable job at several different tasks. She spent the evening mending stockings, and was given a change of clothes so that she could launder her own. With direction, she was able to scrub the old bloodstain nearly completely from her bodice, and the fresher stripes of blood that the cane left behind on her under-breeches. The guards allowed her to pass up to the weather deck, where she hung her clothes to dry.

At the end of the day, her muscles were sore and her fingers had blisters. Adella lay in her hammock while the others slept. She turned from side to side, as the burning pain in the back of her legs prevented her from finding a comfortable position. Only one guard stood at his post by the cabin entrance, while the day guards slept below with the rest of the crew, but she decided not to press her luck that night trying to escape with the boat. It would have to wait for the perfect moment; she would only get one chance. *Matei made that point clear.* Remembering their earlier conversation, she wondered if the things he had said about Valenna were true. *Did we really start the war?*

Adella closed her eyes, feeling the gentle swaying motion of the sea. She hoped that Armand and Teressa had given up by now and were on their way safely back to Elldon. Then, her thoughts turned to Kol. *Perhaps he's back in the Campos.* Adella imagined him camping peacefully under the stars with his black mare grazing nearby. She didn't want to admit it to herself, but she had gotten used to his company, his quiet but reassuring presence. For a moment, the warmth of his skin beneath her fingertips as she changed his dressings surfaced in her mind. *Stop,* she told herself, remembering their argument in the Campos. *He's gone; it's none of my business where he is now.* She turned over on her side, trying to think of other things, and eventually drifted off to sleep.

The next day, *The Accord* drew closer to the southern coast of Belgrand Bay, and approached the scattered formations known as the Teeth. As the ship crept slowly past the massive islands of jagged black rock, Adella felt a homesick ache in her heart, knowing they must be sailing just north along the fields of the Campos. Everyone, crew and passengers alike, stood on the weather deck breathlessly watching the shadowy Teeth appear and float past them in the fog. The wind had suddenly dropped to no more than a breath as they entered the shoals, and the water, as far as they could see around them, had gone still. Without even a ripple, save for the wake behind them, it looked as though the ship sailed over the surface of a mirror. *It's like floating on quicksilver*, Adella said to herself. *I've never seen anything like it.*

A sharp whistle sounded from somewhere toward the bow of the ship, and she watched as the leadsman, hanging by the shrouds, once again lowered the sounding line into the water to measure its depth. He had been doing that at regular intervals since entering the shoals, and Adella didn't envy him the task, dangling out over the eerie, dark waters such as he was. She turned to face Matei, who was standing close by at the rail of the small ship. "Have you sailed this way before?"

"No," he replied. "Though our captain claims he did once, while running from reavers." He leaned over the rail and gazed intently below. "I'm not sure I believe him," he added.

Curious to see what he was looking at, Adella peered over the rail and saw her own reflection staring up at her from the surface of the sea. As she leaned over the water, she was suddenly jarred forward when a great force buffeted the ship. Her heart raced as she just managed to catch herself on the rail to keep from falling. A horrible scraping sound issued from the larboard side of the ship as around them, the entire crew erupted into a flurry of movement and shouting.

"Oh no," Matei muttered to himself, and Adella looked up at him, eyes wide. "It's probably fine," he reassured her. "They can use the bilge pump and make repairs. But," he leaned in toward her and lowered his voice, "I wouldn't go below deck, just in case."

And just yesterday, I believed things couldn't get any worse. Though she didn't know what lay ahead on their journey, she couldn't help but wonder now if they'd even make it to their destination. "Is that reaver ship still behind us?"

He shook his head. "Apparently, they knew better than to come this way."

9

A Sea Change

The day wore on uneventfully, save for the continuous pumping of filthy bilge water over the main deck. Matei refused to go below after the ship had been damaged, and hardly allowed Adella out of his sight after the trick she played slipping away from him yesterday, even going so far as to order another servant to bring them their meals on the weather deck. She would have preferred the risk of being below over his company, but resigned herself to it nonetheless. At least the work he had her do was easy enough, mostly consisting of patching up jacket elbows or stitching on buttons. She was permitted to go briefly into the cabin only to use the chamber pot, and she took the chance to move Kol's knife from inside her boot, where it had formed a bruise against the side of her shin, to the inside of her bodice. She caught a glimpse of herself in a large wood-framed mirror that hung from the bulkhead, and paused before it. Her own sea-blue eyes stared back at her from an unfamiliar face that looked drawn and tired. She stepped back and lifted up to the tip of her toes, trying to see if the shape of the knife showed through her clothes. Adella looked sadly at her figure reflected in the glass; the shadows of ribs were beginning to show above her lean bosom. The layers of fabric she wore obscured its form well enough, but she didn't want to risk losing Kol's knife. It had seemed important to him and, though Adella doubted she'd ever see

119

him again, she wanted to keep it safe in case their paths crossed someday. Retrieving her velvet short cape from the hammock where she had slept, she tied it around her shoulders before returning above deck.

Evening approached and the air turned cold. The wind picked up once more, blowing away the last ragged scraps of mist to reveal an enormous head of rock looming toward them, rising from the southern coast along their starboard side. Two soldiers manned the davits and lowered the ship's boat into the water. They tossed a rucksack filled with supplies into the boat, then unrolled a ladder made from rope and wood planks over the rail.

Matei motioned for Adella to go forward. She wanted to protest, but curiosity drew her silently toward the rail. She knew they were disembarking to search for the Heartstone. *The Heart of the World*, she said to herself. *Isn't that what they call it?* She bit her lip as she looked over at the dark bluffs towering high above the sea. *Could it actually be real?*

Hesitantly, she climbed over the rail and down the rope ladder. As Adella stepped into the boat, it rocked in the waves and she lost her balance, plopping down awkwardly onto a thwart at the stern. Glancing back up at *The Accord*, she was surprised to see Maribel descending next, followed by the cruel older woman she presumed was Princess Dagny, who both took seats at the bow. Next, two soldiers came down and took their places at the oars, and Lucas climbed down the ladder and sat between them. It was the first time Adella had been in his company since their last conversation, and her anger flared up again at the sight of him.

They waited in the boat, bobbing side to side in the water, until Matei came on board. Adella frowned when she saw he carried a lantern in one hand, though sunset was still hours away. He took a seat beside her as the larboard soldier freed the line from the cleat and stowed it beneath him. The soldier pushed off the ship's hull with the oar, and they rowed toward the peninsula as dark grey clouds lowered overhead.

Adella watched the Teeth pass as they wove between them toward the bluffs; little grey shells of limpets crowded at the waterline where the rock had been worn smooth. A lonely gull called out high above them as they came to the base of the cliff, where the surface of the sea was punctured with rocks of every size and height. One soldier tied the line around a thin fang jutting out nearby, and secured it to the boat cleat. They picked their way delicately over the slimy rock toward the sheer face of the cliff wall.

"Look around for anything out of the ordinary," Matei ordered. "A carving, or something metallic, perhaps." The others all began to search, looking down amongst the stones and starfish in the tiny tide-pools that had formed here and there in the cracks.

Adella slid her hand under the tangled mass of her hair and rubbed her neck. Everywhere she looked seemed to be nothing but ordinary rock and water. *It looks like I was right*, she thought, sighing with relief. *There's nothing here. It really is just a silly legend, after all.* Her gaze wandered upward, taking in the full height of the bluffs hanging over her head. She wasn't surprised ships avoided the coast here, now that she saw it for herself. The clouds shifted, briefly surrounding them in golden sunlight, and something caught her eye. Straight above her on the stony face, light briefly reflected off a small, polished surface.

Could that be metal up there? she wondered, looking away quickly. She kept her observation to herself, and pretended to search the rocks at her feet.

It was no use. Matei had also spotted it. "There," he said, pointing up. "Someone needs to climb up there and place the Key inside." He turned, inspecting each person, then faced Adella. "You," he said sternly.

"No," she replied, crossing her arms. "Do it yourself."

He fished something out of the pocket of his jacket and presented it to her. It was the golden disc, Leveret's Key. The linen string hung from it still. "The footholds will be too shallow for me. You are the smallest person, you have the best chance."

"Well," she said casually, ignoring the object he held out to her. "I don't want to do it."

"You're such a spoiled child!" Lucas berated her. He grabbed Maribel roughly by the upper arm, drew a knife from inside his cloak, and pressed the tip to her ribs. Maribel's eyes widened as she looked pleadingly at Adella. "Go," Lucas warned. "Or we'll have *her* do it."

Adella snatched the key from Matei's hand, shooting them both the dirtiest look she could muster, and stuffed the key down the front of her bodice. She knew there was no way she could scale the rock face with skirts in the way, so she untied strings at her waist and removed them. Wadding them up inside her cloak, she tossed the bundle at Matei, and smirked as it hit him in the face. She gathered up the length of her linen shift and tied it at her back, freeing up her legs to climb, then turned toward the rock face. Adella took a steadying breath as she looked up at the sheer height of it, her mouth going dry.

Tentatively, she worked the toe of her boot into one of the cracks on the wall and felt around for a handhold. Pulling herself up a step, she felt with her foot for the next higher grip, and so on as she slowly ascended the cliff face toward the metal spot above.

As Adella neared the halfway point, the lace at the knee of her under-breeches caught on a sharp edge of rock. The sudden catch of her leg caused her supporting foot to slip, and her heart leapt into her throat. Gripping as tightly as she could, she held her entire weight on her fingertips for a moment as her feet scraped and scrambled against the wall. Just when she thought she couldn't hold on any longer, her toe caught a little ledge. She continued upward.

Her fingers ached, muscles burning, and she thought her arms would finally give out when she looked to her left, and realized that she had made it. Her path over the face had diverted to the right, and she had almost passed by it. Adella shifted her weight over to her left leg as carefully as she could, feeling how small and tenuous her hold was through the sole of her boot.

Now what? she asked herself, scrambling to figure out what to do next as her muscles began to burn. Then, a thought hit her. *Oh, of course! It's a key, isn't it?* Grabbing the disc from within her bodice, she stretched her arm out to the side, reaching for the shining metal circle embedded into the cliff face beside her. She pressed the disc into a shallow hole, and rotated it until it slipped into place with a satisfying clack. She hung there, her weakening limbs trembling as she waited to see if anything would happen. Then, a faint murmuring sound hummed around her, and she realized the cliff itself was shuddering.

Adella yanked the disc back out by the cord and tucked it away again, not wanting to lose the precious object, then scrambled down the rocky wall as quickly as she could. The quavering of the cliffside grew stronger; the quiet murmur swelled until it became a high-pitched buzz. Rocks from higher up tumbled down, bouncing past her as she continued to make her way downward. A sudden, sharp clattering came toward her, and she looked up just in time to see a rock bounding down right above her head. Unable to move, she could only flinch and turn her face away as the stone struck her in the left shoulder, tearing at her skin before falling at the feet of the group below. Her fingers, slick with sweat, slipped from their handholds and Adella let go, dropping hard onto her feet on the uneven ground below.

Her ankles jolted painfully at the impact, and she fell backward into the soft bundle of cloth in Matei's arms as he steadied her on her feet. The group retreated toward the boat to avoid the falling stones, but all eyes remained on the cliff above. The golden metal had disappeared, and the rock face around it seemed to be melting away like the wax of a candle.

The entire group stood staring as the rock wall before them sank in on itself. A black cavernous opening spread out from the center, growing ever wider, as the cliffside shuddered. A little stream spouted out from the rock, spraying them with icy water. It continued to increase in volume as the hole in the cliff widened. Soon, it became a veritable waterfall and was still growing.

"What in the hell—" Matei muttered.

"Back in the boat!" Adella shouted over the roar of the water, and they ran across the slippery rock as best they could. The group piled into the boat and one of the soldiers untied the mooring line in a panic, his hands fumbling until the knot gave way. They rowed out, away from the cliff, to watch at a safe distance. The hole in the rock face, now a thundering falls, continued to spill out, forming a rip tide flowing into the sea. When the foamy current reached the edge of their boat, the bow swung round, spinning them in circles as they were dragged along. Finally, a soldier threw a line around a fang of protruding rock and secured it to a cleat at the prow. The line drew taut as the water dragged at the boat but held fast. All they could do was sit helplessly and wait for the deluge to end.

Adella watched the flow of water from the cave dwindle to nothing more than a strong current. The hole that had formed in the cliffside now extended down to the water level and beyond, forming a huge, gaping chasm in the wall of the peninsula ahead.

In the grey twilight, the wind whipped to a frenzy, tearing at their clothes and hair, swinging around the lantern that hung from the hooked rod at the bow of the boat, and their eyes caught a splash of movement at the opening of the cave. A long, black silhouette rose out from the water and arched forward, moving toward them at a rapid pace before disappearing back under the waves beneath the boat. Adella thought she had only imagined it until it resurfaced only a stone's throw away. The serpentine shadow circled through the water around them, dipping in and out of the surface. The golden flash of lantern light reflected in one huge, lustrous eye in the waves beside her before disappearing altogether down into the sea.

Adella froze, stunned with sudden dread that chilled her limbs. She'd never seen anything like it in her life. She turned to look at

Matei, wondering if he had seen what she had, and was surprised to find him cowering behind her shoulders.

He straightened, though fear still shone in his eyes. "Row quickly," Matei ordered over the blast of the wind. "To the cavern!"

They rowed toward the cliffside, drawing nearer to the gaping mouth of darkness ahead. Seawater dripped onto their shoulders as they passed through the high opening. Inside, the heavy, cold air pressed on them like a wet cloak, the radius of light from the lantern never reaching beyond the seemingly endless black before them. Eventually, the walls and roof of rock around them gave way to emptiness, and the soldiers at the oars had to guess their direction after the light from the outside world faded away behind them. Muffled silence hung in the air, broken only by an occasional splash in the distance. Adella shuddered to think what it might be.

"How horrible! I wish I had stayed on *The Accord*," Princess Dagny remarked, the steam of her breath visible in the lantern light. "It's like those old stories—like we're in the belly of Mundil."

"What's that?" Adella asked, shivering in the damp air. "'Mundil?'"

"Do Valennians remember nothing of Andolin?" Matei asked sharply. "Mundil was their name for our world." He paused, but the only reply was the eerie quiet of the cave. "The Andolinians believed that there was a great sea at the center of the world," he went on, apparently to keep the silence at bay. "It's said that the stone Teeth guard the mouth of a tunnel that leads down into the belly of Mundil." Just then, a loud splash came from somewhere outside their little bubble of light and Matei leaned over to look down into the black water, his eyes growing distant. "Perhaps the sea we're floating on even now is unfathomable. Perhaps," he considered dreamily, "if we were to fall overboard, we'd sink down to the very center of the world."

"I wouldn't doubt it," Lucas muttered from his seat in front of Matei. Adella noticed how quiet he seemed, so unlike himself. *But...* she realized, *I don't really know him anymore, do I?* They had always been close as children, but if she was being honest with herself, she had to admit they had been drifting apart for some time now. Before the attack on Elldon, Lucas had been spending more and more time in Raymouth. Perhaps if she had tried harder to be a part of his life, things might have gone differently. *If I had been with him in Raymouth—If I had been a better sister...* Her mind wandered off into dark thoughts as she stared into the black void of the water below.

Adella yawned; they had been rowing for hours, trading places at the oars as they tired. Even Matei and Dagny took their turns together, though not so long as the others. Dagny had spent the whole time moaning and whining about the effort. Adella wondered if that's how she had sounded to Maribel on her first day aboard the ship. She remembered this lesson when it was her turn to row and worked quietly. When it came time for the soldier to take her place at the oar, Adella's whole body ached. She shifted around on the thwart as her legs tingled, wishing she could lie down. Despite the discomfort, she started to nod off, waking suddenly now and then with a jerk of her head.

A spot of light materialized in the distance. As they drew slowly closer, the white glow gradually grew until a shaft of daylight streamed down through the cave ahead.

"What is that?" Dagny asked. "A moon?"

"No, you idiot," Matei murmured sleepily. "It's a hole in the ceiling. The sun must be rising," he noted, then ordered the soldiers to row toward the shaft of light.

"We've been gone all night?" Dagny asked. "How will we find our way out again? We'll die in here for sure."

Matei gave a loud yawn before responding. "Haven't you noticed? We've been rowing against a current the whole way. We'll just follow it back out again." He stretched out on the hard plank of the thwart, resting his head on Adella's lap. Her face burned with anger and embarrassment, but she held her tongue.

Adella focused her attention on the increasing light ahead. As they drew closer, she noticed a solid form jutting out of the water, illuminated in the sunbeam. The two soldiers appeared to be directing the boat right toward it. She craned her neck to watch; the tall object grew more prominent as they neared it until it loomed high above them. Soon, she realized it was a small island and thought she had glimpsed a structure atop its summit. As the boat scraped against the rock, one soldier tied the mooring line around a nearby boulder while the other shouldered the rucksack.

"Wake up," she whispered to Matei, hitting him on the shoulder much harder than she intended. He awoke with a snort, and as he got up, Adella stretched her legs, glad to finally be rid of him.

They climbed out of the boat and picked their way over the slick, wet rock, the soles of their shoes crunching on the shells of barnacles and snails. Matei led the way, lantern in hand, up the dark, precarious slope. As they came to the top, they discovered a perfectly flat expanse of smooth, algae-covered ground stretching out before them, covered in wiggling starfish and other creatures left stranded after the outpouring of the water. In the center, a ray of sunlight streamed from the high ceiling, illuminating shapes carved of white stone. Following the others, Adella stepped carefully across the rocky surface, slipping on wet kelp and catching her toes on coral.

As they came closer, she could see the structure more clearly. Ancient alabaster columns glowed softly in the light from above, supporting a domed roof encrusted with coral and living anemones. Matei raised the lantern higher as they approached the sea-claimed ruins and stepped beneath the shadow. Under the dome lay a long box made of some dark material much like iron but untouched by the effects of time or sea.

"This must be it," Matei guessed, and ordered the soldiers to open it. They tried to shove away the lid, but it wouldn't budge, and resorted to prying at it with their swords before Matei stopped them. "Of course," he muttered to himself. "Adella, the Key."

She stepped toward the strange iron box, carved with many unfamiliar symbols and pictographs. She ran her fingers along their shapes, much like the ones in the sea cave she found herself in days ago, running from the soldiers with Kol, Armand, and Tess. The columns she stood beside reminded her of the broken ones Kol had shown her in the Campos. *They must all be from the same civilization*, she thought. *From the same people.* She wished she could have shown him this. It was a stupid thought, she told herself, but it gave her an idea.

Adella took the disc from around her neck and handed it to Matei. "Do you have any paper?"

"There might be a writing box in the supply bag," he replied, taking the artifact from her. He ran his hand over the top of the iron surface, feeling for a place to set the key.

The soldier dropped the heavy rucksack on the ground, and Adella rifled through it. At the bottom, she found a small writing box, and was pleased to discover some rolled-up parchment and vine charcoal inside. Placing the sheets of parchment over the more interesting pictographs, she rubbed charcoal over the surface to capture the images while Matei continued searching for a place to put the key.

Matei clicked the key into its hollow on a small side of the box just as Adella ran out of clean sheets of parchment. She rolled them up, placed them back in the writing box, and had just tucked it under her arm when, once again, a humming sound began to grow around them. She glanced nervously at the others, unsure what to expect this time, until a nearby grating sound caught her attention. Beneath the dome, the lid of the massive iron box split down the center, and the two sides rotated outward on unseen hinges, coming to a rest at the sides. The golden disc fell downward into the shadows, landing with a soft thud. Matei lifted the lantern, spilling light out over a form within. Inside lay the remains of a woman, desiccated but complete, uncorrupted by rot.

"She's beautiful," Maribel said under her breath.

Glistening gold in the lantern light, the woman's hair lay in perfect waves over her shoulders. Her eyes, lips, and nostrils had been sewn shut, but her copper skin lay unmarred and taut over her delicate bones. Her face was elongated, with strikingly high cheekbones and a pointed jawline. Adella was speechless, overcome with awe as she looked into the countenance of one who had taken her last breath so long ago. She couldn't help but wonder what this woman's world had been like.

Matei stretched out a hand to retrieve the key that had fallen on the woman's lap, landing on the soft fabric of her tunic. He hesitated, his fingers trembling slightly, before reaching down and taking the artifact. "Look for the Heartstone," Matei whispered, shoving the Key into his pocket. "It must be in here." Adella hung back as the others reluctantly prodded around the woman's body. It wasn't long before one of the soldiers found a smaller box of the same strange iron, serving as a rest for the woman's head. Adella grimaced as the soldier lifted the lifeless skull gingerly by the temples and Matei pulled the box from beneath.

Matei set the key into a shallow depression on the top surface of the box and turned it until it clicked into place, then drew his fingers back quickly as the mechanism spun suddenly with a metallic snap. The lid popped ajar, and he peeked inside. A soft, white light emanated from within the lockbox, illuminating his features.

"This is it," he said with a grin. Matei shut the box once more and tucked the Key into his pocket. "Let's head back." He didn't wait for a response before making his way toward the boat.

"Wait," Adella whispered to Maribel as the others walked away. "Help me close this." She looked down at the woman in the iron casket. *She lay here all this time*, Adella thought. *Peacefully at rest for... who knows how long?* It seemed disrespectful to leave her to the elements now. With Adella's direction, the two lifted the heavy sides of the lid, carefully lowering them into place.

As they followed Matei toward the boat, a sharp scream erupted ahead. The two women ran to catch up and reached the boat just in time to see Princess Dagny in the light of Matei's lantern, clawing at the rocks before disappearing under the black surface of the water.

"Dagny!" Matei yelled, kneeling down to search for a sign of movement, but the only answer was stifling silence. He turned to the others. "Get in the boat!" he ordered, and they all scrambled in while the soldiers untied the line, then rowed away as quickly as they could.

Heavy rain pounded in her face as Adella hugged her little cape around herself to protect the writing box in her lap. The thick velvet fabric was so waterlogged it did nothing to keep her dry, though it helped somewhat to block the wind. With the aid of the outgoing current, their journey out of the sea cave was much shorter, but they emerged to face a raging storm. They rowed between the Teeth among the shoals, heading back toward *The Accord*. The still waters from the day before were gone, and the white-foamed waves jostled the boat side to side. They spent most of the return voyage in silence, even as they shared a meager meal from the supplies packed in the rucksack.

As they neared the ship, Adella glanced at Matei sitting beside her. "I'm sorry about Princess Dagny," she said, leaning in to be heard over the storm. "Was she your sister?"

He held his gaze straight ahead. "Half-sister," Matei corrected her. His voice was devoid of emotion, but she noticed his eyes glistened with more than rain.

The boat turned and drew up alongside the ship. Matei sent Adella, Lucas, and Maribel up the ship's ladder ahead of him, dumping the remaining supplies from his bag into the hull to make room for the iron box. He then followed up after them, leaving the soldiers to tend to the boat in the driving rain.

The Accord sailed onward, running north-easterly with the wind rather than returning the way they had come. That way had been too perilous to navigate in a storm, so they sailed forward through a clearer path ahead toward the rim of the shoals. As they passed by one particularly massive Tooth rising from the water like a mountain, a shadowy form emerged behind it, moving toward them through the cresting waves.

The sky above them had grown so dim with clouds and rain that it seemed night already; the unnatural darkness loomed over the sea like a shroud. Adella peered over the taffrail at the ship in their wake, and her gut dropped as she realized it was gaining on them. Not only that, but even in the dismal light of the squall, she could make out the red and black stripes of the sails. *The Tigress. Declan's ship*, she reminded herself to quiet the panic rising within her.

Adella tried not to think about the fact that he didn't know she was on board. *Even if he saw me*, she thought, turning the writing box over in her hand absent-mindedly, *he would probably not even recognize me*. She'd be just one more Sornian servant to him, and his men. *But what if he did?* she wondered. *Would it matter? He's a reaver, a criminal... A murderer*. Adella let out a long breath and made up her mind. As much as it stung her to admit, she couldn't take that chance; she didn't know him anymore.

"Come," Matei said, grabbing her upper arm. "Let's get below. The soldiers will handle this."

They hurried down the steps of the sterncastle and across the quarter deck, Matei pulling her along as they dodged armed men rushing to and fro to make preparations. The box slipped from her hand and she tried to pull away to retrieve it, but he held firm.

"It's no good, Captain," she heard one man shout over the blasting rain. "They'll be upon us soon." Adella could hardly see around her, as she constantly had to wipe away the water running down into her eyes.

"There!" a rough voice answered among the commotion. "We must head for those shoals. Hard to starboard!"

Adella and Matei had nearly reached the companionway when a sudden jolt threw them forward onto the deck. Adella hit her jaw hard as she fell, and the world around her faded to black. She rubbed her eyes and, when her vision finally cleared, she could see all the crew in an uproar, scrambling to their feet and drawing weapons. *The Accord* had somehow stalled in the water, and now the enemy ship drew close, pulling up alongside. Matei was nowhere to be seen.

Adella ran back again across the weather deck, running into crewmen now and again until she reached the quarter deck. Stopping at the top of the steps, she stood open-mouthed as she looked to the larboard. Thick lines secured the two ships together, running from the deck of *The Tigress* to the rail of *The Accord*. A gang-board stretched between them over the turbulent waves, and men wielding swords were crossing the plank, swarming aboard *The Accord*. They slashed and hacked ferociously at the Sornian soldiers, many of whom were caught unprepared. It looked like the fight would be brief until one soldier pushed the gang-board into the water, knocking three crewmen into the dark sea to be swallowed by the waves. Adella didn't stay to watch.

She ran over to the davits on the starboard side where the quarter boat hung, untied the lines that held it, and clumsily lowered it into the sea. Though it dropped roughly into the choppy waters, she was relieved the boat hadn't capsized or broken on impact. Her brow furrowed as she looked down at it, jostling in the rough waves. It was too far to jump.

Adella rushed down the steps to the main deck, pushing and shoving her way through the tumult while dodging swinging blades. Finally, she reached the ship's ladder at the rail. She lifted it, the rope soaked heavy with rain, and unrolled it over the side. Adella was just about to climb over to secure the boat when someone grabbed her wrist.

"There you are!" Matei growled, and pulled her hard toward him. He held the iron box under his other arm. Lucas was beside him, along with a couple of soldiers.

"Please," Adella said, ignoring Matei and turning to her brother. "You know this is wrong. Come home with me." She had to try one last time, for her parents' sake.

"It's too late," he said flatly.

"No, it's not," she said, her throat tight with emotion. "Please."

"You're on the wrong side, Adella." His eyebrows furrowed sadly. "I wish you could see that." Lucas looked away. "I didn't mean for things to turn out this way, but I don't regret my choice."

"Lucas!" a high voice called out. Across the deck, Teressa pushed her way through the fray toward them. Her eyes met Adella's for a moment. Then, Teressa dropped her sword and ran into Lucas's arms.

Adella stood staring in stunned disbelief. *Tess? But... How? Where'd she come from?* Finally, she wrenched her wrist from Matei's grasp and shoved a knee into his groin. He shouted as he collapsed, the iron lockbox hitting the deck with a thud. Adella grabbed for it, but a soldier caught her, his arms squeezing tightly around her waist. Reaching down the front of her bodice, Adella pulled out the knife Kol had lent her and sank the blade deep into the soldier's thigh. As she pulled the knife back out, he shouted and shoved her forward, and she fell to the deck. The knife skittered across the planks, disappearing between the feet of two men fighting on the far side of the ship. Pulling herself up, her eyes darted from the iron box to the ladder, and for a moment, Adella hesitated, unsure what to do. Then, remembering her promise to Kol, she ran after the knife.

10

The Captain

Kol tied his horse to a post and, hurrying along the pier, stopped in front of the gang-board. Though he knew what he had to do, his confidence suddenly fell away at the sight of the sea, and his pulse echoed wildly in his ears. Closing his eyes, he took a deep breath to steady himself. The tangy salt air, spiked with the smell of fish, did little to calm his nerves. Then, he opened his eyes and stepped hesitantly onto the gang-board, only making it a few steps before stopping halfway. As he looked down at the dark waters swirling beneath his feet, a wave lifted the ship, jostling the board on which he stood. *Oh hell,* he thought. *I can't do this...* A sailor in a blue checkered shirt walked brusquely by, raising his eyebrows at him. Embarrassed, Kol composed himself and continued forward.

Stepping onto the ship, he looked around. Sailors hustled here and there, offloading crates and loading large canvas bags. Kol turned this way and that, trying to pick out the ship's captain from the crew, but there was no need. He turned around once more, this time to find a man in a captain's hat pointing a saber at him.

"What could a Sornian soldier be wanting aboard a Valennian ship?" the captain demanded. He stood not so tall as Kol, but had a much stronger physique. The man's bright blue wool jacket, trimmed with cream jacquard at the cuffs, stretched tightly across a broad chest, and though his blond hair was tied back in a neat queue, the hard look in his eye told Kol this wasn't someone to trifle with.

"What makes you think that's what I am?" Kol asked, hoping to sound innocent. He did not want to fight this man.

"Judging by your appearance," the captain answered with a smirk. "Bad haircut, half starved, looking like you haven't bathed in a month."

"You're not wrong on three points," Kol conceded, "but I'm an ex-soldier. Is this Captain Declan's ship?"

The captain nodded.

"And that's you?" Kol asked.

"Yes," Captain Declan replied. "What do you want?"

Kol took a deep breath, choosing his words carefully. "A woman of our mutual acquaintance has just been taken captive aboard a Sornian ship. I was hoping you'd be game to overtake them."

"And the name of this woman?" Declan asked.

"Adella Grimless." Kol shifted uncomfortably as he awaited a reply.

Captain Declan lowered his weapon slightly, apparently thinking it over, then raised it again suddenly. "This must be some kind of trick. There's no way Miss Adella would come all the way out here to this festering backwater. Let's see…" He rubbed his chin. "I'm meant to follow that ship until I'm ambushed by the Sornian Navy, correct?"

"No—" Kol began, but Captain Declan lifted his saber to strike from above. Kol barely had time enough to draw his own cutlass from the scabbard to parry. As Declan spun the blade around in the air to strike from the side next, Kol just managed to block that as well, but the motion and strain sent a sharp pain through the wound in his shoulder. He groaned through clenched jaws as Declan pushed off with his blade, shoving Kol backward.

Captain Declan lunged forward with the point of his blade, but Kol sidestepped it, then deftly wrenched the sword from the captain's hand by the hilt. The sailors nearby froze, watching in anticipation as Kol spun both blades around his hands and pointed them at the captain. Then, he set them down on the deck between them and lifted his hands in the air, showing his palms. "It's not a trick."

"What proof can you give me?" Declan asked, sheathing his saber.

"Proof?" Kol thought for a moment, then pulled the string from around his neck, holding it up to show the gold and coral ring.

Declan took the ring in his hand and looked it over, then narrowed his eyes. "This could have been intercepted."

Kol snatched the ring back from him. "We really don't have time for this."

"Then tell me," Declan prodded, "what does she look like?"

"All right," Kol said, feeling rather annoyed. "Eyes blue like the sea, pouting lips—" He raised his hand to make shapes at his chest. "And firm, perky—"

"Enough," Declan interrupted, drawing his saber once more and pointing the blade toward him. "Pick up your sword again."

Kol let out an exaggerated sigh, and bent to pick it up.

"Captain Declan," a voice interrupted as Armand rushed across the deck toward them. "Oh, I see you've met Mister Kol."

"Ben Armand?" Declan responded. "Good to see you again. Yes, I've just had the pleasure. Charming fellow," he added sarcastically, sheathing his saber again.

Teressa finally joined the group, looking out of breath. "What did he say?" she asked.

"Follow me," Declan ordered. "All of you."

They followed him across the main deck and down the steps into the captain's quarters, where Declan invited them all to have a seat at the round table affixed to the center of the space. Armand explained as quickly as he could how Elldon had been attacked by Sornian soldiers out of uniform, relayed Lucas's capture, and then Adella's. He also mentioned how he'd recovered from the red ague, and that now Teressa was stricken with it.

"I see," Declan said when Armand had finished. "I'm sorry, she'll have to remain quarantined in this cabin for the time being." Armand nodded in agreement. "Also," Declan added, "I don't want the Sornian to go about the ship unsupervised. He must remain in your sight at all times." Armand agreed again. Kol frowned.

"Does this mean you'll help us?" Teressa asked eagerly.

"Of course," Declan replied. "How could I refuse? Miss Adella is my oldest friend." He stood up from his chair and stepped behind it, gripping the back. Heavy gold rings set with large gemstones glistened on his fists. "Please make yourselves comfortable; you are my guests here. Now if you will excuse me..." He pushed in his chair and returned above decks, closing the doors behind him.

"If I am a guest, why do I feel like a prisoner?" Teressa moped, crossing her arms.

"Don't be melodramatic," Armand reprimanded. "You have the plague."

Kol wandered around the cabin, snooping in anything that wasn't locked. He was just reaching out to touch something on the captain's writing desk when Armand shot him a glare.

"Keep your hands to yourself," Armand scolded. "I'm responsible for your actions now apparently, but I won't take a flogging for you."

Kol plopped down on a chair, folding his arms. Soon, Captain Declan returned with the news that they were about to set sail, and Armand quickly went to lead their horses from the docks to the stables nearby. While he was gone, the first mate brought them a tea service with biscuits and set it on the table in the cabin.

Declan sat down at the table with Teressa and Kol and began to pour strong black tea into each cup through a little silver strainer. They drank in silence, the two men glaring at each other over their little teacups until Armand returned with their belongings that had been packed with the saddles and joined them at the table. Looking around, Kol realized he was holding his teacup differently than everyone else. He set it down and tried to grip it by pinching the handle like the Valennians did.

"I see you are wounded," Declan said to Kol. "I would offer you the services of our ship's surgeon, but he was killed a few days ago."

"How unfortunate," Kol replied flatly.

"Indeed. We lost several men to the Sornian Navy, though we did manage to sink their ship." The porcelain clanked as he set the cup on its saucer. "That's our third for May. By my count, I'd say we've reduced their numbers by at least one hundred and fifty men just this month." Declan smiled wryly, watching Kol's face for a reaction.

"Well done," Kol replied. "I've killed a few of them myself lately."

"Hm." Declan finished his tea, then left to return to his duties on deck.

Kol pushed his chair back and got up, pulling his bloodied shirt off to inspect his shoulder. *I've had worse,* he thought, patting it dry with his sleeve, then winced as the wound stung to the touch. He tossed his soiled shirt onto the table, and Teressa wrinkled up her nose at the stench that emanated from it.

Glancing down, Kol noticed that the soiled bandages around his torso had come loose and needed changing, so he pulled some clean rags from Adella's haversack that he had hung on the chair and set them on the table. Peeling the dressing away, he could see the lower portion of the scab was still inflamed and seemed to be weeping fluid. He tried to wrap the clean bandages around himself, but the pain in his left shoulder limited his movement with that arm. With one end pinned under his elbow, he tried to wrap the fabric around his ribs, but it slipped and fell to the floor.

"Do you need help with that?" Armand offered.

"No." Kol picked up the bandage to try again. This time, he managed to wrap it around himself several times before the end came loose and unraveled. He tried once more, and dropped it again. He then picked up the cloth, wadded it angrily, and threw it at the wall before stomping toward the companionway.

"Your charge has wandered off," Teressa said as Kol trudged up the steps. Armand let out a sigh, then scooted his chair back to follow. "I'm not picking up after him," she added loudly.

Looking out to sea, Kol leaned on his elbows against the starboard rail. As *The Tigress* turned about to head eastward, the Sornian ship slowly came into view far off in the distance.

"Something bothering you?" Armand asked as he approached.

"No." Kol squinted at the horizon. Quite a few things were bothering him, but he didn't want to admit to any of them, as they all involved Adella. "I don't like being at sea," he said finally. "It makes me uneasy."

"Ah." Armand looked down at the waves hitting against the hull. "I get a bit seasick myself, sometimes."

They watched the sea silently until Captain Declan joined them at the rail. Pulling open a large spyglass, he surveyed the ship in the distance.

"It looks as though we are going after *The Accord*," he said, watching it through the glass. "A Sornian Navy caravel. We've been after it for years." Then he muttered to himself, "How did you get into this much trouble, Adella?"

"Do we have a chance?" Kol asked.

"*The Tigress* is the faster vessel, for certain," Declan replied. "But the caravel is more maneuverable. I can't imagine where they're headed, but let's hope they steer clear of the Teeth." He closed the glass and turned to them. "Do you care to see the ballista?"

Kol didn't particularly, but he nodded along with Armand, and they followed Declan up to the forecastle deck. A strong wind, damp with seaspray, hit them as they approached a large object at the center of the deck. It appeared to be a giant crossbow fitted to a wooden frame.

"We just got it this spring to replace an older design," Declan began. "It can be loaded with bolts or balls—" He gestured to a box filled with large round stones. "Or the harpax, which we use to winch the enemy ship alongside for boarding."

Kol looked questioningly at Armand. "It's like a grappling hook," Armand explained under his breath. Armand and Declan continued to discuss the weapon, but Kol soon lost interest. Looking aft, he watched the shoreline creep further away behind the ship. He fiddled with the gold ring dangling from his neck, thoughts elsewhere.

Declan eyed Kol suspiciously, looking over the long black scar on his abdomen and the dried blood that stained his arm. "Tell me," he said to Kol, "how did you and Miss Adella meet? I don't recall Armand mentioning that part."

"They hadn't told me," Armand admitted.

"She pushed me onto the floor," Kol replied curtly, looking away.

"And this happened where?" Declan prodded.

"In the dining room," Kol answered. "It's a long story." He didn't want to mention he led the attack on Greywood that night, and was relying on the idea Declan wouldn't want to hear more.

"Sounds like it," Armand said, raising an eyebrow. "Maybe you should keep it to yourself."

Declan frowned, but continued. "There was another item I had sent her along with that ring, which resembled the gear of a clock. Do you know of it?"

"Do you mean Leveret's—" Kol began to say.

"Shh!" Declan interrupted, glancing around them. "Don't speak of it in front of the crew." He lowered his voice and leaned in toward him. "Did she have it on her, or is it in Elldon?"

"Last I saw her," Kol replied, "she was wearing it under her clothes." Declan gave him a hard look, then turned and walked back down the steps to the main deck.

Armand removed his hat and swatted Kol with it. "Knock it off."

"What?" Kol asked innocently.

"He already doesn't like you for being Sornian," Armand replied. "No need to vex him over Miss Adella. Do you think it would kill you to be polite?"

"It does feel that way sometimes," Kol mused.

"Try to be more amiable," Armand urged. "You might find you two have much in common." Reluctantly, Kol nodded.

The passengers, save for Teressa, and the crew of *The Tigress* gathered on the mess deck for supper. Kol sat down beside Armand, placing his bowl on the table in front of him. "What is it?" Kol asked. He held the spoon above the redware bowl and watched as some kind of porridge dripped slowly down.

"Burgoo," Armand gave a muffled reply, already eating. "Stewed oats. And I think they put lard in it as well."

Kol tasted the porridge tentatively. "It has no flavor."

One crewman sitting beside them dug a small cork-stoppered jar out of his pocket and set it proudly on the table. "It's not bad if you put a little nutmeg in it."

"Don't listen to Jon," another crewman chimed in. "He puts nutmeg on everything."

Kol finished his meal quickly despite the taste. As Armand was taking his time, sharing stories and jokes with some of the sailors sitting nearby, he decided to sneak away and look around the ship. Kol snooped around the cargo hold for a while, peeking under tarpaulins and into crates before getting bored with it and heading back up the steps to the weather deck. Crossing to the rail, he looked out over the dark sea and breathed in the cool salt air. Evening was falling, and the sky was just beginning to grow dim. Some of the crew members milled about. Behind him, the western horizon still glowed with the remnants of daylight.

At the sound of clinking glass, Kol turned, and was surprised to find Captain Declan sitting quietly on a barrel nearby. The captain held a wine glass in one hand and a green bottle in the other. His hat and jacket were missing and his sleeves were rolled up to the elbows, revealing a network of scars covering his forearms. Kol hoped the captain hadn't seen him wandering around unattended, and decided to sneak away before he noticed.

"It's not an easy life, you know," Declan began behind him.

Kol stopped and, remembering Armand's advice to be amiable, hesitantly turned back to join him. "How's that?" Kol asked, leaning against the bulkhead. As Declan poured more wine from the bottle into the glass and drank from it, Kol wondered why he bothered with the glass at all, and didn't just drink straight from the bottle.

"Each time I set sail," Declan explained, "I don't know if I will make it back again. Will I die a bloody death? Or will I finally go down with the ship?" Pausing, he took another draught from the glass. "I haven't seen Adella in years. I'm not the man she used to know." He pressed his lips together for a moment, and Kol thought perhaps Declan had forgotten what he was talking about. "But no matter how cruel the sea, or how many men we've lost," Declan continued, slurring slightly, "whenever I came back to port, I always had her letters to look forward to." He looked down at his feet. "Apparently, it meant more to me than to her."

Kol was about to agree that seemed to be the case, but his conscience got the better of him. *Great,* he thought, blowing aside a curl that hung in his face. *I won't be able to harass him anymore after this.* "I think there's been a misunderstanding. There's nothing between Adella and me."

Declan passed him the bottle, and Kol took a drink. The wine was bitter and very dry, but better than none at all. Kol thought about the last time he saw her. Remembering that he'd started their argument, he couldn't help but think it was his fault she'd gotten captured. *And after she saved my life, too.* The guilt gnawed at him. "We did not part on good terms," Kol continued unprompted. "She won't be happy to see me again."

"Oh, good!" Declan replied, clapping Kol jovially on his uninjured shoulder.

Kol and Armand returned to the captain's quarters to retire for the night, with the captain apparently taking a berth elsewhere. When they entered, Teressa was already asleep in one of the two hammocks. Armand pressed his hand lightly against her forehead to check for fever before crawling into the other hammock, leaving Kol with the captain's own berth to sleep in. Kol sat at the edge of the mattress, expecting to feel tired, but a growing uneasiness unsettled his stomach. Trying to ignore it, he lay down, putting one arm behind his head, and closed his eyes. The swaying of the ship seemed to increase in intensity, and images from his nightmares flashed unbidden behind his eyes. He gradually drifted into a fitful sleep before awakening abruptly in a cold sweat to the sensation of falling. He sat bolt upright, rubbing his face. *They're just dreams,* he told himself. *It's not real.*

Kol lay stubbornly back down, pulling the thin blanket over his head. Eventually, he dozed again as the images of sea creatures swam around in his mind. As he snapped awake, gasping for air, he realized he had been holding his breath in his dreams. Kol ripped the blanket off and stood up, kicking the leg of the berth out of spite before striding across the room. Outside the gallery windows, the stars shone faintly in the night sky. One candle had been left burning in the chandelier above the table. Sitting beneath it, he shuffled through Adella's haversack in the candlelight, looking for something to distract himself. Pulling out her heirloom novel, he flipped through it. The print was a little different than he was used to, but he found he could still make out the words. He propped his feet up on a chair to read, giving up on sleep completely.

The three passengers on *The Tigress* spent the morning washing up in a bucket of seawater and mending their clothes as best they could. Kol had to sew a button onto his fall-front breeches while still wearing them, and he nearly gave up the third time he stabbed himself in the hip with the needle.

After that chore was done, he moved on to stitching up the two holes in his shirt where the blades had cut through. When he finished, he pulled it on and stepped in front of a little wood-framed mirror hanging on the bulkhead, then frowned at his unkempt appearance. They had been traveling for so long a dark beard now covered his face. Digging through a box of vanity supplies that Declan had left for their use, he found a folding razor.

When Kol finished shaving, he stared at his reflection. He didn't recognize himself any better now than he had with the beard. *Maybe it's the hair,* he thought. It had been over a year since he had last shaved his scalp, and now his black curls hung over his eyes. Grabbing the wayward tendrils, he lifted the razor to his scalp.

Kol stopped. He wasn't sure why, but cropping his hair didn't feel right anymore. He tied it back instead.

Captain Declan entered and, pushing the clutter aside, spread a map over the table as the others gathered around. "We are here," Declan said, stabbing the parchment with his finger. "Just east of Hedda, here." He tapped the coast of Sornia. "Now, if you were to draw a straight line from Hedda to our current location and continue directly through the Teeth," he ran his finger over the map, "you will come to the Figurehead." He turned to Kol. "That's what we call this peninsula here, along the southern coast."

"I've been to that area," Kol replied. "That's north of Compass Point in the Campos."

"Ah," Armand said. "But why would they be heading there?"

"Because," Declan replied, "they have Leveret's Key and intend to retrieve the Heart of the World."

"They have whose what?" Teressa asked, then tipped back the flask, finishing off the last of the medicine that they had acquired at the apothecary.

"According to legend," Declan explained, "it's a stone that bestows unnatural abilities on whoever holds it in his hand."

Teressa raised an eyebrow. "And you all believe this?"

"My mother was from Andolin," Armand replied. "She taught me this as history. I believe it."

"So what does that peninsula have to do with this key?" she asked, forehead creasing.

"The Key was inscribed with a map of Belgrand Bay on one side," Declan began. "The coastline looks a little different nowadays, but this peninsula is shown on that map with a strange symbol etched above it. I believe it marks the location to the Heart." He straightened, removing his hat. "I have seen the Key myself; we looted it off a Sornian ship as it returned from Andolin. I sent it to Adella for safekeeping." He rubbed the back of his neck. "I did not foresee how much danger that would place her in. I thought it would be safe there," he added, as much to himself as to the others.

"It isn't *you* that should take the blame," Teressa said, glancing sideways at Kol.

The others looked at Kol expectantly. "She's right," he admitted. "I led the squadron that attacked Elldon that night. I saw that I was wrong." He pressed his lips together, not expecting the pain the words brought him. "I am sorry for my part in all this. I've been trying to make up for it."

Declan paused, his brow tense in thought. Then, he relaxed, letting out a breath. "No man on this ship is innocent. What's done is done." He turned his gaze back to the map on the table. "All that matters now is what we do next." He tapped a finger to his lips several times. "I will confer with the quarter master and first mate, and we will speak more of this later." He rolled up the map and tucked it under his arm.

"Excuse me, Captain Declan," Teressa began. "I didn't feel sick at all last night; may I leave the cabin?" She flashed a broad, pleading smile.

"Very well," Declan replied. "You are free to do as you please." With that, he returned above deck.

The crew of *The Tigress* had just finished supper, and the tables had been cleared off to make room for dice and card games. Captain Declan came down to the mess deck with several onion-bottles of wine in his arms and set them on the table where Kol, Armand, and Teressa sat. Crewmen gathered around him, crowding to take a bottle back to their own table. Declan kept one for himself and, sitting down, poured some into a spare glass.

Kol raised a brow. "Don't you have a ship to captain?"

Declan took a drink, shrugging. "Quarter Master Billy is above deck still."

"No, Captain," the quarter master interjected. "I am sitting beside you."

Declan shrugged.

"You call your quarter master by his nickname?" Teressa asked dubiously.

"Billy is my last name," the quarter master explained.

"His nickname is William," Declan said dryly, then brought out a dice-pouch from his pocket and handed a little carved-bone die each to Armand, Kol, Teressa, Billy and one of the crewmen who sat amongst them. "Roll the dice and find the man with the lowest number," Declan instructed, and rolled with them.

They compared dice. "It is I," said the other crewman.

"Ah, Jon. You know this game. You must say something ridiculous with a straight face," Declan explained for the benefit of the others. "If you smile while telling it, you must drink. If anyone laughs, they drink. To skip your turn, drink."

"Jon?" Kol asked, remembering the name. "Nutmeg Jon?"

"The very same," Jon replied.

"Why is it Nutmeg Jon?" Teressa wondered.

"'Twas nutmeg which killed my father," Jon replied. "I eat it in revenge."

As Teressa snorted to keep from laughing, Declan slid the bottle over to her. "It's not a promising start for you, Miss Teressa."

When they rolled again, it was Armand's turn, and he rubbed his chin. "I once asked my mistress why she never blinked when we made love. She said she didn't have time." After a brief silence, Jon laughed and Teressa pushed the bottle toward him.

They rolled again, and this time it was Declan's turn. "I must confess..." he began solemnly. "This ship is being held together by paint." Armand and Teressa looked at each other blankly while the crewmen roared with laughter.

"I knew it," the quarter master muttered with satisfaction. Kol won the next roll, but he wasn't in a joking mood and took a drink instead.

Next, it was Quarter Master Billy's turn. "I saw my mother-in-law the other day, being harassed by six men." He bit his lip to keep a straight face. "My friend told me I should help. I said, 'Why, isn't six enough?'" They had to pass the bottle around to several people after that. Teressa was next, but she laughed at her own joke before she could even get a word out. That caused both Jon and the quarter master to laugh as well, and the three of them had to drink. They continued that game a while, then split up into smaller groups to play cards for a few hours before retiring for the night. Armand and Teressa, having drunk their fair share of wine, fell asleep in their hammocks immediately.

Kol flopped down in the berth and stared at the deck above him. He tried not to think about the dark sea below them, how deep it was, or how far from land they must be by now. He turned his mind instead to the Sornian ship. *I wonder what Adella is doing right now,* he thought, trying to take his mind off the sea and relax. *Is she asleep? Is she... hurt?* He sat up and rubbed his eyes. *That's not helping.* Kol got up, walked over to the table in the candlelight and sat down. He picked up the book he had been reading, found where he left off, and propped his feet up on a chair.

The early morning light slanted in through the gallery windows, illuminating the cabin wherein Kol sat with his forehead on the table, his eyes dry and grainy from the lack of sleep. Teressa busied herself tidying up while Armand lay in his hammock still, awake but hungover.

Teressa picked up the soiled bandages that Kol had left on the cabin floor, and her face wrinkled with disgust. "You should pick up after yourself," she scolded, throwing the rags in the wash bucket. "It's the least you could do."

"No," Kol mumbled, not bothering to lift his head up from the table. "That's the most I could do. The least I could do is nothing, which is what I'm doing already."

"Let him be," Armand interrupted. "He's seasick." It wasn't true, but Kol didn't care to correct him.

"It's not pleasant sharing quarters with you pigs," she muttered.

"How do you think I feel?" Armand replied. "I'm used to sleeping naked."

Kol pushed his chair back from the table, waiting until the others weren't looking to pack away the various items he had strewn about the table. He picked up the antique novel last, running his fingers over the gold foil pattern on the cover before packing the book carefully into the haversack. Then, he pulled Adella's cloak around himself and headed above deck for fresh air.

The wind had picked up significantly from the day before, and the crewmen were busy securing lines and adjusting rigging.

"We need more stays on the mainmast," the captain called out from somewhere behind him. Continuing on toward the starboard rail, Kol surveyed the horizon. *The Tigress* had gained on the caravel ahead, but a fine mist obscured the view, leaving the enemy ship nothing more than a dark shadow in the distance.

"Do you smell that on the wind?" Captain Declan asked, appearing beside him.

Kol took a deep breath. "Fish?"

"No," Declan sighed. "There's foul weather blowing in. And it's as I feared, they're heading straight into the Teeth. Foolish." He crossed his arms. "We'll have to go around and wait for them to come out." He put his hands around his mouth and shouted to the crew, "Put up the storm canvas!"

Kol winced at the sudden uproar, and stuck his little finger in his ear to try to tamp the ringing. When it cleared, he asked, "Could they be heading to shore?"

Declan shook his head. "The cliffs are unscalable here. They would need wings to manage it."

"Then does that mean," Kol furrowed his brow, "that the Heart-stone is in the sea?"

Declan shrugged and walked away, calling out the order to change course.

"Reef the mainsail!" Captain Declan could be heard shouting from above decks that evening as the crew of *The Tigress* hurried to make preparations. They had continued sailing northeast past the shoals, past the Teeth, until they were clear of danger. They heaved to, facing the bow towards the oncoming swell to weather out the storm.

The crew and passengers ate in silence on the mess deck as Kol dipped a stale biscuit into a gill cup of beer to soften it, his hunger unabated by the tension in his gut. His thoughts were not on the storm, but the upcoming attack, when they would face a ship full of Sornian soldiers. He was already in rough shape with the aching slash in his shoulder, and the wound on his side that hadn't finished healing. He put his hand to it, remembering. *If I had been alone when it happened, or she had left me there...* He bit his lip. *If I can't do the same in return, what good am I?*

Armand, sitting beside Kol, caught the look in his eyes and patted a hand on Kol's broad back. "It'll be all right, you'll see," Armand assured him. "The storm will pass, we'll get that Stone, find Adella... Survive another day." The last words came out grim. "Besides," he added hastily, "we outnumber them. Try not to think about it too much." Kol gave a slight nod, but his supper curdled in his stomach.

Teressa, sitting across from Armand, chewed her thumbnail. "Do you think she's still alive?" she wondered aloud, then gasped in pain as Armand kicked her leg under the table.

From the far side of the space, a shrill screech arose as a young crewman produced a violin and began to tune it.

"Play us a tune, Childric!" a voice called out.

Soon, the harsh noises gave way to a softer sound as the sailor eased into a low note. The pitch rose gently, then the young man's fingers played on the strings to produce a light melody. The strain continued, at times loud with courage or tender in melancholy, seeming to echo the prevailing emotions that the crew felt that evening.

The melody wore on, then the fiddler began on a different tune. A quiet voice soon followed the violin, singing along with it. As he continued, others joined in until most of the crew sang in unison to somber lyrics of a love lost at sea. Kol had never heard this song before and marveled that they knew the words. He couldn't remember the last time he heard a song or music, and he listened intently as they went on.

All was quiet when it ended. Teressa was the first of their group to speak, and she did so quietly. "I've never been in a fight before," she mused. "Will they give me a weapon?"

"If you want it," Armand replied. "But shouldn't you stay below?"

Her freckled brow creased. "Of course not. I've come to find someone dear to me, same as you. Would you ask *him* to stay below?" She gestured toward Kol.

Armand glanced at him and shook his head.

"Then why would you expect me to?" she asked sharply.

Kol cleared his dishes and ascended the steps to the weather deck. Gazing up at the darkening sky, he drew a deep breath. A cold tang blew in on the wind. Mingled in the aroma of salt and kelp, a sharp tang brought to mind lightning and thunder. He drew up the hood of the oilskin cloak as the first raindrops wet his face.

The following morning, Kol sat on the edge of the berth, straining to keep his eyes open. He hadn't slept at all since boarding *The Tigress*, and every time he was still for more than a moment, he found himself blinking in and out of consciousness. Captain Declan stood before them with a hand on the cutlass hilt at his hip. Quarter Master Billy accompanied the captain, along with the first mate, a smaller, ginger-haired man Kol had seen around the ship in passing, often at the helm. The table was strewn with various objects; swords and knives lay beside Armand's own bow and quiver, which wouldn't be very useful in close quarters, and Adella's little crossbow that they had stowed safely away until now. Kol walked over to the table to inspect the weapons.

"Trelauny," Declan said, turning to address the first mate, "you will oversee the looting of the ship. Direct your squad to collect any items of interest or valuables as quickly as they can. Look especially for a small lockbox. Anything your squad fails to recover will end up at the bottom of the sea, so work quickly." Trelauny nodded. "Remember," Declan added, leaning in and lowering his voice, "do not mention exactly what it is we're looking for to the crew."

"Yes, Captain," Trelauny replied.

"Billy—" Declan turned to the quarter master. "Business as usual for you and your squad. Kill the men in green jackets," he said with a smirk. "See that none escape."

"Yes, Captain!" Billy replied heartily.

"When you hear the signal," the captain continued to them both, "direct your squads to return to *The Tigress* immediately. Dennick will be on the ballista; watch out for his aim." The men nodded. "You may go now," he ordered, dismissing them with a wave, and they obeyed.

Declan looked to Kol. "It will be up to the three of you to find Miss Grimless, and you must do it quickly," he warned. "I intend to scuttle their ship as soon as possible."

Kol raised his brows at Armand.

"He means to sink it," Armand explained.

"Whether we succeed or not," Kol muttered. He traded his old sword for a better one and buckled it around his waist.

"Indeed," Declan replied. He took a step toward Kol and squared his brawny shoulders. "I must do my duty, and we have standing orders to give no quarter. We're at war, after all."

"I'm sure Adella will understand," Kol replied, his dark eyes narrowing as he looked down at Declan.

The captain pursed his lips, then turned away. "I leave it to you to find her, but stay out of our way. Our mission here outweighs each of us." He looked back over his shoulder. "Even Miss Adella."

"Orders, you say?" Teressa interjected as she picked up Adella's crossbow and looked it over. "But you're the captain."

"Even so," Declan replied. "We're under commission from King Harrian."

Teressa set down the crossbow and picked up a cutlass. "So, you're not reavers?"

"Privateers," Declan replied, then walked away, returning to the chaos above deck.

11

The Battle

Kol waited as *The Accord* was hauled in closer, hearing the mutters and groans of the men as they worked at the capstan. Though the wind and rain blew cold, he could feel himself beginning to sweat under Adella's oilskin cloak. His hand twitched at his side, eager to reach for the hilt of his cutlass, as he made his way toward the men crowding at the rail as the gang-board was lowered into place. Though it was the middle of the day, darkness gathered ominously above. As Billy's squad rushed across the gang-board, the men around Kol jostled shoulder-to-shoulder impatiently.

"Steady, boys," he heard Trelauny order ahead of him as they waited for the gangway to clear enough to press forward. "Remember," Trelauny continued, turning to face them, "we're looking for a lock-box, or any unusual treasure. Leave the dry goods, leave the bottles." One man groaned sadly in response. When Trelauny turned back to *The Accord*, the way was clear. "Go!" he shouted, and Kol pressed forward with the group.

Trying not to look down into the black frothy water as it sprayed up at his feet, he rushed across the gang-board, sword drawn, and stepped onto *The Accord* as a soldier in green ran at him. Raising his cutlass, their blades clashed loudly as he parried. The soldier shoved forward, knocking him back, and Kol stumbled to the side to keep from falling back onto the gang-board.

The Sornian came forward again but stopped short of an attack, instead dropping to the deck. The man pushed at the gang-board, dislodging it, as Kol brought his cutlass down over him. He struck the man in the back, but it was too late; the gang-board fell into the sea, taking three Valennian sailors down with it.

He looked about the weather deck, but the fighting pressed in around him. The sky was dark as twilight, with rain pelting down from black clouds, drenching everything and obscuring his sight. As Kol fought across the deck, the soldiers who came at him were cut down too quickly, leaving him uneasy.

Then, he was rounded on by three soldiers at once. Immediately, they began to slash at him, and he had to turn his sword this way and that to parry each strike with the edge of his blade. He jabbed it forward into the belly of one of the men, sending him downward. Another soldier moved to strike, and Kol winced as he blocked a mighty swing overhead, his abdominal muscles pulling at the scab on his side as they flexed.

The motion left his middle open for attack, and while Kol still held his cutlass up against the second man's blade, the third soldier moved in to slash at Kol's right side. Before the edge could make contact, the man arched backward, then fell. A sword pierced his ribs from behind. Kol pushed away on the blade overhead and swung his cutlass around in an arc, slashing the soldier's torso. Dark red blood poured out, mingling with the rain at his feet. Kol glanced up to see who it was, and nodded in gratitude as his eyes met Armand's briefly before he disappeared into the fray.

The ship rolled sideways, and Kol's feet slipped on the rain-slick deck, slamming him against the rail. Looking down into the sea between the two vessels, he saw a strange shape, massive and serpentine. It stretched out its long neck, as thick as the trunk of a tree, above the water as thin, pointed teeth protruded forward from its lipless mouth.

A large round eye, set far on the side of its massive head, looked up at him, shimmering gold even in the dark of the storm. Kol stood motionless, holding his breath until the creature disappeared again under the surface.

The deck pitched again, almost sending him overboard. As he waited for the ship to right itself, Kol realized that one of the lines securing *The Accord* to *The Tigress* had broken free, and the two vessels were drifting apart at the stern.

Something clattered behind him. Kol, turning just in time to see a soldier slash at him, managed to deflect the strike sideways with the back of his blade. The man spun quickly around to make a strike from the other side, and Kol parried. As the soldier pushed hard against him, steel groaning on steel, the wound in Kol's shoulder strained. Finally, the muscle gave out, and the soldier's hilt slammed into him, knocking Kol backward against the rail with his cutlass dropping to the deck.

Movement behind the soldier caught Kol's attention as a skirt-clad figure ran toward them, then ducked down to grab something by the man's foot. When she stood, a knife glinted in her hand. Squinting in the rain, Kol's heart raced as he recognized the face. *Adella!* The soldier between them raised his cutlass, ready to strike, but Kol grabbed the man's hand and twisted. Something snapped in the soldier's wrist as tendons gave way, the blade slipping from his hand. With his other hand, the soldier pulled a knife from his belt.

Kol hardly had enough time to react. He jerked his arm toward his chest, catching the knife blade in his right hand. The steel sliced into his palm as blood trickled down his wrist. Groaning through clenched teeth, he struggled to push the knife away from his body. Pain searing through his palm, his voice grew into a shout as he grabbed the man's fist with his other hand and turned the knife back on its wielder. With one last thrust forward, Kol jammed the knife into the man's neck, and the soldier fell backward.

He looked over at Adella, who was leaning on the rail to sidestep two other men fighting nearby and didn't seem to have noticed him. Kol was about to call to her when *The Accord* pitched sharply and threw him to the larboard again. He clung to the rail, the effort stinging his injured hand until the sea relented and the ship righted. When he looked for her again, she was gone.

He glanced down over the rail just in time to see her surface. As Adella opened her mouth to take a deep breath, he heard her cry out in pain, then her voice suddenly cut off as she was pulled beneath the rough waves. Kol stared into the black water with rain pelting his face, his heart pounding so fiercely he felt he were in one of his nightmares.

He wavered for only a moment, then climbed on the rail and dove into the sea. The shock of the cold water hit him bodily, and he struggled to keep from gasping as he opened his eyes in the turbid water and looked around. Ahead of him, disappearing into the murky distance, slinked the long, spiny tail of the sea creature, but there was no sign of Adella.

Kol surfaced again, gasping as he struggled among the waves. Grief stabbed in his breast in a way he'd never known as he realized she was lost to the sea. Then, something whistled by his head as a blast shattered the hull of *The Accord,* and he flinched as wood splinters sprayed from a hole at the waterline. *The ballista!*

"Get out of there!" a voice shouted. "Now!" Kol looked up to see Armand leaning over the rail of *The Accord,* pointing toward *The Tigress,* where a ladder hung from the starboard rail. "The captain gave the orders to retreat," Armand called out. "Go!"

Kol labored to pull himself up over the side of *The Tigress* as the last of the crew came aboard, some swinging by rope tossed back and forth, others crossing by a gang-board they had found on *The Accord.* They released the remaining line tethering the two vessels together, leaving the other ship listing heavily to one side, reminding Kol of an injured seabird. Slowly, it sank deeper into the water.

He slumped onto the deck by the ladder, cradling his injured hand in his lap. Around him, the crew was busy tending to the wounded in the rain. He spotted Declan crouching over one man, trying to staunch the blood seeping from his chest. Armand approached Kol, taking his arm to help him to his feet.

Kol pulled his arm free. "Leave me."

"Come on, son," Armand said gently, pulling at his elbow. "Let me help you."

"I said leave me!" Kol shouted, yanking his arm back, and Armand walked away. Kol pressed his hand over his eyes, suddenly feeling the full weight of his exhaustion and failure. *This was my fault,* he thought. *If only I hadn't argued with her on the ridge... Or attacked her home in the first place.* Every part of his body seemed to ache, but none more so than his heart. *She didn't deserve this.* Unwilling to move, Kol lay by the rail as *The Tigress* sailed onward, leaving the foundering ship behind.

* * *

Adella held her breath tightly as she was dragged through the frigid sea, clenching her teeth against the crushing pain in her foot. Her grip tightened around Kol's knife while she strained against the pull of the water, trying to kick or twist her foot free, but to no avail. Adella pushed away her skirts as they flowed, inverted, around her arms and face. Her lungs burned for air; her vision turned spotty at the edges as it faded into blackness.

Adella knew she didn't have much time left. She forced a bend in her outstretched leg and caught the back of her knee with her arms. Struggling against the dragging current, she pulled herself forward, putting the last of her strength into it. Her muscles ached with the prolonged effort, and she nearly gave in, but the thought of dying alone in the sea sent a wave of panic through her. With one last surge of will, she lunged forward and stuck the knife in the creature's large, unblinking eye. The beast recoiled, opening its mouth and releasing her to the sea. A cloud of blood puffed out around her. Her skirts tangled around her legs as she tried to swim toward the surface.

Her chest spasmed, fighting to make a gasp. She cut the waistbands of her skirts with the knife, and they fell away into the abyss as she swam upward, pressing the wooden handle between her teeth to free her hand. Just when she was about to give in and let the sea fill her lungs, she felt air on her face as she came to the surface. Adella pulled the knife from her mouth and gasped for air, coughing up water that had trickled into her throat. She turned about in the cold sea, looking for a direction to swim as she bobbed low in the water. The swells and high waves limited her sight, as did the gloomy haze of the rain. Finally, she saw dark sails close by. After her encounter with the sea creature, she was happy to take her chances with reavers instead. She swam toward *The Tigress*.

Adella grabbed onto the rope ladder that dangled against the hull of the ship. She clung there for a while, catching her breath as it pulled her along through the water, the current tugging at her legs. She carefully replaced the knife back into its sheath at her chest, then she rallied her strength, or what was left of it, and pulled herself up the ladder. Fatigued and sopping wet, her hand slipped as she pulled herself over the rail, and tumbled downward.

"Ah!" a voice uttered in surprise as she apparently struck someone with her fall. Adella tried to stand, but a shooting pain flashed from her foot up through her leg. Collapsing onto the deck in defeat, she flopped onto her back, inhaling slowly. She had spent too much time in the icy seawater, and her whole body ached. Her hands trembled as she placed them over her ribs to try to steady her breath. Adella closed her eyes, oblivious to everything around her, no longer feeling the rain on her skin. She relaxed and let the cold permeate her body, sinking deep into her bones.

"Adella?" a voice on the edge of her consciousness called her name. "Adella!" it said again, this time sounding nearer in her mind.

"What..." A warm hand patted her cheek. "Stop," she muttered, not bothering to open her eyes.

"Your lips are blue," the voice said. It sounded deep, gravelly. *Familiar,* she thought. "You have to get up," it ordered. She rolled over onto her side in defiance.

Adella felt herself being pulled to her feet, and gave up on resting. "Fine, I'm up, I'm—" She gasped loudly as pain surged up her leg.

"I'll lift you," the man said, and warm arms surrounded her, giving heat to her cold flesh.

As her vision focused, Adella recognized the dark eyes that turned upward at the corners, the strongly angled jawline, the sharp cheekbones. "Mister Kol," she said under her breath. "How—No, don't lift me," she protested when she saw his bloodied hand. He set her back down, but she held his elbow to keep her balance. "What are you *doing* here?" He opened his mouth to speak, but was at a loss for words.

Adella's teeth chattered. She looked around the ship, at the wounded crewmen and those who tended to them. One man across the deck met her eyes, standing when he saw her. He was broad and well-muscled, with strands of long blond hair hanging over the chiseled features of his face. The man wiped his hands onto his breeches and strode quickly across the deck, heading straight for her. Adella's stomach dropped and she looked away, pretending not to see him. She turned in toward Kol in a feeble attempt to hide her face, but it was too late.

"Miss Adella!" the man shouted as he approached.

"Captain Declan?" She begrudgingly turned to greet him. "Is that you?" Adella asked in disbelief, squinting up into his hazel eyes. "I didn't recognize you." In truth, she had never expected, or wanted, to see him again. Memories of their last time together, of his warm hands on her skin, flooded to mind and heat rose in her face, flooding her cheeks.

"But you haven't changed at all," Declan said. He removed his wool jacket and threw it around her shoulders, then picked her up, pulling her from Kol's arm.

"Put me down, dammit!" she protested as he carried her toward the cabin.

Declan set her on the berth while Kol and Armand came down the companionway behind him. "You two," he said, turning toward them. "Look after her, will you? I'm needed above."

When he left, Adella set her foot down on the mattress, wincing. Kol sat at the foot of the berth and untied the lacing on her leather boot with one hand. Armand plopped a blanket down over her.

"I'm fine," she insisted. "Just sore, that's all."

Kol pulled the boot away and Adella groaned, grabbing the pillow and stuffing it over her face. He carefully peeled off her blood-stained stocking, and he and Armand stood speechless, gaping at her foot.

"What is that?" Armand asked, pointing to a white object protruding from ragged, bruised skin. "Is that bone?"

"Uh," Kol muttered. "I'm not sure. Maybe you should get the captain."

Peeking from behind the pillow, Adella waited for Armand to ascend the companionway. "Did you find it?" she asked Kol.

"Huh?" He glanced from her foot back up to her face. "What?"

"The stone…" She scrunched her nose, thinking. "The Heartstone. Isn't that why you're here?"

Kol opened his mouth but didn't speak. A pained look crossed his face.

Armand returned with Declan, carrying a box of surgeon's supplies. The captain pulled up a chair to the side of the berth and took a seat, setting the box down beside him. Lifting her left foot and setting it on his knee, he inspected the wound on the top of the arch. As he pressed here and there on the red, swollen skin that surrounded a large gash through the flesh, Adella hid her face behind the pillow again, groaning.

"Hmm," Declan said, lifting a pair of forceps. "What exactly happened, Miss Adella?"

"I was bitten by a fish," she replied, her voice muffled through the pillow.

"A fish?" he asked, raising an eyebrow incredulously. "There is a piece of the creature's tooth embedded in the bone of your foot." He pointed with the forceps to a large, white fragment sticking out from the flesh, which looked more like the fang of a tiger than any fish from Belgrand Bay. "We have to remove it, I'm sorry." He paused to wait for her response. "Did you hear me under there?"

Adella nodded from behind the pillow. Declan grabbed the object carefully and pulled straight back, but it held fast. He adjusted his grip on the forceps and twisted to loosen it while Adella groaned through her teeth. Finally, he gave a good yank and the object came free. Wincing at the sound that came from her, he dropped the tooth into the box beside him and poured alcohol over the wound.

Captain Declan wrapped her foot in clean bandage from the kit. "Well, that's the best I can do for you," he said, rising to his feet, and leaned over to retrieve the box of supplies.

"Wait!" Adella stopped him, uncovering her face. "Mister Kol is injured, too. His hand," she added, pointing. She watched as Declan poured alcohol onto Kol's right palm and quickly wrapped it.

Declan lifted the kit and stood up. "The crew will be celebrating our success this evening," he said, addressing them all. "We'd be pleased to have you all join us. Miss Adella, if you're feeling up to it."

Adella looked up at him. "So," she began eagerly, "does that mean you found it? You've got the Heart?"

"Indeed," Declan replied. "We recovered it, then sent those bastards to the bottom of the sea. And found you—" he added, "all with minimal lives lost. A fortunate turn of events, I'd say." With that, he turned to leave.

"Where's Tess?" she asked. "I want to speak to her."

Declan stopped. Glancing over his shoulder, he shook his head solemnly, then left.

The meaning behind the gesture hit her like a blow to the gut. She clapped a hand over her mouth to stifle a sob. *Minimal lives lost,* she thought bitterly. *Lucas... Teressa. Maribel.* She set her injured foot on the chair and slunk down into the blanket, leaning against the bulkhead behind the berth in exhaustion. Beside her, Kol laid his head back and closed his eyes.

Adella awoke to footsteps thumping down the companionway. "Wake up, you soggy corpses!" a rough voice said. "It's almost supper time."

She hadn't intended to sleep, and it took her a moment to remember where she was. Opening her eyes, she was surprised to see a pair of large stockinged feet right in front of her face. "Ugh," she said, shoving them off the mattress in disgust, waking Kol with a start.

Captain Declan strode over and set a wooden crate on the table. "I had the men donate some of their old clothes so you could change into something dry."

Armand rolled out of his hammock on the other side of the cabin to inspect the items. "I wouldn't mind a change of shirt, myself."

"I don't suppose there were any petticoats," Adella said. She sat up, wincing as her foot began to throb.

"I dared not ask," Declan replied, looking through the clothes. "Here," he said, handing her a pair of knee breeches with a drawstring at the waist. "This might fit you."

Armand and Kol changed their clothes while Declan waited, the men apparently thinking nothing of it while Adella looked away uncomfortably. They then left the cabin to give her privacy, promising to bring back some supper. Adella took the knife from her bodice, set it on the berth, and changed into the clothes Declan left. The breeches, made of tan ticking with indigo stripes, were baggy on her legs, and the drawstring bunched the fabric comically at her narrow waist. She pulled on a white work shirt with a single button at the collar and stuffed the bottom into the breeches. The front opening of the shirt was cut for a large man and plunged much lower on her chest than she would have liked. Adella felt a bit silly to see the cuffs of the sleeves hanging down over her hands, so she rolled them up to her elbows. She delicately tested her left foot and was pleased to be able to bear some weight on the heel. Though it felt better after Declan removed the tooth, it still hurt too much for her to get very far. She sat back down on the berth, her mind reeling from all she had been through.

The Accord, she knew, had sunk. There was no way anyone left behind had survived. Between the storm, the fighting, and the sea serpents, anyone who hadn't made it onto *The Tigress* was surely lost. *My brother...* Adella could hardly bear the thought. *Lucas is...* Her throat burned, tightening with rising, overwhelming grief. *Dead.* She didn't know how to return home, how to face her parents and tell them what happened. *How can I tell them that I failed? That I lost my brother...* Tears sprang up, flooding her vision. Her home, her family, would never be the same again. She could forgive his betrayal, his treason, his crimes, all of it, if only he were still alive. *All I wanted was to bring him home... And I've utterly failed.* Burying her face in her hands, she threw herself onto the berth, taken by her sorrows.

Adella wiped her eyes quickly when Kol returned, carrying a plate piled high with food in one hand and a bottle in the crook of his elbow. He set them on the table and offered his arm, helping her to a chair. As she picked at the boiled pork, Kol pulled the cord with the ring on it over his head and set it down. She picked it up to inspect it, rubbing her thumb over the little peach-colored jewel.

She untied the string and slipped the ring on. "I didn't think I'd get this back," she said, turning her hand over to look at it.

"Why?" Kol asked. "You thought I would lose it?"

"No," Adella replied, raising her eyebrows. "You were leaving, remember?"

He looked down, scratching at the table with his thumbnail. "I was only bluffing." He watched silently for a moment while she drank the wine. "I'm sorry for what I said—"

"Don't apologize," she interrupted with a wave of her hand. "You were right."

"No." He kept his eyes on the table. "I wasn't."

Her brow furrowed as she tried to understand his meaning. "But—" Adella began but stopped herself, not wanting to argue again, and they lapsed into silence. "Oh," she said, filling the gap in the conversation, "your knife is over there." She nodded toward the berth. "It did come in handy, thanks."

Kol went to retrieve it, and sat on the mattress. Pulling the knife from its sheath, he looked it over, and wiped the seawater from the blade with his sleeve before putting it back in. The sun was setting, and rosy light flooded in through the gallery windows at the back of the cabin. He kicked his boots off, dropping the knife into one of them, and laid back to rest.

The storm had died down, and the clouds began to break. Armand stood on the weather deck in an amber-and-coral sunset, gathered with the crew around the bodies of three men, lined up along the rail and sewn into their hammocks. He looked on, peering around and between the shoulders of taller men, to view the captain as he turned to address them.

"Tonight," Captain Declan began, "we say goodbye to our fellow crew members, our friends, our brothers. We commit them into the arms of our mother, the sea. May her gentle embrace comfort them as their souls make their way to the heavens to be received by their ancestors." He walked over to the first body on the deck. "Mister Herkimer Billy, our own quarter master and the best sailor that ever graced the Bay. To you, we say farewell." The crew chimed in their farewells, and then Declan and Trelauny loaded him onto the gang-board and, lifting, slid him into the sea. They moved on to the other two who had died of their injuries after the retreat, then said goodbyes to each man who had been lost in the battle, their bodies unrecovered. The dead crewmen were fourteen in total, and it was dark by the time they had finished. Crates of wine bottles were brought out and distributed among the crew.

"Now," Declan lifted a glass, "let us celebrate in gratitude to still be among the living." The crew all drank, then dispersed about the ship. Many returned to the mess deck to play cards, Armand among them.

He lingered at the tables, playing a couple of games of Brisque and Quadrille before imbibing too much wine and growing melancholy. He wanted to be a part of the merriment, as he always enjoyed a lively celebration, but he soon found his heart was too heavy for it.

Adella still sat in a chair at the table, with Kol sleeping soundly in the berth just behind her. She had been feeling tired but put off going to sleep, lacking the resolve to hobble over to the hammocks that hung on the other side of the cabin. The swelling in her foot had become quite painful whenever she lowered it. Folding her elbows on the table, she laid her head down to rest when Armand returned, his footsteps heavy and slow as he made his way to his hammock and sank into it.

"What are you doing awake?" he asked. "You should be resting."

"I know," she said with a sigh. They were both quiet for a moment.

"We lost Teressa," he muttered, his voice thick with emotion. "It's my fault. She never returned to the ship..." He drew a sharp breath. "I should've made sure she returned."

"No," Adella said quietly. "You were all there because of me." The sound of ragged breathing interrupted the conversation, coming from the direction of the berth.

"What's that?" Armand asked, looking over at Kol. "Is he dying?"

"Dreaming." Adella turned around in her chair and, reaching over, patted Kol's arm just hard enough to draw him out of a deep sleep but not fully wake him. He stirred a little, then was still, his breathing quieted.

Armand raised an eyebrow at her. "You going to do that all night?"

"I don't have much else to do at the moment," she said with a shrug.

12

Aftermath

The sky darkened over the masts of *The Cormorant,* a mass of black clouds gathering over the sea like a wool blanket. Wind whipped the sails into a frenzy while the crew ran about the deck to brace the ship against the sudden squall.

Katarine stood at the taffrail, drawing her cloak tighter around her as the wind pulled and yanked at her clothes, and watched the waves around the ship surge ever higher. "I've never seen the sea so dark," she said.

"Don't fret, Kat." Beside her, her beloved Alfrin pulled her closer and kissed her forehead, his dark mustache tickling her skin. "It's just another spring storm. It'll pass quickly, you'll see. We'll make port before you know it." He wrapped his other arm around her and squeezed her gently. A sudden gust of wind blasted over the ship, and they had to brace themselves against it to keep from being blown down to the deck.

"*The Quest* was supposed to set sail from the Capital when we did, wasn't it?" Katarine asked over the sound of the wind. "Do you think they'll get caught in this storm, too?"

"We need to get below," he replied with a frown as a loud crack issued from the main deck behind them. They turned to see the ship in chaos; the mainsail had broken free of its lines and swung wildly about in the air, lashing across the deck. Another blast of wind sent it reeling around, whipping at the crew and knocking them over. Katarine watched breathlessly as one sailor climbed the mast, carefully working his way upward even as the mainsail slashed at his fellow crewmen, tearing into their flesh, throwing them down. Some didn't rise.

The man on the mast finally cut the flailing canvas free, and the wind carried it out and over into the water. As he began his downward climb, he froze, and raised his arm to point toward the starboard side. "Wave!" he yelled frantically, scrambling down as fast as he could. "Rogue wave!"

Kat spun around. Out in the sea, a giant wall of indigo water rose in the distance. It came toward them, looming upward, dwarfing the ship, at such a great speed that her heart dropped into her stomach.

"Heave to!" the captain shouted from the quarter deck. "For heaven's sake, heave to!" The massive crest of water continued to rush straight toward them, and Katarine knew they didn't have time to turn the ship about before the wave hit.

She looked out over the sea to the west, hoping to find clearer skies in the distance, but the storm seemed to reach out over every corner of the world. "I hope they make it," she said. "For the sake of Valenna."

"They will," Alfrin replied. "They have to."

Kat turned to her husband and looked up into his blue-green eyes, lined now after so many years together. "Goodbye, Alfie," she said. "At least we'll be together, at the end."

"As always." He ran his thumb along her cheekbone, sweeping the tears away. "You know," he said with a chuckle, "it hardly seems important now, but I wanted to tell you—" His words cut off as the icy cold water crashed down upon them. Katarine's last thoughts were of her children.

* * *

Morning sunlight spilled through the gallery windows as Kol paced across the captain's quarters. Armand and Adella were at the table, drinking black tea from a blue and white tea service. They had just finished a small breakfast of hard biscuits and salted butter. The two Valennians apparently liked tea better than he did, as they kept refilling their cups. Kol wandered over to Declan's writing desk for lack of anything better to do, eyeing a small globe on its upper shelf. He spun it with his finger absent-mindedly. Then, he picked up a spiny seashell from the writing surface, its row of long tines resembling a hair comb, and turned it over in his hand before setting it down again. Next, he opened the drawers and shuffled through various letters, opened and unopened, touching his fingers to their elaborate wax seals. He was surprised to find a letter addressed to an A. R. Grimless that was still sealed, apparently never having been sent. It was dingy and dog-eared as though it had been left in the drawer for years, battered from being knocked about, never fulfilling its purpose.

"Adella, what's your middle name?" Kol asked casually.

"Renata." Adella set her cup down, its three little porcelain legs clinking on the saucer. "Why do you ask?"

Kol bit his thumbnail. "No reason." He shoved the letter back inside the drawer and closed it.

Adella was finishing her tea, and trying not to pay attention to Kol rummaging noisily through the captain's things behind her, when Captain Declan and the first mate entered. They carried large canvas ditty bags over their shoulders and set them down on the sole by the table.

"Our plunder from *The Accord*," Declan explained. "We must catalog it, and hold back anything of importance before dispersing the rest among the crew. Would you care to help us?" They nodded. Kol, who had been flipping through a dusty *Encyclopedia of Birds* by the bookcase, came over and began poking through the contents of one bag. Trelauny reached into the pocket of his brown waistcoat and took out a small leather notebook and a brass pencil that held a thick lead in the center. He offered the two items to Kol to make a record.

"Uh," Kol muttered.

"You can write, can't you?" Trelauny asked, arching a brow.

"Of course I can write..." Kol replied, sounding unsure of himself.

"I'll do it," Adella offered, seeing his reluctance. "I want to practice my penmanship." Her tone brooked no argument. Taking a seat nearby, Kol slid the book and pencil across the table to her.

Reaching into a bag, Declan took out a sturdy porcelain container and passed it to Kol, then handed a small wooden box with a brass latch to Armand. "See what's in those," he said as he passed a bronze urn to Trelauny, then pulled out a writing box and began to open it.

"Just dried flowers," Kol said, poking his finger around in the material.

Adella pulled the jar over and peeked in, then began recording in a careful, looping script. *Madorran pea flower tea, one pot,* she wrote.

Declan frowned at the first mate. "I said no dry goods." Trelauny only shrugged.

Armand sorted through the items in his box. "Ladies jewelry," he said flatly. "Carbuncle earrings, three gold chains, two strings of pearls, four gold rings." Adella recorded them as he spoke.

"This urn is filled with gold and silver coins," Trelauny said, taking a seat. "I'll have to count them."

Declan pulled sheets of parchment from the little writing box and unrolled them. They had been rubbed over with charcoal to capture strange symbols.

"Oh!" Adella said when she recognized the images. "Be careful, don't smudge it."

"Did you make this?" Declan guessed.

She nodded. "When we found the Heartstone box. It was in a woman's tomb, and those markings were on her coffin."

"Hm," Declan replied, then rolled up the parchments and put them back in their box. "This could prove interesting." He set the writing box on his desk.

They continued to sort through and record the items in the bags, but found nothing else of significance aside from the strange box made of meteor iron. Declan set the box carefully on the table and they gazed wide-eyed at it, taking in the strange pictographs that covered its surface.

"I'd like to see the damned thing," Armand said, then tried to open the lid, prying at it with his fingers, but it wouldn't budge.

"You'd need the Key," Adella replied.

"Apparently, we did not collect that," Trelauny said, pausing to look up from the coins he was counting. He turned to Adella. "Four hundred and seventy-two gold," he announced, and she recorded it in the notebook.

"So," Kol began, folding his arms as he leaned back in the chair, "how do you know the Heart of the World is in the box?"

"It's either here or the bottom of the sea," Declan replied with a shrug. "As long as the Sornians don't have it, my work is done."

"Are you certain no one escaped?" Adella asked, voice frail.

Declan shook his head. "There were no boats on board, no way to escape. And no one could have survived in those waters for long."

She remembered lowering the ship's quarter boat into the sea at the beginning of it all. Her heart wrenched as she realized that it was her impulsive actions that had doomed her brother, and the others. Adella took a deep breath to steady her emotions. "A man named Matei had the key," she said, changing the subject.

"You mean Matei Azbarian?" Kol asked. "The man who paid for you?"

She nodded. "He was a prince of some sort."

"He's the son of the third-place concubine," Kol explained. "It's common knowledge he's been trying to steal the throne from Crown Prince Gio. Rumors say he tried to poison him last year, but they couldn't prove it."

"Ah," she replied with satisfaction. "So that's why they locked us in the bedchamber at night. I knew he was a snake."

"They what?" Kol asked, brows lowering.

"Not important." She dismissed his question with a turn of her hand. "Wait, how did you know who it was?"

He fiddled with the bandage on his right hand. "I went to find the auctioneer," he muttered.

She leaned in toward him. "You went into Sornia?" she asked under her breath. "Into Hedda?"

"Not alone," he countered.

"Me and Tess went with him," Armand interjected. "How do you think we all got here on *The Tigress*? It was Mister Kol who saw them take you on the ship, and it was his idea to go to Captain Declan for help."

She looked up at Declan and then at Kol in disbelief at the lengths they had gone to on her behalf, until she remembered one detail. "Oh," she said, lowering her eyes. "I see. I had the Key."

They both opened their mouths to speak but Armand cut them off. "Don't lump me in with them." He folded his hands behind his head as he leaned back against the chair. "I, for one, didn't even know you had it."

Adella gave him a warm smile. "Thank you, Armand."

"Five hundred and ninety-eight silver," Trelauny said triumphantly. He had just finished counting the coins and piled them back into the urn, the metal jingling loudly. He looked up at Adella again, who had forgotten her recording duties. "Did you write that down?" Trelauny asked. Adella blinked at him, then scrambled to write the number before she forgot it.

With the cataloging finished, Declan and Trelauny loaded the goods back into the ditty bags and hauled them above deck to distribute, leaving the iron box on the captain's desk. Armand, Adella and Kol were left to themselves at the table.

"Did you find him, Adella?" Kol spoke quietly from beside her. "Your brother." She bit her lip for a moment, then nodded.

Armand leaned forward from across the table. "And?"

"Lost." Her voice was hardly a whisper, but it was all she could manage.

"I'm sorry," Kol said, and Adella buried her face in her hands.

Kol looked over at Armand, unsure of what to do. Armand widened his eyes and nodded toward Adella, but Kol didn't catch his meaning and only shrugged helplessly. Armand, in answer, made a patting motion with his hand outstretched. Finally understanding, Kol put his arm hesitantly around Adella; he was unsure if he should be taking instruction from Armand and wondered how she might react. Kol froze as she leaned into him, resting her head in the hollow of his shoulder, and hoped she couldn't hear his heart pounding. He only let go when she turned away to compose herself.

As Kol walked along the main deck later that afternoon, he took a deep breath, savoring the fresh air and fair weather. Reaching a hand into his pocket, he jingled the little bag of coins Captain Declan had given him in passing as payment for his part in the fighting the previous day. The captain had done it so off-handedly that when Kol opened the drawstring pouch to peek inside, he was shocked to look down into more gold and silver coins than he had ever possessed before at one time. In truth, it wasn't quite so large an amount as he felt it was, but rather that the Sornian army had paid him miserably little. He began to think over everything he wanted to buy the first chance he got, a list that included an oilskin cloak and a wool jacket. He also realized that, of all the desires of his heart that money could buy, what he wanted most was a feather-stuffed mattress to sleep on. But then, he figured, he would need a bed frame to put it on. His heart sank as he realized beds went in houses, and he put that dream away for another time. *A hat*, he thought. *I'll get a hat.*

Kol turned to look out over the sea on the starboard side, watching as a pod of sleek, steel-grey porpoises jumped in and out of the waves alongside the ship. He leaned his elbows on the rail and breathed in deeply. He felt as though a burden had been lifted from his chest now that they were sailing further away from Sornia with the Heart of the World recovered. And, despite his bitter experience in the water the previous day, he was starting to appreciate the beauty of the blue-green waves glinting in the sunlight, the invigorating smell on the briny air. Though the rocking of the ship had still brought on nightmares, he noticed that for whatever reason, they had not troubled him so much last night, and he felt well rested.

"Lovely, aren't they?" The captain had come up beside Kol, joining him as he looked down on the porpoises playing in the water.

"Where are we headed?" Kol asked. By the slant of the shadows on the deck of the ship, he could see they were traveling northeast. "To what port?"

"Raymouth is the nearest port," Declan began. "We should arrive tomorrow, thankfully. We left the Smuggler's Port in such a hurry, we didn't have time to prepare for another voyage." He turned to face Kol, lowering his voice so as not to be overheard by the crew working nearby. "We are dangerously low on supplies, and we need to hire a new doctor. Many of the men are injured and need proper care."

"Raymouth," Kol repeated. "That's in Valenna, I assume?"

Declan laughed. "Of course. Not far from Elldon, in fact. Miss Grimless will be pleased to be back home, I'm sure." He nodded curtly and stepped away again to resume his duties.

Tomorrow, Kol said to himself. *Then what?* He pursed his lips. *Where will I go, then?* he wondered, his memory suddenly flashing to the cold, wet streets of Hedda from his days before the orphanage. Kol shook his head, trying to clear away his thoughts. *Not now,* he told himself. *That's tomorrow's problem.* He turned as heavy footsteps approached.

"Have you seen the captain yet?" Armand asked. "That lunatic just handed me a bag of gold."

Kol nodded. "I got the same treatment."

Armand's eyes took on a wistful, distant look. "Perhaps I could become a reaver. Seems a very lucrative career..."

"You certainly fared better than I did," Kol said with a smirk.

"Indeed," Armand agreed with relish. "I went aboard just behind Declan; he cut them down faster than I could advance. It was truly impressive. He's the very model of what a Valennian man ought to be.

With that massive physique, I bet he could crush a man's skull with his bare hands—"

"Enough. Write a poem if you must," Kol joked. "You only go on like that because he gave you gold."

A sudden uproar broke out behind them, with cries of "Ship!" and "Ahoy!" dispersed among the commotion. Kol and Armand crossed to the larboard side to see what it was about. As Kol peered over the heads of the crew gathered in front of him, he looked out on a ship listing sideways with a broken mast. The top half of the main mast was splintered in the middle and hung down at a dangerous angle over the deck, resembling an albatross with half-folded wings.

"What is it?" Armand asked, lifting up onto his toes in a failed attempt to see over the taller men.

"A ship," Jon replied. He stood nearby, watching through a brass spyglass. "It appears to be foundering."

"What country?" Armand wondered.

"Valennian, for sure," Jon said as he lowered the glass. "It's flying the royal ensign."

"That is *The Quest*," another crewman chimed in from beside them.

Captain Declan gave the command and *The Tigress* turned westerly, sailing toward the ruined ship. They arrived in time to see the meager, bedraggled crew of *The Quest* safely rescued and on board *The Tigress*.

One man from their number came forward to address Captain Declan, introducing himself as Jimothy Ballantyne, quarter master on *The Quest*. "Me and my crew thank you," he said with a voice like gravel. "Had you not come along when you did, we'd have surely been lost." A stark white scar slashed across the middle of his sun-baked face, crossing over his cheekbones and deep into the bridge of his nose. He flashed a smile and the scar tightened, pushing wrinkles up beneath his eyes.

"It's what any Valennian would have done," Captain Declan replied. His own men tended to the many among the newcomers who were wounded or weak with exhaustion. One man who had been brought on board was unconscious and had to be carried. "Please, tell me," Declan said, turning his head to watch as *The Quest* finally ducked under the waves. "What happened?"

"There was a storm," Ballantyne began plainly. "And the sea started going wild, water overtaking the deck. Then, out of nowhere, came a rogue wave—" He lifted his hands in the air for effect. "Bigger than anything I had seen in all my days of sailing—and it crashed down on us. Luckily, we had turned about just in time, but it came down over the bow so hard, shivering our mast. Many of the crew were washed away or battered against the deck. There are only twenty-three of us left now, last I counted. The ship had taken too much damage, our pumps couldn't make up for it, and too few unwounded to man them through the night." He removed a cockaded but misshapen hat and held it over his heart. "Our captain didn't make it." He lowered his head solemnly, his iron-grey hair swinging limply down over his shoulders.

"My condolences," Declan replied. "And your first mate?"

Ballantyne nodded over to where the unconscious man lay as several crewmen struggled to lift him by the arms and legs. "That'd be Moffat over there. He was struck on the head, hasn't woken since."

"I see." Declan watched as more of his men joined them, altogether hoisting Moffat's large frame. "You can take him to the officer's quarters," Declan called over to them, "if you please." He turned once again to Ballantyne. "Did your ship's doctor survive?"

"He did," he replied. "The only ounce of good luck we've had this whole damned journey."

"That is very good, indeed," Declan said. "Where were you headed?"

"Before the storm hit, we were heading—" His eyes darted around the ship. "West," he continued hesitantly. "But being so badly damaged, we had to change course to the nearest port, and hoped to make it before we sank."

"Hmm," Declan replied. "Well, let's get you all looked after. I'm afraid I must ask for the services of your doctor after he has cared for your own, if he is able." Ballantyne nodded.

Adella sat on the captain's berth with her left foot up, trying to ignore the throbbing pain when Declan entered. He stood at the foot of his berth, pulled off his bloodied shirt, and opened the trunk to retrieve a fresh one. Adella let out a small gasp when she saw his bare skin; stretching across his broad, muscular chest was the image of a tiger.

The corner of his mouth pulled into a smile. "I look a little different than you remember?"

"Well..." she began hesitantly, not wanting to seem rude. "I've never seen anything like that. What is it?"

"Ink," he said casually. He stepped closer to the edge of the mattress, then sat down beside her. "I got it when I crossed the Greater Sea."

"May I?" Adella slowly reached out her hand, and as he gave a slight nod, she put a fingertip to the markings. She ran her finger along the blue-black lines, then turned her hand over to see that the coloring hadn't come off on her skin. He laughed.

"You made the crossing?" She raised her eyebrows. "What was it like?"

"Honestly, it was horrible." He grinned. "Took us six months just to get there, and we almost didn't make it. But the land, it's... beautiful. Indescribable." He paused for a moment in thought. "You could come with me next time," he said quietly. "See for yourself."

"Is that where you went, then? All those years ago." Adella looked down, unwilling to acknowledge his invitation. "I thought you had died."

His voice was almost a whisper. "I know." He put a hand to her cheek, looking her in the eyes. "Can you forgive me?"

It was just then that Armand came down the steps to the cabin, with Kol following behind. "Oh, are we interrupting?" Armand asked archly.

"Not at all," Declan said, pulling his shirt down over his head. "We were just catching up."

Armand watched as the captain left, then turned to Adella. "What was that about?"

"Nothing," Adella replied. "You know how Rogero can be." Armand cast an uneasy glance back at Kol, who looked away quickly, seeming not to notice.

13

Raymouth

Spirits were high aboard *The Tigress* the following day, not only for the joy of having saved the survivors from a watery death, but also for the sheer relief of approaching land. Adella sat at the table in the captain's quarters, packing up her belongings. Though she very much wanted off the ship, she found her stomach in knots as they drew closer to Raymouth. She knew the life she would return to would be much different, much darker, than the one she had left behind, with Lucas and Teressa now missing from it. Adella wasn't sure she could face it. *It happened because of me,* she told herself. *There is no escaping that fact, whether I return home or not.* Adella drew a deep breath, hoping to tamp down her emotions for a little while longer. *Not here,* she told herself. *Break down if you must, but don't do it here. At home.* The resolve to return to her beloved Greywood Manor and reunite with her parents lent her strength; the rest she could face after she arrived. She just had to get back home.

As she dabbed the corners of her eyes, Adella was surprised to see Kol standing over her, holding her grandfather's book.

"Here," he said, offering it to her. "Don't forget this."

"Did you enjoy it?" she asked. She had noticed him reading it at times when there hadn't been anything else to do.

"Yes. Well, what I read anyway," he admitted. "I haven't gotten to the end yet."

"Hang onto it, then," she replied. Adella had given it to Lucas when they were younger. She couldn't bear to think the book had made it back home and he didn't.

Kol nodded, but remained standing nearby. "Adella," Kol began tentatively, his brow tense. "I..."

She looked up at him expectantly. "Hm?"

He stood thinking for a moment, then let out his breath.

"Mister Kol." Armand watched the young man struggling and decided to chime in. "Where are you headed next?" Kol didn't have an answer, and Armand threw a pointed look at Adella.

"He's coming with us, of course," Adella said when she caught Armand's meaning. "Aren't you?"

"Am I?" Kol asked under his breath.

"I owe you payment, remember?" she said matter-of-factly. "So you'll have to come with us. At least as far as the banker."

Kol shook his head. "You don't owe me anything."

"We can argue about it on the way," she replied with a smirk.

Their conversation was interrupted by a shout of "Land!" followed by cheers from the weather deck. Kol's face brightened.

"Go see," she said, and Kol hurried up the steps.

Armand sighed pointedly. "That poor boy has nowhere to go, you know that. You might've mentioned all that to him sooner," he chided. "Try to be more considerate. Especially since—" He stopped himself abruptly.

"I know," she admitted, her shoulders drooping. "You're right. I was too self-absorbed to think about it." She paused. "But what were you about to say? Especially what?"

"Never you mind," he replied. "It wasn't my place to say."

"That's never stopped you before," Adella muttered as she stood up, pushing her chair back from the table. She drew air in sharply through her teeth as she set her injured foot down and tried to put her weight on it.

"Where do you think you're going, on that broken foot?" Armand asked.

"I'm tired of sitting—Ah!" she said, taking her first step. "And I want to see—Ooh!" she winced. Her foot began to swell, and she could feel the pressure increase against the bandages. She turned to face him. "It's only a *little* broken."

"Sit back down," he ordered. "You'll make it worse."

She smiled, though her jaws were tight with pain. "It's not your place to say, Armand," she teased, echoing his own words back to him before continuing to limp slowly toward the companionway.

He huffed as he caught up and offered her an arm. "Fine," he said in defeat. "Let's go."

By the time Adella and Armand had made their way up to the weather deck and toward the bow, the mood aboard *The Tigress* had shifted significantly. The crewmen whispered uneasily to each other or stood silent completely. Though it was a clear and warm late-spring day, a dark cloud hung over the port town ahead. As they sailed closer, it became apparent something was wrong. The harbor at Raymouth was usually a merry sight, filled with colorfully painted ships with bright flags jockeying for a place at the docks. Now, it was empty and grey, devoid of any other vessels or the typical crowds that usually gathered to mill about the streets and wharves.

Adella released Armand's elbow and leaned on the rail by the bowsprit, staring in disbelief at the black fog looming over the city. The look of it brought to mind the evening when her stables had been set afire and the way the thick smoke drifted outside her window. *It's smoke,* she said to herself. As they drew closer, a foul reek blew their way. An acrid, charnel smell rolled over them, stinging their lungs.

"What's happening?" Kol asked as he came up behind Adella and Armand. He had gathered up their belongings and brought them up, apparently eager to be off the ship, but unloaded it all onto the deck at his feet to gape at the sight ahead. They only shook their heads at him, unable to give an answer.

As the ship was towed toward the docks, large objects bobbed in the water or were snagged on the rocks by the beach. One floated close by, passing the hull of *The Tigress* as it came in to moor. A fetid stench rose to greet all on board as they sailed into the harbor, mingling with the reek of the smoke. Adella looked down on the foul-smelling thing as it passed by, and she saw that it was a body, bloated and mottled with bright scarlet patches on the skin. *Corpses,* she realized, her blood running cold. *And they died of the red ague!*

While several crewmen tied the mooring lines, a figure appeared from the grey fog of the town beyond and crossed the dock to approach them. "Turn back," he called out. The man wore the blood-red jacket and white tricorn hat of the Valennian Royal Guards. "Harbor's closed."

Declan leaned over the rail. "We must dock here," he replied. "We have to resupply." At the captain's words, two crewmen put the gangboard in place.

"I said it's closed," the man repeated. "All of Raymouth is under quarantine. If any man steps onto the dock, he won't be permitted to leave." Several more Royal Guards materialized from the smoke and gathered on the nearby wharf, each of them armed with sabers.

Ballantyne appeared at the rail, stepping out from the crowd toward the gangway. "Where is *The Cormorant*?" he demanded, shouting down to the guard on the dock. "They should be here by now. Did you turn them away?"

"*The Cormorant* never arrived," the guard answered. "But their flotsam has been washing up all day."

"Any survivors?" Ballantyne asked, desperation in his voice.

"Not a one," the guard replied.

Hearing this exchange, Adella pushed through the crewman gathered around the gangway, approaching Ballantyne. Kol followed closely behind her, grabbing at her arms to stop her. "What did you say?" Adella asked Ballantyne, her heartbeat drumming wildly. "Did you say *The Cormorant*?"

"I did," he answered. "They left the Capital just before we did."

"My father was on board, Lord Alfrin Grimless," she said, not quite a statement or a question. "With my mother."

"Yes, they were," Ballantyne replied. "I'm sorry, Miss."

She wavered on her injured foot, her ankle giving out beneath her as Kol caught her by the upper arm. "Let go," she said to him, but he refused. Adella turned to the guard. "Can I pass through to Elldon?"

"What for?" the guard countered. "Elldon is gone. Burnt to the ground last week," he explained plainly. "A few of the survivors made it here. A lot of good it did them," he added sarcastically. The man turned and walked away, joining the rest of the guards at the wharf. Adella wrenched her arm free from Kol's grasp and continued forward, faltering and stumbling on numb legs but determined.

"Stop," Kol ordered. "Where do you think you're going?"

"I want to go home," she replied. "I'll walk there myself if I must."

"You can't," he said, catching her around the waist as she stepped onto the dock.

"Let go!" she replied breathlessly, trying to pry his arm away. "I have to see for myself."

"I won't let you," Kol replied.

Adella dropped to her knees and Kol followed, apparently trying to keep his hold around her in case she tried to leave again. Her shoulders heaved as she sobbed. "It's all my fault," she said in a hoarse whisper. "They're all gone because of me. Everyone." She inhaled sharply and slumped into the crook of his elbow, her tears soaking his sleeve. "Please, I just want to go and see. See if it's true." Part of her imagined if she could just make it back to Greywood, her family might be there somehow, waiting for her.

"I'm sorry," Kol said, lifting her. As he turned to carry her back toward the ship, he groaned in pain from the strain it put on his wounds.

Adella could feel his left arm shaking beneath her. "Put me down. I'll go with you," she conceded. He set her legs gently back down.

"You idiots," Armand called out to them, pressing through the crewmen. "What are you thinking?! Get back on the damned ship before the guards see you."

At that moment, Declan came down the gang-board, lifting Adella up easily into his arms. He turned and carried her back aboard *The Tigress*.

Declan set Adella on the berth as a fresh stain of ruby red spread across the bandage on her left foot. He lifted her leg carefully, and as he unwrapped it, the wound bled eagerly. He turned to face the others, his shoulders slumping in defeat. "Go find the doctor," he ordered, and Armand left to obey.

"Captain." Trelauny had come down the steps behind them and now was trying to get Declan's attention. He wore a harried expression on his freckled face. "We're out of fresh water."

Declan removed his hat and ran a hand over his head, trying to push back strands of long blond hair that had fallen in his face. He took a deep breath before speaking, his expression grave. "Find every man on board whose home port is Raymouth. See if any would wish to stay behind to be with their families, and be willing to bring supplies to the dock."

"Wait," Adella said, sitting up suddenly. She rubbed the back of her wrist across her puffy eyes. "The plague, it's in the water."

"Are you certain?" Declan asked.

"Yes," she replied. "The Sornians, they are responsible for contaminating the river. They told me as much." She didn't want to mention that it was Lucas who did it. *After all,* she figured, *what did matter now?*

Declan nodded, then turned back to Trelauny. "We must make do with small beer, then. Just enough to get us to the Capital." Trelauny left to follow his orders.

At that moment, Ballantyne came stomping down the companion-way. "Captain Declan, sir," he began. "I must speak with you urgently. In private," he added, looking mistrustfully at Kol.

"This used to be a private cabin," Declan sighed. "Come," he said, gesturing for him to follow, and the two left.

Kol slumped into a chair by the table, rubbing his forehead with his good hand. Soon, Armand returned with the doctor from *The Quest,* carrying the surgeon's kit.

"This needed to be stitched," the doctor said disapprovingly as he prodded the wound in her foot with his fingers. She nodded, and he got to work cleaning and sewing the gap in the skin. She groaned as he pulled the needle through and tied off the string. When he finished, Adella curled up under the blanket, only wanting to be left alone.

The doctor eyed Kol's bandaged hand suspiciously. "If that was given the same care this one got, I'd better have a look." Kol agreed, allowed the doctor to clean, stitch and dress his palm, then asked him to look at the wounds on his shoulder and side. The doctor poulticed the inflamed scab on his abdomen with an herbal salve and cleaned up the cut in his shoulder, though it was too old to stitch. Kol muttered thanks as the doctor packed up his supplies and left, then he and Armand sat silently at the table.

"How?" Armand finally spoke. "Grimless, my old friend." His face contorted in despair. "How can you leave me here alone? Haven't we lost enough? Little Lucas and Tess," He wiped his eyes. "No. No, I don't believe it." He sniffed, drawing a deep breath. He tried to rein in his sorrow but gave in, sobbing loudly into his hands. Kol sat in the chair beside him, at a loss for words.

Adella closed her eyes, giving in to the black despair of her mind. She had no family now, no home. *Elldon is gone,* the guard had said. Everything she'd ever had in her life, everyone she loved, all of it was gone. For the first time in her life, she didn't know who she was. All the things that made up her identity had crumbled away into bitter nothingness.

Later that day, two crewmen who had volunteered to fetch supplies returned to the docks with their cargo and hollow looks in their eyes. The crew pressed them for news of the plague, asking if it was really as desperate a situation in Raymouth as it seemed, but they were reluctant to answer, saying only that it was worse. When asked what the cause of the rancid smoke was, they didn't want to speak of it. The two men gave their solemn goodbyes before turning to disappear in the gloom.

After the supplies were properly stowed away, the captain announced they had a new heading, which he avoided disclosing in detail. The crew had murmured a guess amongst themselves that they should be heading for the Capital, but were dismayed when *The Tigress* instead turned westward. Kol listened in on much of their chatter as he walked about the ship to give his grieving friends some privacy.

In the dusky evening, when Kol was wandering the quarter deck for lack of anything else to do, he overheard some of the crewmen talking on the deck below him.

"Well, I, for one, think he's finally lost his mind," said a rough, throaty voice. "He never was quite right in the head after what they did to his father. Right in front of his eyes, too. It was only a matter of time."

"The only one who's cracked here is you, Dennick," answered another voice, which Kol recognized as Jon.

"Why else would we be heading west, then?" a third voice replied. "If not to certain doom?"

"We're probably going back to Smuggler's Port," Jon replied.

"That's southwest," Dennick said. "We're heading dead west."

"I'm sure he has his reasons," Jon retorted. "He wouldn't be captain if he didn't know what he was doing. Perhaps he doesn't want the others to know where we're headed?"

"Or perhaps," the third man guessed, "it is because of them that we've changed course?"

"I don't trust them," Dennick replied. "Especially that Ballantyne fellow. He has shifty eyes."

"So do you," Jon countered.

"Well, I'm with Dennick," the third man added. "I don't know what's going on with the captain lately. He let a Sornian on board, after all. And now another wench, though it's bad luck."

"She is the daughter of Lord Grimless," Jon replied. "A highborn lady like that goes where she damn well pleases. And if I were you, I'd watch my mouth."

"Foot-licker," the third man interjected.

"It's not about luck," Dennick explained. "We agreed no women on board after what happened to Cook's wife."

"Regardless," the third man said, "you saw for yourself, only enough beer to last us three days. What's a three day sail to the west? Nothing."

"The captain's seen us through worse," Jon replied. "You can be sure he has a plan." The voices dispersed after that.

Kol returned to the cabin after a visit to the mess deck, and set two pewter goblets on the table.

"Is that all you brought us for drink?" Armand said with disappointment, looking up from the hammock.

Kol pulled a glass flask from his pocket and handed it to Armand. "I thought you would say that. I had to trade half my dinner for this."

"Bless you," Armand replied, and took a draught.

Kol then presented from under his elbow a small bundle wrapped in a kerchief, and untied it to reveal biscuits and cheese. "This is all they'd let me carry away." He looked over at Adella, who was still curled up on the mattress. She hadn't stirred since he entered, had hardly left the berth at all since the news of her parents and Elldon. He knew she was grieving, but it was completely unlike the bright and determined woman he'd gotten to know since they met, and he was starting to worry.

"Did the captain say where we're heading?" Kol asked.

"No," Armand replied. "Haven't seen him. Poor fellow has his hands full enough." He took another drink from the flask. "Better be Smuggler's Port. We have to get the horses still."

"What will happen to Adella, now?" Kol wondered.

"Depends," Armand said. "Her father's title is set to pass to her, since her older sister declined when she married." He cleared his throat. "It had always been assumed Miss Adella would do the same, and let the inheritance pass to her brother. If she accepts it now that he's gone, she'll inherit the wealth, properties, and all the responsibilities that go along with it."

Kol glanced at Adella, still a motionless form on the mattress. She didn't seem capable of taking on any responsibilities now. His heart broke for her. "And if she doesn't?"

"If she doesn't..." Armand shrugged. "Who knows. But that's up to her."

Kol took a seat at the table, drinking the beer for a while before he retired to his hammock. His sleep was wracked with fitful dreams of sea beasts with long necks and large mouths until the small hours of the morning, when he gave up and brought out the antique novel once more.

"It's like in that story you told me," Adella broke the silence, her voice weak and hoarse. "When Leveret gets the Heart of the World, and everything goes wrong."

He set the book down. "It does feel that way right now." He wanted to say something more comforting, but he didn't know how. He couldn't tell her that all would be well, because he wasn't sure it was true. Before he could think of anything to say, she turned over and went back to sleep.

14

Discord

Captain Declan came down the companionway with Trelauny close at his heels, and unrolled a map on the desk.

"All I'm saying," Trelauny went on, apparently continuing a conversation as he followed behind the captain, "is perhaps we should let the crew—our crew, anyway—know where we're headed, at least. I'm not asking any more than that."

"They will know it when we arrive," Declan replied, not looking up from the map as he positioned a compass over it. "I have orders to follow, same as you. I may be captain of this ship, but I'm not captain of the world."

Trelauny sighed, giving up for the time being. He looked blankly around the cabin for something to divert his attention until he noticed Kol hunched over the table with parchment and quill pilfered from the captain's desk, an open hand-written book sitting beside him. Trelauny stepped closer, looming down over him, to peek at his work. "What in the world are you doing?" he asked.

"It gets rather boring on this ship," Kol said defensively. "I'm practicing my letters. You Valennians make them a bit differently." Truthfully, he had never learned to write, and didn't want that fact to be discovered.

"You have written the R wrong," Trelauny instructed. "Do that one again. See?" He pointed to an example in the book. "It should join in the middle."

Kol turned the parchment over to write on the reverse. "Thanks," he said, not sounding particularly grateful. "Perhaps you have something more important to do?"

Trelauny pulled out a chair and took a seat beside him. "Not at the moment; this is my off-time. Our new quarter master, Dennick, has it all sorted."

From Trelauny's tone, Kol understood that Dennick did not, in fact, have it all sorted. "Great," he replied flatly.

"Please, continue." Trelauny took a pair of round spectacles from his waistcoat pocket and unfolded them carefully. As he placed them on his nose, his russet brown eyes appeared owl-like behind the glass. "Starting from R."

"Trelauny," Declan said, looking up suddenly from his desk. He got no response, as the first mate continued to oversee Kol's handwriting. "Trelauny," Declan repeated, but still no answer. "Cornelius!" Trelauny finally blinked up at him. "Come look at this," Declan said, tapping the map with the point of his compass.

Kol was relieved when Trelauny got up and left him in peace. He continued his writing half-heartedly, instead focusing on what the two were saying.

"What do you know of this area here?" Declan asked the first mate in a low voice.

"Not much," Trelauny replied. "Shoals and Teeth, as far as I know. Unpassable."

"That's what I thought, as well." Declan rubbed his jaw.

"Do you mean to sail through it?" Trelauny whispered.

"No, indeed," the captain answered. "Not through it."

Their conversation was interrupted by harsh shouting from the weather deck. "Dammit, Dennick," Trelauny muttered as he and Declan left to see what it was about.

Armand sat up in his hammock, where he had been, apparently, only pretending to sleep. "Did you catch all that?" he said to Kol. "Sounds like we're not going to Smuggler's Port after all."

"I don't care where we go," Kol replied, "so long as we get off this ship."

Armand looked over at Adella, still lying on the mattress, and frowned. Rolling out of the hammock, he walked over and sat down on the edge of the mattress, the wooden legs of the berth groaning under his weight. "How's that foot doing?"

Adella sat up and shrugged, wiping her eyes with the back of her hand. "It's fine."

"You know, your father had a similar scar in the same spot," Armand reminisced. "Of course, his wasn't from a fish." He waited for a response from Adella, but she only looked at him blankly. "Did you not hear that story?" he asked. "About the tiger pit?"

Adella shook her head. "No."

"Ah, it's a good one," he related enthusiastically. "We were deep in the forests just north of Enth, and it wasn't going well. They had us routed, and chased our regiment through the trees. I veered away to draw them off," he said, motioning with his hands as though he held reins, "when suddenly the ground gave way under my horse. I fell down into a deep pit with spikes at the bottom—the kind they use to kill tigers. Only these weren't the usual wooden stakes." He shook his head. "No, these were iron. I'd have been impaled for sure, if it weren't for my horse taking the brunt of it. As it was, I only caught one in my thigh, and was pinned to the saddle between the spike and the dead horse." He paused, pressing his lips together.

"Well?" she asked expectantly. "Then what?"

"I was stuck there for a couple of days, my wound starting to fester. I couldn't for the life of me figure a way out. Couldn't call out, being in enemy territory, so I just... gave up." His eyes glossed over with a distant look as he remembered. "Then, on the third day, Grimless shows up at the edge of the pit. He had stayed behind instead of retreating, combing the forest looking for me. Only as he's there looking down at me, the edge of the pit collapses. He tumbles down into it, catching the top of his foot on one of those iron spikes."

"Are you telling me this story to cheer me up?" Adella asked sarcastically. "How did you two get out?"

"Well," he went on, "Grimless pulled his foot off the spike and, luckily, had his sword with him. He cut up the horse to free me, and after we butchered the beast, we were able to make a rope from its guts. We tied that make-shift rope to one of its leg bones and threw that thing out the pit all day, until finally it caught in the cleft of a nearby tree. That's how we climbed out."

"That's disgusting," Adella smirked. "I don't believe a word of it."

"Ah, but it's true," Armand said. He looked at her misty-eyed for a moment. "You're a lot like him, you know. In temperament and personality, anyway," he amended, "not so much in appearance."

Adella gave a small laugh. "Good thing he met Mother when he did, he had pressed his luck long enough with the cavalry."

"You think she was any better?" Armand asked with amusement. "Your mother got into her fair share of scrapes, too. Like that time she was a spy for the Queen and ended up in the dungeon. Was me and Grimless who got her out."

"What are you going on about?" she asked.

"You didn't know? It was right after King Rickan's coronation," Armand began. "Grimless had only met Kat about a month before..."

Kol, though he wanted to listen in on the story, thought he had better go see what was happening up above. He could still hear raised voices from the weather deck. He came up the steps out into the fresh air just in time to see a man in front of him raise his hand, with a knife flashing in the sunlight, ready to strike another crewman. Without thinking, Kol rushed forward to grab the sailor's wrist, and bent it downward over his back, pressing it between the shoulder blades. Kol had a significant height advantage over most Valennians, and this man was no exception. The sailor yelped as the knife dropped to the deck, landing between Kol's feet.

"What is going on?" Kol asked, only managing to sound mildly curious, as he looked about the ship. Declan and Trelauny struggled to lock one man in chains while he kicked at them ferociously. More crewmen stepped forward to catch his legs. The man Kol held pulled at his arm to free himself, which prompted Kol to yank the man's wrist down further behind his back.

"None of your concern, Sornian," Dennick sneered as he stepped out from the crowd that had gathered. "Just a couple of drunk sailors, go back below."

"Fine," Kol replied. "He's all yours, then." He shoved the man toward Dennick, who caught him by the collar of his shirt. The man stomped viciously on Dennick's foot, and a tussle broke out between the two of them. Kol picked up the knife and, sliding it under his belt, returned to the cabin.

* * *

Declan trudged down the steps to the officer's quarters and scanned the large space. He could see Moffat, *The Quest's* first mate, still lying unconscious in a berth across the room. More injured sailors lounged about in hammocks, with bandaged limbs dangling here and there. Then, he spied who he was looking for.

"Ballantyne." Declan marched over toward the man as he sat on a trunk, fastening the buttons at the knee of his breeches. "You had better be damn sure about this," he said, pointing a finger at him, "because if you're wrong—"

"I get it," Ballantyne replied darkly, the deep scar across his face tensing as he spoke. "No need to be jabbing at me. You think I'd come out here for a laugh?" He pulled on his boot. "We'll have bigger problems than a lack of tea if we fail."

Declan let out his breath. "I've got one of your men in the hold, he was drunk and starting fights."

"My apologies," Ballantyne said. "If we were on *The Quest*, I'd have him flogged."

"No need for that," Declan replied, "as I won't be releasing him until we return to Valenna. If your men cause any more problems, I'll be finding you." With that, he turned and left.

* * *

Adella had come up above deck to take in the fresh air, hobbling along with the support of Armand and Kol's arms. A gentle breeze blew, warm with hints of approaching summer. They had stopped along the rail on the larboard side to watch the sunset when she noticed a dark shape passing in the water below.

It broke through the surface only a stone's throw from where they stood, weaving up and down through the waves like a snake. From what Adella could see, its skin was the brownish-green of kelp, and as it raised its massive head above the indigo sea, she saw that it was unlike the creature that had caught her by the foot. Its eyes were bulbous and black, and long seaweed-like whiskers branched out from its snout and above its eyes. Most striking of all, though, was its size. Its head was broader than the quarter boat she had taken into the sea cave, and its body looked so long that she imagined it could wrap around the ship several times over. For one frozen moment, Adella thought it was looking directly up at her, into her eyes.

It slid back under the waves and was gone as quickly as it had appeared. Adella clamped her hand on Kol's arm just above the elbow. "Did you see that?" she whispered, finally turning her eyes away from the water to see his reaction. His face was pale, and she was surprised to see he had drawn out a knife with his other hand. On her other side, Armand gaped, speechless.

The weather had changed overnight, and the crew aboard *The Tigress* woke to a light but chilly drizzle. Kol had been sensing the change in the mood on the ship all the more that morning, despite the fact that things appeared to be quieter. It was a tense silence, and it wasn't hard to imagine that every crewman was silently ruminating on his own unspoken worries and ambitions.

Kol pulled his boot knife from a knot in the wooden bulkhead that formed the wall of the captain's cabin as he passed his time absent-mindedly practicing his throwing skills. The rain had kept him below deck most of the morning, along with Armand and Adella, which he didn't mind. He had never really had what he would consider to be real friends, at least not since the orphanage. Class differences were so much more severe in Sornia than Valenna, and he was from the lowest tier; no one wanted to associate with him. *And that was fine by me,* he told himself. Still, he realized he was growing accustomed to having the two of them around. He enjoyed listening to their easy conversations, their good-natured banter, and wondered what it would be like to be close to someone, to have family.

He looked over at Adella, who was loafing on the mattress, her un-injured leg swinging back and forth over the side while she thumbed through the *Encyclopedia of Birds.* Even though her red-brown hair was strewn in disarray over the pillow and her ridiculously long sleeves hung down over her hands, she didn't look any less elegant to him than when he first saw her in her fancy clothes. He recalled his surprise at seeing who it was that knocked him over that night, but his musing was cut short when she flopped the book down and looked up at him.

"Are you done already?" she asked wryly. "It's only been three hours, and you missed that last one. Maybe you should keep practic-ing."

"I didn't miss," he muttered as he turned back around, one corner of his mouth pulling up into a smile. He threw the knife at the knot once more, this time missing his target by a hand's breadth. *Damn.*

* * *

Declan found Quarter Master Dennick on the main deck, scanning the horizon with his spyglass. The sky was nothing but pale grey clouds in every direction.

"Ah, there you are," Declan began, scrunching his face up against the misting rain. "The men are saying we've run out of beer, now. Is that so?"

Dennick nodded. "We didn't have enough to begin with," he replied.

"They've already drunk enough for three days," Declan countered. "It is your duty to oversee the food and drink, is it not?"

Dennick drew himself up taller, squaring his shoulders. "It's hard to focus on trivialities when I'm being bombarded with opposition at every turn."

"You were chosen for this position because you were a favorite among the crew," Declan said. "Is that no longer the case?"

"I could do my job better if I had all the information I need to do it properly," he said, eyes narrowing into a glare. "All this secrecy is befouling the morale. And that's your doing, not mine."

"I'm beginning to think you were promoted too quickly," Declan said quietly. A group of crewmen had gathered around them, milling about with the intention to overhear their conversation. "It seems to have gone to your head."

"You are speaking of yourself," Dennick replied, rage turning his face scarlet. "Just because you inherited this ship doesn't mean you are fit to be Captain."

"And yet here we are," Declan said, his voice rising. "I *am* Captain, whether you like it or not. This is *my* ship to command, and if you don't like the way I do it, you're welcome to leave at the next landfall. You have no other say in it!" He was shouting by the time he had finished, and the crew around them were openly staring, no longer pretending to work.

"Right. I see," Dennick conceded. "You're the captain, after all."

15

Landfall

The following day saw better weather again, as spring on Belgrand Bay was always fickle. In the afternoon, a call of "Land!" echoed throughout the ship. Kol waited patiently behind Adella as she attempted to ascend the steps without assistance. This goal was thwarted, however, when the entire ship was violently jolted to the side, accompanied by the terrifyingly loud crack of splitting wood. Books and bags that had been left on the table in the cabin careened over the edge, scattering across the sole of the ship. Adella was not spared, and she was thrown backward into Kol, who caught her quite handily. Armand, standing behind Kol, sighed loudly in relief that he didn't have to catch the both of them.

"What in the—" Adella said under her breath, trying to regain her feet. As she finally found her balance, the ship heaved to the side a second time. Again, she heard the sound of splintering wood below as all three of them were tossed onto the sole, sprawling out over the books that slid their way. They waited there a moment, not daring to stand until it was safe.

Shouts issued from the quarter deck above their heads. "Did he say 'rudder?'" Adella asked.

Kol and Armand rushed over to the gallery windows in the stern of the cabin, and flung them open to look out on the sea in the ship's wake, letting in a gust of humid seabreeze. There were no rocks or shoals to be seen; behind the ship, they caught a glimpse of the creature from the day before just as it disappeared into the blue depths. "You again," Kol muttered.

Adella stood by the bowsprit as *The Tigress* crept between the giant stone Teeth that surrounded them. The ship's rudder had been struck and split straight down the middle, half of it being lost to the sea, so their course was precarious at best. Judging by the amount of water being pumped out over the decks from the bilge, Adella understood the rudder wasn't the only part of the ship to take damage. She watched as a large cluster of Teeth up ahead crept nearer, growing ever larger until she realized she was looking at land beyond, guarded by a fierce ring of jagged rock. *An island.*

She had been in a somber mood that day, and Kol and Armand must have sensed it as they let her limp above deck without assistance. Though she appreciated their help, Adella did not want to be so much of a burden as she felt she had been lately. Her injured foot improved a little each day, and though it still hurt quite a lot, she could go a short distance now before it swelled so much that she needed to rest and prop it up. Mostly, though, she wanted to be alone for a moment, as the pain in her heart was greater.

"Listen up, men," Adella heard Captain Declan's loud voice begin from somewhere behind her. She looked around to see the sailors crowding around Declan at the main mast, and stepped closer to overhear, stumping gingerly along on her swollen heel. "We will prepare to row ashore to the island, anchoring within these Teeth." Some of the men cast their eyes toward the rock suspiciously. "No," Declan said, sensing their confusion, "you won't find this island on any map, and we have very strict orders to keep it that way. Understood?" The men all nodded.

"Quarter Master Dennick." Declan turned to face him. "You will put together a scouting party to go ashore in the longboat to find freshwater. First Mate Trelauny." Trelauny stepped forward in response, and Declan continued. "Your men will be responsible for making the repairs to the ship. I will be taking a select few into the island's interior on a private mission. We will head out after Dennick and his men return, at which time Trelauny will be Acting Captain. Treat him with all the same love and admiration that you show me," he said, smiling at his own humor. They all dispersed and Adella hurried to the cabin as quickly as she could.

The scouting party that had gone with Dennick returned with water after only a few hours, distributing it among the crew from the barrels they had filled. Not long after, Declan came down to gather a few items from his quarters. Adella, Armand and Kol had done their best to put the cabin back in order, but it took him a while to find his belongings nonetheless. After he had packed away a few different articles and pulled an oilskin cloak from his trunk, he shouldered his rucksack and turned to leave. Adella stood by with her own cloak in hand, haversack hanging at her side, ready to follow him. Kol and Armand stood behind her, dressed for travel with their swords at their sides.

Captain Declan stopped, his shoulders falling. "What are you doing?"

"Going ashore," Adella replied. "Obviously."

"No." He shook his head. "No, you can't. It's too dangerous."

She raised an eyebrow. "So I should stay on the sinking ship, then? For safety?"

"It's not sinking," Declan mumbled defensively. "Look, you're injured," he explained. "You'll only slow us down."

"Who said I was going to follow you?" She adjusted the strap across her shoulder. "You can leave us behind after landfall, we'll stay by the boat."

"I said no," he replied. "And, since I am the captain, you have to abide by it."

"Let me remind you," Adella began, "that with my parents and my brother gone, my father's title passes to me now, making me a representative of the Crown. As I've been informed you work under commission of the king, that means I have the authority to give *you* orders."

"Not on my own ship, *Adella*." He emphasized her name as he addressed her informally, like he had when they were children.

"The moment you step off the ship, *Rogero*," she said, forcing a smile. Beside her, Kol snorted to keep from laughing.

Declan cast a dark glance at Kol, then sighed. "Let's make a compromise. You come to shore, but you have to stay with my party. I don't want to waste my crew's time looking for you if you get lost. You two," he said, eyeing Kol and Armand in turn, "see that she keeps up."

Adella looked questioningly at Armand and Kol, and they both nodded. She could tell they were as eager to see land as she was, and, like her, would probably agree to anything. "Fine then," she said. Satisfied, Declan offered his arm and she took it.

They came to the larboard rail and climbed down the rope ladder into the longboat, where several other crewmen waited at the oars. Adella was surprised to see Ballantyne on board, as the few times she'd crossed paths with him on *The Tigress*, he seemed to be skulking about the ship alone. She carefully picked her way over the supplies piled in the hull and sat down on the thwart behind Ballantyne, with Kol and Armand following after her. Looking around, Adella saw two other men already seated at the oars.

As they left *The Tigress* behind, each rower moving in unison, they wove side to side around the large, jagged stones that began to crowd in the waves around them. Adella peeked over the side of the boat, down into the water, to see little wide-finned sharks swimming aimlessly around below. The sea here was a soothing turquoise that became shallower the farther they rowed into the Teeth, which seemed as numerous as trees in a forest. The wind died down around them, leaving only the hot sun overhead. Adella's forehead dampened as she continued to work the oar. Glancing over at the other side of the boat, she saw Kol straining to row one-handed.

Ballantyne, seated toward the bow, seemed to be pointing out the direction to Declan. As they passed, a great stone wall rose before them, revealing itself behind the dark Teeth. The shadow of the land fell over them as they approached, cooling the air. They turned the boat and rowed with the wall along their starboard until a chasm opened in the cliff face. Ballantyne motioned, and they turned toward the rift.

Continuing onward, they rowed upriver through the gorge within the shadow of the massive rock looming high above. As the boat floated through the damp passage, the ceiling lowered, the bare rock inching downward over their heads.

Adella's heart sank. *Not again,* she thought, glaring distrustfully down into the dark water. She was quite finished with sea caves. A longing for home overtook her as thoughts of her warm bed at Greywood flickered through her mind. Then, memories of her family surfaced, laughing with her mother and father over tea and playing cards with Lucas. *No,* she reminded herself, trying to push the thoughts away. *It's all gone now.* Her mind reeled on the edge of despair, but she stopped herself. *Not now, for heaven's sake. Keep it together, Adella.* She took a deep breath and swallowed her emotions. There was nothing to go back to; there was only onward, into whatever awaited ahead.

They turned a corner in the cave, and an opening shone brightly at its end. They passed through the cave mouth into a small turquoise lagoon, hemmed about by sandy banks on the sides. Directly ahead of them, a high waterfall spilled down into the lagoon from a sheer rock face, and a stairway, carved into the stone beside the falls, snaked back and forth up the cliff. Adella's eyes followed it upward, her mouth falling open as she saw a massive stone tower sitting at the summit, beside the falls. A thick forest of tall pine and oak grew dense in every direction around the lagoon, even atop the cliffs. Adella sat motionless, taking in the impressive view. It looked like a scene from her wildest dreams. She rested the oar in her lap, leaning over to stick her fingers in the bright blue-green water, and was delighted to discover it was warm.

They rowed across the lagoon until the hull of the longboat scraped against the sandy bank. Setting their oars in the boat, they gathered their supplies and stepped onto the narrow beach. Wordlessly, Ballantyne and Declan pulled the boat ashore and trudged along the bank, heading toward the cliffside ahead. The others followed.

Adella limped heavily in the sand, feeling the flesh of her foot swell. Before leaving the ship, she had put on her torn boot to support the injured foot, leaving the laces open above the arch and stuffing it with rags for padding. Though it seemed to help, she was relieved to have gone this far in the boat rather than on foot.

She stopped walking when she realized where they were going. Adella paused to look up at the steps carved into the side of the stone as a cold, gnawing feeling grew in the pit of her stomach. *It's too high,* she thought, feeling her injured foot throb. It looked to be about five stories or more. Her mouth went dry at the thought of falling onto the rocks at the bottom.

Reluctantly, Adella forced herself to follow at the back of the group with Kol and Armand, passing around the lagoon. The evening sun shone warmly on her face, a pleasant feeling compared to the gloom of the cave. Finally, they came to the foot of the stairway, and the others ahead of her ascended without any apparent reservations about its height. The surface of each step was damp with moisture from the falls, with shallow depressions worn at the center of each edge. There was no rail, just a sheer drop over the side of the cliff. She craned her neck up, eyes following the steeply carved pathway to the top. She looked away again, feeling lightheaded.

Kol had stopped alongside Adella, catching the look on her face. "Do you need a rest?"

She shook her head. "The steps. I don't think I can do it." Her foot was already pounding, the bruised flesh straining against her stitches.

"You can," he said. "You go in front of me; that way, if you slip—"

"Then what?" she interrupted, her brow tense. "We both die?"

He laughed, then stopped himself when he saw she was serious. "After everything that's happened, I don't think it'll be stairs that kill you."

She bit her lip, not taking much comfort from his words. At her hesitation, he offered her his hand. "Then I'll go beside you."

Adella looked down at his open palm, then up at his face, into his dark eyes. She thought back to the time they were pursued by soldiers in the flooding sea cave. *He asked me to trust him then,* she remembered. *And we survived.* Exhaling in resignation, she took his rough, calloused hand and they continued forward and upward.

Adella trudged up one painful step at a time, trying not to lean too much on Kol's arm. He took the outer edge, making her anxious how careless he seemed about the drop. They came to one of the several landings carved into the stone where the steps changed direction, and she admitted she needed a rest.

She sat down on the stone surface to raise her injured foot onto her knee. "You go on," she said. "No need to wait for me." He didn't reply but sat down beside her. Adella suddenly had the feeling something was missing and looked around in agitation. "Where's Armand?"

Squinting, Kol searched the landscape below. "There." He pointed to the forest's edge near the base of the stairs as Armand emerged from behind the foliage, buttoning up the front of his breeches.

"Ugh." Adella turned her face away.

"Look," Kol said urgently, his tone shifting. "What's that behind him?"

Adella looked again to see a strange figure appear at the edge of the forest and walk along the bank on two thin, crooked legs. A long neck lowered to the water at its feet as the creature stopped to drink. She had never seen anything like it before. Kol and Adella both carefully rose to their feet.

"Armand!" Adella waved her hand high in the air. "Come on, hurry!" she yelled, but her voice was swallowed up by the roar of the falls.

Armand ambled along toward the base of the stairway. Behind him, the animal at the water's edge lifted its head high on the long stalk of its neck. It strode along the sandy bank, its head bobbing back and forth with each step. Its pace quickened to a run as it headed straight for him.

Kol and Adella watched breathlessly as the animal opened up a pair of what appeared to be small wings, fluttering them wildly as it came toward their friend. Armand, still heedless of his situation, made it up the steps just in time, leaving the creature scraping its feet at the rock, unable to follow up after him. As it turned and pecked at the ground instead, Kol and Adella breathed a sigh of relief.

"What do you suppose that was?" she asked as they waited for Armand. Below, the animal disappeared back into the trees.

"Some kind of bird, I think," Kol replied.

"Like a... peacock?" Adella raised a brow as she named the most similar thing she could think of. There was nothing like it in the *Encyclopedia of Birds*.

Kol laughed. "Definitely not a peacock."

Armand caught up with them, and they continued upward, weaving back and forth over the face of the stone cliff until they came to the summit. Adella was just beginning to feel more comfortable with the height when her swollen foot slipped on the edge of the final step. Her heart leapt into her mouth as she fell backward until a hand caught her by the upper arm and steadied her. She exhaled slowly to calm her racing heart, and they continued on.

Captain Declan and the others were sitting in the grass on the banks just upriver, drinking from canteens and flasks. Declan stuffed his canteen back into his large rucksack and stood as they approached.

"What happened?" Declan asked Adella. "I thought you were right behind us."

Armand stepped forward. "I had to shit," he interjected matter-of-factly. Declan had no reply for it, and so they all turned, following Ballantyne's lead toward the tower.

As they approached the base of the tower, they could see it was in disrepair. Though crumbled stones littered the bottom and thick vines laced its surface, the curved wall of large stone blocks appeared whole, supporting two rows of arched windows under a conical roof. Adella noticed the windows at the top shone with a golden light, but she wasn't sure if it was perhaps from the sunlight reflecting off panes of glass or lantern light coming from within.

Now that they were closer, they could see the stone tower didn't stand alone; hidden behind the foliage, a high wall topped with a slate roof stretched out from one side. It ran northeast, following the edge of the cliff and disappearing into the trees. On the other side of the turret, the hard ground gave way to the river, churning loudly over boulders before falling over the precipice. At the base, embedded into its rounded wall, was a solid iron door, reddened with age.

Ballantyne approached the door and solemnly reached out a hand. He rapped three times on the rusted iron, which echoed from within. The group waited silently in expectation. Just when it seemed there would be no answer, a large bell rang out from the top of the tower, the heavy metallic sound overwhelming the roar of the falls.

They waited a while after the last peal of the bell died away, until finally the iron door creaked open. A man appeared in the gap, his face wrinkled with age though his back was unbent, his form robust and healthy. Silver stubble glinted on his face; his head was shorn smooth, his tawny scalp unadorned.

He looked the group up and down before returning his attention to Ballantyne. "Go back where you came from," he said in a strange accent, sliding the heavy door shut again.

Ballantyne shoved his foot in the gap before the door closed completely. "Let me talk to her," he said. "It's urgent."

A woman appeared from within, pushing the door open with her hand. "It's all right, Jago," she said to her companion. "I know this man." She turned to face Ballantyne. "Please, all of you, come inside." She opened the door wide to allow their entry. Her skin was fair but deeply lined, and her iron-grey hair, streaked with white, was pulled back into a loose braid. Her shirt and breeches were made of undyed homespun, her tall boots so worn their original color was inscrutable. "We were just about to have tea."

They followed her through the spacious interior of the tower, which contained only a spiral stairwell in the center, and then down a long corridor. She stopped before a pair of windowed doors built into the wall at their left and opened them wide, stepping out into a large courtyard filled with flowering trees and shrubs, shadowed and cool in the evening air. Stone walkways traced lines through the manicured landscape, and they followed one well-worn path to the center of the space. Underneath a tall locust tree, its boughs heavy with white flowers, stood a long table lined with chairs. At the center was a blue and white porcelain tea service much like the one aboard *The Tigress*. A platter of different types of dried fruit sat beside it.

Declan furrowed his brow at the sight. "Were you... expecting us?"

"No," the woman replied with a small laugh. "We always have tea at this hour. Please, sit."

"Where are your other guests?" Declan asked, looking at the table set for eight.

"Jago rang the bell," she explained, "so they'll be meeting him at the armory now. Aren't you all hungry? Help yourself."

Adella stepped forward and pulled out a chair. "Thank you," she replied, and took a seat. The rest of the group followed her lead.

"My name is Ellie," the woman said. "Royal Apothecary. And you've already met Jago, Captain of the Guard. Welcome to the Cairn." She gestured to the ancient fortress around them. Then, she turned to Ballantyne, prompting him with a slight wave of her hand.

"This is Captain Declan, privateer," Ballantyne said, taking her hint for introductions. "*The Quest* was hit by a storm, he brought our survivors onto his ship *The Tigress*. These are his people, save for Tomas over there," he indicated to the sailor that Adella didn't recognize, "who is one of mine."

Declan gestured toward the young brown-haired man sitting across from him. "This is Hugo Jon, our navigator." Jon nodded at Ellie, his mouth full of food. Declan then motioned toward Adella. "My friend Adella Grimless, and her two hired hands." He indicated to Adella's left, "Ben Armand, butler." He motioned toward her other side, "And Kol." He paused. "Mercenary."

"It is lovely to meet you all," Ellie said, pouring tea into the cups. "Now tell me, what brings you here?"

"Royal orders," Ballantyne stated. "There is a plague spreading through the Capital, and so the king sent us to bring you back. But after our ship was wrecked, we had to make a stop at Raymouth. Things were much worse there than the Capital. Looked like the same disease."

"No," Adella whispered, a sudden surge of panic spreading through her at the news. Her thoughts turned to her sister, Margavita, who lived at the Capital. *Please, not Margavita,* she pleaded silently, fighting back tears. *I can't lose her, too.*

Ellie set the teapot down, a weary look overtaking her features. "What disease?" she asked. Ballantyne shook his head, shrugging helplessly.

"I believe it's the red ague," Kol answered, reaching for the teacup in front of him. "It came from Sornia."

"You appear to be Sornian yourself," Ellie replied. "Do you know anything about this illness?" He nodded and she continued, "Good. We will speak more of it later."

The sun sank low behind the stone walls of the Cairn as they finished filling their stomachs. Jago crossed the courtyard toward the table with a punched-tin lantern in hand, and Ellie stood as he approached. "Well, let's get you all settled for the night," she said to the group. "I'm sorry we don't have any spare chambers ready, we don't usually get visitors here. We'll have to make do for now."

They followed Ellie through the other half of the courtyard, another set of doors, and down a second corridor. As they came to an ornately carved oak door at the end, she gently pushed it open. The space within was vast, warmly lit by a crackling hearth in one corner. The walls were covered floor to ceiling in shelves filled with thick, leather-bound books and rolling ladders. The furniture had all been haphazardly shoved toward the walls, writing desks and sofas cleared away to make room for small ticking-striped mattresses scattered across the threadbare carpet. Piles of blankets and pillows had been set on each mattress. The group all began to unshoulder their travel bags.

"Again, I apologize for the temporary accommodations," Ellie said, "but it is getting late, and you all look exhausted. Hopefully, this will suffice."

"It's wonderful," Adella said, looking around the library with admiration. "Thank you for your hospitality, Miss Ellie."

"The privies are in the northern corner of the courtyard. If you need anything, Jago will be around. He never sleeps," Ellie said, a laugh in her voice. Then she left, shutting the door behind her.

"It's certainly better than I hoped for," Declan said after she left, plopping down on the nearest mattress and pulling off his boots.

"A library," Kol mused, choosing a mattress by the wall. "Probably the last place I'd have expected to sleep tonight." Armand chose a spot near the fire, and pulled a flask from his pocket. Jon left to relieve himself in the courtyard while Tomas set a log in the fireplace.

Grabbing a pillow and blanket, Adella sat down on one of the sofas at the edge of the room, and the others all made themselves comfortable while she took in her surroundings. Setting her feet up on the prickly horsehair-stuffed cushions, she gazed at the stars twinkling through large, arched windows. She wasn't sure how she would get any rest in a room full of men who, if Kol and Armand were any indication, were probably all noisy sleepers. Her only hope was to fall asleep first, she thought, but gave up on the idea when she heard a loud snoring coming from near the hearth.

Hours had passed, and Adella still couldn't sleep. She sat up, wrapping the scratchy wool blanket around her shoulders. Every man in the room seemed to be breathing loudly. She looked over at Kol, sprawled out on the mattress with his face smashed into the pillow, curls of black hair falling over his eyes. Even he seemed to be sound asleep, his chest rising and falling slowly, with no sign of the distressing dreams she had become accustomed to hearing in the night. *Good*, she thought.

Adella pulled the blanket tighter around herself and got up from the sofa. She put another piece of wood from the basket beside the hearth into the fire and then crossed over the library floor, stepping carefully around each sleeping figure until she came to the carved wood door. Stepping out into the cool dark of the corridor, she closed the door behind her.

16

The Cairn

Adella had no real reason to leave the library, only a vague hope of wasting time until she was tired enough to sleep through the noise. However, she noticed a faint light illuminating the far end of the corridor, and wandered toward it out of curiosity. As she turned the corner, she could see the source of the light. Ellie stood in the center of the hallway holding the tin lantern; close beside her was Jago, casually leaning on a kind of weapon Adella had never seen before. It seemed to be a polearm, similar to a spear, but the blade atop it had several barbs and spines that she could not guess the use for. The sight of the weapon gave her pause, but Ellie and Jago didn't seem to be discussing anything serious. Jago merely turned to look at Adella when he heard her approaching.

"Is everything all right, my dear?" Ellie asked warmly, stepping toward her.

"Yes," Adella replied. "I just couldn't sleep, that's all."

"I was just about to withdraw to the Great Room." Ellie lifted the lantern and motioned down the corridor beyond. "Would you like to join me?" Adella nodded. Ellie turned to Jago. "See you in the morning, then," she said. Then, lantern in hand, she led Adella down the corridor.

"What is this place?" Adella asked.

"An Old Andolinian monastery," Ellie replied, turning her head to glance backward at Adella. "The ruins were over a thousand years old, but we've been repairing it over the years while using this island as an outpost. It's proved to be more interesting than we had expected."

"How so?" Adella came to a halt beside Ellie as she turned to open a door to their left.

"There are animals and plants living on this island that can be found nowhere else," Ellie said as she led Adella into a spacious chamber. She closed the door behind them and continued. "Medicinal plants of great use to an apothecary. We've been here for eighteen years, studying its resources." The walls on either side of the room were long, and lined with many doors. A row of arched windows ran along each wall, above the doors. On the far end of the space, an enormous stone hearth glowed with the embers of a dying fire. She led Adella to a long, low table surrounded by elaborately carved mahogany chairs, and motioned for her to sit down.

Ellie grabbed a book from a nearby bookcase and brought it over to the table beside Adella and flipped through it. "Now, what do you know about the illness that's been spreading in the Capital?"

"Not much," Adella replied. "Only that it's spread through contaminated water. Mister Kol would know more, he survived it when he was younger. He made a medicine for Armand."

"Mister Kol, your mercenary?" Ellie asked.

"No," Adella began. "Well, yes, but he's not—" She stopped herself, realizing the particulars weren't important. "Yes."

Ellie laughed. "Tell me, Miss Grimless, how did you end up out here in the middle of Belgrand Bay? Last I knew, your family was living in Elldon."

Adella drew a breath to answer, but the words caught in her throat. She could only look away as tears welled up in her eyes. Unable to contain them, she hid behind her hands, hair falling over her face like a curtain.

"My dear child," Ellie said quietly, closing her book. "I am so very sorry."

It took some time before Adella was composed enough to speak again. "We are at war with Sornia," she explained, wiping her eyes on the back of her hand. "I was captured and taken aboard their ship. Captain Declan came to my rescue."

"The dashing blond fellow?" Ellie asked.

Adella nodded. "When we made port at Raymouth, I found out my parents' ship sank, and Elldon was destroyed."

"I am very sorry to hear that," Ellie replied. "I knew your parents, they were good people."

Adella tucked her hair back behind an ear. "You did?"

"When your family lived at the Capital. You and I have met before. Do you not recognize me?" she asked with a twinkle in her eyes, but Adella shook her head. "Well," Ellie reasoned, "you were very young at the time."

Ellie began flipping through the book again, which looked to be an encyclopedia of diseases. Adella brought her hand down suddenly on a page as Ellie was turning it.

"That," Adella said, jabbing her finger at the hand-painted illustration on the page. "That looks like the red ague."

"Hm," Ellie muttered. The drawing depicted a body lying prone, covered in red spots. "This chapter is on diseases with animal origin, there are several illnesses listed here that resemble this. Hopefully your soldier will be able to narrow it down."

Adella opened her mouth to speak, but found herself yawning instead. Glancing around the room, she noticed a particularly large and comfortable-looking sofa in one corner, and gazed at it longingly.

"Go on," Ellie said, catching the look on Adella's face. "Go lie down."

Adella obeyed, pulling the blanket up over herself as she curled up on the plush velvet cushions.

It was in the small hours of the morning when Kol opened the door to the library. Stepping into the corridor, he saw Jago making his rounds through the Cairn.

"Where is Adella?" Kol asked, an edge in his voice. She had been gone for hours. He narrowed his eyes at the weapon in the guard's hand.

"She's safe," Jago replied. "The girl is with Miss Ellie, by the dormitories. Follow me." Kol had become used to the Valennian accent of his companions, but this man sounded much different, and it took him a moment to understand what was said. As Jago led the way down the corridor, Kol followed.

Jago ushered Kol into the Great Room and left, closing the door behind him. Kol looked around, and was relieved to see Adella's sleeping form on the sofa at the far end of the chamber. Ellie sat alone at the table in the center of the room, studying a page in a large book. Littered across the table were more books, piles of blank parchment, and a brass inkwell stand that held a goose quill.

She looked up at his approach. "Ah, I'm glad you're here," she said, motioning for him to take a seat at the table across from her.

"Where is that man from?" Kol asked brusquely, ignoring her invitation to sit.

"Jago is Andolinian," Ellie replied.

Kol raised a brow in confusion. "They still exist?"

"Oh yes." Ellie rested her cheek on her palm, propped up on her elbow. "Small bands descended from the survivors. Not many, though."

His eyes shifted around the room, pausing in the dark corners. "Where are the rest of your people?"

"Asleep—" She waved a hand toward the doors along one wall. "In their dormitories." She waited patiently to see if he had any more questions. It was clear he had woken up in a bad mood.

He looked her hard in the eyes. "There are no Sornians here?"

"None but yourself," she replied with a hint of amusement.

"This island, it belongs to Valenna then?" he asked, and she nodded. "Are you and your people the only occupants here?" She nodded again. He pressed his lips together, satisfied with her answers.

She waited a moment before speaking again. "I apologize if you were worried—"

"I wasn't," he interrupted. Kol finally sat down on the chair. "You wanted to discuss the plague, right?"

She turned the book around to face him, showing him the illustration Adella had pointed out earlier. "Could you look through this chapter?" she asked. "Let me know if anything seems familiar." He took the book and began to read.

"Here," he said after a time, pointing to a page in the book. "It's most similar to this, but not quite a match."

Ellie pulled the book closer, turning it back around to read. "Hm," she said thoughtfully. "How did you survive it?"

"The apothecary in Hedda developed a physic, but the ingredients were too expensive for the lower classes." He lowered his eyes. "So they tried to replicate it with common herbs. When a suitable recipe was found, it was shared among the people. I had to make it for myself while I was ill."

Ellie leaned over, gathering some items from around the table. She set the inkwell and a sheet of parchment before him. "Could you write that recipe down for me? If you please."

"Uh," Kol hesitated. "I will dictate it to you."

When he had finished speaking, Ellie set her quill down and looked over what she had written. "I don't recognize the names of these herbs."

He smiled wryly as he remembered having a similar conversation. "Adella can help you with that." He stood, pushing his chair back under the table. "When she wakes, ask her not to wander off again." He then left, returning to the library.

The bright morning sun streamed through the many large windows of the library, though the others were still snoring. Kol hadn't been able to fall back asleep, but he felt rested enough. He wasn't quite sure how he felt about this place. The Valennians he came here with seemed to trust these people, anyway. He was a little curious about the foreigner Jago and the unfamiliar weapon he carried with him, curious about this strange fortress and the people here. But mostly, Kol realized he was hungry.

At that moment, Adella came limping through the door of the library. She plopped down on the sofa by the wall, resting her injured foot on her other knee while she ate a piece of fruit.

"Where did you get that?" Kol asked suspiciously. Even as he told himself it was too early in the year for fresh fruit, he wondered if there were any more.

"Captain Jago," she replied, pulling another from the pocket of her too-large breeches and offering it to him. "He gave me too many. He said they needed to be eaten up."

Kol took it. It appeared to be something like a plum, but the wrong color, orange instead of purple. He bit into it anyway. "Thanks." Kol sat down on the sofa beside her. "Does Jago not sleep?"

Adella shrugged. "Miss Ellie said he's an ascetic."

Kol didn't recognize the word but didn't want to seem ignorant by asking. "Have you seen any of the other people who live here?"

Adella nodded. "Just briefly as they left the dormitories."

"Are they all guards?" he asked. "Soldiers?"

"Uh," she said, thinking. "Some of them, I suppose." She handed him another piece of fruit.

He turned it over in his hand. "Do you trust these people?"

"Yes," she answered confidently. "Relax for once, will you?"

"I can't, now that you've told me to." Kol looked toward the door as it opened, and Jago entered.

"You all still asleep?" Jago asked, his accent twisting his words. The deep wrinkles in his bronzed forehead shifted as he spoke. "It's broad daylight, you layabouts." He tapped the butt of his polearm on the stone floor impatiently.

Declan awoke, sitting up on his mattress. "What's he saying?" he asked the room groggily. "I can't understand him."

"He says wake up," Adella replied. "And that you're lazy."

"The girl has it right," Jago said. "Come along now, if you want to eat." He left the library, leaving the door open behind him. One by one, the sailors arose, rubbing their eyes or pulling on their boots, and made their way into the corridor. Armand was still snoring heavily on the floor, sprawled out halfway off his mattress.

"Wake him up," Adella said, nudging Kol with her elbow.

"You'd better do it," he countered. "He can't get too mad at you."

"We'll see." She walked hesitantly over toward Armand, and nudged him gently with her boot. "Armand, wake up. Or you'll miss breakfast."

"Dammit, girl!" Armand said, swatting at her. "Don't be kicking me when I'm dreaming." He turned over onto his side and, for a moment, Kol thought he would fall back asleep. "Did you say breakfast?" he asked, sitting up suddenly.

Breakfast was in the courtyard, this time set up with two long tables. One table was occupied by Ellie and Jago, with six unfamiliar people talking quietly amongst themselves. Kol was surprised to see they were all grey-haired, the same age as Ellie and Jago or older. Some of them made Armand look young. It was an even mix of men and women who, despite their age, all seemed to be in good physical condition.

They approached the second table, where Declan and the sailors were already seated and eating. There were platters of fresh and dried fruit, smoked fish and baked tubers with honey. The three of them took seats and ate. When they finished, Ellie made brief introductions before the islanders departed, leaving the newcomers to roam the Cairn as they pleased. They were, however, asked not to leave the safety of the fortress just yet.

Kol noticed that Ballantyne seemed to be distracted. He was continually glancing around him and generally seemed to be on edge.

Though he could relate to the uneasiness of letting his guard down, Kol wondered if the sailor knew something he didn't. *Perhaps he knows about the birds,* he thought. He remembered how the man confidently led their way to the island. Ballantyne must've been here before.

After some time, Jago returned, rounding them up from the courtyard. He instructed them to gather up their belongings they had left in the library and meet in the Great Room.

Ellie emerged from one of the dormitories to their left as the group entered the large chamber, her grey hair tied up in a kerchief. She turned to address their group. "So," she began, "as it will take some time for me to harvest and prepare a medicine against the plague, you may find yourselves here for a while. We will do our best to make you all comfortable, but it's been so very long since we've had guests of any kind." Ellie looked them over, and Adella thought she saw a twinkle of excitement in her eyes.

"I have emptied the dormitories that we have been using as storage," Ellie continued. "Hopefully, you all will find them more comfortable than the floor of the library. As you can see, there are only eight dormitories, and fifteen of us altogether, so I'm afraid we'll have to double up. If there are any of your group you wouldn't mind sharing a chamber with, please pair up now, or you shall be placed with one of us. Miss Adella," Ellie turned toward her, "as you're the only woman in your group, and there's an odd number of us, you shall get the spare chamber to yourself." Adella nodded at Ellie, trying not to smile too broadly at the happy news.

The newcomers all moved to gather up their things and choose a chamber partner while Ellie continued to speak. "I apologize if the presence of posted guards unnerves you. We have been visited by reavers once or twice over the years, though that was long ago now." She paused, a grim look flashing over her face. "However, we also have some unusual wildlife on the island that it would be better not to meet unarmed. For this reason, if you wish to leave the Cairn, you must do so in armed groups, and I ask that you speak with me beforehand." They all nodded. With belongings in hand, they filed along toward their chambers. "I see that some of you are wounded," Ellie said. "Please meet with me here in an hour if you would like my medical services."

Adella withdrew to the farthest chamber along one wall, just to the right of the fireplace. She dropped her haversack onto the cold stone floor and looked about the room, leaving the door open behind her. It was spare, with only a small rough-hewn wooden bedstead in one corner and a battered old wardrobe in the other. Still, the newfound privacy made it feel homey. She was also happy to see a cheery floral-patterned chamber pot peeking out under the bed quilt.

She opened the wardrobe to hang her oilskin cloak on a peg within and was surprised to see it was filled already with women's clothing.

"For you," a woman's voice said behind her. Adella turned to see one of the islanders standing in the doorway. She was beautiful, with stark-white hair piled up in ringlets atop her head. "They're a bit too fine for our tastes, nowadays."

"Thank you, Madame—" Adella said, trying to remember the woman's name from the hasty introductions given earlier.

"Cora," the woman replied. "And Miss is fine, if you must. I am unmarried."

"Right," Adella replied. "Thank you, Miss Cora." Her eyes moved down to the blade fastened at the old woman's waist. "Are you a guard as well?"

"We all take guard duty in turn," she explained. "We like to be prepared, just in case." She threw Adella a warning glance before turning to leave, closing the door behind her.

Seeing how everyone else seemed to be armed, Adella wished she had thought to bring her crossbow along, but she had left it behind on the ship with the rest of her belongings. Turning back toward the wardrobe, she looked the clothes over. The bodices were cut in a style popular decades ago, with a long, pointed front rather than the peplums Adella was used to wearing. The sleeves were pleated at the shoulders, causing them to puff out dramatically. She pulled out a jacket bodice and matching skirt, laying them across the bed to look them over. The light silk fabric was a pleasant sea-blue color. *My mother had a dress like this once,* Adella remembered wistfully. She fished around in the wardrobe for proper undergarments, her hand lingering over a pair of stays momentarily until she recalled how glad she was to be rid of her old ones. She continued until she found some petticoats and a thin linen shift and changed out of the rough sailor's clothes she had been wearing. The neckline of the bodice plunged very low, and Adella felt a bit self-conscious in it. She grabbed a shawl from the shelf in the wardrobe and wrapped it around her shoulders; it was soft and finely made, with figures of prancing horses woven skillfully into the design.

Adella left her dormitory to find Ellie sitting at the table in the center of the room, gently unwrapping the dressing on Kol's hand. His shirt had been removed, with clean bandages wrapped around his torso and shoulder. The older woman had a box of supplies open beside her filled with salves, fresh dressings, and other things. Adella approached and immediately recognized the strong, clean scent of lavender.

Jago entered the Great Room, carrying his polearm in one hand and deftly transporting an entire tea service in the other. His footsteps were silent, and not a single clink came from the porcelain as he walked. *The man is unnatural,* she thought with admiration. He set the tray down on the table beside the medical supplies. Ellie, turning as she noticed Adella, beckoned her.

"Your friend here is in rough shape," Ellie chided. "He looks like a pincushion. I am told you have a wound that needs tending as well?" Adella nodded. "Sit," Ellie ordered, motioning toward the tea, "and drink this."

Adella did as she was told, pouring herself a cup and sipping while she waited. It was not the usual black tea from the camellia plant like she had expected, but instead, a strong, bitter herbal decoction she didn't recognize.

Armand joined them, helping himself to the tea as well. He made a face as he drank it, but said nothing about the taste. He looked over at Jago, who stood by the table still. "Andolinian, aren't you?"

"I am," Jago said. "I take it you've met others before?"

"Indeed," Armand replied. "My own mother was Andolinian. She came to Valenna as a refugee after the War of the Clans."

"As did I. What area was she from?" Jago asked eagerly.

"The Redlands," Armand replied. "Just north of the Iron Coast. From one of the horse tribes."

"Ah," Jago said with recognition. "I was a horseman as well. We ranged southeast of the citadel ruins."

"She spoke of that place," Armand said with a nod. "Told me many stories of Andolin. I'd like to see it myself, someday."

"I would go back willingly," Jago said, "but that isn't up to me."

"No?" Armand prodded.

"That'd be up to Miss Ellie," Jago said, a faint smile crossing his stern face. "Where she goes, I go."

Ellie had just finished bandaging Adella's foot and turned to the two men when she heard her name. "I can't get away from him," she joked. "How many years has it been now?"

"Eighteen at the Cairn," Jago replied. "Thirty-three at the Capital. Fifty-one altogether."

"Was he a soldier at the Capital?" Adella asked Ellie.

Ellie shook her head. "My bodyguard." She turned to him. "The job is easier now, wouldn't you say?"

"Sure," Jago replied. "You don't go out as much."

Ellie laughed, packing up her supplies into the box. "Well, Miss Adella," Ellie began, "I was going to show you and your people around the Cairn, but after what I've just seen, I've changed my mind. I think you need to rest instead."

They had spent most of the day in the Great Room or resting in their dormitories. Kol sat on one of the two little bedsteads in the room he shared with Armand. He stretched his legs across the feather-stuffed mattress and leaned back against the headboard, absentmindedly sharpening his knife with a whetstone.

Armand lay backward on his mattress on the other side of the small space, looking up at the ceiling with his hands folded at his chest. "You know, I was going to retire this year," he mumbled, perhaps more to himself than Kol, as he continued to stare at the ceiling.

Kol paused his whetstone and looked up at Armand, expecting him to continue. When he didn't, he turned the knife over and started on the other side.

"That's probably enough rest," Armand said at length, sitting up on the bed. "For me, anyway. You stay here; I'm going to wander around. Did you see?" he lowered his voice as his eyes darted briefly toward the open door. "This island is filled with beautiful women."

Kol stopped the whetstone in the middle of a stroke, raising a brow as he looked over at Armand. He wondered for a moment if the man had lost his mind. Then he laughed when he realized; "You mean the grandmothers?"

"Voluptuous grey-haired vixens," Armand replied with amusement. "And Miss Ellie most of all." He stood up and made for the doorway.

"Don't get into trouble," Kol warned with a grin.

"Nah," Armand replied as he walked over to the threshold. "Just going to stretch my legs, and find the privy." He threw a look over his shoulder back at Kol. "All this fruit is killing me."

Kol sheathed his knife and stuffed the whetstone into his bag, then lay back on the mattress, folding his arms behind his head. He breathed deeply as he closed his eyes. Aside from the barracks, for the majority of the time he had been in the Sornian army, he had lived in tents, sleeping on a rug on the hard ground with one ear always alert for sounds of trouble. A couple of times he had briefly been stationed in the palace at Hedda, but it was hardly more comfortable as he had to lie on the stone floor in a room full of fellow soldiers. Now, he took a moment to enjoy his surroundings, the dry security of stone walls, the softness of the mattress beneath him. He didn't know how long it would last.

"Mister Kol," a commanding voice came from the door. "Are you asleep? We want to play a card game, and we need a fourth." Kol begrudgingly sat up to see Declan leaning with one shoulder on the doorway, arms crossed.

"I'm not betting," Kol responded. "And I don't feel like drinking."

"No," Declan said. "Just a game. Come on."

Kol followed Declan to the table in the middle of the Great Room. He found himself paired up with Jon, playing against Declan and Adella in a game of Whisk. "Miss Adella is very bad at card games," Declan explained to him as he shuffled. "I had just beaten her at Quinze four times in a row before we called in reinforcements."

She laughed in acknowledgment. "I did warn you."

"I thought you were only being modest." Declan began dealing out the cards. His sleeves had been rolled up to the elbows, revealing the thick white scars that laced over his sun-tanned arms. "You weren't so bad last time we played."

"You mean at the Capital?" Adella asked, scrunching her face up as she tried to remember.

"No," Declan said. "At The Ivy Crown. In Raymouth."

Kol watched her face as she looked down, sorting through the cards in her hand. "Oh, that's right," Adella recalled quietly. "The last time I saw you. I had forgotten, because it was so long ago." Beside her, Jon laid down a card on the table.

"Yes, that time," Declan said, visibly chastened.

Kol glanced over his own cards and set one down likewise. "How long will it take them to repair the ship?" he asked.

"Depends," Declan replied with a shrug, "on how bad the rudder is. We usually carry a spare, but we had to use it during our last voyage."

Jago entered, once again carrying a loaded tea tray steadily in one hand. He set it down in front of Adella and Kol. "For your injuries," he said. "Drink it slowly." Then, he turned and left.

"Am I the only one who can't understand that man?" Declan asked, grabbing a teacup from the stack and helping himself to the teapot. He took a long draught of the tisane and pulled an ugly face, clinking the cup down on its saucer.

"Apparently," Jon replied.

Kol poured and took a sip from his cup. The liquid was a dark but luminous green, like the glass of a wine bottle. It tasted strongly herbal, and as he drank it, he noticed a feeling of warm relaxation settle over him.

"Chamomile," Adella said, peering into the liquid. "And comfrey..." Kol realized she was trying to name the herbs in the tisane. "Madorran poppy," she added with a yawn.

17

The Library

The next morning, Adella stood in the doorway of her chamber and looked about the Great Room. She knew Armand was asleep still because she could hear his characteristically loud snoring coming from the chamber beside hers. Declan and Jon were seated at the table across from each other after having just returned from the library with a set of oversized books on navigation. They were currently looking at what appeared to be a star atlas. Ballantyne and Tomas were heading out to look about the courtyard, Adella guessed from what she overheard. Jago, Ellie and the islanders were off on their respective duties. Kol was stretched out on the sofa, reading from the book she had given him.

Adella didn't wish to remain in her chamber; she wasn't used to being in a room by herself anymore. Her thoughts seemed much too loud whenever she was alone, the ache of her losses only growing heavier in the silence. She wanted to go and sit with someone for company, but everyone looked preoccupied. Declan wouldn't mind, but she certainly would be interrupting. Adella looked over at Kol again; he had nothing of his own, no name, no family, no home, not even a country now. *And yet he carries on, as brave as anything.* If Kol could do it, perhaps she could, too.

She wondered if Kol would mind sharing the sofa. He did seem the type who would rather be alone, but he always greeted her with a smile anyway. As she approached, Kol moved his legs aside to make room and closed the book when she sat down. "I didn't mean to interrupt," she said apologetically.

"I just finished it," he replied. "Though it didn't seem to have an ending."

"It's the first of a series," Adella explained. "*Jonny Reddin-Black* is a classic in Valenna. There is a set in every library in the kingdom."

"Even here?" he asked eagerly.

Adella shrugged one shoulder. "Probably."

"Help me look." He handed her grandfather's book back to her and stood up.

As they entered the library, Adella found a section of the shelving that was filled with popular novels and started to search through their titles.

"Don't you think it's a little strange there's a library here at all?" Kol wondered.

"Everything about this place is strange. Ah," she said, handing him the second novel, "here it is, *Mother Tigress*." She didn't mention there were seventeen books in the set, as she didn't want to discourage him. "This is the one Declan named his ship after," she added off-handedly. Kol opened the cover and began flipping through the pages.

Adella continued to wander around the bright space, illuminated by the late morning sun from the windows above. She walked carefully, as her injured foot began to ache, along the many freestanding bookcases that stood parallel to the shelved walls, looking up and down at the various titles and authors listed on the dusty book covers. Some she recognized, but many she did not. "This place is amazing," Adella whispered, running her finger in awe down a particularly ancient tome. She pulled out one book with odd symbols painted in gold along its spine. "Oh!" she breathed, her voice quiet but edged with excitement.

"What is it?" Kol appeared beside her.

She opened the wide leather-bound book to reveal pages filled with more of the strange pictographs, hand drawn with quill and ink. "Look familiar?"

"It's like the writing in the sea cave," he recalled, "under the images of the creatures."

"And on the woman's tomb from the sunken island," Adella added.

"But," he began, his brow creasing, "why would these people have a book written in Old Andolinian?"

"It isn't." Adella held the heavy tome in one arm while she flipped through the pages. "It's written in *three* languages." She looked up at him pointedly. "Including Modern Andolinian."

His eyes shifted from the book to her face as he realized the implications of their discovery. "A translation."

"Perhaps we can use this to decipher the charcoal rubbings." She closed the book and ran her hand over its cracked leather front. "I'm going to borrow this one."

A faint metallic sound echoed across the library and the sound of hushed voices came from the direction of the door. Though the bookcase behind them blocked her view, from their grim tone, it was clear the newcomers would not like the idea of being overheard. Adella opened her mouth to speak, but Kol placed a forefinger to his lips. While the idea of eavesdropping made her uncomfortable, she realized that, as a soldier, the skill had probably saved Kol's life more than once. She held as still as she could, quieting her breath to better hear the voices that now came from the center of the space.

"And no one else here knows? Not even that captain?" they heard a man ask in a hoarse whisper.

"No, he doesn't," a craggy voice replied. Adella recognized it as Ballantyne's.

"Are you certain?" the second man asked. *That must be Tomas,* Adella thought, recognizing his voice.

"Absolutely," Ballantyne said. "He is no concern to us. He is loyal to the Crown."

"That is good to know," Tomas replied. There was an edge in his voice that Adella caught even from the other side of the room. She thought Ballantyne must have as well, as there was a tense pause in the conversation. As Kol leaned in closer against the shelving beside her, Adella smelled the sharp aroma of Ellie's lavender salve that had been used to dress his wounds, and wondered if the other men would notice it, too.

Footsteps made their way across the floor, the sound muffled somewhat by the threadbare carpets, drawing nearer to where they hid. Adella tried not to imagine what would happen if they were discovered.

"It's our own I'm suspicious of," Ballantyne continued. "I'll need you to ferret out any traitors. See they meet a pointy end in the night." The footsteps seemed to stop on the other side of the bookcase.

"Indeed," came Tomas' reply. "There will be a reckoning, that is certain." Adella could hear one of the men rustling around in the shelving on the other side, just behind her. She recognized the muffled scrape of leather on wood as he removed a book, flipped through it, then shoved it back in place. The force jostled the books piled on top of the shelf above her, knocking some loose. Two smaller books fell to the floor by her feet; another dropped right over her shoulder onto the book she held in her arms. The hefty tome slipped from her hands, landing with a sharp thud on her injured foot. A small squeak of pain rose in her throat just as Kol clamped his hand down over her mouth.

"Did you hear that?" Ballantyne asked his companion. "I don't think we're alone in here." Adella looked at Kol, her eyes wide with panic as her mind scrambled to think of a way out of their situation. Behind them, footsteps traced along the bookcase in both directions as the two men split up to approach from either side. Her heart jumped into her throat when she heard the faint slither of metal as the men drew blades.

Adella stifled a gasp as Kol pulled her into a gap between the bookcases along the wall. She couldn't imagine how the two of them would fit into the small space, but Kol stepped close in front of her, pressing her between himself and the cool stones of the library wall to hide from the oncoming men. She buried her face into the hollow of his shoulder, feeling his heartbeat pound as fiercely as her own. The two of them flattened against the wall into the shadows, hoping the men wouldn't bother coming all the way down the passage.

The footsteps stopped at either end of the aisle, and paused a moment. "You knocked some books down, is what you heard," Tomas said. "See, on the floor?"

"I know that," Ballantyne said, sheathing his blade. Apparently satisfied with a glance down the seemingly empty passageway, the two men turned again and walked away. Adella and Kol listened breathlessly as the footsteps became fainter. Finally, the door scraped to a close on the far side of the room. When it seemed safe, Adella let out a long breath, leaning her head back against the stones in relief.

Kol laughed weakly. "That was close." His shoulders dropped a little as he let go of the tension in his muscles. Loose black curls fell across his forehead as he looked down at her, studying her face.

As Adella met his eyes and paused for a moment, thinking he might speak again, she suddenly became aware of the warmth of his hand, still resting on the curve of her side. She hesitated, then looked down at the floor. "You can let go now," she said under her breath.

"Right." He pulled his arm away quickly and stepped back.

"What do you suppose that was about?" she asked. "Those two."

"I don't know," he said. "But I didn't like the sound of it."

Adella walked over to where the tome had fallen and picked it up, holding it against her chest. She turned to face him. "Let's get out of here while we can."

Adella walked beside Kol down the long corridor toward the Great Room, their footsteps echoing far down the empty space. "Should we mention it to Miss Ellie?" she asked in a whisper.

"No," he replied quietly. "Until we find out what's going on, we don't know who to trust." He thought for a moment, then stopped and turned toward her. "Not even Declan," he warned.

Adella glanced away as he said the name. "I know," she said sharply.

At that moment, they heard footsteps approaching ahead of them. Panic welled up in Adella's chest, but it dispelled quickly when she heard a woman's voice echoing down the corridor. Ellie and Jago appeared from around the corner, chatting casually.

"Ah, there you two are," Ellie said, her face creasing with a smile. "The tables are set up in the courtyard, if you are hungry."

Kol sat between Adella and Armand at the table beneath the locust tree, the sweet scent of its white flowers perfuming the air around them. The food set before them was simple, mainly vegetables, fruits, and an herbed seafood stew. Kol wasn't sure exactly which sea creatures were used to make it. Though the broth was heavy with garlic, he ate it gratefully nonetheless.

"Is this typical Valennian food?" he asked Armand, with a hint of disappointment.

Armand shook his head, pushing his spoon around in his bowl. "Hardly. No bread, no cheese, no meat." He sighed in resignation. "I suppose it comes of being stuck on an island."

After they had eaten, Ellie offered to show them around the Cairn. The buildings were arranged in a square around long stone corridors that surrounded a central courtyard.

"The Cairn has been a Valennian outpost for over a hundred years," Ellie began. "It's been under repairs this whole time. It's a slow process, as there are only a few people in the kingdom at a time entrusted with the knowledge of its location. They used to keep a small standing army here, as it was feared the Sornians would discover the island and try to take it for their own. We are, in fact, located closer to Sornia than Valenna. Over the years, the guard was gradually relaxed, as it turns out the island is rather well protected on its own."

She led them through the corridor to a plain oak door, opening it to reveal an expansive room filled with rough wooden tables. In the corner beside the doorway sat a large copper still, its onion-shaped body and twisting tubes polished to a gleam. One of the old men stood at a table along the wall, chopping garlic. Herbs of every sort hung in bundles from the beams of the ceiling. On the far end of the space was a massive fireplace, and beside it, a stout woman in canvas breeches fed logs into the flames.

"This is the kitchen," Ellie explained, "where you'll often find Cora and Pietro." Cora turned to greet the group with a slight bow of her head. "This is where we keep our medical supplies," Ellie waved a hand toward a glass-paned mahogany cabinet along the side wall, its shelves filled with bottles and tea tins. Next, they followed Ellie out a door at the side of the kitchen that did not lead back into the corridor but outside into a broad green space. Three sides of the garden were lined with the walls of the stone buildings, but the fourth was a tall wrought-iron fence topped with sharp barbed points. The sun over-head shone brightly over the little shrubs and herbs that grew in an or-derly pattern in each garden section, divided into quarters by a stone walkway. Adella breathed in the fragrant air, heady with lavender and rosemary.

"Our kitchen garden," Ellie said. "We also have a greenhouse where we grow our fruits all year. It is near the island's summit and half a day's walk from the Cairn. Evan and Romy are traveling there now." One of the islander men kneeled in the corner, carefully trimming a rosemary topiary into a round shape. "Hayden," Ellie said, nodding at the bearded man. He smiled up at them, waving his shears in the air.

As they followed her back into the long corridor, Adella under-stood they were approaching the Great Room and dormitories. Ellie stopped before a massive iron door and, pulling a key on a string from the inside of her shirt, unlocked the door. With the harsh scrape of rusty iron, she pushed it open. "This door must remain locked. We have not finished the repairs, and this space is not secure. But I do wish to show you," she said, walking out into a large grassy area, shadowed by rock and trees overhead, "the Temple."

Adella gaped in awe as ruined stone walls and partially collapsed arches soared above their heads, intertwined with fresh, spring-green vines. Vigorous weeds grew among large chunks of stone that had collapsed from the walls long ago, and a canopy of trees from the outside forest created a dreamy dappled light around her.

"The Temple," Jago stepped forward from beside Ellie, "is Old Andolian, from the First Empire. According to legend, the First Empire was destroyed by Leveret's greed, when he stole the Heart of the World. Mundil," he said, using the Andolinian word, "in her anger, sent the Twelve Calamities to beset Andolin, until her Heart was returned."

"'Mundil,'" Adella repeated, remembering. "That was their name for our world, right?"

"Yes," Jago replied. "It means world, but it also means sea. To the Andolinians, they are one and the same."

"And which Calamity ruined this Temple?" Armand wondered.

Jago walked over to a large stone archway and reached up to clear a vine that clung to its surface. Pulling it away, he revealed three deep grooves slashed through the rock, like claw marks from some great beast. He turned again to face them with a grim expression. "It came from the water."

They returned to the corridor and continued past the entrance to the Great Room, passing one of the women on guard duty with a poleaxe in hand. "Good morning, Bettlin," Ellie said, leading the group around the corner. Jago stepped forward, this time to unlock a pair of doors covered in an aged and cracked red lacquer, and swung them wide. As the group entered the chamber, a long, wooden rack on the far wall caught their attention, loaded with many different weapons. There were swords of every type and shape, wooden practice staves, polearms, bows, and axes lined neatly along the wall. The stone floor beneath their feet was covered in thick, tightly-woven rush mats, and the room was illuminated by a series of little round windows along the walls high up by the ceiling.

"This is the Armory," Jago said. Kol walked along the racks, inspecting the more interesting weapons that hung from the wall. Jago stood by, waiting for Kol to rejoin the group, then he walked across the room to a small wooden door and opened it. Adella turned back to sneak a peek at Ballantyne and Tomas, who were still eyeing the weapons on the wall behind them. She caught them glancing at each other meaningfully and was glad that Jago kept the room locked. On the other side of the door was a wide chamber, the floor covered again in thick mats. Wooden targets painted with bulls-eyes in various shapes were piled up in the corners. "The Arena," Jago continued, "where we like to keep in practice."

"Jago spends much time here," Ellie said. "If any of you would like to try a little friendly sparring during your stay with us, I'm sure he would be glad of it." Jago nodded.

They left the Arena, walking back through the Armory, Jago locking the doors behind them. "That leaves the Tower," Ellie said, continuing onward. They came to another bend in the corridor and stopped at the broad iron door set at an angle into the corner. She opened it, and they all passed through, gathering in the empty space in front of the spiral staircase. Adella sighed heavily at the sight of it.

Ellie went up the stone steps, running her hand lightly along the iron railing as the others followed along behind in single file. Adella waited for everyone else to go ahead before trudging up. By the time she had reached the top and joined the others, her foot was sore and throbbing angrily.

The top of the tower was open to the air, and a cool breeze hit their faces as they looked out over the landscape below. Ellie pointed out features of the landscape to the group as they admired the view, and Adella leaned on the stone sill facing out over the cliffs to view the turquoise lagoon far below. Beyond that, she could see the opening in the stone cliffs that their longboat had passed through as they came upriver on their way to the island. She squinted as she tried to focus her eyes to the distance, and thought she could make out the shape of their boat on the shore. She looked with longing once again on the placid blue-green waters below, remembering the unexpected warmth as she dipped her fingers into the lagoon the day they arrived.

Crossing over to the other side, Adella could see the layout of the Cairn, with the square courtyard in the center. At the farthest corner, broken arches overlooked the green lawn within the ruined Temple. Far ahead of her in the misty distance, covered in a thick canopy of trees, the island rose steadily to its summit. Ellie joined her, leaning on the sill. "The island, it's much larger than I realized," Adella said.

Ellie smiled. "It's vast, and wild, and full of mysteries that we haven't yet begun to understand." Her smile faded away. "But I shall have to go back to the Capital now."

There was a sadness in her voice that Adella understood all too well. "Will you be able to return?"

"I hope so," Ellie replied, turning to face her. "This is my home."

Adella waited for the others to head back down the spiral staircase that wrapped around the inside of the tower before slumping down against the stone rail, stretching her legs out in front of her. She sighed heavily as she rested her head against the cold rock behind her, looking up at the impressive brass bell suspended from the ceiling beams. She closed her eyes, focusing on the cool breeze playing on her face rather than the ache in her foot, or the deeper pain that threatened to well up again in her heart. She squeezed her eyes shut tighter to keep them dry.

She didn't know what she would do on her return. If she accepted her father's role, she would have a future; the king would be sure she was cared for. But when she'd told Declan she'd taken on her father's title, it had been a bluff. Truthfully, Adella didn't feel she deserved to take on that responsibility. Everything terrible that had happened so far—the plague, the deaths on *The Accord,* the destruction of Elldon, everything Lucas had done—all of it was her fault in some way. Even her parents' deaths, though an act of nature, felt somehow intimately connected to her actions, to all of the choices she had made in her life. She didn't know how to go on. *I can't possibly accept the title when I'm so wholly unworthy. It would be disastrous. And haven't I done enough damage already?*

Adella lost track of how long she lay there when she gradually came to notice the muffled sound of voices coming up from the stairwell. Deciding she had tarried long enough, Adella wiped her eyes, then picked her skirts up to descend the tower. There, she found Kol sitting at the bottom step with Armand, who was recounting an old story from his days in the cavalry. As she came down the last few steps, they turned to her expectantly.

"Ready?" Armand asked, and Adella was touched to realize they were waiting for her. She nodded, and they headed back together.

"So," Kol began, as they walked down the corridor, "if this place is simply a half-forgotten outpost of aged soldiers, why are they rich?"

Adella stopped suddenly. "What do you mean?"

"A bedstead and mattress for each person, porcelain, books." He turned to face her, lightly running his hand down the sleeve of her new bodice. "Silk."

Adella almost laughed, but held her tongue when she saw the earnest look on his face, and her amusement quickly turned to pity. "Do only the rich have those things in Sornia?" He nodded, his eyes darting briefly away. Adella understood he didn't want to talk about the things he lacked in his life. They continued down the corridor.

"Well, you're not Sornian anymore," Armand said as they turned a corner. "You'll have to get used to being Valennian now."

"Is that possible?" Kol raised his brows. "Can I become Valennian?"

"Sure," Adella replied. "It's quite simple. You only need seven respectable Valennians to vouch for your character, a noble to petition for you, then you take an oath at the Capital."

"So many?" Kol asked, his features falling in disappointment.

"Or there's the easy way—" Armand began, but he stopped short when Adella shook her head at him. Kol noticed but didn't ask.

"Seven isn't that many," Adella said encouragingly. "Of course, Armand and I would vouch for you, and I'm sure anyone on *The Tigress* would as well." She smiled at him, but Kol appeared unconvinced.

"You said they needed to be respectable?" he asked. They all stopped before the door to the Great Room.

Adella laughed this time. "They'll be good enough." Armand pulled open the heavy door and went inside.

Kol paused at the doorway, turning to face Adella. "What will you do?" he asked. "When we return. Where will you go?"

Adella let the door swing closed again beside her. "I don't know." She twisted the little gold and coral ring around on her finger. "If I accept my father's title, I will have to take on his responsibilities. I'd have to go to the Capital and face the king..." she paused, biting her lips. "I'm not sure I can do it."

"And if you don't?" he asked.

"I will have to live on my portion of the inheritance," she replied. "It won't last long, but no one will care where I go, or what I do."

"That doesn't sound so bad," Kol reasoned with a shrug.

"No, it doesn't." Adella smiled a little, as she had lately been thinking the same thing. She didn't see how she could take the title in good conscience. However, if she were to refuse it, Adella felt she'd be disappointing not only her parents but also her ancestors, all the way back to Sir Adelo Grimless. She didn't try to explain this to Kol, partly because she wasn't sure he'd understand. Mostly, though, she didn't want to remind him again of what he lacked. Adella opened the door, and they went in.

<h1 style="text-align:center">18</h1>

<h1 style="text-align:center">The Codex</h1>

Adella sat in the Great Room, the musty leather tome she and Kol had found in the library open before her. Evening was falling, and the light from the high windows grew more dim with each passing moment. She yawned as she flipped slowly through the pages; the others had mostly retired to their dormitories, except for Kol and Declan. Kol lay on the sofa on the far side of the room, his stockinged feet on the arm while he read *Mother Tigress,* though Adella wasn't sure how much reading he was getting done; it seemed every other time she looked around the room, he was glancing over at her instead of down at the book. Declan, however, had just entered the Great Room and sat down at the table beside her. She presumed he had just come from the kitchen, since he returned with a bottle of wine in one hand and a pewter goblet in the other. Adella watched as he poured the dark red liquid from the bottle into the goblet and drank.

"Why don't you just drink from the bottle?" she asked curiously.

"Because," Declan said with a smile, "I am civilized." He watched her turn the pages for a moment.

Adella groaned as she rubbed her tired eyes. "I wish I had brought the charcoal papers with me."

"You want to translate the glyphs?" Declan scratched his chin for a moment, where a thick blond beard had started to grow in. "I locked the papers in my cabin, along with the iron box." He took another sip of wine. "Would you like me to bring them back for you? I was thinking of returning to the ship tomorrow to check on their progress."

"Would you do that?" she asked. "Thank you."

"Wine?" he offered, and she nodded. "But—" He waved the goblet and the bottle both in the air. "Are you civilized, or uncivilized?"

She smiled for a moment, his silly question reminding her of their friendship from years ago. Adella reached for the bottle, and took a sip.

"Ah!" he said, feigning surprise. "As I suspected."

They drank together in silence for a time, until Adella spoke. "You never told me what happened."

"I can't." A cold and distant look crept over his face. "Even now, I can't bring myself to speak of it. It would do you no good to know."

She shrugged. "If you say so."

"Do you hold it against me still?" He looked down into the goblet.

"No," she said quietly. "But it was a hard lesson to learn so young."

He frowned. "And what lesson was that?"

She didn't answer, only pressed her lips together. Then, she pulled the coral ring from her finger and held it out to him. "Perhaps I should give this back."

"It was a gift," he said softly. "If you give it back, it will break my heart."

Adella shrugged. "Then at least we would be even." She hesitated, turning the ring over in her hands before finally slipping it back onto her finger. "But I suppose I don't want revenge."

"That's a good sign." He reached forward and took her hand in his, kissing the back of it lightly. "Goodnight, Adella." He stood up, taking the goblet with him and leaving the bottle behind.

"Goodnight, Rogero." She waited until Declan shut the door of the dormitory behind him. Adella took another swig from the bottle and set it down. Exhaling loudly, she rubbed her face. *I never wanted to see him again,* she reminded herself. Five years had passed since they last met, since the night Rogero, her dearest friend, had told Adella he was in love with her. *Five years since we passed that night together...* He was gone before the sun even rose. She hadn't heard from him until a year later, when he began writing to her as if nothing had happened, and her heart had been broken all the while. *Damn.* She slammed the book closed and shoved it away, then, laying her head on her folded arms, closed her eyes.

Adella woke in her own room, and it took her a moment to remember that Kol had roused her from the table and sent her to bed sometime in the night. She dressed, combed her hands through her hair, then left to eat breakfast with the others. The meal was served at the tables in the kitchen this time, as it was a drizzly, grey morning. Cracks of lightning would now and then flash in the windows through the haze of rain on the glass.

Afterward, she sat at the table in the Great Room, studying the large tome from the library again. She drew the horse-patterned shawl tighter around her shoulders against the cold, damp morning air. Kol sat beside her, silently reading from his own little novel, occasionally looking over as she flipped through the pages. The translated text told of the deeds of the High Kings of Andolin, which Adella presumed to date from the time of the First Empire. As she read the story in the Modern tongue, she turned the pages to follow along in the strange glyphs of Old Andolinian. A pattern began to form in her mind of the language's structure, and she began to recognize variations of each glyph. There was a little symbol that was sometimes drawn beneath them, a little wiggling line that reminded her of water. Adella continued to flip back and forth between the two languages, comparing the pictographs to the Modern translation.

"Captain Jago," Adella said as he walked by. "Do you know anything of the Old Andolinian language?"

"No," he replied. "The old words are lost. Only remnants in our names, now." Jago leaned his polearm on the edge of the table and took a seat on the other side of her, gazing with interest at the ancient book.

"Do you know this story?" she asked.

He nodded. "High King *Daw Claer,*" he said, pointing to a painted illustration within the text. "He came from across the sea. He rode the *Haramund*—" Jago paused for a moment. "The Sea Horse." He pointed to a beast drawn along the margin of the page, its serpentine form wrapping around the border. Adella thought it resembled the creature she had seen in the water recently, with bulging black eyes.

"He rode that thing?" she asked in amusement.

"Don't get any ideas, Adella," Kol warned.

She pointed to a pair of combined glyphs, one resembling a horse. "This must be the word *Haramund.* Which means—" She turned to the previous page and pointed to one of the glyphs from the pair, this time written alone. It was one line, spiralled around into a circle. "This must be the other part. *Mund.*"

Jago glanced at the glyph, then smiled as he pulled back his sleeve and showed his wrist, revealing a small image of the same spiral drawn in ink under his skin. It was faded and blue with age. "*Mundil,*" he said. "The Lady of the Deep."

"So, your people," Kol began. "They worship the sea?"

Jago nodded. "She is our Sea, and our World, and our Mother."

Adella tapped her lip thoughtfully. "What was the name for the Heartstone?"

"*Corelimun,*" Jago replied. "Heart of the World."

"What is the name for that weapon?" Kol asked, nodding toward the polearm.

Jago shrugged. "We use the Modern word. Glaive."

Adella flipped the pages, stopping at a colorful illustration of a battle scene by the seashore. She pointed to the image of a fearsome beast that was attacking a rider, as the man fought back with a strange weapon, one very similar to the one leaning on the table before her now. The animal was drawn with teeth protruding grotesquely from its mouth. "What is the name of that beast?"

"*Pelkimund*," Jago said. "Sea Wolf."

"It looks like the fish that dragged you under," Kol commented.

"Yes, it—" She stopped abruptly, her brow furrowing. "How did you know?"

"I jumped in after you," he replied. "But I was too late."

She looked at him in surprise as she realized the implications of what he said. "You did?" she asked incredulously. "You went into the water?" He nodded.

Stunned by the revelation, she watched Kol's face for a moment but could read nothing in his expression. *But he's afraid of the water...* Adella froze, blinking, as she tried to understand. *But why would he...* Realizing she had been staring at him, Adella looked down in embarrassment.

Returning her attention to the book, she located another doubled glyph; one half bore a resemblance to jagged teeth, the other was the same familiar swirl inked on Jago's wrist. "This must be *Pelkimund*." She noticed half of the image repeated often in the text of the next page. "So this by itself must mean... wolf?" she guessed hesitantly. "But there are no wolves in the picture at all." Tapping her lip, she noticed the little wavy line beneath each glyph. "That must change the meaning somehow," she mumbled to herself.

"You two seem clever, I think you'll figure it out." Jago stood up. "I must return to my duties, but I will be around." He took his glaive and left.

Soon, Declan emerged from the doorway of his chamber with a canvas pack on his shoulders. He shoved his cockaded hat onto his head over his neatly tied queue. Jon followed close behind, throwing the strap of a haversack across his chest. They stood by until Ballantyne and Tomas approached them, also dressed for travel.

"Still heading to *The Tigress*?" Adella asked Declan from across the room. She had wondered if they would still go after the change in weather.

"Of course," he said, grinning back at her. "You think I'd mind a little water?" The other men pulled on their oilskin cloaks and turned toward him expectantly, ready to leave. Declan nodded a goodbye to Adella and led the sailors out of the Great Room.

As the last man walked out the door, he held it open for Ellie to enter. Approaching the table, she set her box of medical supplies down on the table by Kol, who pulled off his shirt for her to unwrap the bandages underneath. His wound was nothing more than a thick red scar now, and the cut on his shoulder had healed to a wide black scab. She took his hand and removed the dressing from his palm, inspecting the stitching carefully. "It looks like it's ready," Ellie said, reaching for a pair of tiny shears from the box. "We may remove the stitches now."

"Are you sure?" Kol asked. "It's only a week old."

"The salve I applied accelerates the healing process," she explained. "You'll still have to be careful with it, of course. I could leave them in longer if you want, but the scarring will be worse."

"No, take them out. Please," he added. Ellie alternated between the tiny shears and a pair of tongs to pull the thread from his skin. Kol inspected the scab on his hand, then held it up, grinning as he showed his palm to Adella.

Ellie then sat beside Adella and set her left leg carefully in her lap. She removed the bandages and looked over the slash that ran down the arch of the foot toward the largest toe. "Hm," Ellie said, pressing on the edges of the wound thoughtfully.

"Will you remove mine as well?" Adella asked, eyebrows lifting hopefully. "We were injured on the same day."

"It's not ready," Ellie said, shaking her head. "It's healing well but still too swollen. It needs to be held together a while longer."

"Oh..." Adella's shoulders drooped. "I see." Ellie opened a clear glass bottle filled with a golden liquid. Pouring a little on a cloth, she dabbed it gently over the top of the injured foot. Adella noticed a sweet, floral aroma and inhaled deeply. "That smells lovely," she commented.

"Jasmine and chamomile," Ellie replied, "for the swelling." As she packed up her box of supplies, she noticed the open book. "I see you've found the Codex."

Adella nodded. "I was hoping I could use it to translate some Old Andolinian glyphs we found."

Ellie arched a brow. "That's an ambitious undertaking." She eyed Adella thoughtfully. "I tried to do that myself, years ago."
"And?" Adella prompted. "Did you make any progress?"

"A little." Ellie gave a small laugh. "To be honest, I gave up. But I don't mean to discourage you. I still have my old papers tucked away somewhere, I'll see if I can find them. Perhaps they could be of some use." She then took up her box and left.

Adella looked up to see Kol pulling a face. "What?" she asked defensively.

"You can't have your stitches removed yet because you've been careless," he chided. "Put your foot up."

Adella frowned at him. "That's amusing, coming from you. You let your side rot, remember?" She leaned against the back of her chair, folding her arms. "You're lucky you're still alive."

"I know." Kol looked down at his hands, one corner of his mouth lifting into a smile. "I never thanked you for that."

Adella was taken aback by the change in his tone, as she expected to bicker with him more. "For what?"

"For not leaving me there," he said, raising his eyes to meet hers, "to die."

"How could I?" She dismissed the idea with a wave of her hand "Don't think of it." She set her foot up on the chair beside her and went back to studying the Codex.

Adella glanced over at Kol, watching him flex and relax his fingers as he tested his newly healed hand. She thought about what he had said, about jumping into the water after her. *Was it only because I had Leveret's key?* she wondered. *Or was it because—* Her thoughts were interrupted when Kol looked up to meet her eyes, and she turned away quickly. *Don't be silly,* she told herself. *It's best not to read too much into it.* She had learned that lesson years ago from Rogero.

* * *

Declan set his oar down and grabbed the suspended rope ladder, then climbed up and over the rail, dropping to the deck on the other side. As he waited for the others to join him from the longboat, he surveyed *The Tigress* critically. Tools and supplies were strewn about the decks haphazardly, and filthy water still poured over the deck from the bilge. Some of the men he could see appeared to be hard at work, while a few loafed drunkenly here and there. An empty barrel rolled slowly toward him across the planks.

Captain Declan brought his foot down onto the rounded side of the barrel, putting an end to its migration. He uprighted it, then strode forward furiously, looking for someone to reprimand. "Trelauny!" he shouted, his voice booming across the ship. The other men followed behind as Declan made his way toward the officer's quarters. Beside the steps, two young sailors leaned against the bulwark together, embracing as they kissed. As he walked by, Declan stopped and rounded on the two abruptly.

"Childric!" Declan growled. "What have I told you?"

One of the young men turned to face the captain, his eyes widening in terror. "No dallying on the ship, sir?" he answered timidly.

"Not on the—" Declan repeated through gritted teeth, "*ship!*" He shouted the last word as he threw his hat at the young man. "You," Declan pointed to the sailor behind Childric, who had been one of the crew from *The Quest.* "Swab the quarter deck. Now!" He watched as the man scrambled away as fast as he could, then Declan turned back toward Childric. "Where's Trelauny?" he demanded.

"Well, he's—" Childric began. "You see, there was..." Declan narrowed his eyes at him, and the young man took a breath and braced himself. "He had an accident. Fell from the topmast, as we can figure. He's recovering below." Childric picked up the captain's hat and handed it back. "Dennick has taken over command."

Declan snatched his hat from him and put it on again. "Clean this up," he ordered. "All of it. Clean *everything*." He stomped away toward the officer's quarters with Ballantyne, Jon and Tomas following along behind.

Captain Declan came down the steps and looked around at the injured men resting in hammocks. He found Trelauny by his characteristic ginger hair hanging over the side, and, quieting his footsteps, walked over to him. The first mate's head had been bandaged, the cloth upon his brow stained brown with dried blood.

"Cornelius," Declan leaned down to speak close. "Are you awake?"

Trelauny's eyelids fluttered, then he slowly opened his eyes. Wincing, he turned his head to face the captain. "Moffat," he murmured.

"Moffat?" Declan's eyebrows lowered as he recognized the name of the first mate from *The Quest*. "What about him?"

"Awake," Trelauny replied weakly, then his head rolled to the side.

Declan pressed his fingers against the first mate's neck, then stood to face the men behind him, looking on in concern. "He is dead." Declan narrowed his eyes. "Find Dennick. He has much to answer for."

19

A Bottle or Two

Armand's stomach growled, but his heart sank at the thought of what might be served for supper. Breakfast that morning had been, in his estimation, a tragedy. He didn't think he could stomach any more of Cora's garlicky concoctions and decided he'd better intervene. By his reckoning, it was the second day of June, and the day of King's Feast. If he had been back at Greywood Manor still with Lord and Lady Grimless, there would have been a celebration, with guests and an elaborate meal planned. Their oldest daughter, Margavita, would travel from the Capital with her husband, children, and servants of their own to join them, and some of their closest neighbors would be invited as well. That wasn't happening this year. *Or ever again,* he thought bitterly. The only Grimless he had left to care for now was Miss Adella. She didn't seem to be keeping track of the days, and he wasn't going to let this one be lost amongst the turmoil of the recent events. *I could go in on the pretense of being helpful,* he told himself, *and commandeer the kitchen.* He chuckled mischievously as he walked down the corridor.

He opened the door to the kitchen to find Pietro chopping herbs at the table, and Cora digging vigorously through bottles on the shelf. Her curly hair was escaping from her kerchief, all in a disarray. "Could you two use a hand?" Armand asked amiably.

"Oh goodness, yes," Cora replied, a harried expression straining her face. "It's King's Feast and we've run low on our winter stores. Romy and Evan haven't come back yet from the greenhouse, and I don't know what to do for supper." She wiped her hands on an apron that hung down over her knee-breeches.

"Well, what do we have to work with?" Armand asked. "What's the best meat we can get today?"

"There's not a lot in the way of hunting," Cora said. "There are some good sized birds here, but we're not allowed to eat them." She thought for a moment. "We have ducks here too, but they can be hard to get. We might waste our time trying."

"What about the rock eels?" Pietro offered, looking up from his work. "They're easy to come by and pretty tasty, with plenty of fat for cooking."

"Eels?" Armand asked pensively, scratching a grey sideburn. He remembered the large eel that Adella had caught from the pool in the Campos. It had been surprisingly delicious. "Yes, that may do."

"Pietro and I can go catch them," Cora offered. "They are just in the river cave by the lagoon. If you can get a broth started in the pot," she nodded toward the large iron crucible on the hearth, "and prepare vegetables, that would be great." She pointed to a cupboard on the other side of the room. "I think there are some tubers left, if they haven't sprouted." She sighed loudly as she untied the strings of her apron and hung it on a hook on the stone wall beside her. "Cooking never was my specialty, but I took over the job when Delphine passed." A shadow passed over her expression. "I try my best, but I just don't have a knack for it."

"Don't you worry, just go fetch those eels," Armand replied. "Oh, before you go," he added hastily, "where's the wine?"

Cora paused by the door, pointing vaguely to one of the cabinets that lined the side wall. "Help yourself," she smiled. "It's King's Feast, after all."

* * *

Adella sat at the table, rubbing her forehead in frustration over the Codex when Jago came through the door of the Great Room. He stopped beside the table, setting the end of his glaive on the floor with a sharp tap.

"Miss Ellie says you've healed," Jago said to Kol. "Would you like to spar in the arena? I like to keep in practice." Kol set his book down and glanced over at Adella.

"Go on," she said. "Don't sit here bored on my account."

Kol followed Jago into the corridor, leaving her in the Great Room alone. They hadn't seen Armand since breakfast, and Adella wondered what he was doing. She was just about to go and look about the Cairn for him when Ellie returned with a large writing box and sat beside her.

"Perhaps this will help you," Ellie said, setting the box before her. "I'm sorry I haven't been around much. I've been working on the recipe for the medicine. I think I've got it now; I just need Romy and Evan to return from the greenhouse with the last ingredient." Her forehead wrinkled. "If they aren't back by tonight, I'll head out in the morning myself. We don't have any more time to spare."

"Thanks," Adella said as she looked through the contents of the box. Closing it gently, she let out a sigh. "What will happen when we get to the Capital?" she asked. "You can't make enough medicine for the whole population, surely?"

"Our first duty is to save the king," Ellie replied. "Then the healers. We will teach them how to create the medicine themselves, so they can tend to the people. That's the best we can do."

"The king has no heir..." Adella began tentatively. "Who would be next in line for the throne, if he succumbs to the plague?"

"They would likely call upon the Queen Mother to be steward until a successor is chosen," Ellie replied, frowning. "But, there has been a small cabal of vipers growing within the palace that believe the throne should pass to King Harrian's cousin, Lord Hollen."

"Lord Hollen?" Adella asked pensively. "I've heard my parents speak of him often, and never anything good."

"We'll have to hope for the best, then." Ellie gave a wan smile. "I came here to retire, to live the rest of my days in peace. I didn't think I'd ever return to the Capital."

"You never wanted to go back?" Adella wondered.

"I had lived many years under the weight of my duties," Ellie explained. "To my husband, to my country, to my title. It wears on you."

"I didn't realize you were married," Adella said. "To Captain Jago?"

"No," Ellie said with a laugh. "Jago took a vow of celibacy when he became my guard, and I have had enough of men for one lifetime. My husband died twenty years ago." She leaned forward, resting her elbows on the table. "I loved him, of course, but one was quite enough for me."

"I must decide," Adella began, "if I will accept my father's title or not. I don't think I could live up to it. I'm thinking of refusing. Living a quiet life somewhere, far away from court." She pressed her lips together. "What would you do?"

"We want the same thing. But—" Ellie let out a long breath, leaning back against the chair. "I don't believe life should be so small, beholden only to ourselves. If we are given the opportunity to make a difference in the world, to possibly make the lives of others better in some way, I feel we are obligated to take it. And you may be needed by the Crown soon."

"Do you think so?" Adella looked down at the table. "I understand that the lives of many now depend on you. But what use could anyone have for me? I have no skill in politics, no talent for leadership."

"Those things come with experience," Ellie replied. "What you do have, is an inheritance. Your ancestor took an oath to serve the throne of Valenna, and so bound his descendants in that oath. Each one since has benefitted from his service. Riches, influence, land. You were given much; it would only be right to give your service in return."

Adella fiddled with the gold ring on her finger. "I hadn't thought about it like that."

"That is why I must go, anyway. And stay as long as I am needed," Ellie replied. "But you asked what *I* would do. You must make your own choice."

Kol walked briskly behind Jago as they entered the Armory. Jago stood in front of the weapons rack, leaning his glaive against the wall, and pulled out a couple of wooden practice swords. "That girl," Jago said casually, holding one out to him. "Very pretty."

Kol took the offered weapon. "Yes, I'm aware," he said begrudgingly as they stepped into the arena.

Jago stood to face him in the center of the space. "Are you two—"

"No," Kol interrupted. He tried the weight of the weapon in his right hand. "What's it to you?"

"Just making conversation," Jago replied in his heavy accent. "No need to be defensive."

"Oh." Kol pulled a half-smile. "Well, you're killing me."

Jago laughed. "Not one for small talk?" Not receiving a reply, he moved into a formal on-guard position. "Ready, then?" Kol nodded, and Jago swung his sword around in a low side strike.

Kol parried easily, then brought his sword up in an arc to block a higher blow. He was impressed at the speed at which the older man could move, especially for his age. They continued to spar with the wooden swords for a time, then returned to the armory to look over the other weapons.

"Tell me about that—" Kol nodded toward Jago's polearm against the wall. "The glaive. What's it for?"

"It was designed to be used from horseback," Jago replied, "though it's pretty handy on the ground as well." He walked over and lifted the glaive from where it rested and presented it to Kol. "The hook on the back of the blade is used to pull your enemy from his horse."

Kol took the glaive and looked it over. "Can you show me how to use it?"

"Certainly." Striding toward the far wall, Jago pulled out a wooden target from the pile in the corner. "There are few of us left, now, who know how. I would be glad to pass on what I know."

Armand opened cupboard after cupboard, shoving bottles and jars around to see what he had to work with. He pulled the cork from a green onion-shaped bottle and sniffed; the pungent smell of hard spirits hit his nose, rather than the wine he was expecting. He shrugged to himself, and took a swig from the bottle. It burned as it went down, from his throat all the way to his heart. He took the bottle with him as he crossed over to the hearth, taking another draught from it as he stirred the contents of the pot on the fire. Then he moved to the table to prepare the vegetables, pausing to drink again every so often, humming an old cavalry tune while he worked.

Adella wandered into the kitchen, looking about the room. "I wondered where you'd gone," she said. "I've given myself a headache staring at that book. I wonder if there's something here for it."

"Try this," he said, handing her the bottle.

She took a draught from it. "Ugh, that's awful," she said, grimacing, then took another before handing the bottle back. "That should do it."

Cora and Pietro soon returned with a basket full of large rock eels, which they helped clean and prepare for cooking. After tasting the broth and looking over the vegetables, they saw he had things under control. The two left to set the tables in the courtyard, as the weather had cleared up and the sun shone brightly again through the high windows.

Armand cast a pointed look at Adella. "Are you going to help, or just stand there?" He didn't wait for an answer before handing her a paring knife. "Make yourself useful."

Adella took the knife and, watching to see how he peeled the carrots, tried to mimic his actions. Her grip slipped and the blade ran across the edge of her thumb. "Damn," she whispered as a drop of blood trickled out, and put her thumb to her mouth.

"Don't bleed on the vegetables," Armand reprimanded. She nicked her fingers a few more times before getting the hang of it.

They worked quietly for a while before Adella spoke again. "Do you think, if I hadn't gone after Lucas..." she began tentatively. "Do you think he and Tess would still be alive?"

Armand set the knife down and looked over at her from across the table. "Are you looking for a way to blame yourself for what happened?"

"Perhaps Tess, at least, would still be with us," she said quietly.

Armand let out a long breath. "Tess had been in love with your brother for quite some time. She'd have gone after him regardless."

Adella looked up, a puzzled expression crossing her face. "Really? Why didn't she tell me?"

Armand shrugged. "You're pretty reserved about things like that. She probably figured you don't like to discuss personal affairs."

"Oh." Adella looked down to resume her work, hiding her face by the tilt of her head.

"Try not to dwell on it. Here," he said, handing her the bottle of spirits. "This will help. That's how I get by, anyway."

* * *

Jon shuffled down the steps to the captain's cabin. "Sir," he approached the desk where Declan stood. "Dennick isn't on the ship. No one knows where he is, but the quarter boat is gone as well as several of the men. From both crews."

Declan opened a drawer of the desk and pulled out a small writing box. He turned toward Jon, his mind puzzling to understand. "Why would he..." he trailed off, deep in thought.

"Perhaps they went in search of more timber?" Jon guessed.

Declan opened the flap of his haversack to place the writing box within, but he paused, turning the object over in his hands. Then, a thought struck him. "Where is the first mate from *The Quest*? Moffat, I think his name was."

"He is one of them that's missing," he replied. "Must've gone with Dennick, we figure."

"Dennick," Declan muttered tensely, "left without notice. Without passing on the command." He set the writing box forcefully on his desk, overcome by anger. "I'm going to head back for the Royal Apothecary. We must get her to Valenna at whatever cost. You will remain here in command."

"Yes, sir," Jon replied.

"You must finish repairing the ship before we return. No more breaks for the crew, no more drink until it's completed. I'm counting on you," he said, pointing a finger. "Every life in Valenna is counting on you."

"I give you my word, sir," Jon said with a nod. "It will be done."

As Declan made his way across the cabin, he paused. "If Dennick returns before I do," he added, "put him in chains. I will deal with him later."

* * *

After trying out various other weapons, Kol and Jago took up the wooden training swords to spar once more. No matter how swiftly Jago brought his sword around to strike, Kol brought his own up to meet it.

"Touch," Jago said as Kol stepped forward and tapped his arm with the training sword. According to Jago's rules, they would continue until one of them made five limb touches, or one body strike. Jago blocked a strike from his right, then spun around to parry the next on his left. Kol pushed forward into it, then quickly pulled his weapon back and thrust again to tap the old man carefully in the ribs. "Match," Jago said. "Again."

They stepped back into their preferred defensive stances; Jago nodded, and they began. "Touch," Jago said, as Kol hit him lightly in the arm. Kol retreated, then lunged forward. Jago parried with his sword, but Kol shoved to one side, tapping Jago in the thigh while his other side was open. "Two," Jago said, stepping back into position. They continued to practice, parrying each other's strikes until Kol tapped Jago in the chest. "Match," Jago conceded again. "Either I'm getting old, or you're very skilled." Jago walked over toward the wall and pulled out a third practice sword. "Would you like more of a challenge?" he asked, and Kol nodded.

They stepped into their formal stances again, this time with Jago holding two weapons. He made for a side strike on Kol's left, which was blocked, then he tried again from the other side. Kol swept his sword easily across his body to block that one as well, and quickly ran it down along the other sword, twisting it around as it came toward the handle. The weapon wrenched from Jago's hand and arced in the air above their heads. Kol caught it by the handle with his left hand, and in one smooth motion, brought it down to disarm Jago's other hand as well, and Jago's sword dropped onto the mat.

Feeling pleased with himself, Kol tossed both his weapons simultaneously up in the air, spinning them around before catching them again by the handles. "Ha!" he said triumphantly.

"Show-off," Adella teased from behind him. Kol didn't realize she had been standing there and the sound of her voice startled him, causing him to bounce and fumble both swords before they clattered down to the mat. Jago laughed.

"How long have you been there?" Kol asked, turning to face her.

Adella smiled, still holding the bottle of spirits in one hand. "Long enough to be impressed."

Kol bent to retrieve the swords he dropped. "Just glad to have the use of my hand again," he said with a grin.

"I'm sure," she replied. "Dinner is ready."

Iron cressets filled with burning pieces of wood lit the darkening courtyard under the purple clouds of twilight. Dancing shadows stretched out on the lawn around the two long, rough tables set with porcelain piled full of different foods. The warm aroma of herbs and roasted eel meat overpowered the perfume of locust flowers and green grass while the island inhabitants and guests gathered together, taking their seats. Kol raised an eyebrow as he watched Adella fill her teacup with clear liquid from a green bottle. She was wearing a different dress than she had on earlier, this one a faded pink color. Where she was getting all these clothes from, he could not guess. When Adella caught him eyeing her teacup dubiously, she offered the bottle, and he took a deep swig, stifling a cough as he drank. It had no flavor but burned his nose and down to his gut.

"I can't believe you're drinking that," Kol said hoarsely, handing it back to her. A lopsided grin spread across her face, and he realized she had likely been drinking it for a while. He turned toward Armand on his other side just in time to see him take a swig from a similar bottle of his own. "What is going on?" Kol asked.

"It's King's Feast," Armand replied, a faint slur in his voice. "Valennian holiday, I'll explain later. Here," he said, pressing the bottle into Kol's hand. "Try to relax a little. Don't leave me to drink alone."

"You're not," Kol replied. "Adella's at it, too."

"She doesn't count," Armand said. "She's just a child."

"I heard that," Adella leaned over to look past Kol, narrowing her eyes at Armand. "And I'm almost twenty-three."

"'Almost?'" Armand repeated with a smirk. "Only a child would say that." Adella made a face but was unable to counter his logic. The three of them returned their attention to their food, which Kol found to be very good.

After a time, when all had eaten, the islanders went around and filled the glasses with wine. Ellie stood at the head of the table and lifted her glass to first thank Armand for the meal, then she began to recite a very long and tedious speech, apparently from memory, pleading for the health of the king and the well-being of his country. Kol put up a good effort to listen, but soon grew bored of it, turning to the bottle Armand gave him for diversion. As he drank, it burned the back of his throat so viciously he thought he might choke, and was surprised to see Adella sipping the harsh spirits daintily from her teacup.

When the toast had finally ended and everyone raised their wine glass, Kol noticed Jago was the only one who did not take a sip.

After the toast, games were brought out. Bettlin and Hayden set up ninepins in the grass using empty wine bottles, while Pietro brought out a deck of cards and convinced Armand, Cora, and Kol to join him. Ellie, Jago and Adella sat at the table with them, watching them play at Whisk in the golden light of the cresset fires.

"Mister Kol," Adella began, "what games do they play in Sornia? Do they play cards there, too?" She took a sip from her teacup, which was now filled with wine rather than the clear spirits Armand was still drinking.

Kol shrugged. "The officers did. The rest of us didn't really care for cards."

"So what did you do for diversion?" Armand asked.

Kol paused to think. "We would mostly get drunk and start fights."

"You didn't play any games?" Ellie asked.

"Well," Kol said, smiling as he remembered, "when we were stationed in the Campos, we would ride the horses bareback, and try to knock each other off with sticks."

"That does sound amusing," Adella admitted.

Ellie watched as Armand took a swig from the green glass bottle, and laughed in surprise. "Are you drinking tincture spirits?"

Armand shrugged, his face a rosy pink. "I couldn't find the wine."

"Do you enjoy it?" Ellie asked incredulously. "I use that to make medicine, we don't drink it ourselves."

Kol laughed loudly at that. When he had composed himself again, he turned to Adella. "Why am I always Mister Kol? I'd never been called Mister a day in my life before I met you."

"It's just good manners," she replied. "Do they not have manners in Sornia?"

"Apparently not," he said. "But just Kol is fine." Adella nodded in acknowledgment.

"All right," Armand slurred. "Kol it is, then."

"I meant that for Adella," Kol joked. He was not nearly as drunk as Armand, but he was beginning to feel the wine.

Armand set a card down on the pile, then looked over at Ellie, sitting across the table from him. She, like Adella, had changed into evening clothes before the feast. "That dress looks great on you," Armand commented. "As a matter of fact," he muttered off-handedly, "so would I." The whole table fell silent for a moment, the islanders all glancing nervously around at each other. Ellie's stoic face softened in amusement, and then she began to chuckle. The others followed likewise, and soon everyone broke into laughter. Kol looked anxiously at Jago, wondering if he'd have to break up a fight between two old men, but Jago appeared as amused as the others.

"Perhaps you should switch to water," Ellie suggested after she caught her breath. "It seems as though you aren't feeling yourself."

"I suppose I'm not," Armand agreed. "Could I feel you instead?" Once again, Ellie laughed heartily, dabbing at the corner of her eye. Adella hid her face behind her hand, and Kol thought he heard her snort.

Ellie pushed her chair back and stood. "Romy and Evan haven't returned yet from the greenhouse," she explained. "I'll have to head out early in the morning to retrieve the last ingredient. I'm afraid you'll have to excuse me now, I have a long list of things to do." She bowed her head to them, and turned to leave.

"Pencil me in, will you?" Armand called after her. Ellie didn't turn to respond, but her shoulders bobbed with laughter as she disappeared into the Cairn, with Jago close behind.

Adella removed her hands from her face. "I've never been so mortified," she scolded Armand, but the effect was lost behind her large grin and cheeks pink from laughter. "You're lucky they're so good-natured."

"Don't know what they found so amusing," Armand paused to yawn. "I was dead serious."

Adella and Armand took over the game of ninepins after Bettlin and Hayden retired. Together, they tried to recruit Kol and Cora to play with them, but the game was cut short when Kol shattered one of the bottles with the wooden ball. The four of them had just returned to the tables to refill their cups when the bell in the tower clanged loudly.

Cora got up, but Armand stopped her with a gesture. "It's just Declan back with his ruffians," he guessed. "He doesn't need us all to greet him at the door like pups." Cora didn't need much convincing before she sat back down, and the two lingered there in conversation.

Armand threw a pointed glance at Kol, but it took a couple of times before he got the hint that Armand wanted to be left alone with his new friend. Kol took Adella's hand, putting a finger to his lips to forestall her questions, and led her back across the courtyard. He expected her to drop his hand at her first chance, but they walked like that for a while down the corridor before she moved her hand to his arm.

Kol led her into the Great Room, and found it empty. The fire in the hearth was dying, filling the space with an orange glow. "I wanted to speak with you," Adella said quietly, releasing his arm as she turned to face him.

"You are," Kol replied.

"If Ellie leaves in the morning for the greenhouse," she began, sounding hesitant, "I think you should go along, too."

"Why do you say that?" he asked, though he felt he could guess the answer.

"I was thinking about what we overheard." She twisted the ring around her finger. "We don't know what's going on, but it didn't sound good. You said as much yourself. And, well, Ellie has to get to the Capital, there are too many lives at stake. My sister and her family, also, live there," she added.

"You want me to help protect the apothecary," he stated plainly, and Adella nodded. "You expect me to leave you behind," he continued, exasperation tinting his words, "with Ballantyne and his lackey here."

"I can't very well spend a whole day walking," she reasoned. "Besides, Captain Declan will be here, too."

"Declan only looks out for himself," Kol countered.

"Kol, please," she said under her breath. "You know as well as anyone how grave the situation is."

He blew a long breath out through the side of his mouth. "Fine. But you," he ordered, pointing a finger at her, "stay far away from Ballantyne. Where he is, you're not." He reached down to his boot, pulled out his knife in its sheath and offered it to her. "Keep this on you, at least."

"I almost lost that last time," she admitted.

"I don't care." He watched her for a moment as she took the knife. "I guess this is goodnight, then," Kol said. As Adella hesitated, he stepped in closer, drawn in by the sea-storm color of her eyes. The deep ache of longing, a feeling he'd tried so hard to ignore until now, panged in his chest. Slowly, he brushed his fingers along her cheek, and her lips parted to draw breath. Kol touched his thumb to her lower lip, running it softly along the outer edge as he leaned in.

Metal scraped behind him as the door to the Great Room opened. Ellie and Jago entered, followed by Declan, Ballantyne, and Tomas. Kol dropped his hand to his side and turned to leave, but Adella caught him by the wrist. "Goodnight," she whispered, then let go. Kol returned to his dormitory and, glancing out through the doorway, saw Adella still watching him as he closed the door. Leaving it cracked for light to see by, he lingered there as he pulled off his boots. After hearing the door of Adella's chamber close shut beside his, he laid down in his bed. Heart racing, his mind swirled with hopes and anxieties as he wondered what might've been, if only the others hadn't returned at that moment. Letting out a long breath, he closed his eyes, the softness of her skin lingering on his fingertips.

20

The Greenhouse

Kol woke in a cold sweat, panting. His nightmare had been different this time. It wasn't himself lost to the sea, nor some faceless, shadowy figure. This time, it was someone he knew, which made it that much worse. He sat and rubbed his eyes, waiting for his heartbeat to calm, then stood and pulled on his boots. It was dark, but he knew Armand hadn't returned to their dormitory since he couldn't hear any snoring. Kol wondered if he was still with Cora somewhere. He tucked his linen shirt into his breeches, buckled on his sword belt and scabbard, then opened the door.

A hearthfire illuminated the Great Room, but the high windows were still black with night. Ellie stood with her belongings strewn over the table, dressed in knee breeches and boots.

"Mister Kol," she said as he approached. "I'm surprised to see you up this early."

"Adella asked me to go with you," he replied. "If that's all right."

"Certainly." She packed a waterskin neatly into a white canvas rucksack. "We will be glad for more company. Leaving this early, we risk running into avoa."

Kol frowned. "I don't know that word."

"That's because Jago made it up," she explained with a smile. "It's his name for the large birds that live on the island."

"Are they dangerous?" he asked, remembering the animal that pursued Armand to the steps.

"Yes, they can be." Ellie finished packing the bag and fastened the flap with three pewter buttons. "They have large talons, and the inner claw on each foot is armed with venom." She pulled the rucksack over her shoulders. "They usually aren't active in the daytime, though, so we don't often have trouble with them."

Soon, Jago entered from the corridor, bringing with him various weapons. He handed Ellie a light, two-edged sword of a type Kol had never seen before. She buckled it onto her waist.

Jago turned to Kol. "You coming along?" Kol nodded, and Jago held out a short bow. "How are you with one of these?"

"Mediocre at best," Kol replied, taking the bow in hand.

"That will do." Jago passed him a quiver with a handful of arrows, and Kol slung it over his shoulder. Jago led them to the kitchen, stopping to pack up some quick provisions before going out the door into the herb garden. Ellie took out her large keyring and unlocked the tall iron fence separating the garden enclave from the wilderness outside. They stepped through the gateway and into the chilly morning fog as the first glimpse of grey light seeped above the horizon.

Kol followed them down a well-worn path in the dirt, bow strung at the ready in his left hand. Tall trees loomed above, dark against the early dawn sky. Unseen creatures rustled in the underbrush, making strange calls that echoed in the gloom beneath the canopy.

* * *

As Adella opened the door of her dormitory, she was relieved to find the Great Room empty. She had made a habit of waking before sunrise to empty her chamber pot in the privy of the courtyard, but all the drink from the night before caused her to sleep in until late morning, and she woke with a pounding headache. She carefully lifted the lidded porcelain pot from the floor and, holding it out away from her body, made her way across the Great Room.

Glancing around, she noticed the doors of several of the other dormitories hung open, with no sound of any occupants inside. The door leading out to the corridor was ajar, and only needed a push from her hip to open it.

As she walked down the sunlit stone path through the courtyard gardens, a strange feeling overcame her. She hadn't passed anyone in the corridor, no islanders on guard, no crewmen from *The Tigress* wandering idly. *Where is everyone?* she wondered. *Where is Armand? Rogero?* She pulled open the door to the privy and, holding her breath, emptied the pot into the hole in the wooden seat.

Overcome with curiosity, she set the chamber pot in the grass to take a look around. The sun was already high in the blue, cloudless sky, shining warmly down on her face through the boughs of the locust tree. The tables from the night before had been cleared and the cressets put away. *Perhaps they all went along with Ellie to the greenhouse and left me behind to sleep?* she wondered, but a nagging in her gut told her otherwise. The Cairn had always had an islander on guard since the day she arrived, she recalled; they wouldn't desert it now. Adella walked softly across the ground, her eyes darting from one flowering shrub to the next as goosebumps rose on the back of her neck.

Turning this way and that as she looked around, her foot came down with a squelch on a soft spot in the dirt. Lifting her boot, she found a stain of dark liquid beneath. *Blood.* Adella drew a slow breath to settle her nerves and continued across the courtyard. As she passed between two large camellia bushes, heavy with white flowers, she nearly tripped on something underfoot.

Adella turned to see what she caught her foot on. A cold dread spread through her as she looked down on the form of a man, half buried under the foliage. She stooped down and, rolling him over by the shoulder, looked down on the face of Tomas, Ballantyne's crewman. A gaping wound slashed through his gut, seeping dark red blood into the grass. She didn't have to check for a heartbeat to know the man was dead.

Seeing there was nothing she could do for him, Adella continued to search the courtyard, making her way slowly to the other side. As she approached a sprawling rhododendron bush, she was startled by a harsh sound, like the snarl of an animal, low and rough. Adella pulled Kol's knife from her boot, brandishing it as she stepped silently around the shrub. Behind, lay a familiar figure, curled up on his side.

"Armand!" Adella shouted, dropping to her knees beside him. "Are you hurt?" Her heart pounded wildly as she shook him by the shoulder.

Armand snorted loudly. "Good heavens, girl!" he muttered. "I'm only sleeping. What's the matter?"

She let out a sigh of relief. "Tomas is dead," she said, tucking the knife away again. "Where is everyone?"

Armand sat up and blinked at her. "What do you mean?"

"You're the first living person I've seen since I woke." She took his arm to help him up. "Did you sleep out here all night?"

"None of your business," he said guiltily. They walked across the green grass of the courtyard to the door nearest the tower. As they approached, it swung violently outward, and a frantic figure ran toward them.

It was Cora, with fresh blood running down her forehead, her grey hair hanging loose and disheveled. "They've come for her," she said, her eyes wide with fear as she grabbed Adella by the forearms. She was breathing hard and her words came out between gasps. "Pietro—" Tears welled up in her eyes as she turned to Armand. "They killed him. They disarmed me and I ran. We have to save her."

"Who?" Armand asked, grabbing Cora by the elbow to steady her.

"Miss Ellie," she replied, wiping away the blood that dripped into her eye.

"Who is after Miss Ellie?" Adella asked.

Cora shook her head. "I don't know. Strange men." She leaned against Armand's arm, exhausted. "But someone must've let them in."

Adella looked upward, raising her eyes to the tower above them. "I have to warn the others."

"No!" Cora said. "Those men, they'll know you're up there."

"Get away from here," Adella said to Armand. "Go now, I'll be right behind you." Reluctantly, he obeyed, leading Cora with an arm around her shoulder as she stumbled along beside him. Adella pushed open the glass-paned door that led from the courtyard into the Cairn. Looking around, all seemed quiet. She turned the corner and approached the iron door to the tower, which hung open, beckoning her into the darkness beyond.

It was nearly noon when Kol, Ellie, and Jago emerged from the trees and walked up the rise at the island's summit. It wasn't that the distance had been so great, as a bird flies, but rather that the path they traveled along wove back and forth around stone outcroppings or thick tangles of impassable forest. They also went slower than Kol was used to, and stopped to eat or drink rather than do so while walking. If he had traveled alone at his accustomed marching pace, he could've arrived in half the time. He tried not to be frustrated, reminding himself these two were old enough to be his grandparents, and perhaps he was a little too used to hard travel.

Atop the rise perched a long and low-sloping building, its glass panes gleaming in the sunlight. Two short walls of brick stretched down its length to form the longer sides; the rest of the building was composed entirely of glass set into white-painted metal framing. Ellie opened a pair of glass-paneled doors and walked inside; Kol and Jago followed.

Inside the greenhouse, the air was warm and damp. The space was packed with many strange plants that Kol had never seen before, adorned with flowers and fruits of every shape and size. However, what caught his eye was the unexpected presence of many large, multicolored butterflies, their wings catching the light like pieces of stained glass as they fluttered around their heads, alighting on their shoulders and hair. A large blue one came to rest on Kol's forehead, tickling as it crawled its way down toward his nose.

Kol blew at the butterfly, waving his hand to shoo it away. Undaunted, the little animal crawled toward his eye until Kol put his hand up and it walked onto his fingers. He gently shook his hand to dislodge the butterfly, but it stubbornly held fast.

Ellie laughed as she watched him. "Aren't they amusing? This is my favorite place on the island."

Kol shrugged indifferently, but thought that Adella would probably have enjoyed it. Finally, the butterfly flapped its wings and flew off. As they walked through the greenhouse, they realized they were alone; Evan and Romy were nowhere to be seen. Ellie and Jago passed worried looks between them but said nothing.

Ellie crossed to the back of the greenhouse and, pulling an empty sack from her pack, began to harvest the clusters of white blossoms from a little, stunted tree in a large ceramic pot. Jago and Kol followed her lead, dropping the blooms into the bag. The tree was similar to the one Kol had used to make medicine for Armand. He paused, trying to remember the name of it, but it eluded him.

"I think that should be good," Ellie said, appraising the contents of the sack. "If we head out soon, we can arrive at the Cairn by sunset." As Kol followed the other two out the doors into the open air, a clear, metallic sound rang out in the distance.

"The bell." Ellie's face was pale as she looked at her companions. They listened; it was not the usual gentle chime or two that the islanders used to summon each other. The peals echoed harshly over the island, clanging desperately before falling silent again.

Kol's stomach dropped as he considered the implications of the alarm. "Something's happened," he said. "We need to go back."

* * *

Adella gathered her skirts as she ran down the spiraling steps of the tower, heedless of the throbbing pain in her foot. She stopped at the bottom, clutching her stomach, unsure if she was ill from nerves or from drink the night before. As she shoved open the tower, something crashed into her side. A large hand clamped down over her mouth and an arm wrapped around her middle.

"Shh," a raspy voice said into her ear as she was dragged through the corridor. "Keep quiet and I'll release you." She nodded her head as the man pulled her back into the bright light of the courtyard and behind a large shrub in the corner of the garden.

The hand lifted away from her mouth, and, turning, she looked into a weathered and deeply wrinkled face. A large, white scar stretched tightly across the sun-tanned skin, biting into the bridge of the nose. *Ballantyne!* Adella scooted backward, pulling the knife from her boot and pointing it at him.

"No need for that," he whispered hoarsely. "I mean you no harm."

Adella wasn't sure she believed that. "Was it you who attacked Miss Cora?" she asked sharply under her breath.

"No," he said, shaking his head. "It was them."

She narrowed her eyes. "And I suppose you didn't kill Tomas either?"

"I killed him," he replied. "He was one of them."

She lowered the knife slightly. "One of whom?"

"Traitors from aboard *The Quest*," he growled. "I had my suspicions, but I wasn't sure." Crouching, he peeked through the foliage to the courtyard beyond, then turned and beckoned with a flick of his hand. "Let's go. Quickly."

Though her mind was awash with questions, the earnestness of his tone compelled her. Adella reluctantly followed Ballantyne as they scrambled across the grass and through a door leading into the corridor on the other side. Soon, they approached the Armory, with its red lacquered door smashed and splintered, hanging from the hinges.

Entering, they could see that many of the weapons on the wooden rack were now missing, with others scattered on the floor. Adella sheathed Kol's boot knife and ran to the far side of the room where the bows were stored, lifting from the rack a small wooden crossbow similar to the one she had left on the ship. Hanging beside it was a carved-wood quiver filled with bolts, which she fastened at her waist. Then, with one foot in the stirrup, she pulled back the string and loaded the crossbow.

Ballantyne, who was busy stuffing blades of every kind into his belt, looked over to eye her choice. "Good thinking," he said, approaching to choose from the ranged weapons. He picked up a heavy steel crossbow, grabbing its quiver of thick bolts, and readied the weapon.

Adella grabbed a long knife that had been left behind on the floor and slid its sheath into the waistband of her petticoat. "Where's the captain?"

Ballantyne shook his head. "We were outnumbered, and got separated. He was injured, last I saw."

Adella rounded on him. "And you left him?!"

The heavy creases in his brow deepened. "By his orders. We have to save Miss Ellie, no matter the cost." Ballantyne turned, heading into the corridor. Adella's breath caught in her throat as she reluctantly followed.

Emerging into the open air of the courtyard, they were spotted by a group of three men passing through the center beneath the locust tree, shouting as they ran toward Adella and Ballantyne with swords raised. Ballantyne widened his stance as he lifted his crossbow, and Adella followed suit. Ballantyne's bolt pierced the gut of the closest man, dropping him to his knees with a cry. Adella stayed her hand until the other two men were closer, remembering that her smaller weapon had a shorter range. Ballantyne drew his sword as Adella pulled back on the iron trigger.

Her bolt flew a bit wide, catching the man in his right shoulder. He continued to charge toward her, though his sword arm now moved stiffly. He raised his cutlass for a downward strike, but was too slow. Adella darted sideways and, drawing the long knife at her waist, plunged it up under his ribs. He collapsed into the dirt with a gasp as Ballantyne dispatched the last man with a stab to the gut. Hands shaking, Adella placed the knife back into its sheath at her side.

Ballantyne turned toward her. "Where is Miss Ellie?"

"She left for the greenhouse early this morning," Adella answered, her voice unsteady. "I know Kol went with her, at least."

"The Sornian?" He looked at her incredulously. "And you trust him?"

She thought about it, and was surprised by her answer. "More than anyone."

"Good." Ballantyne hoisted his crossbow against his shoulder. "We must find her."

Adella opened her mouth to protest. More than anything, she wanted to find Rogero, but she remembered the lesson she had learned with Lucas and the Heartstone and knew Ballantyne was right. Kol's words echoed in her mind; *Some things are more important than one person.* Adella nodded in agreement, and hated herself for it.

21

Into the Wild

Kol walked behind Ellie and Jago, swearing under his breath as they marched downhill. He felt guilty about rushing them along, but he couldn't ignore the urgency of the bell. When he'd heard it, he fought the urge to run ahead and leave them behind. After all, they were in no immediate danger themselves, but clearly, something was wrong at the Cairn. What it was, he couldn't imagine, but his mind kept returning to the conversation he overheard in the library. Now his friends were in trouble, and he wasn't there to help. He spat at the ground. *Whatever happened, we wouldn't be there in time to do any good,* he thought. *But... they must've known that when they rang the bell.* Kol's stomach turned as he realized. *It wasn't a call for help; it was a warning to us!*

"We have to get off the trail," Kol said, urging the other two into the forest. "Hurry."

"This way," Jago said, leading them through the underbrush. They followed him over a little babbling stream and through a thick tangle of knotted vines that they had to hack with their blades to get past. Eventually, they found themselves at the top of a high cliff face, with a sheer drop into the canopy below their feet.

Standing at the ledge, they looked out over the island. Though a breeze blew across their faces, the air was warm and thick with moisture. In the distance, Kol could see the river that ran alongside the Cairn cut a swath through the forest. He squinted, trying to locate the bell tower through the trees to no avail. A wide valley stretched out between them and their destination.

"If we find a way down," Kol began, "we could get back sooner."

"True," Jago replied. "But the valley is rife with avoa nests. Even in the daytime," he said, scratching the white stubble of his neck as he considered it, "they can be very territorial."

"I wouldn't go that way," Ellie replied, "unless—" She was interrupted by a crash through the foliage somewhere behind them. Then, they heard voices in the distance.

Kol pulled an arrow from the quiver over his shoulder and nocked it. "Go," he whispered and ushered them along the ridge, stepping carefully over the vines and roots at their feet. It was clear now that they were being pursued as the sounds behind them grew louder. *It's no good,* he thought, *they're too close behind us. We're not moving fast enough...* He stopped suddenly, eyeing a particularly large and gnarled oak tree growing right up against the cliffside. "Down this way," he ordered, sending them clambering down through the branches. He'd much rather deal with birds than the unknown number of men hunting them down.

Kol followed the others down the tree, pulling the bow over one shoulder and carefully stepping from one broad limb to another. He was relieved the bark was rough and dry, providing good traction under their boots and palms as they descended. Finally, he saw Ellie and Jago waiting on the ground. As he swung downward by his hands, Kol dangled in the air for a moment, then let go and fell hard onto his feet, landing in a crouch.

Jago led the way carefully across the waist-high ferns that covered the forest floor. At the back of the group, Kol kept alert for signs of their pursuers. Rather than voices, however, he became aware of a low gurgling in the shadows around them. As the noises grew nearer and more menacing, Ellie and Jago stopped and glanced nervously around.

"That's the avoa," Ellie said. "It is their warning call. Tread lightly, no sudden movements."

Kol nodded. The three of them crept slowly through the valley, keeping alert to the presence of the unseen animals until the calls faded away behind them. Kol let out a breath of relief as they approached the far side of the valley and the ground began to slope upward once more.

A sharp, high-pitched squeal rang out from the forest behind them, then trailed off into a low rattle. Kol, Jago, and Ellie stopped in their tracks to look around, listening. More shrieking calls erupted in the distance. The three froze as the last rattling echo died away.

"That's probably not good," Kol said under his breath. His eyes roved from the bole of one large tree to the next, as the uneasy feeling of being watched crept over him. "Let's keep moving."

The hair on the back of Kol's neck raised as the uneasy feeling grew. Looking through the trees to a dense patch of dark ferns behind them, his eyes settled on a shadow beneath the emerald leaves. A small, metallic flash glinted briefly from within the foliage, then was gone. In one smooth motion, Kol raised his bow and drew back an arrow, loosing it into the bracken. A harsh cry came from the underbrush, then echoed around him as men armed with blades sprang out from the forest.

Kol looked back at his companions. "Go!" he ordered, then nocked another arrow as the two turned to flee. He shot it into the nearest man's chest, dropping him to the dirt. Drawing another from the quiver, Kol spun to his other side and let it fly. The arrow pierced low in the second man's gut as he ran, and, stumbling, was lost in the ferns. More were advancing, and two were upon him before he could grab another arrow. The blade of a cutlass came whistling through the air above his head as Kol hefted his bow up in both hands to meet it. The steel bit deep into the leather-wrapped grip, and the wood splintered and gave. He gave a forceful shove upward against the blade, sending the swordsman reeling backward.

A second man rushed Kol's other side, dagger flashing in his hand. Kol swung the bow around, crashing it against his head; the top half of the bow shattered away on impact and the man was knocked unconscious. The other swordsman had regained his footing and came at him once again, swinging his blade for a forward strike. Instinctively, Kol pulled back the jagged, splintered end of the bow left in his hand and jabbed it forward into the man's belly before he let the ruined weapon fall to the ground along with the gasping man. Kol drew his sword.

A strange sound rang out from the trees, and the men surrounding him hesitated, looking nervously around. Then a large bird stepped out from behind one trunk. The wrinkled skin of its long neck was bright blue; its body was covered with glossy black feathers, and its legs and feet were large, thick, and grey. Its small head, held high on the thin neck, lowered as the bird approached, spreading its small wings threateningly. Opening its dagger-like beak, a guttural drumming sound issued from its throat. Its call was answered by more of its kind appearing from the foliage. Kol wished he hadn't broken his bow.

Glancing at the faces of the attackers, he realized they were ones he recognized. Some were from the original crew of *The Tigress*; others had come aboard after the foundering of *The Quest*. The man who stood now foremost, with sword arm ready and off-hand twitching, Kol remembered as the crewman named Dennick.

The large birds advanced toward them from the ferns, necks low and wings outstretched, circling around them. The men all turned to face the avoa, weapons at the ready. Seeing things at a standstill, the leader turned back to face Kol. "You again?" Dennick glared at him. "Still meddling in Valennian affairs? It's time I taught you a lesson."

"Try it," Kol dared him. Dennick's sneer dropped into a scowl, and he charged forward, sword raised. Kol blocked the high strike with a loud clang of steel, and again when Dennick swung at him from the side. Kol pushed his blade free, grabbed Dennick's wrist, and twisted. He could feel the release of tendons beneath his fingers as the other man's sword dropped to the ground. Kol jabbed his cutlass forward, the point of the blade bursting through cloth and skin as it plunged into Dennick's side. As he drew it back out, the sailor crumpled to his knees. The remaining men, having turned their attention from the birds back to Kol, all rushed at him. Kol didn't pause to think, relying instead on instinct honed through experience. He grabbed Dennick's sword from the ground in his left hand and, following through one smooth motion, raised both blades to parry a strike from each side. While holding the block to his left, he shoved with the blade on his right, and as the man's sword reeled backward, Kol slashed the first man across his midsection. Arcing the blade tip across, he thrust it forward into the second man's side. The two sprawled out on the ground, groaning in pain as their blood pooled at Kol's feet. The last sailor hesitated and, with a downward glance at his companions, turned and fled.

The man ran, crashing loudly through the bracken and drawing the attention of the avoa. The birds hissed and gave chase, bounding after him in a flock of legs and necks until they were lost to sight within the forest. Kol took a deep breath and looked around, noticing for the first time since the fighting began that his companions hadn't left when he told them to; they stood by only a stone's throw behind him, waiting with weapons ready.

"Why didn't you run?" Kol asked, looking from Ellie to Jago for an explanation.

"We couldn't," Ellie explained. "The avoa are vexed by movement; we were surrounded by them until just now."

They continued toward the Cairn while the sun sank lower behind the trees at their backs and the light under the canopy grew dim. Soon, they heard the river splashing through its rocky bed and, as they came upon it, followed its banks as it wove through the forest. Stopping by a large stone outcropping not far from the riverbank, they rested their tired backs against the cool, damp stone and drank from their waterskins. Kol let out a long breath and leaned back, closing his eyes beneath the warm golden light that filtered through the trees. He hardly had time to calm his breath when the snapping of a twig came from somewhere behind them. Kol drew his cutlass and, motioning for Ellie and Jago to stay put, snuck silently over the wet soil to peek around the stone.

Prowling along the river's edge was a line of armed crewmen. Soon, the men would come upon the tracks they had left behind on the riverbank. There were too many to face with just the three of them, and Ellie was a healer, not a warrior. If they got a head start, Kol figured, they could lose them in the forest.

He turned back to his companions. "We have to run," Kol said under his breath, and they nodded. "Now!" he whispered, urging them on with a light shove to the shoulders. Tucking the sack of herbs under her arm, Ellie took off at a sprint. Kol and Jago followed, with the voices close behind.

The three of them were breathing hard as they made a sharp turn through a high stand of wild lilac bushes, thick and heavy with late-blooming purple flowers. They seemed to have lost their pursuers, as there was no longer any sound of footfall or voices behind them, but they kept running. Kol glanced behind, and was relieved to see no one there. Before he had time to look ahead again, he collided into something.

He realized it was a person when it softly gave way. As Kol hopped to his feet, drawing his blade, he froze at the sight of a familiar shade of long brown hair. "Adella!" Kol said in surprise and gripped her upper arm, helping to lift her from the ground. He realized she wasn't alone as Ballantyne stopped short behind her. "What is going on?"

She rose to her feet with a huff. "The Cairn is under attack."

Kol leaned down to whisper in her ear, "Didn't I tell you to keep away from Ballantyne?"

She shook her head. "We were wrong about him, he's on our side," she said quietly. Adella bent to retrieve her crossbow from the ground, looking past him at his companions. "Miss Ellie! Thank goodness you're safe, we've come to find you."

"No time for a chat, we're being chased," Ellie replied, looking back behind them for signs of their pursuers. The distant sound of voices once again filled the silence.

Ballantyne raised his crossbow. "You three go on ahead. Me and Miss Grimless will slow them down."

"No," Kol said. "There are too many, you can't reload fast enough."

"But my foot—" Adella replied. "I won't be able to keep up with you."

"You will," Kol promised, taking her by the arm again. "Let's go."

Adella's injured foot pounded as she ran beside Kol, who was now pulling her along, her ankle threatening to give way with each step. Just as she felt she could go no further, the group came upon the Cairn silhouetted in the evening sky. Approaching from the southwestern wall, they followed closely along the stones around the fortress. The last rays of fading sunlight bathed everything in gold as they entered the tumble-down sanctuary of the Temple.

They followed Ellie over the soft grass, stepping around massive blocks of stone toward the iron door. "We do not know how many are in the Cairn," Ellie began, turning to face them. "Even if we lock this door behind us, they could enter through another way and we may face the same group again, plus more. We must face them here."

Each readied their weapons and took a position in hiding. Adella crouched behind a short remnant of wall close to where they had entered, peeking out over a low point of the barrier with her crossbow aimed at chest level. Ballantyne lurked in the shadows behind a column of stone across the gap from her, the two preparing to ambush the men with bolts before they entered the Temple. Adella glanced behind her to where she knew Kol hid only a few paces away, in the open but unseen, as he blended into the deepening shadows beneath the arches. Jago, with his glaive, waited at Ellie's side, not far from the door, in case they needed to make a retreat.

Adella's heartbeat pounded in her ears as she waited. Soon, she heard the muffled padding of boots in the dirt, and the dark shapes of men appeared before her. In her panic, fingers trembling, she let the first man slip by, but squeezed the iron lever when the second stepped in close range. The little bolt plunged deep into his ribs, and the man let out a rasping gasp as he fell. As quickly as she could, Adella turned and braced her right foot into the iron stirrup at the front of the crossbow, drawing back the string with both hands to load another bolt. She didn't have time to steady her aim before another attacker came around the wall straight toward her, cutlass in each hand. She pulled back on the lever and released her breath when the oncoming man collapsed close by, groaning and clutching his middle. *That was too close,* she chided herself. Adella scrambled to her feet and loaded the weapon again, this time standing.

A massive weight dove down on her, knocking her weapon from her arms as one man jumped onto her from the wall at her back, and they fell to the ground. As he rolled away from her and rose, Adella reached out to grab the crossbow. Gripping the handle, she dragged it toward herself when a boot slammed down over her hand.

Adella looked up to see a grizzled crewman glaring down at her. He lifted his sword as he pressed his weight into his foot, crushing her fingers against the wood and iron of the crossbow. She bit down on a groan, not wanting to call out and distract her companions. She tried to pull her hand back, but her fingers only stretched and cracked. Adella shut her eyes, anticipating the edge of his blade.

The strike never came. Adella heard a heavy thump instead, and the weight on her fingers lifted. She opened her eyes to see the crewman dead on the ground and Kol standing over her with a bloodied sword. She hardly had time to breathe when she glanced beyond his boots and saw another swordsman running toward them.

Still stretched out on the grass, Adella carefully aimed the crossbow through the gap between Kol's legs; as the sailor came into range, she loosed the bolt deep into his gut, then clamped her lips shut over a scream as warm pain flooded through her right hand. The man dropped to the ground, and Kol finished him with a downward thrust.

"That was a risky shot," he commented with a nervous laugh.

"Sorry," she replied, wincing.

Kol crouched beside her and offered a hand. "Are you injured?"

"I'm fine," she said breathlessly, rising delicately to her feet. "The others?"

"Well enough," he replied, glancing around. "That looks to be it, for now."

They met up with their companions by the iron door of the Cairn. Jago held his side, dark blood soaking through his shirt, but all were standing. Ellie tucked her bag under one arm and, drawing out her key, unlocked the door. They stepped cautiously into the dark corridor.

The first thing they noticed was the acrid smell of smoke. The corridor appeared deserted; the only sounds to be heard were the ones they made themselves. Jago led the way to the doors that led into the courtyard, and as they stepped out into the evening air, a blaze of light hit their eyes. Across the Cairn, the library was being consumed in a raging fire, with black smoke billowing out in a column overhead. Over the roar of the flames, a clang sounded from the bell tower. There was a pause, then another peal of the bell. They continued down the corridor.

No one spoke as the group approached the tower door. It hung wide open, and the slow scrape of limping footsteps grew louder as someone came from the darkness beyond the threshold.

The figure stepped into the orange light that flooded in from the courtyard doors behind them, and they were relieved to see it was Armand. "Thank heavens," he said as he eyed the group, his voice steady and hale despite his limp. "We must get to the lagoon. The other survivors are already gathered there." They followed him through the darkness of the tower to the heavy rusted door that led outside the

Cairn. He shoved it open with a grating creak, and they stepped into the night air, now thick with smoke.

Though it was a moonless night, the glow of the burning library made shadows on the ground as they tread carefully toward the cliff. They came to the top of the stone stairway leading down toward the lagoon when a dark figure rose up from the steps before them.

"It ends here," the man growled, aiming a heavy crossbow into the midst of the group. He took a step closer. "All of it. Harrian. The Haspen Dynasty," he paused, glaring at Ellie. She took an involuntary step back. "You."

"Moffat," Ballantyne spat. "I should have known you were behind this, you bastard." Adella saw the twitch of movement in Moffat's finger over the lever and lifted her crossbow. Not sparing a moment to aim, she squeezed the lever; at that same moment, Moffat launched a bolt into their group as both Jago and Ballantyne stepped into motion. Beside Adella, a figure collapsed with a gasp just as Moffat was hit in the side. Stumbling backward, Moffat disappeared with a sharp cry over the edge of the cliff.

They gathered to turn the wounded figure over, and beheld the scarred face of Ballantyne. "Leave me be," he said, his voice less than a whisper. He had stepped in the path of the bolt in front of Jago and Ellie, and it pierced deep into his chest. "Just get her to Valenna."

Reluctantly, they made their way down the stone stairs and met up with the few survivors at the edge of the lagoon. Peering through the darkness, Adella saw that the boat they used to pass through the sea cave was missing and realized they must all be gathered here waiting for its return. Ellie and Jago joined their friends from the island who were seated on the river bank, happy to see Cora, Evan and Romy alive.

Adella slumped down onto the grass, finally allowing herself to rest. She became keenly aware of the swelling in her foot, and realized she could not move two fingers on her right hand, which pulsed with a bone-deep pain. High up on the cliff behind them, the roof of the library collapsed into the stone walls of the Cairn.

"I left my travel bag in the dormitory," Armand said sadly, sinking down to the ground to rest beside Adella. "Too late now, I suppose."

Adella laid back into the cool, damp grass and closed her eyes.

She opened them again when she heard the murmuring of the others, and the splash of water. Sitting up, she saw the small light of a lantern approaching slowly from across the lagoon. As it drew nearer, Adella could see that it was being held aloft at the prow of the boat by a man.

She rose to her feet when the hull scraped against the sandy bottom of the lagoon, wincing as the throbbing in her hand and foot returned. The man stepped onto shore. "Is this everyone?" he asked, holding out the lantern to appraise the group in the light. His other arm hung idly in a sling.

Adella thought she recognized the voice. The sight of his face confirmed it. *Rogero.* Relief flooded over her. *He's alive!* She looked around at the other faces in the lamplight, but one was missing. "Where's Kol?"

"I noticed he was missing some time ago," Armand admitted, "though I don't know where he got to."

"Get in," Declan ordered. "The wounded cannot wait, I will come back for him later." He helped Cora into the boat with his good arm as a crewman at the stern reached forward to steady her.

Adella took a step back. "I'm not going without him."

"Get in the boat, Adella," came a voice behind her. Kol stepped into the circle of lantern light, holding a bundle of items in his arms. "I'm here."

22

A Homecoming

Adella lay in the hammock, watching as the morning light filtered through the dirty windows at the stern of the captain's quarters. Romy and Cora were still sleeping soundly, but Ellie had risen at first light to check on the injured elsewhere aboard *The Tigress*. It was their third day at sea since departing from the Cairn, and the ship was sailing with a minimal crew. Adella had offered to do her share, but Declan sent her back to the cabin after seeing her hand. The two center fingers of her right hand were now bruised black and green, swollen to nearly twice their size. She kept them wrapped together in scrap cloth after that, but didn't want to bother the apothecary with it. Ellie seemed busy enough as it was.

Tilting herself carefully out of the hammock, Adella stepped over to the table in the middle of the cabin. Running her hand over the soft fabric of her shawl that sat on its surface, she unfolded it to reveal the object wrapped inside. The night they departed, Kol had gone into the Cairn to recover some of their belongings from the dormitories, even though he himself had nothing to go back for. She was touched to see him return Armand's bag, her haversack that had belonged to Lucas, their oilskin cloaks, and, wrapped in her shawl, the Codex.

She picked up her petticoats from the seat of a chair and, shaking out the wrinkles, pulled them over her shift. Adella had just finished tying the lacing on her jacket bodice when she heard boots coming down the passageway toward the cabin, and looked up to see a young man carrying a tea service. He went slowly, gripping the porcelain handles tightly with a terrified look in his eyes.

He sighed with relief as he set the tray onto the table. "I was sure I'd drop it," he said, and grinned at his accomplishment. He was short, with straw-colored hair tied back loosely in a blue ribbon. His age, and something about his demeanor, reminded Adella of Lucas.

"Thank you," she said. "I don't think we've met."

"No," he replied, "but I've seen you around the ship, Miss Grimless. Childric." He placed one arm behind his back and gave a slight bow. "Yul Childric."

Adella tapped her chin with a forefinger. "Childric. Why does that name sound familiar?" she asked herself.

"My family is from the Capital, if that helps you," he offered. "Our manor is in the Hartwicks, just north of the Ansebulet."

"Ah!" Adella waved her finger in the air. "Now I remember! I've seen your surname in my mother's family book. I believe you and I are cousins of some sort."

"That's right," he said with a wide grin. "I didn't want to mention it and seem too familiar. It's a pleasure to meet you finally."

"Likewise," Adella replied, and they spent some time chatting over recent events. Soon, Romy and Cora roused from their hammocks and Ellie joined them for a simple breakfast of hard biscuits and black tea while Childric returned to his duties.

Ellie watched as Adella fumbled with her teacup in her wrapped right hand. "I wish you'd let me look at that."

"It's fine," Adella replied. "Only bruised."

"No one wraps a bruise," Ellie countered, and held her palm out expectantly. Adella gave in and gritted her teeth as Ellie tended to the broken fingers, carefully repositioning the shattered bone and wrapping them against the healthy fingers for stability.

"I want you to know," Ellie said, smiling softly, "that you can always come to me for anything. Not just your injuries, but for advice or support, whenever you may need it." She paused as a look of weariness passed over her face. "We shall be arriving at the Capital soon, and things might seem different after that. But remember, I will always be there should you need me."

"I will remember," Adella said quietly. "Thank you."

It was afternoon when Kol first spied land from the crow's nest. He had been put on lookout duty that day as it was one of the simpler tasks, like swabbing the decks, that didn't require much experience. He gave the call of "Land!" and watched as the deckhands below all crowded at the bow. Kol climbed over the edge of the platform and worked his way down the ratlines, pausing to watch the long, black shape in the distance. He was surprised at the feeling that rose in him now. A new land awaited him, and he was eager to see it.

Looking down, he spied Armand among the crew, waddling toward the rail with the help of a cane. Kol stepped onto the deck to meet him, and leaned on the rail as they looked out to sea.

"It's quite a relief, isn't it?" Armand said absent-mindedly. "The sight of land."

"Certainly is." Kol grinned. "If I ever set foot on a ship again, it'll be too soon."

"Never say never," Armand muttered. "Who knows what's to come?"

Kol stared into the deep blue waves, wondering what sort of life awaited him in Valenna. *The gold Declan gave me will last for a time,* he thought, *but soon I will have to find work if I want to eat.* He knew he didn't want to be a soldier anymore, but he was unsure what else he might be fit for. His thoughts were interrupted when he saw an ominous shadow below the waves in the distance.

A dark, snaking body rose to the surface, cresting above the water. Slowly, its large, elongated head emerged from the waves. Kol elbowed

Armand. "Look there," he said, pointing out the creature. "Is it the same one as before? Do you suppose it's following us?"

"Perhaps a different one," Armand guessed with a shrug. "Maybe the sea is rife with them now."

"Great," Kol commented flatly. He looked around at the group that had gathered, all watching with hopeful faces as the shore of Valenna crept closer. He spied Adella and put up his hand to wave to her, but stopped and turned away again when he realized she was being accompanied by Declan. It was too late. Adella, noticing the gesture, left Declan's side to wedge herself between Kol and Armand at the crowded rail.

Adella linked her arms around their elbows. "Civilization at last." She grinned. "And look!" She pointed toward the jagged outline of buildings taking shape before their eyes. "No heavy black smoke. Surely that's a good sign."

"What's it like there?" Kol asked. "At the Capital."

"Well..." Adella paused to consider it. "The people are all very formal and stuffy. And everything is just covered in gilding, it's quite gaudy," she admitted. "But the city is beautiful in its own way, and there's much to do. I think you might like it."

"After everything is settled," Armand began, "The first thing I plan to do is find an old friend of mine. Of the female persuasion, if you get my meaning," he said with a wink.

"Lovely," Adella replied sarcastically. "For me, it will be a hot bath or two, then eat pastries until I'm sick of them." She grinned. "Then perhaps another bath. And maybe I'll go to the evening dance, though I hate dancing."

"I don't think either of you should be doing any of that during a plague," Kol said wryly.

"I've already had it," Armand replied.

"This isn't like the pox," Kol countered. "You can catch it more than once."

"It will be all right," Adella assured him. "We have the Royal Apothecary now." They leaned against the rail, enjoying the sea air as they watched the silhouette of buildings grow slowly larger. "What about you, Kol? What would you like to do?"

Kol considered it before answering. "I'd like a hot meal and a beer." Across the water, the shape of a turreted fortress came into view, its peaks protruding skyward from a rise in the land. "What's that?"

"The Ansebulet," Adella replied. "Otherwise known as the Royal Palace. That's where we'll be headed when we escort Miss Ellie back to her duties."

"'Ansebulet?'" Kol repeated.

"The word is Andolinian," Armand explained. "Though no one remembers what it means anymore."

As *The Tigress* sailed toward the shore, the details of the port became clearer. They could see flags fluttering in the warm breeze as sunshine glittered on the waves around the various ships moored at the docks.

"It doesn't look like they're under quarantine, at least," Kol commented, squinting in the bright sunlight. "What are the flags for? I can't see a design." Though colors were beginning to grow clearer as the land drew closer, he could not make out any detail on the pennants that hung in the air above the wharf. They appeared to be solid black.

Adella shielded her eyes from the glare of the sunlight as she peered out over the water. "Oh, no."

"What does it mean?" Kol asked. "A celebration?"

Armand shook his head sadly. "They're flags of mourning."

"It means—" Adella turned to face Kol, frowning. "The king has died."

Adella clutched the heavy Codex in her arms, wrapped up in her cloak with her little crossbow she had found in the Campos, and stood by the doorway of the captain's cabin. The haversack over her shoulder was heavy with the burden of the ancient iron box, which Declan had entrusted to her to deliver to the Crown.

The sight of the mourning flags at port had sobered the joy of land-fall; what began as a happy moment turned to one of grief. Though Adella felt numb by now after so much loss and pain, the death of the king struck her sharply. The Valenna they returned to now wouldn't be the one she remembered and never would be again. The others on the ship seemed to feel the same way, as all grew somber and quiet, especially those from the Cairn.

Adella waited for Ellie, Cora, and Romy to ascend the steps to the deck above, then followed slowly behind. On the main deck, they met up with Kol, Armand, Jago, and Evan. Jago's shirt was missing, his bare torso wrapped with clean bandaging, but he still held his glaive at his side. Over his shoulder, he carried Ellie's bag of medicine for the ague. Armand joined them and took the bundle from Adella's arms as she rubbed her wrist in relief and stretched her fingers gingerly.

Her group stopped at the rail by the gangway, each saying a word of appreciation to the captain as they left. Armand and Kol each shook his hand, and waited for her. Adella was the last to approach, and, stepping closer, looked up into his hazel eyes. "Rogero, I can't begin to thank you—" Her voice caught in her throat, and she looked away quickly.

"We'll be docked here for a while." Declan put a finger under her chin and lifted it gently to meet her eyes. "This isn't goodbye." He leaned in toward her and pressed his lips softly against her cheek, and his rough beard prickled her skin.

Adella could only nod in response and turned to join Kol and Armand. She followed along on the plank walkway and stopped before a young porter, who stood with a book and brass pencil in hand.

"Welcome to the Capital," the porter said as he approached them, scrawling the name of the ship onto the paper. "Be warned, there is plague here."

"We know," Ellie replied. "The flags. Is it true? Has the king died?"

"I'm sorry to say," the young man confirmed. "His Majesty's funeral was just yesterday. It was the illness, I heard."

"He died of the red ague?" Adella asked, and he nodded. Guilt struck her like a blow to the gut. The very illness that her brother had inflicted upon Valenna had now killed their king. *I could've prevented this. I should have...* Adella couldn't help but feel wholly responsible.

"Who is on the throne now?" Jago asked.

"The Prince Regent," the porter replied. "Lord Hollen." Adella caught the uneasy glance that passed between Ellie and Jago.

"Prince Regent?" Ellie frowned. "According to whom?"

"According to himself," the porter said. "And what's more, the Royal Guard. I'd watch your tongue, Madame, if you don't want to be accused of treason."

"We shall see about that," Ellie replied, walking away.

"Wait a moment," the porter called out, jabbing his pencil in the air. "Is that a Sornian?"

Kol turned to approach the young man, towering above him. "*That?*"

Adella grabbed Kol's elbow before he stepped any closer. "He is."

"Someone must vouch for him," the porter said weakly, taking a step back. "I need a name, please."

"Adella Grimless," she replied.

"Oh," he said, eyeing her sympathetically before adding her name into his book. "My condolences on the loss of your parents. Lord Grimless was a good one." His tone was earnest, and Adella nodded her thanks. "Please—" He gestured toward the path leading up toward the city. "Carry on."

As they walked along the cobblestone streets, weaving their way through the rough stone buildings of the Capital, Adella noticed there were few people out and about. A black lacquered carriage would pass by every so often, but otherwise, the streets were empty. The taverns and shops all had closed doors and dark windows. Though she hadn't lived there in years, she would often visit with her family, and the quiet of the city now unnerved her compared with the bustling crowds she remembered.

They soon approached the massive outer wall of the Ansebulet. Adella shaded her eyes from the hot midday sun as she peered upward at the towers rising above them, looking as though they would pierce the sky. They paused at an arched gate in the stone wall where guards in scarlet and white jackets stood before an ornately-wrought iron portcullis.

Ellie turned to face the others. "If what the porter said was true," she said in a hushed voice, "I cannot enter here. Lord Hollen is not a friend of mine. Come, we must enter by another way." They followed her, creeping beneath the shadow of the wall, until they passed under a grove of hemlock trees. As she led them through the cool, fragrant air beneath the boughs, they came to a little stone building. They all watched breathlessly as Ellie pulled out her keyring and approached the door.

Kol raised an eyebrow at Adella, but she could only shrug, not knowing what would happen next. The door gave a sharp, rusty squeal as Ellie pushed it open and entered. The others crowded around the door, watching as she rolled away a dirty rug and pulled up a large section of the plank-wood floor.

Ellie looked back at them briefly, her face resolute. "We're sneaking in," she said, eyes twinkling mischievously. Then, she stepped into the hole at her feet and disappeared into the darkness below.

Jago followed immediately, then the islanders behind him. Armand glanced between Kol and Adella, then cracked a smile. "A bit exciting, isn't it?" he said, then turned and hurried after the others.

Adella peered into the square hole in the floor, where stone steps disappeared in the blackness beyond. Goosebumps tingled her skin, raising the hairs on her arm. She had no idea what they were getting into. Her thoughts drifted to her near-miss in the flooding sea cave, and her breath quickened. She lifted her eyes again to Kol, her brow furrowing as she spoke. "I really don't want to," Adella murmured. It wasn't a refusal, just a quiet confession to a friend.

Kol looked around the little space; sunlight streaming in from the open door shone on the woodlice that crawled around at their feet. "Shall we stay here, then?" he said, feigning sincerity. "It is pretty cozy." She only frowned at him.

He held out his hand. With a resigned sigh, Adella took it and carefully lowered a foot onto the stone stairs. They made their way down slowly, step by step until they were surrounded entirely by darkness.

As they came to the bottom of the stair, their footfalls went silent on the hard-packed soil. "Is that everyone?" Adella heard Ellie ask, and Kol responded. "Don't be afraid," Ellie assured them. "It's a short passageway; there are no turns."

Adella ran her hand along the damp stone to her left as she walked, feeling her way with her feet, and gasped when she felt fingertips at her back.

"Sorry," Kol said with a laugh. "I can't see anything. I didn't want to bump into you." Adella continued forward once more, this time colliding into something soft in front of her as her toes stubbed on the back of a boot.

"Back off," Armand grumbled. "Don't shove me."

"Oh, sorry," Adella whispered.

The ground beneath them rose gradually until they reached the end of the tunnel, as Adella discovered when she jostled blindly into the people in front of her. She heard the metallic clank of the key in a lock, and a slit of glaringly bright light filled the space in front of them. Ellie stuck her head through the gap, then swung the door open wide and stepped through. "Hurry," she urged, motioning for them to follow.

They emerged into a hallway, brightly lit with warm sunlight from the high-arched windows. As Ellie closed the door behind them, it seemed to disappear into the design of the ornately-carved and gilded wainscoting of the wall. Adella followed the others, passing under many-armed brass chandeliers and painted murals of clouds and flocks of birds on the ceiling. Beside her, Kol moved a hand to the hilt of his sword.

As they turned a corner, they saw two guards at the far end of the corridor, walking in their direction. Ellie didn't hesitate, only continued to walk with her head high as they approached the two men in scarlet jackets. The others followed her lead, and Adella held her breath as they passed by the guards, expecting to be stopped and questioned on their ragged appearance. Thankfully, they seemed in a hurry, not sparing a glance at the group as they continued.

Soon, they came to a vast hall, opulently decorated with a floor of white marble and vaulted ceilings held aloft on tall, fluted columns. Great black pennants draped the walls, and people dressed in dark mourning clothes milled about the area, giving no notice as the group approached. On the far side, a wide swath of steps led up to a series of gilded doors set in a curved, pilastered wall protected by armed Royal Guards.

Ellie strode across the room, the others following behind as she approached one of the guards. "Allow me entry," she said plainly.

"Is the Prince Regent expecting you?" the guard asked.

"Certainly not," Ellie replied.

"Then by whose authority do you demand entry?" he asked sharply, eyeing them each in turn. "You look an unfortunate lot."

Jago stepped forward and spoke to him in a low voice. The guard's eyes widened as he looked Ellie over in astonishment, and hastily pulled open the door for her without another word.

"What did he say?" Adella whispered to Kol, who only shrugged as they followed behind Ellie and the others. Adella's pulse quickened as she recognized the spacious room, generously illuminated by massive windows stretching to the soaring, domed ceiling. Heavy hardwood tables occupied the floor, with well-dressed but somber courtiers sitting around them. On the far side, a double-winged staircase led to a balcony high above an ornate, gilded throne on a raised dais. Scarlet-coated Royal Guards in their white cocked caps stood along the walls, eyeing their group. Memories of her younger days at the Capital surfaced, of time spent with her parents at the opulent gatherings among the crowds of finely-dressed courtiers.

The wall backing the dais below the balcony was hung with a massive, dark tapestry woven with the images of kings and queens so magnificent that they dwarfed the figure on the throne below, but at Ellie's approach, he stood.

"Ellinora," the man said under his breath, barely audible in the echoes of the space. Then, pointing a finger at Ellie, he spoke more clearly, "Guards, arrest them." Men in scarlet rushed from their posts at the wall, drawing their swords as they surrounded Ellie's party. Adella, at the back of the group, heard a commotion behind her.

Turning to look, she saw the guard from the doorway run into the chamber. "Release her, you traitors!" he shouted, brandishing his sword in the air. "Bow to your Queen!" Some of the guards who had come to their arrest lowered their weapons and stood dumbfounded.

"Did he say 'Queen?'" Adella asked sharply, watching incredulously as several of the guards turned against the others who had not yet given up their orders. Beside her, Kol drew his sword. Armand passed Adella's bundled-up crossbow back to her, then drew his as well. Shouting and the ringing of steel echoed in her ears as fighting surrounded them.

The courtiers, who all had been sitting peacefully at the tables, shoved their chairs back and scrambled to their feet in a panic, some fleeing to the doors, others taking up bronze candlesticks as weapons and joining the fray as the doors flung open and more guards poured in. Adella clutched the bundle to her chest and looked around, searching for Ellie in the chaos.

Kol raised his cutlass, steadying it in both hands, as two red-clad guards pressed together in combat right in front of him. They were hacking and clashing their blades together, and he had no idea which one was on his side until one man collapsed to the floor, slashed through the gut, and the other turned on Kol.

The guard thrust at him, and Kol didn't dare to dodge it, knowing that Adella was behind him. He swept his cutlass down and across, pushing his opponent's blade safely toward the floor and leaving him open long enough to stab him in the midsection. The guard grabbed his belly and doubled over, and another guard stumbled backward on top of him. Kol moved to put his sword into that one as well but stopped himself as he realized he didn't know if the man was an enemy or ally. "Adella, what's happening?" he asked, completely bewildered but determined to be useful.

The guard hopped to his feet and was just about to strike at Kol when a bronze candelabra came down hard upon the crown of the guard's hat, and he fell to the floor once more. Behind the guard stood an elderly courtier with bunches of lace at his neck and wrists, hat and wig askew on his head. Kol nodded at him in gratitude.

Behind Kol, Adella dropped her bundle of belongings as a Royal Guard collided with her side. She hesitated, unsure whose side he was on, until he drew back to strike, a menacing look on his face. She grabbed her haversack at her side and shoved it at him, blocking his sword with the iron box inside. The impact rang painfully through her injured fingers. The guard frowned at her unexpected shield, then drew back to strike again. From Adella's left, Kol lunged forward and stuck the guard through the ribs before the man could finish his strike.

"Thanks," Adella said, turning toward him. "We have to protect Miss Ellie." She looked desperately around, her eyes searching through the confusion. "Where is she?"

"Adella—" Kol grabbed her wrist, catching her attention. "What the hell is going on?"

"Politics," she said. "Look out!" Two guards, locked in combat, backed up close beside Kol. One dispatched the other, then turned toward them. Kol pulled back his elbow, ready to strike.

"Stop!" the guard pleaded, raising a palm. "I'm with you."

As Adella bumped into someone behind her, she turned to see Armand parrying a Royal Guard's powerful blow. The guard got the better of him, knocking Armand's sword from his hand. Clutching the strap of her haversack, Adella swung, bringing the iron box inside down upon the man's head with a crack. He doubled over with a cry as Armand snatched his sword back up from the floor. Groaning, Adella cradled her injured hand, which throbbed furiously.

She scanned the room, eyes roving frantically from one figure to the next, but saw no sign of Ellie. Then, she spotted her slight form being dragged backward toward the left stairway, a knife to her throat by a sunken-faced old man. *Hollen!* Grabbing her bundle of belongings, she pulled out her crossbow and quiver.

Despite the shooting pain in her foot, Adella ran as fast as she could, passing by an unconscious Jago lying on the floor with blood trickling from his head. She arrived at the bottom step in time to see Ellie and Hollen disappear at the top of the landing. *Damn!* Clutching the rail, Adella thumped up the stairs after them.

The pain in her foot was so intense she was crawling when she neared the top. Sitting, Adella stuck her good foot into the crossbow stirrup and drew it back to load the bolt. As she stepped onto the balcony landing, she leveled her weapon. Ahead, Ellie struggled against Hollen's arm, trying to keep his knife from her neck. She threw herself backward and pinned him against the railing, their upper bodies leaning precariously over the edge.

"No!" Adella shouted.

Drawing up his strength, Hollen threw himself forward onto the safety of the landing.

"Adella, get out of here!" Ellie shouted

With a renewed grip on his knife, pressing it to her throat, Hollen turned on Adella. "Stay back," he said, narrowing his eyes at the crossbow leveled at his chest. He looked her over with an appraising glare. "Mind your own affairs, chambermaid."

"I'm not a chambermaid," Adella replied coolly. "Let her go."

"Might as well be," he scoffed, shielding himself with Ellie's body. His eyes glanced nervously to the wall opposite the railing, where a narrow passageway led away from the landing. "Who are you, then? I've never seen you in court. The throne of Valenna doesn't concern you."

The question struck her. *Who am I?* A wave of grief flooded over her, and she ached for what was gone, for the loss of who she'd been once and was no longer. *No, I know who I am,* she reminded herself. Her back straightened with resolve. "I'm Adella Grimless," she replied. "Descendant of First Knight Adelo Grimless." Her voice grew stronger as she stepped closer. "Heiress of Lord Alfrin Grimless. And the fate of Valenna is very much my concern." She raised her crossbow, aiming it at his brow above Ellie's head. "Let her *go*," she ordered, clipping out each word clearly.

Hollen stood speechless, eyes darting around for a way out. Then, he grabbed Ellie by the arms and shoved her toward the rail. For a brief moment, she teetered in the air over the throne room, then disappeared over the side.

"No!" Adella screamed. Without a thought, she rushed to the railing. Just below, Ellie clutched the top of the tapestry, legs kicking desperately against the wall as she hung in the air above the throne. "I'm here," Adella said, straining to reach her. "Take my hand."

Ellie struggled to pull herself up. "I can't," she said, letting herself dangle limply again. "It's too far."

"You can't give up," Adella ordered. "Try again."

Ellie groaned as she pulled her body upward, then shot out a hand quickly in one final effort to make contact.

Adella grabbed her wrist. "I've got you!" She pulled upward with both hands around Ellie's arm, squeezing her eyes shut against the pain that seared through her broken fingers. Her grip gave out and Ellie slipped out of her hands.

Adella opened her eyes and was surprised to see Ellie still dangling below. Standing on either side of her were Kol and Jago, holding Ellie's arms as they pulled her up. "Oh, thank heavens," Adella sighed, stepping out of the way. She slumped to the floor as they helped Ellie over the rail. Lord Hollen was nowhere to be seen.

"Come on," Kol said, offering his hand to Adella. "Let me carry you this time."

Exhausted and teary-eyed with pain, Adella didn't have the will to protest. She nodded weakly and let him carry her down the stairs.

Kol set her down gently at the bottom, and she clung to his arm as they walked behind Ellie and Jago. The tumult in the throne room had died down as the treasonous guards found themselves outnumbered. Many dropped their weapons and stuck their hands in the air while others ran out the doors.

"Hail the Dowager Queen!" a voice called out. One by one, the remaining guards lowered to a knee, forcing their prisoners to do likewise.

Adella watched breathlessly as everyone in the room lowered, bowing in their direction, even Jago and the others from the Cairn. The only one who remained standing was Ellie. As a realization hit her, Adella dropped carefully to one knee, pulling Kol down by the arm when she saw the lost look on his face. "Bow," Adella whispered. "Our Miss Ellie, she is the Queen."

"Please," Ellie began, addressing the room, "let's not waste time with formalities. Summon all the healers in the Capital; bring them here to me." At that, several of the Royal Guards scurried to their feet and dashed off through the open doors.

"The Queen?" Armand said in disbelief as he rose to his feet, his cheeks blushing at the realization of exactly who he'd been flirting with at the Cairn.

"Mister Armand," Cora said, "you look unwell. Are you not 'feeling yourself?'" Armand stood speechless, face bright red as Adella, Kol, and the others laughed at his expense.

"Damn," he muttered. "I thought she looked familiar."

"Damn," he muttered. "I thought she looked familiar."

23

New Beginnings

Adella walked briskly to keep in step with the others, cradling the iron lockbox in her arms. She held her injured fingers away from the object to keep from jostling them, but they ached with each step as she followed behind Ellie, now Queen Ellinora, with Jago, Kol and Armand. Behind them marched armed Royal Guards.

"The Heart of the World is more than just a legend," Ellie explained. "Whether you believe the old stories or not, this artifact does have a certain power: the power over the minds and hearts of all descendants of Andolin, Valennian and Sornian alike. Though our two colonies have diverged greatly since the Great War that split the Empire, we all hold this artifact sacred. It is a battle cry, a rallying banner for whichever nation possesses it." Her steps echoed across the stone floor as they walked down the corridor.

"If Sornia were to get a hold of the Heart," she continued, "it would indeed give them a significant advantage—the belief that their cause is just and their forces invincible. The Azbarian Dynasty of Sornia has long harbored the desire to restore the glory of Old Andolin under the rule of their own empire. Thankfully, they can never use this for that purpose now." She led them to a heavy iron door and brought out her large keyring.

The Queen took a lantern from one guard who stood at the ready as she turned a key in the lock and swung the door open. They made their way down a stone block staircase, through an unfurnished and musty subterranean hallway, walking by a series of identical doors until they reached one at the end of the passageway. Shadows danced in the flickering lantern light as Ellie unlocked the final door, opening it with the low, grating moan of old iron. Inside the dark chamber, treasures and precious metal objects glittered in the orange light from their resting places on shelves protected behind iron bars.

Ellie unlocked a shelf at the back of the room, swinging the metal grate open as she motioned for Adella to approach. She stepped forward, cradling the ancient artifact in her arms. Adella took a deep breath and set the lockbox gently down in an empty place on the dusty wooden shelf, her hands lingering on the cold metal surface. She ran a finger over the strange embossed symbols before drawing back again. Ellie closed the bars over the shelf and secured them in place with a key from her large keyring, and they turned to leave.

An odd sensation crept up over the back of Adella's neck, and she turned to look at the lockbox one last time. The shadows around the room deepened as Ellie reached the far side of the treasury, but Adella hesitated still, eyeing the box as a gnawing feeling rose up in her gut. A dark emptiness settled over her thoughts as she stood motionless. Trying to shake off the feeling, she turned on her heel, putting the artifact behind her and walking briskly to catch up with the group.

"What is it?" Kol asked as she came up beside him.

"Nothing," she replied. "Just glad to be done with it."

Kol stood outside the chamber door, rapping on it with a knuckle. "Adella, hurry up, or we'll be late." He waited, but there was no answer.

Armand stomped across the floral carpet of the sitting room and knocked on the door with his cane. "Come on, girl," he chided. "It's not like the Queen'll wait for you."

The door opened slightly, and Adella peeked through the crack. "It was hard to lace it up by myself," she said, wincing apologetically. Then, she opened the door and stepped into the room, shaking the wrinkles from her skirt. "It doesn't fit very well, but it was the best they could lend me on short notice," she explained, smoothing the black-and-gold brocade of her bodice.

"No one will be looking at you, anyway," Armand assured her. "Let's go, before we miss the coronation."

Kol offered Adella his arm and, following Armand, escorted her down the corridor. Her hair was pulled up high on the back of her head, and the sweeping neckline of her dress lay low on her bare shoulders. "You look..." He tried to think of a better word, to no avail. "Beautiful."

"Thank you." Adella smiled warmly at him, and he felt a nervous flutter in his gut. Kol didn't know how much longer he would be able to enjoy her company. He still had no clear plans for his future, and he wasn't sure he'd ever see her again after this.

They took seats at the back of the crowded throne room, which had been cleared of tables and filled with rows of benches instead. On the gilded throne, raised on the dais for all to see, sat Ellie, dressed all in black. Jago stood beside her in the scarlet and white jacket of the Royal Guard, with his glaive in hand and a feathered hat atop his bald head. Kol found it amusing to see them in formal clothes, with plenty of lace hanging off them in every place it could, rather than their usual rough homespun and worn-out leather. Kol still wore his old clothes, aside from an oxblood-colored velvet jacket he consented to wear at Adella's insistence. It was too tight across his shoulders for his liking.

He watched the ceremony absent-mindedly, occasionally catching a few sentences here and there whenever his thoughts drifted back to the present. Soon, Ellie knelt to take her oath from an ancient long-wigged courtier before rising again, a bejeweled crown upon her head. The room stood and erupted in cheers before the Queen hushed them down again.

"Now that that's done," Queen Ellinora said matter-of-factly, "we may move on to the rest of today's business." She pulled out a sheet of parchment from the pocket of her black silk skirt and unfolded it. "I have a long list here, so let's begin. Firstly, Miss Adella Grimless. Please approach the throne."

Adella glanced at Kol before rising to her feet and making her way toward the front of the room. She stopped before the dais and, holding out her skirts, lowered herself to one knee. Ellie stood and approached her, lifting a ceremonial sword aloft for all to see.

"Adella Renata Grimless," Ellie began, loud enough for all to hear. "Do you wish to take up the mantle of your father's title and allegiance, swearing fealty to the Haspen Dynasty, as your father and your father's father have done, all the way back to your original oathbearer, First Knight Adelo Lucius Grimless? Do you swear to serve your Queen and all her heirs for the rest of your days, in whatever way may be demanded of you, on your honor and your life?"

Adella lowered her head. "I swear it," she uttered solemnly, heart swelling with pride.

Ellie touched the tip of the sword gently to Adella's shoulders. "Rise, Lady Adella Grimless, Equess Primorri, First Knight of Valenna." With a smile on her face, Adella rose and returned to her seat to the sound of clapping. A shrill but joyful whistle emanated from the back of the room, stopping abruptly when Kol jabbed Armand in the side with his elbow.

The Queen raised her palm, and the room quieted once more. "Kol of Sornia," she called out. "Please approach the throne."

Kol threw Adella and Armand a questioning glance, but they only prodded him up from his seat. His pulse throbbed in his throat as he hesitantly rose and walked down the space between the chairs toward the dais. He hadn't expected to be called forward, or he might've changed his clothes after all. Kol stopped before the Queen and tried to remember exactly how the others had made their bows. He lowered to his knee and hoped it was the correct one.

"Mister Kol," Queen Ellinora began informally. "Based on the outstanding courage and loyalty you have displayed in service of the Crown, you have earned the right to citizenship. Do you wish to take the oath of allegiance and become a citizen of Valenna?"

"Yes." Kol bowed his head. "I do."

"Kol of Sornia," she said, raising her voice again. "Do you swear fealty and allegiance to Valenna, and to the Queen and all of her heirs, for the rest of your days? Do you swear that you renounce all allegiance and loyalty to any foreign ruler or nation you may have held before, on your honor and your life?"

"Yes," he stated firmly. "I swear it."

She tapped his shoulders with the sword, and a warmth spread through him, raising goosebumps on his arms. "Rise, Kol of Valenna, Citizen with Honors." He stood and turned to face the room, searching over the faces of his new countrymen for his friends, and found them clapping as they rose from their seats. He had been given a new homeland, and his friends were here to see it. A sudden tightness rose in his chest, catching in his throat. He had never felt so proud in his life. *A new beginning,* he told himself. Kol could hear a sharp whistling, and tears welled up, clouding his vision. He blinked them away in time to see Adella smacking Armand's arm.

After the ceremony concluded and they were filing out the doors, Kol was surprised to see Ellie, now with a glittering crown upon her grey head, waiting for them in the corridor. Jago, as always, stood at her side.

"Lady Grimless, Mister Kol," Ellie began. "Armand," she added with a wry smile. "Would you care to come with me? The healers have been summoned."

They followed her through twisting corridors to a more remote part of the Ansebulet, away from the bustling activity of the day. By the savory smell of roasted meat, Kol realized they were near the kitchens. Jago stood guard outside as Ellie led them through a small, plain wooden door into a wide room with a low ceiling supported by thick, ancient wooden beams stretching overhead. At the many tables within, men and women of every age gathered around small copper stills. Set in little bowls on each table, Kol recognized the ingredients they had collected from the greenhouse.

"Thank you all for coming on such short notice," Ellie addressed the room. "I'm sure you all have seen how dire the situation is. This man," she said, gesturing toward Kol, "is Mister Kol, formerly of Sornia, now a citizen of Valenna. He is here to show us how to make the physic against the plague." Kol swallowed hard as every eye turned toward him.

He cleared his throat. "The ingredients are simple; eternity root and eldritch flower—" Kol froze as his mind went blank. He glanced at Adella, who returned his look with an encouraging nod. "Or peony root and elderflower, if you're Valennian," he went on, smiling as he remembered. "The most difficult part is gathering the ingredients, since the blossoms can only be found for a few weeks in the spring..." He strode over to one of the tables where supplies had been gathered and took a whole peony root in his hand, all the while explaining how he had made the physic himself during the plague of Hedda when he was young.

As the healers followed his lead, chopping roots and readying their little stills, he moved about the room to be sure they were all doing it as instructed. "Slice it more finely," he said, coming to one table where a young woman in an undyed apron worked. He took the knife to the peony root. "Like this." She nodded, and Kol turned to survey the others' progress.

His eyes lingered in one spot across the room, where Adella was talking to one of the healers, a smile illuminating her face as she chopped herbs in her pearls and silk. He didn't know how long he watched her when Ellie appeared at his side.

"What are your plans?" she asked. "Will you be staying here in the Capital?"

"I don't know," Kol replied, frowning. "Is Adella staying here?"

Ellie smirked. "Will that make a difference?"

"No—No, not at all," he blurted out, trying to sound nonchalant. "Why, did she mention me?" Ellie chuckled, and Kol wished he hadn't asked so eagerly.

Adella looked up from the table and, glancing around, noticed Kol speaking with the Queen across the room. She paused for a moment, remembering how they'd met. It was surprising to think the man who started the attack on Valenna, on her own Greywood Manor, would be here now, helping to right the wrongs of her brother. She smiled to think how much Kol had changed, from the surly, quiet soldier she didn't believe would even survive the trek across the Campos to a citizen of Valenna and a friend of the Queen. After the chaos of that first day in the Capital, Adella had sent Armand to the docks in the evening with a request for Captain Declan and his crew. Their response had been swift, and the very next day, with the help of seven respectable privateers, Adella petitioned the Queen for Kol's citizenship. It had been partly why she had accepted the title, to help him make a better life for himself. That, and to use her inheritance to do what she could to right her brother's wrongs, be the person he couldn't be, and honor her parents' memory by carrying on their legacy. After all, if Kol could face an unknown future so bravely, she could, too. She smiled with pride as she watched him now.

With his help, and with the Queen on the throne, Adella felt hopeful for the future of Valenna. *But, what will Kol do now?* she wondered. *Where will he go?* He would make a great Royal Guard, she figured. *Perhaps he will stay in the Capital.* She was surprised to feel a pang of sadness at the thought. After spending so much time together, Adella realized she would miss his company.

* * *

Kol stretched out on a floral damask sofa, his stockinged feet resting on the arm as he turned a page in the *Mother Tigress* novel he had rescued from the Cairn. They had been given this sitting room and its four attached bedchambers for use during their stay at the Capital.

Each chose a bedroom, then piled their belongings haphazardly in the fourth chamber, scattering weapons across the bedstead.

The rooms were decorated extravagantly, with gilding covering every surface that could be gilded. Adella had warned him about that, Kol remembered with a smile. He felt quite comfortable here; the bed he slept in was massive, with heavy, ruffled curtains hanging from the posts, the featherdown mattress piled with silk quilts and pillows. Though he thoroughly enjoyed it, Kol knew better than to get used to the place; he didn't know exactly how long they would remain in the Royal Palace. He wanted to ask Adella about it, but doubted she had any idea, either, and anyway, he was waiting for her to mention it first.

There was a knock at the door, and Armand rose to answer it. The Queen entered, carrying a small wooden box, followed by Jago. Kol jumped up from the sofa, pretending he did not just have his dirty feet on the most expensive piece of furniture he'd ever sat upon.

Ellie, seeing the nervous look on his face, laughed politely. "Good morning to the both of you," she said. "Don't get up on my account, I've come to see Miss Grimless."

Kol pointed a thumb toward the door of Adella's bedchamber, which hung partly open. Ellie nodded to him and crossed the room to enter while Jago braced his ribs with a hand and lowered himself gingerly into an armchair to wait, leaning his glaive against the marble-topped side table.

Adella leaned on the balcony rail, breathing in the crisp morning air. Beyond the walls of the Ansebulet, past the crowded stone buildings and the ships at the docks, she could see the waters of Belgrand Bay, calm and turquoise in the bright sunlight. She turned at the sound of footsteps behind her.

"I thought I would check on your stitches this morning," Ellie said. Adella followed her back through the balcony doors to take a seat on the bedstead. She watched as the Dowager Queen removed the boot and bandages, then cut away the threads that wove through her skin.

"There you are, good as new." Ellie watched Adella run her thumb over the scar appreciatively. "What are your plans?" she asked. "Will you be staying at the Capital now?"

"To be honest," Adella replied, pulling on her stocking, "I intend to return to Elldon. To see what's left of it."

"I thought you might," Ellie replied. "I was hoping to find someone who might scout it out and report the situation back to me. I didn't want to ask it of you, though, considering what you've been through. And it will be dangerous to return there now that we are at war with Sornia."

"I know," Adella replied. "But I'm going, regardless."

Ellie looked at her sympathetically. "Might I make a suggestion? Hire a personal guard. Someone you already know and trust."

"Hm..." Adella hesitated. She didn't like the idea of dragging anyone else back into danger with her. She'd had enough of that.

"If you don't have anyone in mind," Ellie added, "there are a few among the Royal Guard I can recommend."

"I'll consider it, thank you." Adella laced her boot as Ellie finished packing up her supplies, then followed her into the sitting room, where the others lounged about in conversation. "It feels bleak to see the Capital so empty," she commented sadly, glancing out the tall arched window across the room. "Did the plague hit the city so hard?"

"Fortunately not," Ellie replied. "My son had the good sense to allow the people to retreat to the countryside. Given the waterborne nature of the illness, he likely saved many lives."

"He was a good king," Adella replied.

Ellie nodded, her eyes glossy at the edges. "Now that we've closed the contaminated wells and the apothecaries are distributing the medicine throughout the city, it will soon be safe for the people to return," she said. "You all are welcome to stay here in the Palace as long as you please, and are free to come and go as you like. You three will always have a home here."

"Thank you." Adella looked at Kol and Armand, who seemed to approve of the idea. "I think we may stay here a little while until we are fully rested."

* * *

Kol flopped his book down into his lap, sighing dramatically. He glanced at the large clock in the corner of their sitting room. "What can she be doing?"

"She's getting ready," Armand answered gruffly, tying a silk cravat under his chin in front of the gilded mirror. "Like she said she was doing." Armand made faces in the mirror as he ran a comb through his grey sideburns. "And just when are you going to get dressed? We're expected to be in the ballroom within the hour."

"I am dressed," Kol replied.

They turned as the door behind them opened. Adella stepped out of her chamber wearing an evening dress of dove-grey silk embroidered with a pale gold scrollwork pattern. A long strand of little, perfect pearls grazed her collarbones, hanging past her neckline. Her dark auburn hair was arranged simply, twisted up into a high bun and wrapped with a wide cream-colored ribbon with a large bow tied elegantly at the back. "What do you think?" she asked them. Grabbing the full, heavy skirts in her hand, she stepped her left foot forward, revealing a little slip-on shoe with a pointed toe in a creamy golden color. "And look, it covers my scar."

"I suppose it'll have to do," Armand joked.

Adella frowned at Kol. "Aren't you going to get dressed?"

"I am dressed." Kol pulled his jacket of oxblood velvet over his stitched-up black linen shirt, which had long ago faded to a dark grey. He had tied his hair back and tried his best to remove the travel stains from his doeskin breeches, but that was the sum of his efforts. Sighing, Adella led the way.

Kol followed the others through the open doors leading into the ballroom. The ceiling arched high above them and, for a moment, he felt as though they had stepped outside, as the top half of the room was painted the blue of a summer's day, interspersed with fluffy white clouds. The effect was a little unnerving since he knew it to be evening, though there were no windows to confirm the hour. They had arrived just in time to see the Queen, accompanied by Jago and several Royal Guards, make her way down a flight of carpeted stairs. She stopped on one balcony where the twin staircases met high above the ballroom.

"Friends," Queen Ellinora began from her perch above the crowd, looking out over the ballroom floor. Men and women gathered below her, dressed in their finest clothes, their jewelry sparkling in the light of the many chandeliers and sconces illuminating the space. "I have asked you here this evening for a purpose. We have all experienced much sadness of late, myself included. We are all grieving. However, it is important that we not only take time to mourn our losses, but to celebrate our victories as well." She paused, searching over the room. "The plague—" she continued, "the red ague, as it is named—has been quelled here in the Capital, and even now, our apothecaries are on their way to help the people of Raymouth. By all accounts, the worst is over." She paused to wait for the sounds of murmuring to abate. "I do not ask that we forget our sadness, only that we take some time for joy as well..."

Kol's mind wandered until clapping erupted around him as Queen Ellinora finished speaking. He'd never been one for speeches. An orchestra began to play from the corner of the room, filling the air with a gentle, lilting tune. Couples made their way to the center of the floor to dance, while others retreated toward the tables. Armand disappeared on the arm of a well-dressed older woman with a beauty mark drawn in ink by her mouth, winking at them as he went. Kol led Adella to the tables along the walls, which were filled with plates of food and bottles of wine. He noticed she looked distracted, her eyes roaming here and there about the room as though searching for something.

"I'm not dancing," he warned her.

"I'm not asking you to," she replied. "Keep your eyes open for little round pastries. You can only find them here at the Palace. They're the whole reason I come to these silly events." He nodded, then turned his attention to the cold meats sliced and arrayed on a silver platter nearby.

Kol soon realized someone was standing close at his side and, turning, was surprised to see it wasn't Adella. The woman was several years older, with light chestnut hair forced into ringlets and a look of expectation that hinted she wasn't used to being overlooked. Kol pretended not to see her, returning to the plate of ham instead.

"Ahem," she said, waiting for him to acknowledge her presence.

"Can I help you?" he asked plainly, not bothering to turn and face her.

"I saw you came here with Adella," she said, looking around the ballroom. "Where did she run off to?"

"I don't know," he admitted. "She absconded to look for pastries."

"How like her. Oh, there she is," the woman said, craning her neck toward the center of the room. "Dancing with an exceedingly handsome fellow."

Kol looked around and spotted Adella among the dancing couples, groaning to himself when he saw who she was with. "You're mistaken, that's only Captain Declan."

"Little Rog? It can't be," the woman mused, tapping a finger to her chin. "He used to wear spectacles. How good he would look on my arm. Come," she said, taking hold of Kol's elbow, "let's ambush them and switch partners."

"Let go," Kol replied, irritated at the woman's impertinence. "I don't know how to dance."

"Just follow my lead," she said, pulling him toward the middle of the floor. "Don't be a coward." Sighing, Kol gave in and followed along; he was not opposed to her accomplishing her goal. He did what he could to keep up as they made their way across the floor toward Adella and Declan.

"You must be the man they call Kol," she said, making conversation as he found his footing.

He looked down at his feet, trying not to crush her shoes. "How did you know?"

"Everyone in the Capital is talking about the Sornian who helped save the Queen," she replied, raising her skirt slightly from the floor. "They say you are the one who provided the recipe for the medicine."

Kol glanced around the room at the couples dancing, at the people standing by the walls. It was strange to think any of them would be speaking about him at all, let alone anything good. Some of them smiled at him or nodded as he caught their eye.

"Oh!" She stopped dancing suddenly, wincing. "My foot." Kol didn't have time to apologize before he heard Adella's voice nearby.

"Margavita!" Adella called out, releasing Declan's hand to greet her. "It's good to see you." The two women wrapped their arms around each other. "Kol, this is my sister," Adella explained.

"I should have guessed," he said under his breath.

"Are you here with Rolan?" Adella asked her.

"He's here somewhere," Margavita replied slyly. "He doesn't like to dance, but if I make him jealous enough, he will."

"Margo," Adella began, her eyes beginning to glisten. "I'm afraid I have much to tell you. Mother and Father—"

"I know," Margavita said, her countenance darkening. "Let's catch up afterward. We can't stop in the middle of the floor. I confess," she added, her tone becoming light once more, "I've come to steal your dance partner." She took Declan by the arm, allowing him no say in the matter. "He will do quite nicely."

"How rude," Adella laughed. "I'll find you after the last dance." She turned to face Kol. "I didn't mean to disappear," Adella began apologetically. "Apparently, the Queen invited the entire crew of *The Tigress*. Declan caught me by surprise." The music changed to a slower movement as more couples joined in, hemming them in on the dance floor. Without replying, Kol held out his hand to her.

"You said you weren't dancing," she quietly reminded him, placing her hand in his.

"I changed my mind." His other hand he set gently on her side, pulling her closer as he followed her lead. The pace of the music was easy, and he soon figured out the steps as they relaxed into a pattern together.

His hand slid over the delicate silk of her gown as he drew her in, and Adella glanced away, biting her bottom lip. It was something he had noticed her do many times before, whenever she was nervous. *But what could she be nervous about?* This was her world, after all. Letting his questions go, he gave into the moment, and they moved together, spinning over the marble floor, the world around them shrinking away until all that remained was the two of them under the painted summer sky and the sound of violins.

The music came to an end, and the moment passed. A livelier tune began to play as they made their way back toward the buffet tables, Adella pulling Kol by the elbow toward a plate of round pastries with colorful icing. She stood by and ate one after the other before she stopped suddenly, her eyes widening.

"What is it?" he asked, glancing around the vast, lavishly decorated ballroom.

"I just remembered something," she said. "If we hurry, we can get back before anyone misses us."

Adella led him through the open doors and down the steps leading out into the wide antechamber, through groups of people who stood about in conversation, wine glasses in hand. They passed through another set of tall, ornate doors, pushing them open to step outside in the cool air. With her hand on his arm, she guided him down the cobblestone pathway to the iron gates of the Ansebulet. Whispering a word to the guards, she led him to the city streets under the dark night sky dotted with stars. They made a couple of turns, passing by open-air carriages and groups of people walking idly down the street lined with storefronts and shops closed for the night, until finally stopping at a greasy wooden door. In the warm glow from the nearby casement window hung a sign shaped like a shield, with the name *The King's Garters* painted on it in red and gold.

They entered and sat down on a bench toward the end of a long table, one of several that stretched from one side of the dimly lit room to the other. Seafarers and rough-clothed men with missing teeth were grouped here and there along the benches, muttering among themselves. Eventually, a young woman in a stained apron approached the two of them.

She looked Adella over and arched a brow. "It's meat pies tonight," she said, setting two stoneware tankards on the table.

"We'll have two," Adella replied. "And a pitcher of beer, please." The woman nodded and left.

"Ah," Kol said, leaning his elbows on the table. "You've brought us here on my account."

"You wanted so little," Adella replied, remembering their wishes when *The Tigress* made port. The tavern maid returned and set a pitcher between them before disappearing into the kitchen. Kol filled their tankards and they drank in silence for a while.

"You should know," Adella began, "I don't plan on staying in the Capital. It's lovely, but..." Her words trailed off.

"It's isn't your home," he offered, finishing her thought.

She nodded. "It could be yours, though, if you wanted. Or—"

"Or?" he prodded, not trying to guess at her meaning this time.

"The Queen has advised me to hire a bodyguard." Adella paused to take a drink from her cup. It hadn't taken long after the Queen's suggestion for her to realize she already knew exactly the man for the job.

"And you want to hire me?" He rubbed his chin thoughtfully, trying to hide a smile. "Why do you think I'm suited for it?"

"Well," Adella began, taken aback by the question. After all, in her estimation, he was more suited to the task than anyone else, and he certainly needed the job. "You're highly skilled, clever, trustworthy—"

"Good-looking?" he suggested.

"I didn't say that," she added quickly. "Oh, I see. You're fishing for compliments."

He grinned shamelessly. "I will do it."

"I plan to return to Elldon," she warned.

"Wherever you go," Kol replied, "I will go with you." Though he spoke in response to her question, Adella looked at him closely, feeling like there was more behind his words. She was touched that he was so willing to join her. He could've chosen to stay in the Capital and live an easy and comfortable life, yet he was willing to follow her back into the unknown, into danger. His answer brought an unexpected warmth to her heart, and she was grateful that, no matter what lay ahead, she wouldn't have to face it alone.

Adella and Kol had finished their meal and returned to the ballroom of the Ansebulet while the orchestra was still playing. Adella spied Margavita on the dance floor, this time accompanied by her husband, looking pleased with herself. A servant in a coiled wig walked by, carrying a tray full of cordial glasses, and Kol snatched a couple as he passed. He held one out to Adella as he sipped the other, grimacing as he forced it down. The bright red liquid was syrupy sweet, tasting strongly of tart cherry. Pulling a face, he passed the second glass to her as well. Adella took them both, sipping from each glass in turn.

They were joined by Declan as the music ended. He glanced at the two glasses in her hands, then looked reproachfully at Kol. "I've been looking for you," Declan said to Adella. "We're setting sail in the morning, and I wanted to say goodbye."

Adella passed the two little glasses back to Kol and turned to Declan, taking his hand in hers. "Rogero," she began. "I—" She paused, at a loss for words.

"Please," he said. "I cannot leave without knowing we have parted on good terms. Please," he repeated, his voice softening, "will you forgive me, for what happened between us back then? I had never meant—" He stopped himself as she replied with a nod.

She looked down toward the floor. "I forgive you," she said quietly. "You must write to me still," she added.

"Of course." Declan turned to face Kol. "If you should ever be looking for work, you always have a place on *The Tigress*."

"Thank you for the offer," Kol replied.

Declan turned Adella once more. "This is goodbye, for now. You won't forget me, will you?"

She opened her mouth to reply but Declan leaned in toward her, lifted her chin and kissed her, his lips lightly pressing against hers for a brief moment. Declan bid them a hasty farewell, then turned and vanished into the crowd. Adella was left standing speechless, with color rising in her cheeks and the taste of wine on her lips.

Kol tipped back one of the little glasses, downing the sticky liquid as quickly as he could. He didn't notice Armand coming up beside him.

"You know," Armand began thoughtfully, his voice low, "there's a simple solution to your problem."

"What?" Kol asked, though he was not quite sure which problem he meant.

"The three of you—" Armand raised his bushy eyebrows suggestively.

"Ugh!" Kol's face wrinkled in disgust at the thought. "I'm sorry I asked. Don't you have some woman to annoy somewhere?"

Armand's smile fell away. "Turns out, she's married now." Kol handed him the other cordial glass in consolation.

Elldon

Adella shifted uncomfortably on the leather seat, trying to keep her balance as the stagecoach rocked back and forth. They had been traveling for days with a coach and team lent to them by the Queen, stopping off at various little towns on the way to rest and change horses. They would have simply borrowed riding horses instead and, by that way, traveled much faster, but Armand still walked with a limp due to the injury in his knee incurred at the Cairn. It would be too much for him to ride.

Feeling the rough bump of planks beneath the wheels, Adella pressed her hand against the glass to look at the landscape. They were now crossing the bridge over the River Ray, which was so broad that only one bridge had been built, just to the southeast of Raymouth town.

As they drew closer, Adella could see the charred, crumbled remains of buildings here and there, where the smallholders and crofters had once lived and tended their flocks and gardens. They passed by the home of one smallholder, Misses Asher, who had always stayed for tea when she came to pay her rent to Adella's father. Her heart sank to see the little house was only four blackened stone walls now, its roof wholly gone. She glanced at Armand to see his reaction, but his eyes were closed, and his head nodded sleepily.

Soon, they approached the southern edge of what remained of the town, and Adella watched breathlessly as they neared the distant hill whereon Greywood Manor had stood. The coach passed under the shadows of elm trees, and she craned her neck to get a clear view of the crest. As they passed through a row of lilac trees with spent blooms lining the pathway and came out the other side, Adella gave a cry of surprise. There, silhouetted on the hill beneath the elms, stood Greywood Manor, whole and unruined.

"Stop," Adella called out. Without waiting, she opened the door and stumbled onto the hard-packed dirt of the road. It was no great feat since the coach rolled along at an infuriatingly slow pace as it was. She could hear Kol sighing in exasperation as she closed the door behind her. Turning toward her home, she gathered up her skirts and ran. Her heart rose within her, and soon she was sprinting all the way up the carriage path, stopping only as she reached the front doors of the manor. They had been repaired, she noticed, since the night they had been smashed in. *The last time I was here...* She reached toward the brass handle, pausing to catch her breath and prepare herself for what might await inside.

Finally, she pushed the doors open wide. Inside stood the round pedestal table, with an earthenware pitcher sitting where the blue and white porcelain vase had once held lilacs. Passing under the staircase, Adella walked down the hallway toward the main room. The tall-case clock by the doorway chimed, seemingly in welcome, as she looked around. The furniture that had been in her family for generations could still be seen, hiding their familiar shapes beneath linen sheets. She ran her hand over the back of the shrouded sofa, her eyes taking inventory of what was left of her life. Though it was more than she had hoped for, her breath caught painfully in her throat, eyes flooding with tears as she realized that this was all she had; her family would never return home again.

Adella heard soft footsteps behind her, and turned to look. In the doorframe, waited a stout woman with plaited grey hair in simple dress, smiling at her warmly.

"Misses Asher," Adella whispered. "How—?"

"It's good to see you again, Miss Grimless," the woman said, her face solemn but kind. "We thought we lost you as well." She motioned for Adella to follow, leading her to the window at the back of the room, then pulled the curtain aside, revealing the meadows behind the manor that led out into the Campos.

Adella stepped toward the glass, her mouth falling open as she saw several large tents arranged around a smoldering campfire. Seated on logs at the fire, Adella recognized the faces of her neighbors, many with make-shift weapons at their sides. Horses were interspersed among the tents, grazing. She recognized her own gelding, Shy, and the red and white Ember among them.

"We gathered here," Misses Asher explained. "Those of us who did not flee. We've been fighting back against the Sornian raiders, holding them off."

The heavy thump of boots echoed from the hall, and Kol appeared in the doorway. Misses Asher startled at the sight of him, her eyes shifting nervously toward Adella.

"It's all right," Adella explained, placing her hand gently on the woman's arm. "Kol is one of us now. He is Valennian."

Adella clipped a stem from the coral-pink rose bush that climbed the stone walls of Greywood Manor, careful not to prick her thumb on the little thorns. Placing it into her arm with the rest she had gathered, she carried the fragrant bouquet up the steps toward the pair of oak doors. At the threshold, she paused to look out to the horizon, eyeing the dark clouds that seemed to be blowing in from a strange direction before turning back to the manor and bumping the doors open with her hip. One by one, she set the blooming branches into a plain stoneware pitcher on the little table in the foyer, arranging them thoughtfully before continuing down the hallway and through the open doors of the dining room.

She walked over to the center of the room where her mother's tea service sat in the middle of the dining table amongst scattered papers and books, steam rising from its spout. She raised an eyebrow at Kol, who was just putting up his stockinged feet on the table as he flipped open *Mother Tigress*. Without looking up from the book, he took his feet hastily down again at her approach, and one side of Adella's mouth pulled into a smile as she helped herself to tea. Across the table, Armand was already sipping his, holding his little finger out in affectation.

Armand, like Misses Asher and several other of Greywood's neighbors, stayed at the manor as a guest now, until their homes in the surrounding countryside could be rebuilt. The work was slow, however, due to the unseasonable summer storms and a dearth of supplies and workers from the nearest town of Raymouth, which was still recovering from the plague.

Adella adjusted her skirts as she sat and opened the Codex, which sat on the table along with the sheets of her translation work. She had thrown herself into it in an attempt to keep her mind busy now that she faced the loss of so many people in her life. A new feeling of emptiness now darkened the rooms of Greywood Manor for her. She knew her home would never feel the same, but it was all she had left.

Taking a sip of the lavender-flower tea, she flipped over a new page just as the sound of hoofbeats on gravel arose from the open window. Both Adella and Armand clanked their teacups down onto their saucers and rose from their chairs in unison.

"You needn't get the door anymore," she reminded him.

"I haven't got anything else to do," Armand sulked. "I don't want to just sit around and rot."

"It's been pretty quiet out in the Campos lately," Adella replied. "Perhaps when we have a stretch of good weather, we can fetch the horses from Smuggler's Port." She glanced over at Kol as she made the suggestion, as this was her first time mentioning it. He looked up at her pensively from his book but didn't reply.

Armand grunted his approval and disappeared down the hallway, returning a moment later. "It's some raggedy-looking sailor from *The Tigress*," he announced.

"Thank you for that introduction," a youthful voice said from behind Armand. Yul Childric stepped into the dining room, cradling a canvas haversack under one arm. His hair ribbon was half untied, and blond strands hung about his face.

Adella motioned toward a chair across from her. "Please, sit and have some tea. How was your voyage?"

"The weather was very bad," Childric replied, helping himself to a teacup. "The crossing took twice as long, but nothing worse than that."

He lowered himself into a chair and took a sip. "Aside from the sea serpents."

Across the table, Kol raised his brows. "Do they give you trouble?" he asked, lowering his book slightly.

"Occasionally," Childric replied. "It's the damnedest thing, the appearance of these beasts." He paused to take a sip. "No one's ever seen the like of them before, and now suddenly they populate the Bay. Where could they have come from?"

Adella pressed her lips together, trying to ignore the feelings of culpability that crept up within her. *It was after I opened the sea cave,* she thought, *wasn't it?* She shrugged innocently and poured more tea into her cup. "How is the captain doing? Is he well?"

"He has been in a bad temper," Childric said, turning to shuffle through his haversack. He pulled out several envelopes and a small box wrapped in brown paper and string. "He speaks of you often, though. I imagine he misses you."

"Not enough to visit," she noted.

"He has his hands full with the new crew," Childric explained. "They're all very stupid. He asked me to give you this," he added, handing her the little package.

Adella untied the string and unfolded the paper quickly, remembering the last time Declan had sent her a gift and the trouble that followed. She pulled the lid off the box to reveal a white, many-tined seashell, then examined the paper it was wrapped in for markings. She let her breath out in relief, a smile crossing her face. "It's a shell." Above the pages of his book, Kol rolled his eyes.

"A sea comb," Childric explained. "Also, you have a letter from the Queen," he said, placing an envelope sealed with gilded wax on the table before her, "which was given over to us as we passed another ship at sea." He placed a second envelope, sealed with red wax, on top of that one. "One from the notary in Raymouth." He set down a third letter, this one dog-eared and water-stained, on top of the others. "And this one was among those sent to Valenna from Smuggler's Port. It is two weeks old by now."

Adella shuffled through the letters. The one from Raymouth was addressed to Lady Grimless of Elldon. *There is no Elldon anymore,* she thought bitterly, tossing the envelope aside. *How can I be the lady of a place that no longer exists? I am only Adella... Adella of the Campos.* And yet, she would be here at Greywood Manor, waiting to fulfill whatever duties were required of her by the Crown.

She turned the second envelope over in her hands, thumbing over the wax seal bearing the Queen's coat-of-arms. Setting that one aside as well, Adella paused to examine the third letter carefully. Though the ink was smudged and faded with water stains, she recognized the bold, simple script that adorned the face of the envelope. Her breath caught in her throat, and she touched her fingers to her lips as she swallowed the lump of emotions. When she was finally able to speak again, her voice was nearly a whisper. "I know this writing. This letter is from Tess."

To be continued...

www.ingramcontent.com/pod-product-compliance
Lightning Source LLC
Chambersburg PA
CBHW070533120726
47909CB00007B/2127